P9-CFQ-007

7/24/13

A Dangerous Fiction

A
Dangerous
Fiction

A Novel

Barbara Rogan

VIKING

VIKING
Published by the Penguin Group
Penguin Group (USA) Inc., 375 Hudson Street,
New York, New York 10014, USA

USA I Canada I UK I Ireland I Australia I New Zealand I India I South Africa I China

Penguin Books Ltd, Registered Offices: 80 Strand, London WC2R 0RL, England
For more information about the Penguin Group visit penguin.com

LIBRARY OF CONGRESS CATALOGING-IN-PUBLICATION DATA
Rogan, Barbara.
A dangerous fiction : a novel / Barbara Rogan.
pages cm
ISBN 978-0-670-02650-0
1. Psychological fiction.   I. Title.
PS3568.O377D36 2013
813'.54—dc23
2013007097

Printed in the United States of America
1 3 5 7 9 10 8 6 4 2

ALWAYS LEARNING   PEARSON

For Benny

Acknowledgments

I am grateful to many people who contributed to the writing of this novel. My expert on protection dogs (and breeder of my own beautiful German shepherds) was Yvette Piantadosi, CCRN. Detective Gina Sarubbi, NYPD's Deputy Commissioner of Public Information, provided essential information. My first readers, Ben Kadishson, Jonathan Kadishson, and Daniel Kadishson, combined bedrock support with savvy critique. I owe much to my dear friends and walking companions, Laurie Rozakis and Gudren Calabro. Without them to prize me away from my desk, my legs might have atrophied altogether. My many friends on the Compuserve Writers Forum kept me company on the long road. Special thanks to my agent, Gail Hochman; my editor, Tara Singh; Rachelle Mandik; and the rest of Viking/Penguin team.

A Dangerous Fiction

Preface

"Start at the beginning, Jo," he said, opening his pad just like a TV detective. "What happened first?"

As if I knew when it began. Endings are unambiguous—a slammed door, a final chord, the vacant, glassy stare of the dead—but beginnings are always a matter of perspective. Sometimes you can't tell where a story begins until you reach the end. That's fine if you're writing fiction, but in real life, it's too late.

I explained this. He said, "You're making it too complicated."

"'Just the facts, ma'am'?" I said.

He smiled as one does at an oft-heard joke. I looked at him properly for the first time. The boyishness was gone, but the lines around his eyes and mouth suited him, lending gravitas to his face. His eyes were green, but a darker, warier shade than I remembered, rain forest instead of meadow. I wondered if he'd ever married. His ring finger was bare, which meant nothing. Hugo and I exchanged rings when we married, but Hugo never wore his. It chafed him when he wrote, he'd said.

"A series of incidents occurred," I said. "But I don't know how they're connected, if they even are."

"Just tell me what happened," he said. "Let me make the connections."

How strange, I thought, that Tommy should be giving me the very advice I give my writers. "Just show what happens," I tell them, "don't explain it." He waited patiently, his pen motionless against the pad. I saw that he was a man who understood the uses of silence.

"It began," I said unforgivably, "on a dark and stormy night."

Chapter 1

In the well-ordered world of fiction, murder and mayhem never arrive unheralded. For as long as men have told tales, disaster has been foreshadowed by omens and signs. But if there were portents the day my troubles began, I never saw them. True, the city sky was overcast; but if every passing rain cloud is to be taken as a sign of impending calamity, we might as well all close up shop, don sackcloth, and take to Times Square with hand-lettered signs.

If anything, the day had been remarkably ordinary. It was the first Wednesday of July, and we'd all stayed late for our monthly slush-pile session, gathering in my office around a battered old conference table piled high with manuscripts and query packets. I presided at the head of the table in what I still thought of as Molly's place. To my right sat Harriet Peagoody, currently the only other literary agent in the firm. Harriet was a pale, bony, gray-haired woman with long, restless hands, an Oxbridge accent so well preserved it smelled faintly of formaldehyde, and an air of martyrdom for which I was to blame—for until my prodigal return, she had been the presumptive heir to our little queendom. Her assistant, Chloe Strauss, sat on her other side. Chloe was an Eastern cultivar of the West Coast Valley Girl, dressed in a short, swingy skirt and one of those baby-doll shirts all the girls wear these days. Opposite her sat Jean-Paul Devereaux, our intern and resident hipster. Beneath his sports jacket, his T-shirt read: ETERNITY: WHEN WILL IT END? Twenty-two years old and fresh out of college, Jean-Paul was a tall young man possessed of such extravagant good looks that our bestselling client, Rowena Blair, had asked him to pose for the cover of her latest blockbuster, an offer he had declined. He had dark eyes, olive skin, and luxuriant black curls. Chloe, two years older, was pale, blond, and petite, and I thought they'd make a pretty couple, but Jean-Paul never paid the poor girl any attention.

Lorna Mulligan backed into the office clutching a loaded tray in plump, efficient hands. Today she wore a boxy white blouse and a plaid skirt, a parochial-school outfit that added fifteen pounds to her not-insubstantial frame. Although Lorna was my secretary—she scorned the title "assistant"—it wasn't actually her job to make coffee. Office policy was that whoever finishes one pot makes the next; it lent an egalitarian gloss to the agency, though of course the distribution of profits was anything but. Still, Lorna had herself taken on the task of fueling our monthly conferences. She distributed the mugs and handed around a box of doughnuts. I took my favorite, lemon-filled: a little tartness to balance the sweet. Harriet, as always, chose the old-fashioned doughnut with no cream or glaze, then looked enviously at mine. Chloe passed, and Jean-Paul took two. Lorna never ate any herself, though she must have had a sweet tooth; she took her coffee with four sugars. Now she seated herself at the foot of the table and opened her notebook.

We began, as usual, with the hopeless cases. Other literary agencies don't bother keeping notes on rejects, because office time is better spent serving actual clients than discussing those we'd rejected. But Molly had always kept records, saying that sooner or later every agent overlooks a great book, and when it happened

in her shop, she wanted to know whom to torture. After she retired, I kept up the tradition. Eventually I'd put my own stamp on
the agency, and these meetings would be the first thing to go; but
for now I preferred to follow closely in my mentor's size-9 footsteps.

Jean-Paul and Chloe took turns reading out titles, explaining
in a sentence or two, sometimes from the work in question, why
they recommended rejecting it. They were our first readers of all
unsolicited submissions, and most often they were the last.

Chloe opened with a book called *The Autobiography of a
Nobody*. "The title says it all."

Then Jean-Paul. "*The Secret Life of Gerbils*. You don't want
to know."

"Oh, but I do," Chloe said. "Is it kinky?"

"If you're into rodents."

"Speaking of gross, my nomination for submission of the
month: *To Pee or Not to Pee*, by Dr. Wannamaker."

Even Lorna the Dour laughed.

"You made that up," Harriet said.

"I swear on my mother's urethra," Chloe said. And so it went,
with much joking and laughter, for another couple of hours, by
which time we had disposed of the hopes and dreams of scores of
aspiring authors. Outsiders, listening in, would have thought us
heartless, but outsiders never had to wade through a literary
agent's slush pile, which for people who love literature and language is as much fun as vivisection is for animal lovers.

My thoughts wandered. I looked around my office, thought
about redecorating, and decided once again against it. I'd kept all
of Molly's furniture, even her desk chair, which was too big for me,
because it made me feel as if she hadn't entirely left. The only personal items I'd added were half a dozen framed photos of Hugo,
including one by Annie Leibovitz that I particularly treasured, and
the pearl-handled dagger that he bought me in Morocco, which

served as a letter opener. Molly had disapproved of the photos. "They give the impression that he's the reason you're sitting in this office." As if he weren't; as if I'd be running my own agency were I not the widow of the great Hugo Donovan. Only Molly, who loved me like a mother, could imagine otherwise.

The little sliver of sky visible between the towers of Third Avenue was turning green. There was still an hour to go before sunset, but a summer storm had been threatening all day. A burst of hail pelted the window, and it brought back a vivid image from our honeymoon in Paris: the two of us in bed, my head on Hugo's chest while hailstones clattered against the tiled roof and he recited Emily Dickinson. *Wild Nights – Wild Nights!/Were I with thee/Wild Nights should be/Our luxury!*

Inside my office, the atmosphere had also changed. Chloe was leaning forward, speaking eagerly. "I know it seems, like, gimmicky? I know it won't appeal to everybody? But at heart, it's really an old-fashioned epistolary love story updated to the electronic age. The pages are funny, fresh—the best I've ever found in the slush pile."

"A first novel?" I asked. Chloe nodded, and I sat up, because good first novels come around as often as tax cuts for the poor. "What's it called?"

"It's clever, but . . ." Her voice trailed into silence and she looked at Jean-Paul, who immediately took up the baton.

"Titles can be changed. Personally, I like it. If I saw it in a bookstore I'd pick it up."

"The title?" Harriet demanded.

Chloe held up the title page. "I LUV U BABY, BUT WTF?" it read. "A novel by Katie Vigne."

I laughed and glanced at Harriet. I was braced for fireworks, but she just looked puzzled.

"Chloe. Do you *mind*?" My secretary sounded put-upon, and Chloe hastened to turn the page in her direction.

Lorna read it silently, moving her lips, and copied it into her notes. "What's 'WTF' mean?"

Chloe and Jean-Paul exchanged glances. Lorna was twenty-three years old, their contemporary; how could she not read basic texting? "It means," Chloe said, "'I love you, baby, but what the fuck?' The whole novel is written in texting shortcuts; tweets, actually."

Harriet gave her assistant the look Cleopatra must have given the asp. "And you're recommending that we read this gobbledygook?"

"Harriet, the girl can totally write."

"But she can totally not spell."

"It's a whole other language, thought and emotion pared to the bone, like poetry." The pitch was fluent, no doubt rehearsed, but Chloe had wrapped a strand of blond hair so tightly around her finger that the tip had turned white.

"It's unreadable," Harriet said flatly.

"Not to people who grew up texting," Jean-Paul said. "In Japan, there's an entire industry of cell-phone novels."

Chloe added, "Even people who don't text will pick it up from the context. Or there could be a glossary."

I looked from one to the other. Chloe had excellent taste; and it was interesting that she and Jean-Paul had joined forces on this submission. I was curious, but Harriet was unmoved.

"I do not read books in which 'love' is spelled L-U-V. I do not read books with 'fuck' in the title." She turned to Lorna, who sent out all our rejections. "Add a line to the form. Say that while her work in its present form is inappropriate for us, we would be interested in seeing anything she writes in standard English."

In the silence that followed, I stared at Harriet's adamant profile in amazement. Even for her, this was way over the line. If she wasn't interested in this novel, fair enough; every agent has places she won't go. But she had no right to speak for the agency—to speak for me.

"Ask for a partial," I told Lorna.

Harriet's head whipped around so fast I was reminded of *The Exorcist.* "*Excuse me?*"

"The first fifty pages. Chloe, you read them. If you still like it, I'll have a look."

"*Thank you,*" Chloe mouthed.

My fellow agent had gone bright red. "Far be it from me," Harriet said, "to question your judgment, *Joanna.* But as someone who has worked in this office longer than you have, let me remind you that there is a reason we represent the kind of writers we do. This agency has a reputation to uphold. That novel is symptomatic of the devolution of the language that we of all people must oppose."

Harriet often took it on herself to lecture me, but "Joanna" was a particularly nice touch; I hadn't been called that since the age of nine, when I first read *Little Women.* Her resentment had nothing to do with this particular novel, which was just one more in a long line of proxy battles. She saw me as a usurper, although in fact I'd joined the agency before her. Working as Molly's assistant was my dream job, but I kept it only for a couple of months before meeting and marrying Hugo. Harriet came on board a year or so later, and she'd settled in for the long haul, hoping, perhaps even believing, that one day the business would be hers. But when I returned to the agency after Hugo's death, it was as a partner; and when Molly retired last year, I bought her out and became the sole owner of the Hamish and Donovan Literary Agency, while Harriet remained an employee—well-compensated, but an employee nonetheless.

"The language is always in flux," I said mildly, "and good writers like to play. At least it's not something I've read a thousand times before. If the kiddies think so highly of the first few pages, I think it's worth a look."

"The *kiddies?*" Jean-Paul sounded offended. I raised an eyebrow. At twenty-two, he was thirteen years my junior. How else could I see him but as a kid?

It was dark out by the time we finished, and the hailstorm had dwindled into fitful rain. We said our good nights and the others filed out, carrying stacks of rejected proposals like little baby corpses. We'd rejected 122 submissions and decided to ask for more pages from two, the texting novel and one other: about average for a slush-pile session.

There was no time to go home before my evening engagement, a book launch in a SoHo restaurant, where I hoped to get something to eat in between air kisses and paying court to Rowena. I'd dressed that morning with the evening in mind, in black silk trousers and an unstructured jacket, cinched over a lacy white camisole. All I had to do was slip on high heels and fix my makeup. There is such a preponderance of women in publishing that many don't bother anymore. Not me. An agent needs every bit of leverage she can get, and looks are leverage.

In the private bathroom adjoining my office, I brushed my hair to a dark sheen, removed my makeup, and started from scratch. The face in the mirror was pale and smooth, unmarred by lines of worry or sorrow. No gray showed in the sleek black hair that fell straight to my shoulders. At thirty-five, I was older than I looked but younger and prettier than I felt. There was something Dorian Grayish about this disparity, but I couldn't regret it. That was the face Hugo had loved. Not just the face, of course; but I knew my husband too well to imagine he'd have married me if all my other assets had come wrapped in a plain face and dumpy body. A person who grows up on her own learns to make the most of whatever she's got. Sooner or later, what I was would catch up to what I seemed to be, and then there'd be a reckoning. For now I was living on the cusp: young enough to possess a young woman's power and old enough to know how to wield it.

I left my office and walked down the hall. As I entered the

dimly lit reception room, a figure rose suddenly from behind a desk. I let out a shriek. Jean-Paul came forward, hands raised. "Sorry, Jo, sorry. Didn't mean to spook you."

"I thought everyone was gone."

"I wanted a word, if you have a moment."

"A moment is all I have. Tonight's Rowena's launch, and she'll never forgive me if I'm later than she is."

I locked up and we turned toward the elevators. In addition to my purse and umbrella I was carrying a heavy manuscript bag. Jean-Paul took the strap from my shoulder and put it on his. I smiled my thanks and in the dim light of the corridor thought I saw him blush. The elevator arrived, and we got in.

"Jo," he said, "I was wondering if I could stay on after the summer, not as an intern, but as your full-time assistant."

"What about law school?" I asked, for he'd been accepted to several.

"I can defer for a year or two. If I even go."

"You're having second thoughts?"

"I never really had first thoughts. The thinking was done for me."

I considered it. When Molly retired, I absorbed her entire list. Six months later I fired Charlie Malvino and took over a dozen of his clients as well. My workload was Sisyphean. I needed another assistant, one who read submissions. Lorna didn't, which I couldn't really complain about because she'd been upfront about it. "I'm a first-class secretary," she'd said. "I'll organize your files so you never lose anything again. I'll screen your calls, answer your correspondence, keep your schedule. The office will function like it never has before. But I'm no judge of writing and I won't pretend I am."

Not your usual agency hire. But my last assistant had just left me for a subrights job at Viking, and the one before that had run off to start her own agency with an editor friend. I was tired of

smart, ambitious kids with minds of their own, for all that I'd
been one. Lorna was young, but one had only to look at her, with
her sensible flats, bargain-basement clothes, clunky glasses, and
the excess weight that encased her like an old down coat, to know
that she was the very antithesis of her flighty predecessors. She
had worked for a temp agency that specialized in publishing, so
she knew the business; and because she'd temped for us on occasion, I knew she was a hard worker and brighter than she looked.
And she was happy to work for the salary I offered.

Jean-Paul wouldn't last long, I thought. He'd come to his
senses and go to law school, or he'd accumulate a bit of experience and find a job that paid better. But he'd undoubtedly be an
asset for as long as he stayed. He had a nice touch with clients,
friendly but respectful, unlike Lorna, who, despite her youth,
seemed to regard them as unruly children.

"I'll think about it," I said. "But you should too. Publishing's
a tough racket, and the pay's ridiculous compared to what you'd
make as a lawyer."

"I don't care about that."

"You should. Money matters. Have you talked to your parents
about this?"

I knew at once I'd said the wrong thing. Jean-Paul scowled.
"I'm old enough to know my own mind."

"At twenty-two?"

"*You* did."

Meaning, I supposed, that I'd married Hugo at twenty-two.
What a strange turn this conversation had taken. I was relieved
when the elevator shuddered to a halt and the doors slid open.
The building was prewar, but the lobby had been sleekly redone,
all glass and polished black marble. The night man was reading
a magazine at the security desk. He glanced up as the elevator
opened, then shoved the magazine into his desk, stood and
touched his cap. "'Night, Ms. Donovan."

"Good night, John." There would come a day, I thought, when I would enter a room and no man would notice; but that day was not here yet. I started opening my umbrella as we left the building, but there was no need. The rain had let up, for now at least, and through a parting in the clouds a bright crescent moon shone down on the glistening avenue. After the rain, the Manhattan air smelled as fresh and clean as a sea breeze.

Jean-Paul handed me my tote bag, and we parted on the sidewalk. As I walked south, a man burst from the alley beside our building and rushed toward me. "Jo! Jo Donovan!"

I stopped and turned to face him. He wore a belted trench coat, sopping wet, and a fedora tilted down over his face, so that in the dark I could hardly make out his features. He'd spoken as if he knew me, but I didn't recognize him except from old Bogart flicks. "Sam Spade, I presume?" I said.

"What time do you have?"

Reflexively I glanced at my watch. "Seven fifty."

"Mark the time, Jo. Remember this moment. Both our lives are about to change." His voice throbbed with emotion. It was the sort of voice that sounds good on the radio, deep and smooth. I noticed a parcel under his left arm that looked suspiciously like a manuscript.

"Let me guess: you're a writer."

"Not just a writer," the voice said, "any more than you're just an agent. I know what you really are, Jo. And soon you'll know what I am."

One has to make allowances for writers, especially the unpublished ones. Rejection gets to everyone after a while, and those poor bastards swim in a sea of it.

"Look," I said, "if you have something to submit, use the guidelines on our website and I promise we'll read it. This isn't the way."

"I did. It never reached you. *Someone* in your office intercepted it and sent it back unread."

"Why do you say that?"

"Because if anyone had bothered to read it, they'd have recognized it for the work of genius that it is. Also, you failed the test."

I sighed. "Let me guess: an upside-down page?"

"Which came back the same way."

"What page?"

"Two hundred sixty-two."

I laughed, couldn't help it, though I knew it would only make him angrier. Presumption, thy name is Writer. Our guidelines ask for synopses and the first five pages only, no more material except by request. At least a quarter of submitters ignores those guidelines and sends us their full manuscripts. Clearly Sam Spade was one of those. Even so, it was impossible not to feel sorry for him. A person can pour his heart and soul into a book and still end up with something only a mother would read.

"I'm sorry you didn't get the answer you wanted," I said, "but we take on very few new clients, and once we determine that a book is not for us, we don't continue reading. We get hundreds of submissions a month; if we read them all in full, we'd have time for nothing else, as I'm sure you understand. But of course you should try elsewhere. I'm just one agent. There are any number of good ones out there."

"Not for me." He held out the manuscript. "You'll understand once you've read it."

There's a reason agents barricade themselves behind assistants and secretaries. Rejection is unpleasant for the rejecter as well as the rejected; a little distance makes it easier to bear. But I had no intention of being bullied into reading something we'd already turned down.

"I can't help you," I said firmly. "And for future reference, this is hardly the way to recommend yourself to any agent."

"You still don't get it. No other agent will do." He slid closer.

"I know what you are, Jo. You were Hugo's muse. Now you're going to be mine."

A jolt of fear ran through me. I had misjudged the situation. This wasn't the usual writerly egotism. This was something else.

You can't live in New York without occasionally encountering crazy people. They used to scare me till I learned the protocol: keep moving, look straight ahead, and feign deafness until they go away. I was good at feigning deafness, having practiced it often when Hugo's old girlfriends called.

He stood in my path. I stepped to the side, but as I made to pass him, he reached out and grabbed my arm.

I didn't stop to think. The umbrella was in my free hand and I swung it, striking him solidly across the chest. He flew backward into a lamppost and came back at me.

I faced him squarely, fear banished by anger. *How dare he touch me? How dare he mention Hugo, compare himself to Hugo!* Dropping my tote, I grasped the umbrella stock with two hands and struck a batter's stance. I heard steps, running hard; then hands clutched me from behind and pushed me aside. Nose to nose with my accoster, Jean-Paul shouted, "Get the fuck away from her!"

Too angry to welcome interference, I tried to slide past him, but Jean-Paul wouldn't budge. He shoved the writer hard in the chest. "Grab me, why don't you?"

Sam Spade backed away, cradling the manuscript to his chest. "Kid, you just made the biggest mistake of your life." He inclined his head toward me, shadowed eyes groping. "I'll see you later, Jo."

He turned and walked away. Jean-Paul lunged after him, but I grabbed his arm. We looked at each other. His face was flushed, fists clenched. I could smell his rage. "Are you all right?" he asked.

"I could have used a few more whacks."

"Who was he?"

"Nobody. Some idiot who can't take no for an answer."

"A writer? Someone we rejected?"

"Apparently."

"What an asshole!"

"Comes with the territory," I said, but that was just to calm him. Overeager writers were indeed a fact of publishing life, and I'd met my share at writers' conferences; but this felt different, creepy, and far too personal.

Jean-Paul mastered himself with a visible effort. "I never realized agenting is such a contact sport. Nice umbrella work, by the way." He picked my tote up from the sidewalk and slung it over his shoulder. "I'll see you to the subway."

"I'm fine," I said, but he walked me anyway.

Chapter 2

Within an hour of its occurrence, my encounter with the crazy writer had been absorbed, processed, and edited into a story that I recounted to a clutch of colleagues at the restaurant, eliciting uneasy laughter from the females, protective noises from the males. Left on the cutting-room floor was Sam Spade's invocation of Hugo, which had left me feeling more violated than the vilest obscenities could have done. Jean-Paul, all agreed, had behaved admirably. It occurred to me that I had not been altogether gracious to my would-be rescuer. The boy had undoubtedly meant well, even if the one he ended up protecting was my accoster.

I snagged a glass of white wine from a passing waiter and looked around to see who else was there. It was difficult to see much, since the restaurant was fashionably dark. Maison D'être was its name, and it billed itself as an existential café. The menu was eclectic and the food delicious, though what it had to do with existentialism I couldn't begin to guess. Maybe the small portions. Housed on the ground floor of what had once been a coach house, the restaurant consisted of a single large room with a bar near the entrance. Sconces shone upward, illuminating the tin ceiling. The main source of light in the room was a spotlight at the far end trained on a floor-to-ceiling pyramid of Rowena's new book, *Alexandrian Nights*. The pyramid was flanked by two huge arrangements of white roses, her favorite flower. *Alexandrian Nights* was Rowena's twentieth book in twenty years, every one of them bestsellers, and Pellucid Press had gone all-out to celebrate this anniversary book. The Pellucid contingent was there in force, of course, led by publisher Larry Sharpe; Rowena would expect no less. In the crush I spotted editors from other houses, a smattering of agents, and some hungry-eyed writers circling the crowd like wolves. Plenty of press, but no book critics. Rowena was not beloved of the critics, nor they of her.

In this, Rowena Blair was not the typical Hamish-Donovan client. Our fiction list tacked toward the literary, while Rowena trod the path blazed by Judith Krantz and Jackie Collins: that is, she wrote big old-fashioned potboilers set in exotic locales, with lots of steamy sex and a spunky heroine whom no adversity could defeat. In my admittedly biased opinion, Rowena got a raw deal from the critics. She wasn't a great literary artist, but her books were always fun to read, which was more than could be said for many of our more lauded authors. She was an honest craftswoman and a hard worker who always delivered on time, if a bit of a prima donna, as evidenced by the fact that one hour into the party, there was still no sign of the guest of honor.

Rowena liked to make a grand entrance, and no one minded, as her publisher had ensured that her guests would not want for food, drink, or entertainment while they waited. There was an open bar, roaming waiters with trays of hors d'oeuvres, and, running down the center of the room, a large buffet table engulfed by an impenetrable scrum of bodies. They were young bodies for the most part, publishing assistants and interns who supplemented their meager or nonexistent wages by scrounging the free food at every book launch they could get into, as I'd done myself before Hugo. The entertainment came from the spectacle of the waitstaff dressed in tight black pants and T-shirts, all of whom looked like models or actors and probably were, and by the exchange of publishing gossip that was the main currency of these gatherings.

I heard a burst of familiar laughter and spied Charlie Malvino heading in my direction, arm in arm with a Pellucid publicist. Gathering tidbits for his damned blog, no doubt. I hadn't met Charlie since I fired him and had no wish to meet him now. But as I turned away from him, I found myself face-to-face with another man I'd been strenuously avoiding for weeks.

"Jo," he said, beaming. "What luck."

Luck my ass, I thought. Ambushed twice in one day. I should have stayed home, as if that were an option. "Hello, Teddy."

Despite pudgy, dimpled cheeks and a Tweedledum figure, Edward Warren Pendragon was not nearly as cuddly as his nickname suggested. He had good manners and pleasant looks and a Mississippi drawl that reputedly had cut swaths through the ranks of New York's female editors, though you couldn't tell it by me; having grown up in Appalachia, I was cornpone-proof. But Teddy also had a sharp eye and a sharper pen. By trade he was a biographer who specialized in writers. Last year, *Vanity Fair* had commissioned him to write a profile of Hugo to coincide with the third anniversary of his death. I gave Teddy an interview. Big mistake. Feed a biographer and it only makes him hungry for more.

"You're a difficult lady to reach," Teddy said.

"Sorry, I've been swamped."

"Did you get the tear sheets?"

"I did, thank you." I sipped my wine to bridge the awkward silence where praise should have come.

"You didn't like the piece?" he said, with the ready insecurity of even the most successful writers.

"Haven't had a chance to read it yet, I'm afraid."

He looked as if I'd slapped him.

"Sorry, Teddy. It's still hard for me, even after three years." Pathetic, playing the grieving-widow card, but I had a reason. There is only so long you can detain someone at a function like this, and Teddy knew the rules as well as anyone. One moment of commiseration and I could let the human tide bear me away.

He didn't offer any. "The thing is, Jo, I really need to talk to you, not as Hugo's widow, but as his executor. The *Vanity Fair* piece stirred up a lot of interest. Random House approached me about doing a biography."

I knew this. Hugo's editor, David Axelhorn, had called me, too, to feel me out. I'd told him I'd think about it and stopped returning his calls. Sooner or later it was bound to happen; but knowing as I did Hugo's opinion of literary biographers—"coyotes battening on the remains of their betters," he once called them, in a letter to the *Times*—I had no intention of helping the process along.

"This week's crazy," I said, edging away, "and next week I'm doing a writers' conference in Santa Fe. Personally, I'm not convinced the time is right for a bio. But call me at the office after that and we'll discuss it."

Teddy seemed skeptical, with good reason; he'd never get past Lorna. Then salvation arrived in the form of a six-foot-tall Jewish goddess in a caftan and a very chic turban.

"Molly!" I cried, throwing my arms around her. It felt like hugging a skeleton. She winced a little and I let go immediately. "What are you doing here?"

"Hey, kiddo. What do you think? Rowena threatened my life if I didn't show."

I should have anticipated that. Molly had been Rowena's first and only agent, until she retired. Over the course of twenty books and twenty years, they'd formed a close friendship that continued after Molly retired and I took over Rowena's representation.

"But how'd you get here?" I asked, for Molly lived in West-chester and could no longer drive.

"Rowena sent her car. You should see her driver. *Mamma mia!*"

I led her away from Teddy, who showed signs of wanting to join in the conversation. Molly leaned heavily on my arm as we passed slowly through the crowd, all of whom, it seemed, needed to greet her. For forty years she'd been a literary agent, a match-maker of writers and publishers. She'd midwifed thousands of books, launched hundreds of careers, and now all her babies were coming home to roost. It was some comfort to see how much she was loved and missed, though I cursed their inconsideration in keeping her standing. At home she'd been using a cane since the last surgery, but she was too proud to use one here.

At last we came to an unoccupied table near the pyramid of books, and I urged Molly into a seat. She reached up to adjust her turban.

"You look beautiful," I said. In fact she looked haggard. In one year she'd aged twenty. Though the caftan disguised the gauntness of her body and the turban her baldness, nothing could soften the stark features that had once ruled her face in stately harmony but now occupied her face like outposts in a barren wasteland. The strange thing was that no matter how often I saw Molly, which was once a month at least, I never seemed to assim-ilate the changes in her appearance, so each new encounter came as a shock.

Only her eyes were unchanged, deep brown pools of intelli-gence whose penetrating gaze was fixed on my face. "Such a liar," she said. "I hate this damn babushka. But the wig is even worse."

"Can I get you something, Molly?" The crowd by the buffet table was only two deep, and here and there I could glimpse ac-tual dishes. The smell made my mouth water; apart from Lorna's doughnut, I'd had nothing to eat since breakfast.

"Sit." She patted the chair beside her, and I sat, swallowing a sigh. "Talk to me. What did Teddy Pendragon want?"

"He cornered me, the prick. The *Vanity Fair* piece wasn't enough; now he wants to do a bio."

I fully expected her to join in my indignation. She had been Hugo's agent, after all, his dear friend and our accidental match-maker. She would hate the idea of our lives being pawed over and hung out for display. So I could hardly believe it when Molly said, "You could do worse."

I gasped. "*Et tu,* Molly?"

"Someone's going to write one," she answered matter-of-factly. "You can't prevent it, so you might as well find someone good. Teddy's first-rate. Did you read his Vonnegut?"

I had read it and it was good. It was the reason I'd agreed to the interview, that and the incessant nagging of Hugo's publisher. But there was a huge difference between a magazine profile and a book, and I was amazed that Molly couldn't see that.

"Didn't you like his *Vanity Fair* piece?" she asked.

"I didn't read it."

"Well, you should, it was very flattering. He called you and Hugo the greatest literary couple since Scott and Zelda."

"You call that flattering? Look how Zelda ended up!"

"You're made of sterner stuff. Anyway, if Teddy doesn't write it, someone else will. I've heard rumors."

"What rumors?"

Molly lowered her voice. "I heard Gloria Vogel's been shopping a proposal."

I couldn't take it in. Gloria Vogel wrote celebrity bios—gossipy, titillating, speculative trash. Impossible. Molly must be wrong.

Except that she was never wrong. Even secluded in her house in Scarsdale, Molly Hamish collected information the way TVs collect dust. She heard everything about our incestuous little world: who's moving where, who's stealing whose authors, who's cheating on whom in the boardroom and the bedroom. If Molly said it, it was true.

I felt sick to my stomach. First Sam Spade, then Teddy, now Molly. The first two I could have taken in stride. Desperate writers come with the territory, and as for Teddy, fending off pests had been one of my jobs as Hugo's wife; I could do it in my sleep. That was just business.

But Molly was different. Molly had given me my start in publishing, choosing me out of a hundred applicants to be her assistant. She'd introduced me to Hugo. After he died and I was drowning in grief, she pulled me ashore, taking me back into the agency, piling on work to fill the unbearable emptiness. It was useful work, I was good at it, and it gave me a reason to crawl out of bed even when I didn't want to. I loved Molly. She was the mother I'd never had, just as I was the daughter she'd longed for. How could she take Teddy's side, against Hugo's wishes and my own?

I yearned to go home, crawl into the big bed I'd shared with Hugo, and pull the covers over my head, but I couldn't leave before congratulating Rowena. Suddenly a blare of trumpets sounded, silencing the room. The doors to the restaurant were flung open, the lights raised, and two trumpeters marched in. Behind them, half-reclining on a litter carried by four huge men, was our very own Rowena. She was dressed as Cleopatra in a flowing, draped gown of gold and Nile green, thick jade wristlets, and a gold head cloth that covered the crown of her head and fell squarely to her shoulders. Her eyes were ringed with kohl. A large fake snake—I hoped it was fake—was wrapped around her neck.

My eyes met Molly's, and we burst into laughter. Our client's flair for over-the-top drama wasn't confined to her novels. The launch party for her last book, which was set in a circus, had been held in the Big Apple Circus, and Rowena had made her entrance on an elephant. But tonight she'd surpassed herself. If nothing else, it was a bracing antidote to the usual staid book launch.

"Did you know?" I asked Molly when I could speak again.

She was laughing so hard that mascara was carving rivulets in her powdered cheeks. "She never said a word! Bless her for making me come. I'd have died if I'd missed this."

The crowd parted before Rowena like the Red Sea before Moses, flashbulbs marking her passage. The litter bearers, clad in short togas and leather sandals with straps that wove around their calves, carried Rowena to the pyramid, where her publisher awaited. Larry held out his hand, and the Queen of the Nile graciously descended.

The room rang with laughter and applause. Rowena spread her arms to embrace us all. Her outfit was perfect, down to the very sandals Cleopatra would have worn if Manolo Blahnik had lived in ancient Egypt. In her natural state, Rowena, née Marylou Hubbard, would have made a creditable farmer had not ambition and talent propelled her far from the Kansas wheat fields of her youth. She had broad shoulders and a sturdy physique that not even the most rigorous diet and exercise regimen could render sylphlike, and her nails were polished works of art mounted on thick, blunt fingers. But everything that could be changed had been: boobs, butt, tummy . . . The face framed by that golden headpiece had been expertly improved and updated. Rowena was fifty-three, admitted to thirty-nine, and could almost get away with it.

Waiters came around with Champagne. Larry's toast was both effusive and sincere, befitting an author whose books accounted for a hefty percentage of his company's gross revenue. In her response, Rowena lauded her publisher, swore undying love for her editor, and thanked what seemed like the entire Pellucid sales force by name. Then she said, "Finally, most importantly, I'd like to take this opportunity to thank my two extraordinary agents, Molly Hamish and Jo Donovan. Molly believed in me before I believed in myself, and she terrorized other people into believing as well. She has been my champion, my teacher, my protector, and my friend. When she told me she was retiring, I was devastated, first for her but also, with true writerly selfishness, for myself. I knew no one would be able to take her place, and indeed no one ever could.

"But Jo Donovan stands in a place of her own. We all know the kind of writers Jo has worked with. We know the level. I was—I admit it—intimidated. As young as she was, to have done so much: what would she make of my scribblings? What I discovered, when I turned in *Alexandrian Nights*, was an agent/editor par excellence. She treated my twentieth book as if it were my first. She saw through what was on the paper to what was in my heart, and she would not rest until she had cajoled and bullied me into producing the best work I had in me. And then she sold the hell out of it." Beside her, Larry shrugged in rueful acknowledgment. Rowena raised her glass in our direction. "To have had two such agents in a lifetime is a blessing indeed."

Molly blew her a kiss and I bowed my head in thanks. I knew perfectly well that before Molly's chair had even cooled, Rowena's phone had been ringing off the hook with suitors. That this woman, who could have had any agent she wanted, should have felt nervous about showing me her work spoke again to the appalling insecurity of fiction writers. Tightrope walkers, Hugo once called them, crossing chasms on strings of words. I couldn't do it. Give me the business end of publishing any day.

I assured myself that Molly had a ride home, then said goodbye before she could start in on me again. Rowena was surrounded by people, but a lane opened for me. We hugged. She smelled of something expensively exotic.

"Nice entrance," I said.

"I wanted a horse-drawn chariot, but the restaurant wouldn't go along. Some stupidity about the health code."

"This was better."

She grinned. "It was, wasn't it?"

"Thank you for those lovely words. Molly was touched too."

"I meant every word, my dear." She squeezed my hand. Then the crowd exerted its pressure and I was rotated out. I made for the exit before anyone else could jump me and was waiting for my tote at the hatcheck counter when Molly appeared, leaning on the arm of one of Rowena's tunic-clad litter bearers.

"Bit young for you, isn't he?" I asked.

She veered toward me and rapped my knuckles with her umbrella. "This is Manny, Rowena's driver. He's taking me home."

I looked him over. "Like that?"

"It's New Yawk," Manny said. "Who's gonna notice?"

Chapter 3

It was too early to check into La Posada, so I left my bags and slipped out for a walk through downtown Santa Fe. Once the writers' conference began, the world would shrink to the size of the hotel, and between workshops, panels, pitch sessions, luncheons, and dinners, I would have no time to indulge myself. Blazing sun glanced off the adobe buildings and flooded the streets; the air tasted of pine and dust. It was just past noon and very hot. Island-dweller that I was, I felt the altitude as a lessening of gravity, as if a single strong gust would send me soaring, Chagall-like, over the adobe walls into the deep-blue distant sky.

Over the course of a year, I, like most agents, receive a dozen or more invitations to attend writers' conferences. Most I turn down, because it's rare to find a publishable writer among the attendees, much less one whose work I loved enough to take on. But this Santa Fe conference held two big attractions. The first was that one of my favorite clients, Max Messinger, was among the presenters; the second was Santa Fe itself. I'd been there with Hugo, a year into our marriage, and if I kept my eyes straight ahead, I could imagine him striding beside me, hear his voice in my ear.

I found my way to the plaza, which looked exactly as I'd

remembered it and probably not very different from the way it had looked two hundred years ago. In the portal of the Palace of the Governors, Native American women sat on low stools behind blankets covered with crafts: jewelry for the most part—silver and turquoise and coral—but also woven blankets and rugs, baskets, pottery. The women did not hawk their wares but rather sat in dignified silence, speaking only when addressed. On the last day of our visit, Hugo bought me a silver pendant set with turquoise and coral from a woman who mistook me for his daughter. I wondered if she was still there. Resisting the lure of the shady cottonwoods, I crossed to the portal and made my way down the line of vendors. I studied each one in turn, but if the seller was among them, I didn't recognize her.

Well, I thought, twelve years. Anything can change in twelve years. Isabel Delgado, Hugo's friend and collaborator, might have sold her house on Canyon Road, though I hoped not, for it suited her so well. It had adobe walls a foot thick and rounded windows, hand-carved vigas, and kiva fireplaces in all the principal rooms. The terra-cotta floors were strewn with bright Navajo rugs, and niches in the walls displayed her collection of Indian pottery. There was a separate adobe outbuilding fitted up as a state-of-the-art music studio, where she and Hugo worked on the project that had brought us to Santa Fe: a rock opera based on his first novel, *Distant Cries*. Every morning, before they started working, the three of us drank coffee on the patio beneath a trellis of orange trumpet vine, surrounded by pots of periwinkle, sage, and desert marigolds. Afterward I'd leave them and go off on my own to explore the city.

In the early days of my marriage, I had been wary of other women. Hugo was a famous playboy, and I did not yet feel myself an equal partner in our marriage; I didn't even feel equal to the worldly, accomplished women who orbited around him. But Isabel Delgado didn't worry me, because the composer was old, forty-five at least, well past the age of dalliance. (That Hugo was even older never occurred to me; in my eyes he was ageless.) She was a fine-looking woman for her age, tall and slender with strong features and long black hair, filigreed with silver, that she wore in a single braid down the middle of her back. Though she was as acclaimed in her world as Hugo was in his, she lived simply and without airs. And she was kind to me in an Auntie Mame sort of way. She gave me things: an embroidered shawl, turquoise earrings, and a Hopi bowl . . . When Hugo died, she flew to New York for the memorial service.

I should call her, I thought. But somehow I didn't care to.

I had checked in with the conference organizers and was just getting my room key when a hand clasped my shoulder. At once I flashed back to Sam Spade grabbing me on the street and, without thinking, I knocked the hand away and spun around.

Max Messinger raised both hands. "Easy there, bruiser."

"Max!" I cried, and we fell into each other's arms. Max was a legacy from Molly, but one I'd long since made my own. He was six-foot-two with a gleaming bald head, a trim goatee, and one gold hoop earring. Before he took to writing thrillers for a living, he'd been an FBI profiler, and before that a field agent. I kept expecting the sedentary life of the writer to take its toll, but the body pressed to mine was as soft as a refrigerator.

He held me at arm's length and inspected the goods. "You're a breath of New York air."

"My new scent: Eau D'exhaust."

He laughed. "Come have a drink."

I asked the desk clerk to send my bags to my room and hooked my arm in Max's. We strolled out to the garden and chose a table beside a fountain. There was something so comforting about being with Max; it was like walking a mastiff.

"How's Molly?" he asked.

People asked me all the time, and I usually said she was doing fine, holding her own. I couldn't lie to Max, though. "Not great. It's in her bones now."

He said all there was to say, which was nothing. Dragonflies darted through the spray of the fountain. A waitress came and took our orders: white wine for me, beer for Max.

When she left, Max said, "Barry sends his love and two pots of jam from our very own strawberry patch. Can you believe those words coming from a New York Jew? Life is so incongruous."

"Who does the canning?" I asked.

"Elves. You didn't think Barry would stain his lily-whites, did you?"

Barry Roth was an entertainment lawyer and Max's husband. Molly took credit for the match, having sent Max to Barry when the movie rights to his first book sold. Within a month they were living together; and days after gay marriage was briefly legalized in California, Molly and I flew to L.A. for their wedding. At the dinner we sat next to Max's mother, Estelle, a plump little widow from Queens, who danced the hora with gusto and confided, after a few White Russians, "I always hoped he'd marry a nice Jewish girl. But two out of three ain't bad."

Of course, by then Max was out of the FBI. They'd known he was gay—Max was too big to fit in any closet—but marriage might have strained his colleagues' grudging acceptance to the breaking point. Or so I imagined, for while Max made prodigious use of his years in the bureau for his thrillers, he rarely talked about his own time there. Couldn't have been easy, I imagined, being gay and Jewish to boot. But writers do tend to be outsiders, and whatever else he was, Max was a writer to the bone.

Over our drinks we discussed his new publisher. I had moved

him over to Random for a three-book deal with a 50 percent bump in his advances and a fresh marketing plan to back up their investment. The first book was due out in a few weeks and Random had already gone back for a second printing. There was a twelve-city tour in the works, along with a national radio campaign. Max should have been over the moon, and a part of him was, but another part of him worried. "What if they don't earn out? What if I don't make the list?"

Writers. Every one I'd ever met was bipolar, the poles being arrogance and insecurity. Even my Hugo had had his moments of doubt. I never knew what would trigger them. A clueless review, the success of a lesser writer (not even great writers, I'd learned, were immune to jealousy), a significant birthday. It was better in Paris, where we spent six months of every year, but the troughs between books were always fraught with danger. I'd come home from shopping on the Boulevard du Montparnasse, carrying our daily baguette, fruit, and cheese, to find him sprawled across our brass bed, wiry gray hair furrowed with tugging, surrounded by balled-up sheets of loose-leaf paper.

"I'm done," he'd say. "I'm finished. I'm out of words."

"They'll come back," I'd promise. And they always did.

Max had opened a menu and was studying it closely. "I'm starving. Eating for two now, you know."

"Excuse me?"

He gave me a sly grin. "Didn't I tell you? We're pregnant."

"Highly unlikely."

"And yet true, thanks to an egg donor and a lovely surrogate named Pamela."

I was speechless, but Max, secure in my delight, rattled on without noticing. He'd always wanted kids, he said. Barry was the hold-out, but when he hit forty, something changed. "We don't know which of us is the biological father. Better that way, don't you think?"

"Much better." I managed a smile. It's not that I wasn't happy for them. He'd taken me by surprise was all.

"If it's a girl, we're naming her Molly."

Something cold and hard throbbed in me, like the beating of a dead heart.

"You don't think she'll be offended?" he asked. "Technically Jews aren't supposed to name children after the living."

"She'll be thrilled and honored. It's a lovely name. If I'd had a daughter, I'd have called her Molly." I don't know why I said that. It felt like sticking a fork in my hand. There was a time when I thought Hugo and I would have a child. It didn't happen. Since then I'd put fruitless longing behind me and moved on. Still, now and then it flared up, like malaria or some hidden disease of the heart.

Max probed my face. At certain angles, you could still see the detective in him. "What's going on in your life, Jo?"

"Same old same old. Fighting with publishers. Doing their job for them."

"And? Anyone special?"

That again. Max was as bad as Molly, always urging me to start dating, get back in the game. I'd had offers, from men far more attractive than the oily Teddy Pendragon, but none of them were Hugo; none of them compared.

"You know," I said, "ever since you found wedded bliss, you've turned into an awful yenta."

"I come by it honestly," Max said. "You met my mother."

"You should be glad I'm married to my work. No distractions."

"It's not all about me."

"Shhh!" I said, looking around. "Don't let the Authors Guild hear you."

"I mean it, Jo. Listen to Uncle Max. The best book in the world won't keep you warm at night. You need a man for that."

"You think? Goose down's warmer, and a lot more malleable."

"Always with the jokes," he said, sighing.

My suitcase was waiting in the room. I unpacked and took a long shower. When I came out of the bathroom, I went to check my e-mail and realized only then that my laptop was missing.

I called the desk. The clerk took the particulars and promised to send the computer over at once. I finished dressing, dried my hair, and did my makeup; then, as the computer still hadn't arrived, I took the conference folder outside to read on the patio, which was shaded by a large oak and surrounded by sweet-smelling banks of geranium, sage, and lavender. The folder contained a list of presenters with bios; a schedule of all events, with a digest of mine; and four novel synopses to be read prior to Sunday's one-on-one pitch sessions. Among the writers on the presenters' list was one whose work I admired, and I made a mental note to seek her out. I don't poach writers from other agents, but it never hurts to plant a seed. There were editors from Doubleday, Crown, Morrow, and a few smaller houses. The agents were a mixed bag: some one-man shops, some junior agents from large agencies, and a smattering of regional agents I didn't know at all.

I put the file aside. It was time for the cocktail party, and I was ready for a drink. From the pool area came the sound of children laughing and splashing, but the garden was deserted.

The phone rang. I went inside and answered. The hotel manager's voice sounded spongy, like plush carpet laid over a waterbed. He was so sorry; he couldn't explain it—this never, ever happened—but somehow my laptop had disappeared from the luggage room.

"Find it," I said.

"Yes, ma'am. Absolutely. We'll search the entire hotel if we have to. We'll—"

"I'm going out," I said. "I'll be gone for an hour. When I return, I expect to find my laptop in my room." I hung up. I hadn't raised my voice, hadn't tapped the arsenal of invective amassed over a decade of New York City cab rides. I know disaster when I see it, and this was no disaster. Nevertheless I was furious. How dare they? My entire life was on that computer. I couldn't have felt more exposed if I'd walked naked into a ballroom.

"They *what*?" Max said.

"You heard."

He couldn't stand up—he was already standing. But he gave the impression of doing so. "Allow me to deal with this."

I put my free hand on his arm. The other held a double scotch. "I gave them an hour. Let's not haul out the big guns just yet."

"Is something wrong?" said a voice behind me.

I recognized that smarmy tone at once, though his name hadn't been on the list.

"Charlie," I said. "What a surprise." Charlie Malvino, my former employee, was the only man in the crowded hospitality suite dressed in a suit and tie, and I had to admit it suited his sleek, foxy looks. Give him a cane and a top hat and he could have doubled for a young Fred Astaire.

"Last-minute thing," he said. "I'm pinch-hitting for Janie Aldridge."

"Is she all right?"

"She is. One of her brood has chicken pox or measles or whatever rug rats get these days." He turned to Max with a charming smile and outstretched hand. "Charlie Malvino, Mr. Messinger. We met when I worked for Jo."

"I remember," Max said in a markedly cool tone. I never told him about the business with Charlie, but Max keeps his ear to the ground. Or maybe he hadn't cared for the rug rat remark.

"You sounded upset, Jo," Charlie said. "Is something wrong?" He looked concerned, but I saw the smirk hovering below that blond wisp of a mustache. I considered the possibility that he had hijacked my laptop just to mess with me. Unlikely, I decided. Charlie preferred the safety of cyberspace. After I fired him, he'd led a chorus of attacks on me by bloggers, which was picked up by Gawker, Mediabistro, and various publishing gossip sheets. I was scourged as "a top literary agent who defends free speech for writers while denying it to her employees." The charge stung, though it wasn't exactly true. I hadn't objected to Charlie's pseudonymous "Jack the Ripper" blog, only to his using it to make fun of writers we'd rejected.

It was a mean-spirited blog, but funny and full of insider gossip. Like most people in the industry, I read it now and then for a laugh and joined in the speculation about the Ripper's real identity. I'd had my suspicions—the voice was familiar—but I wasn't sure until the day he posted a sampling of that month's slush-pile rejects.

I read the blog on a Wednesday night, six months ago. The first thing I did was call Molly. By then she'd turned the agency over to me, but Charlie was her hire and he'd worked there longer than I had. We talked it through and agreed on what had to be done. The next morning, I went in early, copied Charlie's files, and started sorting through his list. Lorna saw me doing it, but Lorna's loyalty was to me alone. At ten o'clock I heard Charlie stroll into the office. A moment later he tapped on my open door.

"Lorna said you wanted to see me?"

"Come in," I said. "Shut the door."

He took the visitor's seat and arranged his narrow face into a look of polite interest that told me he knew damn well why he was there. Carelessly, recklessly, he'd blown his cover.

"What were you thinking?" I said.

He stroked his mustache, a recent acquisition. "About what, Jo?"

"Let's not waste time. I read your blog."

I watched as he considered playing dumb and wisely decided against it. "Were you amused?" he asked.

"I was the first time you said those things, in this office. It was a lot less funny online where anyone could read it, including the writers you ridiculed."

"I didn't use names."

"You summarized their stories; you quoted from their work. You don't think they'll find out?"

"What are the odds?" he scoffed.

"Quite good, I should think. Unpublished writers read agent blogs."

"You should read what they write about us. I could show you some sites—they rip into literary agents like we're all a bunch of goose-stepping little Hitlers conspiring to squash their creative genius."

"I've read them. So what? It's just writers blowing off steam. Rejection hurts, Charlie. Why would you think of pouring salt on the wounds?"

"Hey, it's a tough business. If they can't take the heat, let 'em self-publish." He leaned back in his seat and stretched out his legs.

I would have fired him anyway, because sooner or later he was bound to be outed as Jack the Ripper, and when he was I didn't want his name associated with my agency. The arrogance of his posture just made it easier. Charlie had never been a writer, never lived with one. He had no idea what that life is like, starting with all the rejection on the front end, which is like hazing except that it continues even after you make the club. For every yes, there are a dozen nos. Once Hugo started publishing, rejection was not a concern, but he still bore the scars, along with every other writer in our large acquaintance.

"Pack your stuff and get out," I said.

Charlie was too astonished to argue. If he'd imagined this encounter, none of his scenarios had ended this way. He left the room without another word, and a short while later I heard him stomp out of the office. By then I was already on the phone to one of his clients.

I called only those I wanted to keep, good earners or good writers or, in a few cases, both. "Charlie's leaving the agency," I told them. I didn't say why, and though they probed and hinted, none came right out and asked. "I'm not sure what he'll be doing next, but I wanted to let you know that you won't be left hanging. We value our association with you, and if you choose to stay with Hamish and Donovan, I will undertake to represent you myself."

Some agreed on the spot. Others, to their credit, asked for time to consider—time for Charlie to make his case. But in the end, every one of them accepted my offer. Charlie had the relationship, but I had the agency, the name, the connections, and the reputation. It was no contest. And there was no malice to it, not on my end. Those writers were agency clients; I had as much right to them as he did. If I'd wanted to hurt him, I could have taken his whole list.

Charlie, of course, didn't see it that way. He was furious, but there was nothing he could do except bitch online. According to Molly, with whom he stayed in touch, things didn't work out badly for him. He took his remaining list and set up shop in his apartment. Someone at Mediabistro put two and two together and outed him, but far from hurting, the publicity from the blog and his firing brought in a flood of submissions. I heard he'd even sold a book or two since then.

I could see that he still hadn't forgiven me. He smiled, and spite glinted in his eyes. He asked how I was doing and I said fine and he said he was glad to hear it, because he'd hate to think of anything bad happening to me. I said grow up, why dontcha, and we smiled some more. Max interrupted all this smiling by slinging an arm around my shoulders and walking me away.

"Sweet guy," he said.

"For an asshole."

"If your laptop doesn't show up, I know where to look."

"He's not stupid," I said. Then I had a vision of my computer lying at the bottom of the pool and my stomach clenched.

Chapter 4

When the presenters' reception ended, we were gently but efficiently herded toward the banquet room to be formally introduced to the conference attendees. My attempt to slip away was blocked by a genial giant with a Texan accent and an organizer's badge. He didn't actually say, "Git along, little dogie," but it was too close for comfort. One by one, the anesthetized editors, agents, and authors filed into the banquet hall, which was airy and light and full of flowers, with picture windows framing the turquoise sky. The attendees, already seated, were buzzing with excitement but fell silent as we made our way to the reserved tables in the front of the room. Faces turned to us like flowers to the sun.

Over dinner I fell into conversation with a Doubleday editor named Marisa Deighton, a delightful girl, smart and funny. She said she loved fiction in any genre as long as it came in a distinctive voice, and I immediately thought of Keyshawn Grimes, a young writer I recently took on. Keyshawn had written a semiautobiographical novel about a black kid from Bed-Stuy who wins a full scholarship to an overwhelmingly white, Groton-like prep school and is suspected when a series of crimes occurs. It wasn't a big book, in industry parlance, just a promising one, and I hadn't yet found a home for it. The book was a genre cocktail: one part mystery, one part coming-of-age story, and two parts novel of class and race. This had presented definite marketing challenges, since editors tend to prefer their genres straight up. But the writer's voice was strong and original; it spoke to me, and I thought it might speak to her. A youngster like Marisa would have more room on her list than the senior people I usually worked with. Young writer, young editor: could be, as Molly would say, a match made in heaven.

We exchanged cards and promised to stay in touch. It was a pleasant dinner, but I was edgy, worried about my laptop. Over coffee, the presenters were introduced to the attendees; I stood when my name was called and smiled blindly into the klieg light of hopeful gazes. Then there were speeches and announcements, until at last, well past eleven o'clock, I was able to return to my casita.

Max walked me back to see if my computer had shown up. It was sitting on the desk, perfectly dry and looking no worse for wear. Beside it was a bottle of Sauvignon Blanc and a note from the hotel manager. I read it aloud. "'Dear Ms. Donovan, I am so sorry for the delay in delivering your laptop, which was misplaced within our luggage room. Please accept this small token, and if there's anything I can do to make your stay at La Posada a pleasant one, do let me know.'"

Max sniffed disgustedly. "I'm going to talk to this guy."

"Don't bother. No harm, no foul." I yawned, jet lag setting in. It amazed me how often men felt compelled to play the protector around me, most recently Jean-Paul and now Max. As if I needed protecting. That had been my role in Hugo's life, and they hadn't called me the Dragon Lady for nothing. It must be my size, I thought. Five-foot-three was not an impressive height, however high one's heels.

Thinking about Jean-Paul reminded me that I hadn't yet given him an answer. I ought to have said yes on the spot, before he started looking around—there were three or four of my colleagues who would snatch him up in a moment if they heard he was available—but I still worried about aiding and abetting such a reckless decision.

"Do you remember my intern, Jean-Paul?" I asked Max, who had taken a seat at the desk and was examining my computer.

"Who could forget that lovely?"

"He wants to come work for me full-time instead of going to law school in the fall."

"Of course he does. The kid's gaga for you."

"Be serious, Max. Do you think I should hire him?"

He looked up, considering. "Is he as useful as he is ornamental?"

"Yes. Takes initiative, speaks three languages, very bright and good with people. I could absolutely use him on staff."

"So what's the problem? A pretty face never hurt anyone, as you may have noticed yourself."

"Are you suggesting that I got where I am on looks?"

"Absolutely. That and being the best at what you do."

I blew him a kiss. "Have I ever told you you're my favorite client?"

"Every payday," Max said.

I didn't check my e-mail until the next morning. There were several dozen messages, including one from Molly, which I read first.

Look, kiddo, I got hold of Vogel's proposal. It's called *The Secret Life and Loves of Hugo Donovan* and it's exactly what you'd expect from her. I'll send you the

outline if you're not convinced, but I promise it'll make
you sick. Only one way to stop her and YOU KNOW THIS.
Call me!! M.

She was right, of course: the only way to stop Gloria Vogel
was to get a better book out there. So much for privacy. My life
would be an open book. Hugo's, too.

Once, a month or two after I moved to New York, I was
groped on the subway. It was rush hour and the uptown local was
jammed. A man rubbed himself against my ass. I spun around
and smashed my knee into his groin, but his pain didn't assuage
my sense of disgust and humiliation. The prospect of some
stranger picking and prying at my life with Hugo hurt me in the
same deep place. It's not that I had anything to hide. Ours had
been a whirlwind, romantic courtship followed by ten years of
love and perfect companionship. Though we'd had no children,
Hugo had given birth to four novels during our years together, a
prodigious output and by all accounts the best work of his career.
He called me his midwife; we were partners in every sense of the
word. The thought of an outsider dissecting that perfect time,
deconstructing the life we'd created to tell some lesser story of his
own, filled me with the most intimate disgust.

I called Molly.

"So?" she said. "What do you think?"

"There must be another way."

"Let's hear it."

I gazed out the window as I tried to come up with an answer.
A steady trickle of people passed on their way to breakfast. I recognized Charlie Malvino, arm in arm with a leggy brunette who
wore an attendee's badge around her neck. Naughty Charlie.
Writers' conferences were notorious hunting grounds for horny
agents and authors; my own barricades had been assailed, though

never stormed, on many such occasions. But the protocol was that you stick to your own kind; no casting couches, no screwing of aspiring writers.

"I could threaten to boycott any company that bought her book," I said. No idle threat, not with a list like mine.

"At the expense of your clients who work with that publisher? It wouldn't work, anyway. Vogel's last so-called bio was on the list for five months. Don't kid yourself, Jo: if the numbers are right, even your best friends will bid."

"I'll refuse her access to Hugo's papers."

"Like she needs them! She's writing about his life, not his work."

"It'll be a hell of a dull book. We led a fairly quiet life, you know."

There was a pause, then Molly said carefully, "He had a long and eventful one before he met you."

As if I didn't know. Three marriages, countless lovers, several scandals. "Those stories have been done to death."

"Then she'll make things up, with just enough truth blended in to give credence to the lies."

"I'd sue her and her publisher from here to Kingdom Come."

"For what?" Molly said incredulously.

"Slander."

"Hugo's dead. You can't slander the dead. Not to mention she'd love you to sue. The publicity alone would sell a million copies."

She was right, as usual. There was only one thing that could stop Vogel's project in its tracks, and that was a better book in the pipeline. The trouble was, I didn't want any biography, good or bad. What Hugo and I had was unique and beautiful and private. When I died, the vultures could write what they wanted about us. They could already write what they liked about Hugo's work. The writer belonged to the world, but the man was mine and mine alone, in death as in life.

"Talk to Teddy," Molly commanded.

That morning I gave my standard "Writers and Agents" presentation to a standing-room-only crowd of aspiring writers. A stripper at a frat party could not have commanded more rapt attention. Molly always claimed that agents go to writers' conferences not to find clients but to feel like rock stars for once in their lives. Maybe so, but to me it felt uncomfortable to be the focus of such avid desire; dangerous, too, for as any rock star knows, the B-side of adulation is resentment.

And even as I thought this, I felt it: a concentrated beam of malevolence, directed at me, hidden amid that mass of admiring gazes.

I am not a fanciful person. I don't see ghosts, I don't have visions, I don't believe in angels. Clarity, not imagination, is my forte. So it was strange to feel so convinced of something for which I had no evidence at all; and yet that was what I felt, as clearly as one hears a single flat voice in a choir.

After the lecture came the Q and A, all the usual questions until the last one: "What if you know the perfect agent for your work and you can't get her to pay attention?"

A shiver ran through me. That deep voice was infused with an intensity tinged with hostility. The room fell silent; people craned in their seats, seeking the speaker. I searched too, for I'd recognized the voice, but I could not distinguish its owner.

"You move on," I said.

At lunch I sat at a presenters' table beside Sikha Mehruta, the writer whose acquaintance I'd intended to make during the conference.

She was a striking woman of about forty, with a regal bearing and long black hair gathered in a bun at the base of her neck. Her first novel had won the PEN/Faulkner Award for fiction, and her second, which came out a few months ago, was even better. I introduced myself and told her how much I'd enjoyed them both. We talked for a while, then Max joined us and the conversation turned general. I was content. One day, not too long from now, Sikha would discover what I already knew, that her agent, Percy Ailes, planned to retire at year's end; and then perhaps she'd think of me.

I was busy for the rest of the afternoon—the conference was lavish with amenities but not the time to enjoy them—and it was growing dark by the time I made my way back to my casita. I poured a glass of the manager's wine and took it and the conference folder out to the patio. Santa Fe was hotter than I'd expected in June, but a fresh breeze had come up, and the mingled scent of sage and lavender was delicious.

I settled in to read the synopses of the four writers I'd be meeting tomorrow. The first was another zombie mash-up, yesterday's news. The second was a Harry Potter clone. So many of the proposals we see are poor imitations of successful books that I should be inured by now. Instead it seemed as if the more I saw, the more they irritated me, the way exposure to allergens can trigger the development of allergies. Some degree of imitation can't be helped. How many tough private eyes were spawned by Dashiell Hammett and Raymond Chandler? Generations of them: the DNA of Sam Spade and Philip Marlowe is in the genes of contemporary detectives whose authors never even read their stories. But this proposal was outright theft, set in New England but otherwise lifted lock, stock, and broomstick from Rowling's original.

Sighing, I refilled my wineglass and turned to the next synopsis.

An artist, famous but long past his prime, meets a
beautiful young woman named Clio who becomes his

model, his muse, his lover, and his wife. The artist is inspired to a final, frenzied burst of wild creativity, doing his best work before dying suddenly. Devastated, the young widow buries herself in the anonymity of New York City. One day she is sitting in a diner when a thin man with haunted eyes walks in carrying a canvas. "I'm starving," he tells the owner, whose name is Gus. "I will trade you this painting for a bowl of beef stew." "Get outta here," growls Gus, not an art lover.

As the thin man trudges past, Clio glimpses his painting of a clown so sad it brings tears to her own eyes. She knows genius when she sees it, and she's seeing it now. "Wait!" she cries, but the artist has already left. She throws some money onto the table and chases down the painter, who can't believe that this beautiful woman is talking to him.

"Are there more?" she demands, pointing at his painting.

"Many more," he replies morosely. "A lot of good they do me."

"Show me!" she exclaims.

He takes her home to his studio. There are paintings everywhere. When he ran out of canvas, he used the walls. There is genius in every stroke, yet something is missing. The painter watches as Clio moves from one painting to the next, and suddenly he sees what is missing.

"I need to paint you," he blurts out.

She turns and gazes deeply into his intense eyes. "Yes," she murmurs. "I see that."

He shoves a pile of canvases off a divan and covers it with a red silk cover. "Take your clothes off," he demands. He can hardly believe his own words, but he

knows it's right, and so does she. She undresses with-
out embarrassment in front of him. She has a body like
Madonna's in "Body of Evidence."

"How do you want me?" she asks.

"Let me count the ways," he thinks to himself. He
arranges her on her back, arms flung over her head,
one leg bent, heel resting on the couch, the other trailing
off it. He stands at his easel and starts to paint, but his
hands are shaking so bad he can barely hold the brush.

She sees what is happening. "Come here," she beck-
ons. He crosses to her side like a man walking in his
sleep. She reaches out with greedy abandon, pulling his
clothes off impatiently, and gasps when his throbbing
manhood stands revealed.

"My God," she cries, "you're even bigger than—"

These are the last words she speaks before his lips
close on hers. They make brilliant, passionate love for
hours before he rises to paint her portrait as she lies in
exhausted sleep. When he finishes, he steps back and
sees the best work he has ever done. At long last, the
artist has found his muse.

With a shaking hand, I turned back to the first page and read
the title: THE HAND-ME-DOWN MUSE, a novel by Sam
Spade.

I didn't see Max until dinner, where we were seated at separate tables. When I spotted his bald head glistening under the
lights, I went over and put my mouth by his ear. "Buy you a drink
later, big guy?"

"Sure thing." He looked at me. "What's wrong? It's not Molly,
is it?"

I could have kissed him for that. Nine writers out of ten, sensing something amiss, would have asked first about their book deals.

"It's not Molly," I said.

We cut out early and ended up in the bar of La Fonda on the plaza. It was Saturday night and the place was jumping, but blessedly not with writers. Up front a first-class bluegrass band was playing. Max commandeered a booth in the back. It was the perfect spot: we could hear each other just fine, but no one else could overhear. Over drinks I told him about Sam Spade, starting with the ambush outside my office and ending with the synopsis, which I handed to him.

Max put on a pair of glasses and held the pages close to the candle on our table. The band broke into "Blue Ridge Mountain Blues" and I couldn't keep from tapping my feet. It was a song I heard a lot growing up, and though I had no nostalgia for those times, I never held it against the music. The second scotch was kicking in.

"How do you know it's the guy from outside your office?" he asked, handing back the pages.

"I called him Sam Spade, because of his fedora and trench coat. He must have adopted it as a pseudonym."

"When was the first encounter?"

"Ten days ago."

"And Jean-Paul ran him off. Was that before or after he asked for a job?"

"The same day. Right after." A moment passed. "Don't be ridiculous, Max!"

"I'm just saying. The kid gets to play the hero and clinches the job."

"No way. He's a good kid. Besides, Sam Spade's here, he followed me."

Max nodded. "What do you make of him, based on those pages?"

I hadn't expected the question but didn't have to stop and think. "He's no writer, that's for sure. He's never published, but my guess is he's tried and been roundly rejected; hence his search for the missing element, his muse. He's not illiterate, probably even college-educated, but he thinks in clichés and his aesthetic is totally hackneyed: the sad-clown paintings and that tacky Madonna reference. And he's nuts, of course. Grandiose and delusional."

"Would you know him if you saw him?"

"No. I never really saw his face. The night he waylaid me, it was raining and he wore a trench coat and a fedora tilted down over his face, Bogart-style. That's why I called him Sam Spade. But I'm scheduled to meet him tomorrow, to discuss this dreck."

"If he shows. Guy strikes me as the shy type."

I didn't like the sound of that. "You're the profiler; what do you make of him? Do I need to worry?"

"You? You're golden." Max leaned back, hands clasped behind his neck. "Boyo needs to worry."

Chapter 5

On Sunday, Max arranged for hotel security to place several people in the conference room where presenters met one-on-one with attendees, while he himself lurked behind a screen in one corner of the room. Sam Spade was the fourth and last of my scheduled appointments.

He never showed.

On Monday, Max flew back to New York with me. There was no talking him out of it. The strange thing was that, having convinced him to take my stalker seriously, I now found myself incapable of doing so. It wasn't as if this were the first I'd ever dealt with. Hugo had attracted a whole following. Fans and aspiring writers used to send letters, hang around the building, or leave manuscripts with the doorman. Women, too, called the apartment, demanding to talk to Hugo, refusing to leave messages. Some were so persistent that I was finally forced to change our number. Especially when he was writing, my husband relied on me to protect his privacy, and I felt a . . . I won't say "sacred duty," for that sounds slavish, but an absolute imperative to do so. People had no consideration and would disturb him day and night if I didn't intervene. I'd dealt with his stalkers as efficiently as a

farmwife deals with flies. Why should Sam Spade be any different?

From Kennedy we taxied into Manhattan, weaving through
rush-hour traffic. The sky was pewter-colored, and the air smelled
of rain and exhaust. I opened my window to the polyglot babel,
horns, sirens, rumble, and clatter that was home for me. It was
nearly six by the time we reached my office, but everyone was
there, gathered around the conference table. Harriet looked
pointedly at her watch as we entered. Jean-Paul brought in an
extra chair for Max, who sat beside me at the head of the table.
Lorna, as usual, anchored the foot with her trusty steno pad at
the ready. They must have ordered in Chinese; my office smelled
of fried rice.

Max filled them in on the events in Santa Fe, then handed
around copies of Sam Spade's novel summary. We'd argued about
this on the plane, and I lost. It would be as obvious to them as it
was to me that the muse in Spade's story was a stand-in for me,
with the author cast in the role of Well-Hung Starving Artist. It
disgusted me to be the object of this perv's sexual fantasies, and
I felt that letting my colleagues read his story would diminish me
in their eyes. But Max said that someone in the office must have
read some pages of the manuscript when Spade originally submitted it, and the summary might ring a bell.

Chloe, the first to finish, pushed the pages away with the tip
of one finger. "This is so creepy. Who *is* this guy?"

"At the very least," Max said, "he's someone with boundary
issues and a fixation on getting Jo as his agent."

"Not just as his agent!" Jean-Paul said. His face was
bright red.

"Right," Max said calmly. "Which is why we need to figure
out who he is."

"Then it's a shame you didn't check with the conference organizers," Harriet said. "He must have been registered."

I was used to her patronizing tone, but Max, who wasn't, answered coolly. "Sam Spade was a walk-in registrant. He paid cash and registered with a nonexistent New York City address and phone number. If he was staying at the hotel, it wasn't under that name. But I doubt he was; the hotel had been booked up for months."

"So how do we find him?" Jean-Paul asked.

"Well, the guy claims he submitted a manuscript to the office and it was rejected. We can assume this happened not long ago, say within the last six months. Someone in this office read his submission. Did anything sound familiar in the pages you just read? Either the content or the voice?"

They all shook their heads except Lorna, who never read.

"Do you keep track of all submissions?" Max asked.

She looked up from her pad. "I do that."

"Even rejections?"

"Every submission, with the date received, who read it, how and when we responded."

"Excellent," Max said. "I'd like a copy of that log."

"It's confidential," she said repressively, with that mulish look she got whenever anyone trampled on her secretarial turf.

"Max has appointed himself our chief of security," I said.

"He appointed *himself*?"

I frowned at her, but Max laughed and said, "No, she's right. Jo, give me a dollar."

I looked in my wallet and, finding no singles, handed him a five.

"Even better," he said. "No one should say I work cheap. Now we're official. All right, Lorna?"

"No problem."

"Is there some reason," Jean-Paul cut in, "why Jo shouldn't go straight to the police and get a restraining order?"

"Against whom?" Max said.

"Let them find out! He's stalking her; that's got to be illegal."

"Unless bad writing is a crime, and writing as bad as his should be, nothing Sam Spade has done so far is actionable. And we want to keep it that way, which means that apart from IDing this guy, our goal is to prevent another approach. We need to make Jo impossible to reach."

"He'll never get past me, I can tell you that!" Lorna said stoutly. She had forsaken her notebook for once and was gaping at Max. It wasn't a good look for her, not that she'd care. Ever since she'd come to us, I'd been trying tactfully to get Lorna to do something about her appearance. She had lovely skin and youth to offset those extra pounds, but she hid her face behind thick glasses and mousy brown bangs and her body in shapeless corduroy slacks and calf-length skirts. For her birthday I'd taken her shopping at Bloomingdale's and bought her two charming outfits, youthful but professional, perfect for work. She'd thanked me earnestly and repeatedly, but what she did with them I don't know; she certainly never wore them to the office.

She was an exasperating child, but I could have hugged her now. I could have hugged them all, even Harriet, who despite her supercilious tone was gazing at me with concern. It moved me to see it, and it opened my eyes.

I grew up without a family. My parents died when I was three; I have no memories of them. My mother's mother took me in. She was a God-fearing woman with a heart of carbolic acid who knew her duty and set about it grimly. I got a cot, secondhand clothes, enough food to survive, and nothing else: not a kind look, not a hug, not a word of praise, even though for years until I wised up I nearly killed myself trying. Luckily for me I found other sources of approval and a way out. I graduated high school at seventeen with a full scholarship to Vassar in my pocket, and once I left, I never went back.

When I married Hugo, he became my family. He was my father, my mother, my husband, and my child. His death left me orphaned anew, widowed, bereft in every possible way. I thought I was down for the count. And yet here I was three years later, still kicking. As I looked around at the room, I realized that somehow this agency had become my home, these people my family.

The panic I'd felt in Santa Fe had evaporated completely. Sam Spade was no threat to me; he was barely a nuisance. I tried to explain this. Everyone listened politely. Then they turned back to Max, and Harriet spoke for them all. "Tell us what to do."

Max ran through a litany of security measures, most of which I'd already heard on the plane, while Lorna's pen flew furiously over her pad. All calls were to be screened, all doors kept locked, all computer passwords changed. He was meeting the head of building security that evening, while I was delegated to brief the doormen in my apartment house. "Most important," Max said sternly, turning to me, "you need to vary your schedule. No more runs around the reservoir, for the interim, anyway. Work at home more; come into the office at odd hours. Don't be predictable."

Just past Max's shoulder, Hugo gazed at me from his portrait, smiling slightly as if to say, *So much fuss, my dear!*

"Is all this really necessary, Max?" I said. "Isn't it overkill?"

"Think of it as an ounce of prevention," he said. "Stalkers can be incredibly persistent; that's what makes them stalkers. Trust me, you'd rather have bedbugs in your apartment than one of these bastards fixated on you."

A few minutes later, the meeting ended and Max took off. I asked Jean-Paul to stay for a moment. He took the seat beside mine, and I looked at him with a pleasure akin to that aroused by a beautiful Greek sculpture. Sitting so close, I had to resist the temptation to run my hands through his black curls. It wasn't a sexual impulse. In museums, too, I had a hard time keeping my hands to myself. For his part, Jean-Paul seemed to avoid looking directly at me. The charm I'd seen him display toward others was eclipsed in my presence by an awkwardness I could only attribute to my being his boss.

"I've thought about what you asked me," I said. "If you're still interested—"

My door opened, and Chloe's smiling face peered around it. "Ready?" she asked Jean-Paul.

"What?" he said blankly. "Oh, right. Sorry; go without me."

The smile faded fast. "You're kidding."

Boys can be so dense, I thought, and pointed to the door. "Go. You have plans. This can wait till tomorrow."

"No, it can't." He looked back at Chloe. "See you tomorrow, OK?"

"Whatever." She backed out, not before casting me a look I can only call lethal.

Poor child, I thought. She really had it bad if she saw me as her rival. But Chloe would have to learn to deal with her little crush if our intern became a staffer.

"You were saying, Jo?" he said.

"I could use a good assistant. Lorna's wonderful, but she's strictly secretarial."

"You're offering me the job?"

"I am."

His face shone. "I accept."

"Hang on, we haven't talked about salary yet, or what you'll be doing."

"Whatever it is," Jean-Paul said, "I'll take it."

Chapter 6

The next day Max drove up to Westchester to visit Molly. That evening, with no further sign of Sam Spade and with many exhortations to contact him immediately if anything happened, he flew home. We followed his orders like good little soldiers. The office door was kept locked; visitors and deliverymen had to buzz to get in, and with Lorna on the gate I could not have felt safer. We all changed our computer passwords. Max had said to use random digits and letters, but I knew I'd never remember such a password, so I changed mine from Hugo's birth date, which was ludicrously obvious, to a date that was equally meaningful but only to me: 7/10/1996, the day we met.

I changed my schedule, too. Instead of running in the park, I ran on a treadmill with a manuscript propped up in front of me. I went to work late, came home early, caught up on reading. Life in the agency returned more or less to normal. On Wednesday I e-mailed the Keyshawn Grimes novel to Marisa Deighton at Doubleday; she sent back a lovely note thanking me and promising a quick read. On Thursday, I received an unexpected offer on a book, a combination memoir and how-to book on dog training. I don't normally handle either genre, but this one came with a unique voice and a story worth telling. The author, Gordon

Hayes, was an ex-Marine and former monk who now bred and trained protection dogs. The journey of a man with such an eccentric résumé was a big part of the story. Everyone liked the book, but no one had a clue how to market it, and after twenty rejections I'd nearly given up hope. Now I got to do my favorite part of my job: I called my client and told him we had an offer.

On Friday, Teddy Pendragon called the office. I'd finally read his *Vanity Fair* profile the night before, lying in the big brass bed that I'd shared with Hugo and had been unable to fully colonize in the three years since his death (even if I managed to fall asleep in the middle, I invariably woke up hugging the left edge). Molly had called the piece flattering and it was, in a smarmy sort of way. Teddy wrote almost worshipfully of Hugo's work, which he'd discovered as a precocious, lonely adolescent, the age when we are most susceptible to seductive voices. In the piece, he idolized Hugo and romanticized me, quoting writers I'd worked with and altogether portraying me in such a flattering light that the cynic in me wondered if he hadn't written it with a biography of Hugo in mind. Still, it was a promising start, if start there must be.

To Lorna's surprise, I took his call.

"I read it," I said. "I liked it; how could I not?"

"I'm relieved to hear it," Teddy said, and he did sound relieved.

"Molly thinks I should cooperate with you on a bio."

"What do you think?"

"I won't lie. It feels like a damned intrusion. But I'm convinced that if it's not you, it'll be someone . . . else."

Someone worse, I meant, and he seemed to know it, for his dulcet voice hardened to the consistency of cold maple syrup. "I gather you've heard about Gloria Vogel's little project?"

"Never happen," I snapped. "No one who knew Hugo would give her the time of day. It's a pipe dream."

"Of course," he said soothingly, but I felt, as he surely did, a sudden, slight pitch in the balance of power. He knew why I needed him, and that gave him leverage.

"I'm prepared to move ahead with this," I said. "You could have your agent talk to Random." That was clumsy. I was a lot more interested in having the book sale announced than actually facilitating its writing, and Teddy would know that.

He didn't say, "Not so fast." He wasn't that crass. But I heard it in his voice nonetheless. "I think it would be a good idea if you and I talked a little more first. Why don't I take you to lunch one day and we'll put our heads together?"

I had no lunches free for weeks, so we made it for dinner the following Tuesday. I spent much of the intervening weekend fretting about it, trying to decide what I'd give him and what I wouldn't. Then something happened that put Teddy Pendragon right out of my mind.

Sunday night I went out with some friends from Paris, the Lepetits. Valerie was a painter, originally from Chicago, and her husband, Yves, was a jazz pianist. Hugo and I met them soon after we moved to Paris, in a jazz club on the Rue des Lombards. They were sitting at the table next to ours, and we couldn't help noticing them, for they were an odd-looking couple: a stunning black woman nearly six feet tall and a diminutive white man some twenty years her senior. Midway through the set, Yves was called up onstage and introduced; then he sat in on a couple of songs. After the set, Hugo struck up a conversation. They knew Hugo's work, of course, and admired it. Before long we were sitting at the same table, chatting like old friends. Hugo and Yves bonded over the music they both loved, while Val and I found common ground as Americans in Paris, both married to older men. After that we met often and grew close, even vacationing together several times in the south of France. For Hugo's birthday,

I commissioned a portrait of him from Val; it still hangs in his
study. When Hugo died in Paris of a sudden massive heart attack,
I would have been lost without Val and Yves, who saw to all the
arrangements. When I decided to sell the Paris apartment, they
handled that, too. We hadn't met since Hugo's memorial service
in Paris, and I'd missed them badly.

They were already seated when I arrived at the restaurant on
West Fourth, and a great chord of gladness sounded in me when
Val saw me and waved exuberantly. I blew past the maître d' in
my hurry to reach them. Yves kissed me on both cheeks, then Val
enveloped me in a good old American hug.

After dinner and a couple of bottles of wine, we went on to the
Blue Note and the Vanguard. We drank some more, and in between sets talked about Paris and the old days with Hugo. Yves's
English was weak, so we spoke in French. When he left us to
talk to a musician he knew, Val slid over till her thigh touched
mine.

"Dear Jo," she said, switching to English, "I feel so close
to you."

"You *are* close to me."

"I've thought of you so often. I always meant to call."

"You should have."

"*You* didn't. And I was so afraid you were upset with me."

"Why would I be?" I asked, surprised.

"You know."

"I don't."

"That night at the hospital . . ."

All at once I realized what she was talking about. Hugo had
been stricken at around eleven p.m., on his way home from a
movie theater. I hadn't gone, which is something I'll always regret, but it was one of those noisy American films based on comic
books that I loathed and he loved. The first I knew of his collapse
was a call from the emergency room of the Hôpital Européen

Georges-Pompidou. I grabbed a taxi and offered the driver double the fare if he could make the hospital in ten minutes. He did it. I paid, jumped out, and was approaching the door to the ER when it opened and Val emerged.

We exchanged a few quick words. She'd brought in a neighbor who cut herself on a carving knife. I told her about the hospital's call. "They wouldn't say what's wrong with him," I said.

"I'm sure it's nothing," she replied. "You know men." I must have expected her to turn around and walk back inside with me, because I was surprised when she didn't. But the incident was so thoroughly eclipsed by the disastrous news to come that I'd forgotten it until this moment.

"That was nothing," I said. "You couldn't have known. I can't believe you worried over that."

Val hugged me with one arm. She smelled of paint and French perfume. "I'm so glad. You know I loved you both. Hell, I owe my career to your husband!"

"You do?"

Her eyes brimmed with whiskey tears. "Before I met you two, I was struggling to show my work, let alone sell it. Then you commissioned that portrait, and when it was done, Hugo made a point of showing it to his friend Henri Roux, who has galleries in Paris and New York. Henri loved it and he came to see more. That's how I got my first solo show."

"I never knew that," I said.

"No one knew. It was just Hugo being kind."

How typical of Hugo to do a good deed secretly. Strange, though, that he hadn't told me, for there were no secrets between us. Maybe he had said something and I'd forgotten.

Yves returned to us then, and we switched back to French. Val ordered another bottle, but I'd had enough. By the time I got home it was past two. I took a couple of aspirin to stave off a hangover and fell into bed.

I jerked awake to full daylight. The phone shrilled. I ignored it. Damn thing kept ringing.

Finally I picked up. Groggily: "Hullo?"

"Jo?" It was Lorna. I heard office noises in the background, but her voice was hushed. "Are you OK?"

I sat up too quickly and winced. Preemptive aspirin doesn't always work. I rubbed my temples. "What time is it?"

"Ten."

"What do you want?"

"Did something happen I don't know about with Nancy Kurlin's book?"

"No, why?"

"Did you sell TV rights to the Gordon Hayes book?"

"What the hell are you talking about?"

"Jo," she said, "you'd better get in here."

The smell smacked me in the face the moment I opened the office door. For a moment I was back in the funeral parlor, sitting in state beside Hugo's coffin with the suffocating stench of lilies all around me; but this was a different room full of flowers and gaping faces. Jean-Paul and Chloe were huddled around Lorna's desk. I got the sense of excited speech that had ceased the moment I walked in. There was a crystal vase full of red roses on Lorna's desk, a spray of irises on Jean-Paul's, two more bouquets and a bottle of Champagne on the credenza. I plucked the card from the roses. "Thank you, thank you, thank you!" it exclaimed, and it was signed "N." I looked at Lorna.

"Nancy Kurlin," she said. "I checked with the florist."

The card on the irises was from Jenny Freund, whose first novel I'd been unable to place. "Bless you, Jo. I can't tell you what this means to me." The Champagne came from Milo Sanders, whose fascinating biography of Bob Dylan ought to have sold and would have, if another one hadn't just been made into a PBS series. His note said, "To the world's greatest agent, with boundless gratitude."

I couldn't speak. Writers often send flowers and little gifts as thank-yous, but there was no reason for any of these particular writers to be thanking me. Something burned in the pit of my stomach, and my limbs felt weightless. I didn't quite know what was happening yet, but I knew it was bad.

"There's more," Lorna said, breaking the long silence. "Check your messages."

Harriet stepped out of her office as I passed; her English complexion had lost the peaches and was all cream. She regarded me without a word. I went into my room and shut the door. The light on my phone was blinking and the counter showed six messages. I hit PLAY.

"Jo, it's Marty. My God, I can't believe it. Steven Spielberg? Call me—this is unbelievable—we have to celebrate!"

The next one was hard to make out because of the crying. "It's Edwina. Jo, you can't imagine what this means to me. I'd pretty much given up hope. God bless you, Jo."

I couldn't listen to any more. My head was pounding and there was an ominous churning in my gut. Except for a ringing phone, quickly stilled, the silence outside my door was deafening. Now I knew the shape of this disaster, but I didn't yet know its scope; indeed I felt unequal to knowing.

I am a coward. I admit it. When the ER doctor came out to tell me about Hugo, he'd hesitated for a moment before speaking. That momentary pause and the look in his eyes revealed all; yet he, determined to break the news gently, listed all the steps they'd taken to save my husband before admitting they had failed. And I let him stall. That is the point: I let him. I even interrupted with a cogent-sounding question or two, because I couldn't bear to hear the words I knew were coming.

Now the message light blinked on and on, and I buried my face in my hands. I'm not sure how long I would have stayed like that if my secretary hadn't come in. She stood before my desk until I was forced to look up.

Lorna is not an expressive girl. Molly once said, unkindly but accurately, that she has as much affect as her computer. But I hardly knew her now. Her back was straight, sallow cheeks pink with indignation, bovine eyes gleaming behind their glasses.

"How are you?" she asked.

"Bad. But not as bad as my poor clients are going to be."

She came around to my side of the desk, and for one awful moment I thought she was going to embrace me. Instead, she opened the bottom drawer where I keep a bottle of Johnnie Walker and a couple of shot glasses for celebrations. She filled one glass to the rim and placed it in my hand.

"Lorna, it's not even noon."

"You've had a shock."

I downed half the shot in a gulp and felt its warmth spread through my body. That felt good, so I finished it off. Liquid courage. There's a reason clichés become clichés.

"Sit," I said to Lorna, still hovering about me. "Did you listen to the messages?"

She took the client's seat and glanced at the blinking light on my phone. "You didn't?"

"Just the first few. What's happened, Lorna? Can you explain it to me?"

"E-mails," she said. "Sent over the weekend. Each with some kind of offer, apparently. Each signed by you."

"How? Someone hacked into our e-mail?"

"I don't know. They weren't sent from any of our e-mail accounts. I checked everyone's sent mail."

"Have we seen any of these e-mails?"

"Not the ones our clients got. I couldn't ask them to forward them without saying more than I thought I should. But there's one addressed to you, too. Check your personal inbox."

I grabbed the mouse and logged into my e-mail account. There were a dozen new messages. I scrolled down the list of senders until I came to one named "JDonovan."

"That one," Lorna said, startling me. She was behind me now, looking over my shoulder.

I opened the e-mail. "Can you hear me now?" it said. No salutation, and no signature; but in my head I heard the words in Sam Spade's voice.

I looked longingly at the Leibovitz portrait of Hugo on the opposite wall. If he were alive, none of this would have happened. I'd been safe with him, for the first and only time in my life. "Does Molly know?" I asked; I don't know why.

"We haven't told anyone. Jean-Paul wanted to call Max, but I said to wait for you."

My lips felt numb and my fingers were icy. I wanted another drink, but I knew that would be a mistake. After Hugo died, I'd tried drinking myself to sleep every night. Whatever worked, I'd thought. In India, they give widows opium. I got pretty good at solitary drinking, but I quit when Molly took me into the agency and I had to get up mornings. Hadn't missed it, till now.

The phone rang and Lorna picked up. "Hamish Donovan Literary Agency." She listened for a moment. "No, sorry, still out. She's got meetings all morning. I'll tell her you called. . . . No, I don't know anything about it. . . . I will." She hung up and looked at me. "Gordon Hayes. Wants to talk to you about the Animal Planet deal."

"What Animal Planet—oh God. This is a nightmare." Slowly, so slowly, it was starting to sink in. I'd known from the first how devastating this disappointment was going to be to my writers. Now I began to realize what it could do to the agency. The victimized clients would blame me. I could lose them all. I could lose

Harriet, too. Ever since Molly retired, that tie had been fraying; this could sever it entirely.

I felt assaulted, violated, too shocked even for anger, though that would surely come. But Lorna was looking at me anxiously, and I felt the weight of the silence outside my door. Later, safe in my empty apartment, I would howl and curse and lick my wounds, but right now someone had to deal with this mess, and there was nobody else.

I braced myself. "How many?"

"Based on the gifts, the voice mail, and this morning's calls, twelve." Lorna hesitated. "Twelve we know of."

Of course; there could be others who hadn't checked in yet. Part of me wanted to curl up in a ball under my desk. Another part of me smacked that part in the face and told it to buck up. Step by step, I told myself. That's how I got through Hugo's funeral, and if I could get through that, I could get through anything.

"I need a list of the twelve clients, with phone numbers. Then a full client list, also with phone numbers."

"I thought you might." She pointed to a file on my desk.

"You're a godsend. Ask the others to stay in the office and say nothing to anybody. I'll see everyone in a little while, including Harriet. Max may want to talk to them, too." A thought struck me. "Were any of Harriet's clients involved?"

"Not that we know of." Lorna edged toward the door, relieved, I suppose, that I hadn't actually dissolved into a puddle.

"And get rid of those flowers," I called after her.

Chapter 7

I Skyped Max. It was early morning in L.A. and he was at his desk, dressed for work in jeans and a graphic tee with a picture of the Brooklyn Bridge on it. Behind him I could just make out a large picture window with a view of Benedict Canyon. His and Barry's house was a graceful concoction of iron, cement, and glass, cantilevered over the cliff at an angle that defied God and gravity.

I'd set up my computer at the head of the conference table, where I usually sat. Harriet, Chloe, Jean-Paul, and Lorna sat in a semicircle around me, close together so Max could see us all.

I filled him in. When I finished, there was a long silence. Max looked like he'd broken a tooth.

"We need those e-mails," he said at last.

"I know," I said. "As soon as we get off I'm going to start making those calls."

"Forward me the one you got right away."

"That's it?" Jean-Paul burst out. "You want to look at e-mails? We've got to stop this bastard!"

"Which bastard is that?" asked Max, as calm as Jean-Paul was agitated.

"The stalker, of course; Sam Spade, who else?"

"Did he sign that e-mail?"

"He didn't have to," I said. "It's obvious from the content. 'Can you hear me now?' That's been his demand from the start. I have to hear him. I have to pay attention."

Max's face was inscrutable. "So it seems. Lorna, did you pull together that submission log?"

"It's done," she said. "You want me to e-mail it?"

"Hold on to it. I'm flying in."

"Absolutely not," I said firmly, for I'd expected this and was prepared. "You have a book tour starting in three days. You have a million things on your plate. I can handle this."

And Harriet for once backed me up. "That's a very kind offer, Max, but at this point, Jo clearly needs to go to the police. I only wish she'd done it sooner."

"She *is* going to the police," Max said. "And I'm going with her."

"I don't need you to hold my hand," I said.

"Too late, doll. You hired me."

"For five bucks!"

"And I'm going to earn every penny. Jean-Paul?"

Jean-Paul straightened, nearly saluted. "Sir?"

"You'll see Jo safely home tonight."

"Yes, sir!"

"At ease, soldier," Chloe muttered.

After Max logged off, I moved to the head of the table. "We have to assume that this guy has hacked into our computer files and e-mail accounts; I don't see how else he could have learned enough to pull this off. For the time being, we're going to have to avoid using e-mail. Harriet, I suggest you and Chloe go through your contact list and let everyone know that until further notice, any communications from us will be by phone or messenger." Harriet nodded. I went on. "Lorna and Jean-Paul, you can divide up my contacts and do the same. If any more phony offers turn up, pass those calls to me. I'm going to ask you all not to talk about what's happened. Clients who were victimized will have to be told the whole story, of course, but I'll make those calls. The others need only be told that our e-mail's been hacked. The longer we can keep the whole story quiet, the better."

The young 'uns nodded solemnly, but Harriet arched an eyebrow. She knew as well as I did that it couldn't be for long. Too many clients had been duped; God knew how many people they'd already talked to.

Chloe hugged herself. "This whole thing is so . . . I mean, cue the spooky music, right?" Jean-Paul put a hand on her shoulder and she shot him an upward glance. I wondered what would happen if Harriet left me. Would Chloe go with her, or would she stay?

"Buck up," Harriet said reprovingly. "Look at Jo: cool as the proverbial cucumber."

"Just numb," I said. "Wait till I start making the calls." One more thing remained to be said, though I feared the consequences. "This is going to get ugly, guys. It's already ugly. If any of you feel it would be better to disassociate yourself from the agency, I will be very sorry, but I'll understand and accept it."

Four faces stared back at me. No one spoke. Outside, a phone rang twice and stopped, shunted to voice mail.

"You don't have to answer now," I said. "You can see me later if you—"

"How can you even ask that?" Jean-Paul said, his dark eyes blazing.

Chloe nodded fervently. "It's insulting."

I looked at Harriet, to whom my words had been primarily addressed.

"Not to worry, Jo," she said. "We'll see you through this." Though hardly open-ended, this commitment was more than I had hoped for, and I knew Harriet was as good as her word. I gave her a grateful nod. Only Lorna had not yet spoken, and I hardly felt she needed to. But the others all turned to her expectantly.

"Me?" she said, looking surprised. "I'm not going anywhere."

And then there was nothing standing between me and the phone. I asked Lorna to reschedule my appointments for the day and closeted myself in my office.

The twelve victims were a mixed bunch, weighted toward fiction, as my list was. It included first-timers and old hands, midlist and bestselling writers, male and female. Some of my favorite clients were on the list, though Sam Spade could hardly have known that. Or maybe he did; he'd certainly figured out the best way to strike at me.

Publishing is a big, tough business, and a writer's agent is all that stands between him and the machine. So great is the dependence of writers on their literary agents that a reciprocal response is all but inevitable. Even those writers who are decades older than me became my children, to be guided, encouraged, and protected. I had many clients, and there were days when I felt like a mother bird with far too many hungry chicks. But nothing in my working life was sweeter than delivering good news, and nothing hurt more than disappointing them.

I started with Gordon Hayes, my ex-Marine, ex-monk dog trainer. There was no Animal Planet deal, but I had just sold his book, so he'd have something to fall back on. Besides, he was a gentle, taciturn man; with him there'd be no tears.

He answered his phone on the first ring. I heard dogs barking in the background.

"Jo Donovan," he said, "you are rapidly becoming one of my all-time favorite people."

"Not for long," I said, and broke the news.

When I finished, he asked, "Was it just me, or were there others?"

"At least a dozen."

"Who the hell would do that to you?"

"Me?" I said, startled. "It's not about me. I'm just so sorry about your disappointment."

"Of course it's about you. Do you have any idea who's behind it?"

With a dozen difficult calls yet to make, I didn't want to get into details. I asked him to forward the e-mail he'd received and tried to get off. But Gordon kept asking questions, and his normally soft voice went so alpha-dog that I couldn't refuse. I told him about the stalker and Max and the police and my protective staff.

"It's not enough," he said. "I can help with that, at least. Will you be in your office tomorrow?"

"Tomorrow we're seeing the police. But Gordon, please don't—"

"The day after, then. I'll call." And he hung up on my protestations.

I put the phone down and looked at it. That hadn't gone at all as I'd anticipated. Most writers are egoists, even the most charming of them. They need to be, to survive in this business. I'd expected anger. I hadn't expected it to be on my behalf.

The next call was tougher. Edwina Lavelle wept buckets, while I writhed in sympathetic agony. Her first novel was a beautifully written story about a family of Haitian immigrants living in Brooklyn. When I offered to represent her, I'd known plenty of editors who might take a chance on a talented newcomer, despite what they might see as limited demographic appeal. But that was before the economy crashed. Now half those editors were gone, and the rest were in no position to stick their necks out.

I told Edwina, by way of consolation, that she was one of a

dozen clients who'd been victimized, but that only seemed to upset her more. In between sobs, she read me the phony e-mail she'd
received. "Betsy Miller from Knopf called—said she can't get
your book out of her mind, so decided to make offer after all.
$80,000 advance. More info to come. Congrats, Jo."

If it hadn't been so tragic, I'd have laughed. The scenario was
absurd. For one thing, editors, like agents, don't look back. They
might agonize over a submission, debate its merits and salability,
but once they make the decision to pass, it is full speed ahead and
on to the next. For another thing, no editor these days would pay
$80,000 for a small first novel. This one had already made the
rounds without attracting an offer.

But Edwina didn't know that. Edwina must have thought she'd
hit the lottery.

"I'm so sorry," I said. "I know how devastating this must be."

"It's not that. I'm proud of my book even if it never gets published. I'm proud you liked it enough to take it on. But when I
think about you sitting there, having to make twelve calls like this
one . . ." Her voice broke again.

It was a moment before I could speak. "Come on, Edwina,
don't worry about me. I'm a tough old bird."

"Not old, and not so tough, either. Jo, baby, tell me: what can
I do to help?"

And so it went on every call. Hurt though they were, and bitterly disappointed, none of my clients blamed me. For some reason this made me feel guiltier, though I knew I was as much a
victim as they.

After the fourth or fifth call, I took a break, went online, and
pulled up the e-mails my writers had forwarded. The sender
clearly knew what manuscripts each of them had in play, as well
as the authors' sales histories, for the offers he'd come up with,
unlikely as I knew them to be, were just plausible enough to pass

muster with writers who lived on hope anyway. Gordon Hayes had been told that Animal Planet had offered $75,000 for the television rights to his book, *My Life in Dogs*. Nancy Kurlin was a midlist novelist with declining sales whose last book hadn't sold at all. Her e-mail said that Viking was launching a new line of women's fiction and they wanted her book to inaugurate the series. Poor Marty Gillman was told we'd received an offer from DreamWorks for his upcoming thriller, and that Steven Spielberg himself was interested in directing.

The cruelest hoax of all was played on the client I loved the most. Alice Duckworth, a dear old friend of Hugo's, took me under her wing when Hugo and I first married. She was old enough to be my grandmother, yet we became fast friends, both of us being at loose ends: she because she'd just been widowed and I because Hugo was immersed in a new book. Alice was also a writer, much acclaimed for her first novel, published when she was only twenty-two. I'd read it as a girl; it was that book that first inspired in me the determination to live in New York. Despite critical praise, none of Alice's subsequent books sold as well as that first one, and of course she paid dearly for that. By the time she came to me for representation, she hadn't published in ten years, although she'd kept on writing, and her old books were long out of print.

I'd managed to sell her latest novel to Pellucid Press, who owed me for Rowena, but was unable to persuade them to put any juice behind it. It was slated to come out in a month with a tiny print run and no publicity budget. Alice, no neophyte, was rightly concerned for her book's prospects.

"Dear Alice," the e-mail said. "Great news! NYT committed to a front-page review. Pellucid's going back for second printing. They want to reissue your entire backlist in a uniform trade edition. Congrats—this is long overdue. xoxo, Jo."

I was reading that e-mail when Lorna walked in and caught me without my game face on. She stopped short halfway across the room. "Jo?"

I passed a hand over my face. "What now?"

"I'm sending out for sandwiches. What'll you have?"

"Nothing, thanks."

"You have to eat."

I could see by the flat-footed way she stood there that it was no use arguing, and anyway, I knew she was right. Part of getting through things, I'd learned, was eating even when you didn't want to.

"Soup," I said. "Beef barley. Lunch is on me today. Take it out of petty cash."

"I brought mine. I'll tell the others." Then she left, easing the door shut behind her the way one does in a sickroom.

Sometime after six I got off the last call. Jean-Paul had waited, and we rode the elevator down together. My head was throbbing, and I had it in mind to walk home through the park, since I had an escort. It was a warm evening, and the sky between the buildings was streaked with pink. The sidewalk was mobbed, workers pouring out of office buildings into eddies of shoppers and tourists. We wove into the southbound stream, and it came to me suddenly that Sam Spade could be out there, watching. No sooner did the thought occur than it morphed into a certainty. Of course he was watching. Seeing my reaction would be half the fun. I stopped in my tracks. Jean-Paul was carried onward a few yards before he managed to get back to me.

"What is it?" he asked.

"He's here," I said.

His head whipped around. "Where? Did you see him?"

Ahead of us, a lone man peered into the window of a jewelry

shop. Across the street, a crowd of people waited at the bus stop. He could be any of a dozen men standing there; and since he could be any of them, he was all of them.

"I wouldn't know him if he was right in front of me," I said. "I just feel it."

Jean-Paul opened his mouth and closed it without speaking. Poor kid, I thought, for this he deferred Harvard Law? From our little cove by the building, I looked out at the great mass of pedestrians moving in sync, like shoals of fish. One step at a time, I told myself, but I couldn't take the step.

"Maybe a taxi after all," I said. "Do you think you could grab one?"

"It's one of my greatest talents," he said and proved it.

In the cab, I couldn't help checking behind us. No one seemed to be following us, though I could hardly tell; the traffic was so slow he could be trailing us on foot.

Or waiting outside my home. I had a good look around before stepping out of the cab. There were plenty of people, but no one seemed to be loitering. Jean-Paul got out with me. "I'll just go up with you, make sure everything's cool."

I didn't argue. Logically I knew there was no way anyone could get past the doorman. But that Sam Spade creep had penetrated so deeply into my life that suddenly no place felt safe.

I collected my mail, then we took the elevator up. The apartment was dark and still; I'd rushed out that morning without opening the blinds. From the entrance hall I turned left toward the living room and turned on the overhead light.

Jean-Paul whistled. "Wow! My whole apartment would fit in here."

"My first place was like that. They called it a studio, but it was the size of a dog kennel." The home Hugo had given me was on the opposite end of the scale, a three-bedroom, two-bath, fifth-floor apartment in a prewar brick building on the corner of

Seventy-Ninth and Central Park West that he'd purchased when he was flush with movie money. Jean-Paul followed me through the dining room into the kitchen, which we'd redone, updating the cabinets and fixtures but keeping the old subway tiles, the year before Hugo died. It was dark. I switched on the light, sensed sudden movement, and turned in time to see something small and dark scuttle under the stove. Shrieking, I jumped backward into Jean-Paul. His arms closed around me. My whole body was shaking, and my heart was beating so fast I could feel it. I hate roaches. My kitchen is immaculate, never a crumb left out; I have a weekly cleaning woman, and an exterminator comes bimonthly, and yet it still isn't enough. You can't keep the bastards out.

"Easy, Jo," Jean-Paul said. "It's just a little bug."

"I hate roaches."

"Strange, most New Yorkers love them."

I laughed. Jean-Paul's arms were still around me and it felt good, too good. I moved away. We checked the rest of the apartment and found no bogeymen lurking. Back in the living room, Jean-Paul seemed in no hurry to leave. I offered him a drink.

"Whatever you're having," he said.

There was a small bar in the bookcase. I poured two whiskeys neat, because I wasn't going back into my kitchen until the exterminator came, and handed one to the kid. I sat on one of two facing sofas flanking the fireplace while Jean-Paul wandered around the room, examining the photos on the wall and the mantelpiece. "You guys knew everyone, didn't you?"

"Hugo did."

"Bit daunting, really."

"Daunting?"

"All the pictures." He blushed. "I mean, if you ever had a guy up here or something."

I managed not to laugh. "I suppose it would be."

He flung himself onto the facing sofa, legs splayed, arms stretched out over the backrest, taking up as much room as three women would. "I like this one," he said, picking up the silver-framed wedding photo from the side table. Hugo and I stood arm in arm on the steps of City Hall; behind us and two steps above, Molly, our inadvertent matchmaker, gazed down at us like a proud but wary fairy godmother. I wore an ivory silk suit she'd bought me that morning, urging me all the while to reconsider. *You want to sleep with him, kiddo, be my guest, but don't sacrifice your whole life!* I was too happy to take offense and anyway could only laugh at such absurdity. Molly might as well have accused Cinderella of sacrificing herself to her prince. In the picture I looked every inch the radiant bride, while Hugo was gray-bearded and distinguished, authorial in a tweed jacket. It was, oddly enough, my dream wedding. The girls I grew up with had envisioned huge white weddings with bridesmaids, tiered cakes, wedding bands, and bouquets, but my fantasies had always been of a ceremony at New York's City Hall, followed by drinks in a tavern with rowdy bohemian friends. And that is exactly what I got, which so rarely happens in real life.

Jean-Paul replaced the photo. "It didn't bother you that Hugo was so much older?"

A strange question, I thought; but it had been a strange day. "Never. There was no difference. He was young at heart, you see, and I'm an old soul." Hugo's line, oft-repeated.

"I totally get that. Age is irrelevant." Jean-Paul looked at me intently. There was a speculative edge to his gaze, and suddenly he didn't look so young to me, but just like any other man on the verge of making a move. My heart sank. The kid had misinterpreted the scene in the kitchen, and that was all my fault. What an idiot, throwing myself in his arms over a damn bug! What was wrong with me?

He finished his drink and set the glass down with a decisive little click. "Jo—"

"It's late," I said quickly. "I've kept you long enough. Thanks for the escort."

"I could stay if you like."

"No, thanks. I'm fine on my own." I cobbled up a smile as I walked him to the door. "What a mess. Poor guy—not exactly what you signed on for, is it?"

"I don't care about that," he said. "I'm glad I'm here. You don't have to worry, Jo. Nothing's going to happen while I'm around."

But he was wrong. It already had.

Chapter 8

The precinct interview room was tiny and square, three paces each way. The only furniture was an oblong table, bare but for a box of tissues, with four chairs set around it—not folding chairs but comfortable upholstered seats with arms. Mounted high on the wall near a corner of the room was a small video camera of the sort used for security. I wondered if we were being watched.

Max lounged in one of the armchairs, his briefcase on the floor beside my laptop. "You're making me dizzy," he said.

"How long are they going to keep us waiting?"

"It's been all of ten minutes, and we were early."

"Sorry." I dropped into the chair beside his. "I'm a wreck."

"You don't look it."

I hoped not; I'd spent enough time on my makeup that morning, trying to conceal the circles under my eyes. Like Max, I'd dressed conservatively for the occasion: in his case a jacket and tie, in mine a little sheath in black cotton chambray, with an old Coach bag in leather so soft it made me want to cry every time I touched it. Four-inch heels, but only because I needed the height. Not Crazy is the look I was going for. Solid Citizen. Woman in Distress Showing Admirable Restraint.

While we waited, we talked about Molly. I hadn't told her about the e-mails. Last night, after Jean-Paul left, I'd been sorely tempted to call her and spew out all my troubles, but pity stopped me, and shame, too: for I could not escape the feeling that I'd been an unworthy shepherd of the flock she'd entrusted to my care.

"You have to tell her," Max said. "She'll find out anyway. Better she hear it from you."

"I can't do it over the phone. I'll have to go up there. Tonight, maybe." Then it struck me that I had something planned for tonight. I checked my BlackBerry and Teddy Pendragon's name leapt out at me. God help me, I thought. As if stalkers and cockroaches weren't enough. My first thought was to put the biographer off, but I'd stalled him too long to get away with that now.

The door opened and a tall, slender man strode in. Our eyes met, and he smiled. I gasped and stared like a tourist on Broadway. He was a strikingly handsome man, but it wasn't that.

Max rose, hand outstretched. "Detective Cullen, I presume?"

"You must be Max Messinger. Nice to meet you. I'm a big fan."

"Really?" Max beamed. "That's good to hear." Writers, I thought. Max stepped aside. "Jo Donovan, Detective Tom Cullen."

"Hey, Jo," the detective said.

"Tommy." I stood and took a step toward him; there was an awkward moment before we settled on a handshake.

Max looked from him to me, eyebrows raised. When neither of us volunteered anything, he said, "You two know each other?"

"Used to," Tommy said cheerfully. "Have a seat, won't you?" Max and I sat side by side, across from Tommy. I examined him properly for the first time. He was as fine-looking as ever, but the boy I'd known was gone. It wasn't just the tailored suit. There were lines around the corners of his mouth and his eyes and a harder cast to both. His sandy hair was shorter now, and his eyes were a darker, warier shade of green, rain forest instead of meadow. His ring finger was bare, I noticed, not that that meant anything. When Hugo and I married we exchanged rings, but he never wore his.

Max took a buff file from his briefcase and placed it on the table. "We've documented everything. There's a timeline—"

"I'd like to hear it from Jo, if you don't mind." Tommy produced a small notepad, just like a TV detective. "Start from the beginning," he said. "What happened first?"

As if I knew when it began. Endings are unambiguous—a slammed door, a final chord, the vacant, glassy stare of the dead—but beginnings are always a matter of perspective. Sometimes you can't tell where a story begins until you reach the end, which is fine if you're writing fiction; but in real life, it's too late.

I explained this. He said, "You're making it too complicated."

"'Just the facts, ma'am'?"

Tommy smiled reflexively, as one does at an oft-heard joke.

"A series of incidents occurred," I said. "But I don't know how they're connected."

"Just tell me what happened. Let me make the connections."

How strange, I thought, that Tommy should be giving me the very advice I give my writers. *Just show what happens,* I tell them, *don't explain it.* He waited patiently as I thought about this, his pen motionless against the pad. I saw he was a man who understood the uses of silence.

"It began," I said unforgivably, "on a dark and stormy night."

Tommy took notes as I told him about the encounters with Sam Spade outside my office and in Santa Fe, the laptop that went AWOL, and the e-mail attack. It made a convincing narrative to my ear, and I thought to his as well, though it was hard to tell what this new Tommy was thinking. Now and then he glanced at me, never for long. He must find me greatly changed, I thought. It was more than the passage of thirteen years; it was marriage and widowhood and the lifetime compressed in between. I wasn't the same. But he, too, was different, I could see that already. Prom King, I used to call him; you wouldn't now.

When I finished, Tommy turned to Max. "What's your connection to all this?"

"I'm a client and a friend. I happened to be at the Santa Fe conference when the stalker showed up there. I offered to help."

"What did you do?"

"Had a word with the hotel manager. He swore her laptop never left the luggage room, which is a small room on the side of the reception desk, accessible through doors from the back office and the lobby. But he also claimed that the lobby door is kept locked. When I tried it, it was open."

"OK, let's see what you've got."

Max slid the file over across the table. It included copies of the e-mails, Sam Spade's novel summary, Lorna's submission log, and a detailed timetable of occurrences. While Tommy read through the file, I watched him and wondered: How could it be that of all the damn cop shops in the city, I walked into his? He wasn't even supposed to be in New York. His plan after graduating had been to work a few years for the NYPD, then go home to Kentucky with some big-city creds, which had sounded as crazy to me as a prisoner escaping from Alcatraz, then taking the next boat back. And yet here he still was, thirteen years later.

When he came to Sam Spade's synopsis, his face tightened, and a little tic pulsed in the corner of his jaw. Finally he closed the file and looked at me.

"I'm sorry, Jo. This is ugly."

"It was heartbreaking for my clients. I had to tell them the offers were bogus."

"Your clients believed them, then?"

"Absolutely. Those offers were designed to play straight to their wildest dreams."

"It's a major escalation," said Max.

I'd forgotten he was there. Tommy looked as if he had too. "It is, assuming it's the same person," he said to Max, and turned back to me. "Let's leave this stalker aside for a moment. Is there anyone in your life with a grudge? Anyone who'd want to hurt you?"

"No one I know of." I supposed they had a checklist they have to go through, but it seemed to me he was veering off track.

"Anyone who might feel betrayed or rejected by you?"

"Betrayed, no. Rejected . . . that's part of the job. We decline ninety-nine percent of submissions, and, unfortunately, many writers take it personally."

"What about your personal life? Are you seeing anyone?"

"No."

"Had you been? Any recent breakups?"

I shook my head. "There's been no one since Hugo."

"Really?" Tommy's eyes flickered toward Max.

Max laughed and raised both hands. "I'm flattered, Detective. But I'm happily married to a wonderful man."

"No one," I said firmly. "Look, Tommy, isn't it obvious what happened? Sam Spade followed me to Santa Fe, seized the opportunity to grab my laptop, and hacked into my agency files."

Tommy nodded but continued along his own turgid path. "Who else has access to those files?"

"No one, only me and my staff."

"Tell me about your staff."

I bristled. "They're incredibly loyal and supportive and they have nothing to do with this."

"He has to ask," Max said. "Besides, you know, we wondered ourselves."

"Not about them!"

"No, but about how Sam Spade could have pulled this off. About the specificity of the offers, the tone, the publishing savvy in those e-mails."

"Well, he's obsessed with getting published, isn't he? He probably follows the agent blogs. He had access to my files. There's all sorts of ways you could pick up the lingo." I knew I sounded defensive, but I felt that Tommy and Max were ganging up, bullying me and casting aspersions on people who had earned my gratitude.

"I still have to know everyone who's ever had access to your work files," Tommy said, "if only to eliminate them."

"Fine!" I ran down the list: Harriet Peagoody, Chloe Strauss, Lorna Mulligan, and Jean-Paul Devereaux.

"Tell me about them. Where do they come from, how long have they worked for you?"

"Harriet's worked for the agency for eleven years. Before that she was with an agency in London. Chloe's her assistant, with us two years, right out of college. Lorna joined us about a year ago, after working for a publishing temp agency. I took on Jean-Paul two months ago as an intern, also straight out of college."

"Anyone else? Accountant, IT person?"

"Our accountant, Shelly Rubens, comes in once a week and works on the spare computer in the file room. Shelly's seventy-two and has been with the agency since Molly started it. We don't have an IT person. We use an outfit in California that provides networking and hosting services to small businesses. I've never even met them in person. There's no one else."

"Don't forget Charlie Malvino," Max prompted.

Tommy raised his eyebrows.

"Former employee," I said. "I fired him six months ago."

"Why?" Tommy asked, and I told him about Charlie's blog.

"He didn't take it well," Max said. "He started trashing her online, anonymously of course. He also showed up at the Santa Fe conference, even though he wasn't on the original list of presenters."

I hadn't realized he knew about the cyber-sniping, but it didn't surprise me. Max was almost as good as Molly at knowing things. "He's not happy with me," I told Tommy, "and Charlie does have a mean streak. But it couldn't be him."

"Why not?"

"Because that would mean that at the exact same time I'm being stalked by a crazy writer, someone else is hacking into my files and sending malicious e-mails. I don't believe in coincidences."

"They happen," Tommy said, with a flash of his old smile. "Though this might not be one. Who knew about this Sam Spade stalker?"

"Lots of people. It wasn't a secret. In fact, when he first ambushed me I was on my way to a client's launch party, and I told some people there about it. It was a good story; I'm sure it made the rounds." It occurred to me then that Charlie had been at Rowena's launch too. I decided against volunteering that information. Tommy was veering off track already; there was no point leading him further astray.

"Was Malvino there?" he asked.

I sighed. "Yes."

"So that's one person with a motive. How about the others? Because I'm getting the feeling here that whoever sent those e-mails knows a good deal about you and your business. Stalkers often know their victims."

"No one I know would do this."

"OK," Tommy said. "But let's try a little thought experiment. Apart from Malvino, there are five people with ready access to your electronic files. Imagine this is a mystery story, and you have to come up with a motive for each of those people. What would it be? Start with Harriet Peagoody."

"She'd never do it. The woman's an agent to the bone. The idea of Harriet tormenting a bunch of writers—it's like trying to imagine a kindly old vet torturing kittens."

"Or a kindly old priest molesting kids?"

"OK," I said. "But Harriet would never do anything to hurt the agency. It's all she has."

"Is it?" Tommy looked interested. "No family, kids, lover?"

"Family in England, no kids, no partner. There was a man, years ago, according to Molly, but Harriet was very mysterious about him, so Molly assumed he was either married or a client. The affair ended in some vaguely tragic manner. In the three years I've been back, she's been alone as far as I know. But what difference does that make? The point is, Harriet has no motive."

"Then she must have done it," Tommy said, looking at Max. "The least likely suspect: isn't that how it works in fiction?"

"In bad fiction," Max said.

Tommy turned back to me. "If you had to give her a motive, though, what would it be?"

It was like brainstorming with a writer. I didn't want to play this game with Tommy, but we needed his help, and I figured that the sooner we got through his list, the sooner he could get down to catching Sam Spade. "A Machiavellian plot to usurp the agency."

"Now we're cooking. What about Jean-Paul?"

"A set-up so he can play the hero."

"Chloe."

"Jealousy."

"Shelly Rubens."

"Dementia."

"Lorna Mulligan."

My mind went blank. Finally I said, "She's an anarchist who hates all bosses. Are we done, Tommy?"

"Almost," he said. "One more. Sam Spade."

"That's obvious: he's crazy."

"Even crazy people have motives. What's his?"

"He wants me to recognize his genius and be his agent."

"And how does sending those e-mails advance that cause?"

"It doesn't," I said tartly. "That's where the crazy comes in."

"Most stalkers are obsessed and controlling, not crazy. If he sent those e-mails, he had some goal in mind, however moronic it may seem to us." Tommy spoke with a practiced calmness that I found at once reassuring and infuriating. His professional dispassion hurt my feelings, or perhaps just bruised my ego, although there was no reason in the world why he should take a personal interest in my problem, nor any why I should want him to.

He was waiting for my answer, but I didn't care to put myself in Sam Spade's head. At last I said, "Maybe he hoped I'd lose clients and need replacements."

"Or," Max put in, "he started off wanting Jo for his agent, got rejected, and now wants to punish her."

Tommy gave him a nod. "Which would explain the escalation."

"That and a touch of erotomania."

"Yeah, I noticed that, too."

They were talking over my head like a doctor and parent discussing a child. I broke in. "Will you help, Tommy?"

He leaned back in his chair and regarded me through those deep, hooded eyes. "Sure," he said. "It's my job."

Meaning if it weren't, he wouldn't? I felt an unexpected pang.

Beside me, Max exhaled deeply. He must have been relieved, not only for me, but also for himself. Finally he could turn this over to the proper authorities and get back to his life. I wished I could do the same.

"What happens next?" I asked.

"Next," Tommy said, "I visit your office with a team from the

computer crimes unit. While they inspect your computers, I'll
talk to your staff."

"I've already questioned them, and so has Max. There's nothing they can add to what we already told you."

"Including the accountant, if you can arrange that."

"I don't see why," I said.

Tommy gave me a look of fond exasperation, without the
fondness. "Let's make a deal, Jo. I won't do your job and you
don't do mine."

"Tommy?" Max said as we walked toward my office.

"He didn't mention knowing me when you first spoke?"

"Not a word. I'd have told you."

"How did he get the case?"

Max shrugged. "I called the precinct commander. He said he'd
assign his best detective. Your Tommy was the one who called
back."

"He's not my Tommy."

"Are you going to talk, or do I need to torture you?"

"There's nothing to tell. We were friends a long time ago, before I met Hugo."

"Friends with benefits?"

"How rude!"

"Only half-rude. The other half is relevant."

The ground rumbled beneath our feet, and steam rose from
a grate. Max took my elbow and steered me away. It was noon,
and the office towers were exhaling their inhabitants into the
streets. I let the current carry me forward. I didn't want to talk
about Tommy to Max. Max is a true friend; I'd trust him with my
life, but not my life story. He's a writer, after all, and writers can't
help themselves around other people's stories. But I knew he'd find
out about Tommy anyway. If I didn't tell him, Molly would.

"We met the summer before my senior year at Vassar. I was interning for Molly and waiting tables in a steak house at night to make ends meet. He worked the bar, a part-time gig while he studied at John Jay."

"You dated?"

"We hung out," I said. "We had fun. Neither of us saw it as a long-term thing."

"Why not?"

"Because I knew him. The moment he opened his mouth, I knew everything about him, because I grew up with guys like him. Tommy came up a good-old country boy, a big fish in a tiny pond, with all the confidence that comes with it. Prom king, high school football star, major stud. He'd have wreaked havoc in whatever small town he came from."

"And yet you were immune?"

"Early inoculation. And I'd made it to New York, you see; I had the internship with Molly and a good chance at a job when I graduated. My life was opening up, everything I'd dreamed of and worked for. I liked Tommy a lot; everyone did. But I wasn't about to settle for the boy next door."

"And he felt the same way?"

"Of course. Absolutely. I'm sure he did. We were totally different people. Tommy was gregarious and outgoing, at ease with himself, a social magnet. I was an intense little bookworm whose idea of a fun night was a bubble bath and a Jane Austen novel. We wanted different things. He planned to go back home and be a sheriff like his daddy. I was never going back. We were two kids with no money, exploring the city. It was fun while it lasted, but that's all."

We'd reached my office building. Inside, the elevator disgorged a carful of people. Max and I rode up alone.

"It can't hurt, can it," I said, "that Tommy and I were once friends?"

"Shouldn't think so," he said judiciously. "Might even help, if he takes a personal interest."

"Right," I said, relieved. "There couldn't be any hard feelings after all this time."

"Why should there be?" The elevator juddered to a halt and the doors slid open. "Assuming you didn't break his heart."

Chapter 9

The wine, a seductive French Burgundy, was outrageously expensive, but I drank it with a clear conscience, for I'd come to be seduced. If someone was going to write Hugo's biography, which according to Molly was inevitable, better Teddy Pendragon than that gossip-hag Gloria Vogel. At least he respected Hugo's work; I doubted she'd ever read it.

Our hors d'oeuvres seemed to appear without human intervention, so discreet was the service. We were dining at Michael's. At lunchtime it was an upscale publishers' mess, full of table-hopping and gossip. (Editors might be laid off in droves, production outsourced to India, and lists slashed to the bone, but the publishing lunch will never die.) At night, though, the room took on a warm, intimate glow. Honey-colored walls seemed to pulse in the candlelight. Crystal and silver glistened against snow-white linens, and waiters, gliding soundlessly through the dining room, bore platters so beautifully arranged that the thought of eating them seemed sacrilegious. Tantalizing aromas swirled around us. My senses encountered nothing that did not please them. It's easy, living in New York and traveling in the circles I do, to take such sights and service as one's due. But I had grown up poor and sometimes hungry; I took nothing for granted.

I was hungry now, ravenous, in fact; I'd eaten nothing since breakfast, and no dinner last night. No wonder the wine was having its effect. I savored the foie gras, garnished with Champagne strawberries, while Teddy Pendragon prattled charmingly in his sonorous Southern drawl. He was an old-fashioned dandy with a waistcoat and fob watch, Capote-esque in style but bent the other way; bit of a tomcat whiff about him. A natural raconteur with a wicked gift for mimicry, Teddy knew everyone in publishing, admired them to their faces, and mocked them mercilessly behind their backs. His greatest regret in life, he confided, was never having met Hugo. "And not for lack of trying, I assure you. I wrote him letters worthy of a besotted schoolgirl. I badgered Molly for an introduction. I befriended his friends. Yet somehow he eluded me."

"Well," I said, "you've caught him now."

"So I have," he said, and something crossed his face, a predatory gleam that came and went in an instant; but it woke me to my purpose.

"We should talk about the book," I said.

"Yes, indeed. Shall we have another bottle of that pleasant Burgundy, or would you like something lighter?" Without waiting for an answer, he signaled the waiter. I wondered if tonight's dinner was on Random House. Teddy's next words showed his mind moving on a parallel track. "Do you realize that if you and I had an affair, it would be entirely tax-deductible?"

I laughed so hard I inhaled a bit of strawberry and started to choke. Teddy darted around the table and pounded me on the back until I begged him to stop. No one even looked our way, which is not indifference in New York, but manners.

"A simple 'No, thank you' would have sufficed," Teddy said as he resumed his seat, looking a bit pink in the face. "Choking seems excessive."

"Sorry, Teddy. It really was the most original proposition, and so practical, too, given the tax benefits."

"More idle supposition than proposition, though one can always hope. But truthfully, Jo, the intimacy I seek from you is not carnal. It may be harder to give."

It could hardly be that, I thought, stifling another laugh. I knew I had to be careful of Teddy. All writers are opportunists, but none more so than biographers. Nevertheless, I felt reckless, giddy. It was the wine, no doubt, combined with stress and lack of sleep; it was the surprise encounter with Tommy Cullen that morning and the unsettling scene in my office that afternoon, full of intrusive detectives and the bewildered faces of my staff. I felt only that I couldn't allow this biography to become another ordeal; I couldn't let it become adversarial. A person can fight on only so many fronts at one time.

I was like a bull weakened by picadors, and Teddy must have scented blood. Dinner was served. We ate and talked and drank. Somewhere around the middle of the second bottle, I started to think old Teddy wasn't such a bad guy after all. This spirit of harmony pervaded our negotiations. Teddy wanted permission to view and photocopy Hugo's drafts and manuscripts, which Hugo had left to NYU, his alma mater. "I'll arrange it," I said. He wanted introductions to our friends; I promised to write them. He wanted Hugo's publishing correspondence, and I agreed to provide it. It was only when Teddy brought up Hugo's personal correspondence that a vestigial sense of caution reasserted itself. My husband was a great writer of long, old-fashioned letters. He corresponded with most of the important writers in the world, and he'd saved copies of nearly every letter and e-mail he'd ever written or received. Given his oft-stated distaste for biographers, I'd sometimes wondered why he bothered. But Hugo always had a well-honed sense of his place in the literary pantheon, and I supposed he'd known this day would come.

Here at last I dug in my heels. Hugo may have forfeited his right to privacy by dying, I said, but his correspondents still had theirs.

The biographer, replete and glowing, seemed indisposed to argue. "We can cross that bridge when we come to it. By that time, Jo, I hope you'll have come to trust me. After all, we have the same interest at heart."

"Have we?" I said, doubting it.

"You may not have wanted a biography to begin with, but I'm sure you feel that if one is to be written, it should be a true portrait."

"And you think you can draw that portrait, Teddy? You think you can encompass Hugo?"

"Encompass him?" He smiled, but his eyes were wary. "That's not how I'd put it."

"Isn't that what biographers do? Oh, you pretend to be selfless, a transparent lens on your subject's life, but really you impose yourself with every choice you make: *your* values, *your* theories, *your* obsessions. You want to cut Hugo down to size and stick him in your pocket. The whole enterprise is shot through with hubris. To the extent that your work succeeds, his is diminished."

My voice had grown sharp. The same diners who had tactfully ignored my choking raised eyebrows at my tone. Only Teddy seemed unperturbed.

"You read my Vonnegut," he said calmly. "Did it diminish him?"

"No, it didn't," I said, deflating at once. Fair is fair. Teddy's biography of Vonnegut was a good book; it took nothing away, and it shone a light. I came away from it with a desire to reread Vonnegut, and a bio can't do more than that.

"I understand your concerns," Teddy said. "They're not uncommon. There's bound to be a tension between the artist and his family, who want his work to stand and be judged on its own merits, and the biographer, who draws attention to the fingerprints in the clay. But connections do exist between the life and the art, and they're interesting connections."

"Interesting the way gossip is interesting. They don't explain anything. All the biography in the world can't explain one line of Hemingway."

"And biographers would be the first to admit that. Your husband was a great artist, Jo, and great artists belong to the people."

"Why are we even talking about this?" I said. "I've already agreed to cooperate."

Teddy leaned toward me, and I caught a whiff of musky cologne. "We're talking because I want more than your grudging cooperation. I want openness, confidence. You're a big part of Hugo's life, the last great act. I need to understand your marriage."

"I already told you our story when you did the *Vanity Fair* profile."

"You gave me the official version, and a beautiful story it was; but it has the sheen of editing about it."

I felt a twinge of dislike penetrate the Burgundy glow. Teddy picked up the bottle of wine and gestured toward my glass. I covered it with my hand. "There's only one version," I said.

His smile was condescending. "There's never just one version. That's half the biographer's job: triangulating the truth."

"I told you the truth."

"As you recall it, perhaps," he said.

"You can take my recollections to the bank. I remember every day of the ten years I spent with Hugo."

"And yet others remember things differently."

Just then our waiter approached to inquire about dessert. Teddy ordered some chocolate monstrosity; I asked for coffee. The waiter left.

"What are you talking about?" I demanded.

"Do you remember telling me about the first time you met Hugo?"

"Yes, of course. You used that story in the *Vanity Fair* piece."

"You said Molly sent you out to Sag Harbor to deliver his manuscript."

"That's right."

"You stayed for a drink. Drinks turned into dinner. After dinner the two of you sat up all night talking about his latest book. At dawn you went for a swim."

"Yes," I said. "That's what happened."

"Molly remembers it differently."

Coffee appeared before me. I tasted it, strong and bracing. "Molly wasn't there."

"It's a small detail, but the discrepancy is interesting. According to Molly, she didn't send you to Sag Harbor. You were supposed to messenger the manuscript, but you chose to go yourself."

I stared into the cup. Molly couldn't have told him that. Teddy had got it wrong. And so had I, when I agreed to allow this biography. Hugo would have hated it. *I* hated it. Who the hell was Teddy Pendragon to decide what was true?

"Why don't you leave Molly alone?" I said. "She doesn't need you badgering her."

"Badgering her?" Teddy looked wounded. "Really, Jo, badgering? Molly was eager to talk to me. She has her own stories to share about Hugo. He was important to her, and she to him."

After that I had nothing more to say to him. I'd said too much already, agreed to things I shouldn't have agreed to. I'd compromised myself, but in the end the seduction had failed, because I was damned if I'd let this travesty proceed.

The next morning I sat in the porch swing while Molly reclined on a chaise, her long legs covered with an afghan despite the heat—close to eighty degrees already, and not yet ten o'clock. A light breeze carried the scent of lavender. Molly's husband, an avid gardener, had transformed their suburban lawn into an English country garden full of lavender, hollyhocks, pansies, and delphiniums. After he died, she kept it up, first for his sake and then for her own. Gardening became her therapy, and I could tell by the dirt under her nails and the smudge on her nose that she'd been at it earlier that morning.

I told her about Sam Spade, starting with his appearances outside our office and in Santa Fe. At first Molly wasn't terribly disturbed, since all agents have tales of overeager writers. She told me one about a friend who was handed a manuscript at his own wife's funeral.

But the news about the phony offers shook her. "Oh, kiddo," she said. "Oh, jeez." She'd gone pale and shivery under the afghan.

"Forget it, Moll," I said. "The police will get him. Let's go in and I'll make us some lunch. I brought bagels from Zabar's and that maple cream cheese you like."

"I'm not hungry." But Molly allowed herself to be led inside and settled in an armchair in her bright, farmhouse-style kitchen, with gingham curtains and pots of basil and thyme on the windowsills. I toasted a bagel, spread on a schmear of cream cheese, and served it to Molly on a plate. It could have been boiled boot for all the interest she showed, but she took a dutiful bite before setting it aside. "I'm worried about you," she said.

Her hair, which was starting to grow back, covered her head like a cap of silver down. She'd lost so much weight that the hollows in her cheeks had deepened to gorges. When I first met her, Molly had been a beautiful, bold woman with a raucous laugh, a forthright manner, and a handshake the equal of any man's. Even now she was beautiful, but it was a haggard, stripped-down sort of beauty that reminded me of the vogue some years back for heroin-chic fashion models. There was a war raging inside her, and we both knew how it was going to end.

"That's rich," I said, "coming from you."

"What's to stop this guy coming after you?"

"Not gonna happen. There are serious barriers in place."

"What barriers?"

"Lorna, for one," I said, and Molly smiled, Lorna being no small impediment. I cast about for some further distraction. "Do you want to hear something funny? I know the detective assigned to the case."

"Who is it?"

"A guy named Tom Cullen."

Her jaw dropped. "*Your* Tommy?"

"He wasn't my Tommy. You remember him?"

"Are you kidding? I never forget a handsome face, and he was some looker. Nice guy, too, and crazy about you. I thought something might come of it. But then you met Hugo and the rest was history."

"It was never serious," I said. "But how weird is it meeting him again under these circumstances?"

"How's he look now?"

"Older, of course. More gravitas. But still damn good."

"Married?"

"Why, you interested?"

Molly snorted. It was good to hear her laugh, but my heart was still in deep shadow. I told her about the detectives' visit to the agency the previous afternoon. Two men spent hours going over the computers while Tommy interviewed my staff one by one in my office, which he'd commandeered. Jean-Paul had emerged from his interview red-faced and tight-lipped; for the rest of the day he busied himself in the file room. Chloe came out looking excited, Lorna sullen, Harriet offended. Shelly Rubens, our accountant, schlepped in all the way from Brooklyn, his broad brown face perspiring from the unseasonal heat, and made his usual joke when I introduced him to Tommy. "You were expecting maybe a nice Jewish lady?" When the detectives finished their detecting, Tommy called me and Max into my office and laid out the results in language that was nominally English but Greek to me. Anonymous remailers, masked and spooked IDs, keyloggers, and rats . . . Max translated for me afterward. The detectives had found no sign of tampering or spyware on any of the office computers. They were taking my laptop for further examination. The e-mails had been routed through a service that scrubbed them of identifying markers. The police would try but probably fail to trace their source.

"A lot of nothing," Molly summarized.

"Precisely," I said. "Which is why this whole biography thing is such a nonstarter at the moment."

"Excuse me?"

I'd hoped to slip it past her. Stupid of me. Nothing gets by old Argus Eyes.

"I feel besieged," I said. "Sam Spade's infiltrated the agency files, Tommy Cullen's combing through my laptop and my life; the last thing I need is Teddy Pendragon undermining the foundation."

"The *foundation*?" said Molly, an odd look on her face.

I regretted the word instantly, not because it was inaccurate but because it was too revealing. I'd built my life on my marriage. Everything I was, I was because of Hugo. But this was not something I could say to Molly, who has her own image of me. In even the closest of friendships, there must be some pockets of reticence.

"You can't stop him," she said. "He's already signed with Random."

I didn't ask how she knew. Molly always knew. "He can't write it without my cooperation."

"He'll write it anyway; it just won't be as good. Is that really what you want?"

"That's his problem."

"What have you got against the man?"

"I don't like biographers in general. And I don't like Teddy in particular. He's presumptuous." Even to my ears, the last bit sounded petulant.

"Presumptuous how? Did that scamp make a pass at you?"

"Not really, though he did mention that if we had an affair, it would be tax deductible."

Molly threw back her head and roared. "Oh, God bless him," she said, wiping her eyes. "What a thing to say. Don't tell me that offended you."

"That didn't," I said, but I stopped there. If Molly really had told him that skewed version of how I first met Hugo, it could only be the effect of her illness. I was determined not to mention it.

"Well, you can't back out now," she said. "And you shouldn't. Teddy's the best literary biographer working today, and he adored Hugo."

That she could take Teddy's side hurt me in a place only Molly could reach. *She's eager to talk to me,* he had said, and I saw now that he was right. Molly had loved Hugo—not as I'd loved him, of course, but in her own way. She'd nurtured him, scolded him, guided his career. She had stories she needed to tell while she still could.

"What makes you think Teddy's trying to undermine you?" she asked.

"He claims I don't know the truth about my own life. He says the truth is arrived at only through a biographer's 'triangulation.'" I let out a derisive snort, but Molly just looked at me thoughtfully.

"Is it the biographer you object to, or the whole process of unearthing and reexamining the past?"

"There's no need to unearth what's never been buried," I said.

"Then what are you so afraid of?"

I drew myself up. "Can you really believe I'm afraid of Teddy Pendragon?"

"You're sure acting like it, and that's not like you."

"Is it really so hard to understand? I don't want Teddy's grubby paws on my life and marriage."

"But it's not just your life," Molly said. "It's Hugo's, too, and that doesn't belong to you alone."

I looked away, stiff with resentment. Why did everyone act as if I had something to hide, when all I was doing was trying to protect my husband's legacy?

A moment passed. Then Molly said, "Let's have some chai."

I got up to put the kettle on, glad to have my back to her. It didn't take long to make the chai, for I knew her kitchen as well as I knew my own—a true measure of intimacy among women, it seemed to me.

"Such a comforting drink," she said as I set two steaming mugs on the table. For her, maybe, but I was steeling myself. When a doctor lays out alcohol swabs and a Band-Aid, you don't have to be a weatherman to know a needle's coming.

"Want to know what I think?" Molly said.

"Do I have a choice?"

"I think you've created this canonized image of Hugo, and you're afraid to let anyone deconstruct it."

"That's ridiculous," I said. "And rude."

But Molly was just warming to her theme. "In fact, the more excuses I hear from you, the more I think this biography is just what the doctor ordered. I loved Hugo to death, you know that, kiddo. But the man was no angel, and it's absurd and even disrespectful to pretend he was."

"I never said he was an angel! But I won't tolerate anyone maligning him. I knew Hugo better than you did, and I sure as hell remember more clearly."

Molly looked bewildered. "What are you talking about?"

"Do you remember how I first met Hugo?"

"Of course. You took his manuscript out to Sag Harbor."

"You sent me."

She laughed. "As if! He'd gone out there to be alone and finish the novel. The last thing I'd have done would be to wave *you* under his nose. Good Lord, didn't I know the man? You were supposed to messenger that manuscript, not go out and spend the damn weekend."

"So you really did tell that story to Teddy!"

"He asked me how you met. I told him."

"But it's not true, Molly. And telling the story that way makes it look as if I schemed to meet the great Hugo Donovan, as if I were some kind of stalker."

"Nonsense," Molly said. "I never held it against you. If anything, I admired your enterprise."

"But my version's better and has the advantage of being true."

Molly raised her eyebrows but didn't answer. We sipped our chai, not as comforting as usual. Something else she'd said was nagging at me. Finally I realized what it was.

"What did you mean he 'went out there to be alone'? He could have stayed in the city for that."

"No, he couldn't," Molly said. "What's-her-name was there."

"What's-her-name?"

"His mistress. And the kid."

Chapter 10

Lorna glanced at her watch and frowned as I walked into the office. It was nearly noon.

"I went to see Molly," I said, wondering, not for the first time, why I felt compelled to answer to my secretary. I certainly didn't answer to anyone else. Publishers call me a tough cookie, which I was and took pride in being. Yet Lorna, all of twenty-three, ran the office and me with an iron hand; and she was no easier on herself. She'd never missed a day, taken time off, or even come in late. Last winter she dragged herself in with the flu; I sent her home, and damned if she wasn't back the next day. Whoever said the younger generation lacks dedication never met my staff.

"A ton of calls," she said, with an air of forbearance, as she handed me a stack of message slips.

"Did the police call?"

"No, but Charlie Malvino did, twice, and he sounded mad as heck."

And that was another thing about Lorna: she didn't swear, though I'd noticed no other signs of religiosity. Perhaps, like me, she'd been raised by people who didn't care for cursing; only in her case, the training had stuck.

"Must've heard from the cops," I said.

Her eyes widened behind her thick-rimmed glasses. "You think it was him?"

"No, I'm sure it was that idiot writer, Sam Spade, but the police have to talk to everyone."

"Gordon Hayes called a few times too. Says he's in the city and needs to see you today. I told him you're jammed up, but he's real insistent."

I remembered then that Gordon had said something about coming down when I called him to tell him there was no Animal Planet deal. I sighed. Work was piling up on my desk, I had a thousand calls to return, and I hadn't even briefed Jean-Paul on his new duties yet. The last thing I needed was a meeting with a client, even one I liked. But Gordon lived all the way up near Saratoga Springs. If he'd already made the trip, there was no way I could refuse to see him.

I told Lorna to set up a late-afternoon appointment, then hurried down the hall to my office without seeing anyone else. I felt rotten. My conversation with Molly had been as close to a quarrel as we'd ever come, except for the time she'd urged me not to marry Hugo, and it had left me sick at heart. I wanted to call and put things right, but I wasn't the one who'd put them wrong. Things she'd said still played in my head like a song I couldn't shake. "Canonized image of Hugo" my ass: as if I didn't know my own husband, warts and all! And that nonsense about a mistress and child.

"Not his!" Molly had added hastily, seeing my face. "Hers."

She was out of her mind, of course. When Hugo and I met, he was as free as I was. There was no child. There was no live-in mistress. Women there were, and plenty; some had left souvenirs, and they weren't shy about calling the apartment, either. But I'd moved in with Hugo right after he returned to the city from Sag Harbor, and, besotted though I was, if there'd been a woman and child in residence, I'm quite sure I'd have noticed.

Work was the best remedy for misery, so I rolled up my sleeves and plunged into my e-mail. The first message I read drove everything else from my head. It came from Harvey Millstein, Max's new editor at Random House. "Jo, did you get my fax? I sent over an advance NYTBR. First page, baby! We're going back for another 30K. Call me!"

I suspected the e-mail at once. If Sam Spade could prank my clients, he could do the same to me. But then I found the fax, buried in my inbox, of the front page of next week's *New York Times Book Review*. I read the first paragraph: "Max Messinger's six previous books were clever entertainments, fast-paced thrillers notable for the verisimilitude and attention to detail one would expect from a former FBI agent. His seventh, 'The Gatekeeper,' is a work of another order altogether. Nothing in his previous writing, as competent as it's been, gave any indication of this writer's true depth and ability." I let out a whoop. Footsteps pounded in the hallway; my door flew open and Jean-Paul appeared, Chloe right behind him. "Jo," he cried, "what's wrong?"

"Nothing," I said, "it's good, it's great—here, read this!"

Lorna and Harriet drifted in to listen as he read the review aloud. The last line was "'The Gatekeeper' adheres faithfully to the form and conventions of its genre but transcends it in the depth of characterization and the lucent clarity of Messinger's elegant prose." I had to swallow hard to keep from bawling. This couldn't have happened to a more deserving writer. A year ago, Max had delivered his latest novel. I read it in one night. It was a first-rate thriller, certainly up to the level of his past books, but it was just a hair off being a much better book than that. We talked. Max listened a lot, spoke little, and took the manuscript back. Two complete revisions later, it went to Harvey Millstein, who worked with him on a final draft that in my view amply deserved the reviewer's praise. No wonder Harvey was over the moon.

This was huge for him, too. It wouldn't escape the notice of anyone in the business that Max had written his breakthrough book *after* switching houses.

I took the bottle of scotch from the bottom drawer of my desk. "We have to celebrate."

"Absolutely," said Harriet. Jean-Paul hurried out and came back with five glasses. We toasted Max in absentia, and I gazed fondly at my stalwart, motley crew. Lorna was frowning slightly, no doubt fretting over the waste of office time. I asked her to scan the review and e-mail it to Max and Molly.

"We can e-mail again?" she asked.

I hesitated. Although we still didn't know how Sam Spade sent those phony e-mails, we knew they hadn't been sent through the agency's e-mail account. There was no telling how long it would take the cops to catch this guy, if they ever did; till then, the stalker might strike again at any time. But how long could we function without e-mail?

Jean-Paul seemed to follow my thoughts. "We could send out a general notice warning people to check the headers on any e-mail they get from us."

I'd rather have said nothing. I was sick of Sam Spade; if it were up to me, I'd bury the whole incident for good and never think of it again. But there was no wishing this leech away. Something had to be done to protect the agency and its clients, so for lack of a better idea, I accepted Jean-Paul's.

I spent the rest of the afternoon on the phone, starting with Harvey Millstein, who told me that the major chains and distributors had already reordered, and the publicity director was working on a television campaign. No sooner was I off with Harvey than I got a call from Marisa Deighton at Doubleday, who raved about the Keyshawn Grimes novel. We strategized about lining up support on the editorial board. These days it was hard to sell even established writers; publishers were even warier of untested commodities. "Is there anything about the author that might help?" Marisa asked. "Does he have a platform?"

"Does drop-dead gorgeous help?" I said. "How about smart, outgoing, and funny? Not to mention his arc: from Bed-Stuy to Swarthmore."

I left the young editor very happy and myself hopeful that her enthusiasm would carry the day. But I would say nothing to Keyshawn yet, for many an offer founders in the shoals between an editor's enthusiasm and the cold, hard calculations of marketing.

Another half a dozen calls later, I was more behind than ever, because for every call I made, two more came in. There was a special project I was eager to launch, but I despaired of ever finding time for it. I need help, I thought desperately, and finally it dawned on me: I had a brand-new shiny assistant I hadn't even unwrapped yet. Jean-Paul was still doing the work he'd done as an intern, reading slush-pile submissions and helping Lorna with clerical chores, because I hadn't yet made time to deploy him on other tasks.

I rang Lorna's extension. "Send in Jean-Paul, would you, and hold my calls?"

A moment later my new assistant knocked and entered. He advanced slowly, looking nervous. It occurred to me that we hadn't been alone together since that night in my apartment, when I lost my cool over a cockroach and he drew the wrong conclusions. I'd hustled him out before anything foolish could be said or done, but the fleeting moment when that possibility existed seemed to have opened a Pandora's box of discomfort for him. I indicated a chair across the desk from mine; he sat as if it were upholstered in cactus.

"I've got a project for you," I began, and at once Jean-Paul relaxed. "I want you to pull the files of the twelve clients Sam Spade hoaxed. Familiarize yourself with their publishing histories, submissions, reviews—everything. Read their books. I want you to come up with a new marketing plan for each of them: lists of houses we didn't try, subsidiary rights we didn't place, other media outlets. You'll have to dig. If it's obvious, I've already tried it. Let's see if we can't make some lemonade out of Sam Spade's lemons."

"Brilliant," he said, with such fervent admiration that I blushed with gratitude. At least I hoped it was gratitude. He really was the most attractive young man. If I were Chloe's age . . . but I had never been Chloe's age.

A commotion seemed to have broken out in the reception room. I heard Lorna say, "Oh, no you're not!" followed by a deeper voice that answered calmly but insistently. Both voices were growing louder as the speakers approached my office.

My eyes met Jean-Paul's, and the same thought must have hit us simultaneously. I grabbed the letter opener from my desk and strode toward the door, but Jean-Paul got there first. He flung it open, filling the doorway. Beyond him I could see Lorna, her back to us, arms outstretched as she faced down the intruder, who was hidden from me. I tried pushing Jean-Paul aside, but it was like shoving an oak. "Who is it?" I demanded.

"It's Gordon, Jo," the intruder said. "Gordon Hayes."

"Oh for Chrissake! Lorna, Jean-Paul, let the man in."

"He's not alone," Lorna said stubbornly. She didn't budge, but Jean-Paul stepped aside, and finally I saw what all the fuss was about. Gordon had one of his dogs with him, a huge black German shepherd sitting calmly by his side.

"Jo," Gordon said, "this is Mingus. Say hi, Mingus."

The dog stood and approached my outstretched hand. I'd shooed the others out; we were alone in my office, though I sensed Lorna hovering protectively right outside the door. Mingus sniffed my palm, paying special attention to the pulse point on my wrist where I apply perfume. I stroked his sleek head and ran my fingers through his ruff. He had a lustrous black coat, broad shoulders, intelligent eyes, and a noble head, graying at the muzzle.

"Nice to meet you, Mingus," I said. He wagged his tail, then walked off to explore the office.

"Hope you've got no contraband," Gordon said. He'd dressed up for the city in slacks and a sports jacket, but even cleaned up he wasn't nearly as pretty as his dog. He was a hefty six-footer, rock-solid by the look of him, bullet-headed with just a tonsured fringe of grizzled hair, a skewed nose, and a long, thin mouth. He was forty-five but looked ten years older.

"He's a police dog?" I asked.

"Retired. Once a cop, though, always a cop. You like him?"

"Who wouldn't? He's beautiful."

"Good. He's yours for as long as you need him."

I stared at my client. I didn't know him well, except through his book, but I knew him well through that. He'd been with the agency for about a year, brought to me by a client who'd purchased one of Gordon's dogs and ended up reading his manuscript. The title, *My Life in Dogs,* was quirky enough to be interesting, but I'd started reading only out of courtesy to my client; I had no interest in a book on dog training.

But it was much more than that. I wasn't two pages in before I knew the writer was a writer. Each chapter began with a story of a German shepherd the author had trained, and those sections did include practical guidance in understanding and training dogs. But those stories segued into others, drawn from the author's peripatetic life, a journey that had included a long stint in the Marine Corps and another in a monastery before depositing him in upstate New York, where he now made his living breeding and training German shepherds.

It was a book that shouldn't have worked but did, because the dogs' qualities—loyalty, bravery, rivalry, pack discipline—mirrored similar qualities in Gordon's comrades-at-arms and brothers, and because the author was as astute an observer of men as of dogs. The composite of all the stories added up to a sort of pointillist self-portrait: hence the well-conceived title, which we kept.

The book was an original but difficult to categorize; it garnered more compliments and fewer offers than any I'd ever handled. Nothing but pure bullheadedness compelled me to keep going until, finally, my twentieth submission struck gold.

It seemed as if I'd cast my bread upon the waters and it had come back to me in the form of a four-legged guardian angel. I was touched by Gordon's generosity and tempted to accept. As a lonely child, I'd longed for a dog but wasn't allowed to have one. Thwarted desires never really go away; they just burrow in deeper.

It was impossible, though. I couldn't take care of a dog, and I told Gordon so.

"You've got it backward," he said. "The dog takes care of you."

"I can't accept."

"You need him. And I need you to keep doing what you do, instead of looking over your shoulder. A trained dog's the best security there is. Any other weapon can be taken away and turned against you, but nobody turns a dog against his master."

I thought about the night Sam Spade emerged from the shadows and grabbed my arm. I looked at Mingus, who had finished exploring and settled on the floor beside Gordon's chair. In response to my gaze, the dog thumped his tail and panted, baring long white fangs. He was as big as a wolf.

"But I'm not his master," I said.

"He's a professional. He'll work for you."

"I've never owned a dog in my life."

"I won't leave until I'm satisfied you can handle him. You're not afraid, and that's a start."

We left the office and walked to Central Park. Gordon made me hold the leash, and I began to enjoy the way the rush-hour crowd parted before us. Clearly Mingus had the Moses touch. Nevertheless, I still intended to refuse Gordon's generous but impractical offer. I wasn't Mingus's mistress and thus had no authority or control over him. That he walked so calmly beside me, sitting when we stopped for lights, I put down to Gordon's presence at my side . . . his silent presence. Gordon didn't speak once the whole way to the park. Like many writers I'd known (Hugo having been the great exception, he was as shy and taciturn in speech as he was eloquent on paper.

In the quiet, enclosed haven of Strawberry Fields, Gordon took the leash and put Mingus through his paces. Then he taught me the command words and hand signals and gave the leash to me. We practiced sit, down, stay, come, and heel over and over while Gordon called out corrections, not to the dog but to me. At first I felt overmatched. Mingus was not only big but muscular, an armored tank on legs. He obeyed me, I felt, on sufferance only, or by way of obeying Gordon. And yet the longer we practiced, the more responsive he became, until he seemed almost to antici- pate my commands. When I walked, he kept pace; when I stopped he sat by my side; when I called him he came. He clearly enjoyed the routine, throwing himself into it so that his movements seemed to flow from my will and extend its reach.

Gordon's instructions grew less and less frequent. After an hour or so, he said, "Not bad. I'm getting hungry."

"Me too," I said. "How about you, Mingus? Are you hungry?"

"He's a dog; he's always hungry. Come on, I'll buy you a hot dog."

We headed back toward the ball fields. I offered Gordon the leash. He shook his head. "German shepherds need to bond with their handlers to work for them. Normally that's a process that takes weeks or months. We don't have that, so we're going to take some shortcuts. From now on, this dog is attached to you at the hip. Where you go, he goes. Every necessity of his life—food, water, shelter, affection—has to come from you alone."

"But I have to work. I have to go into the office every day."

"Of course. He goes with you. What good would he do sitting at home?"

We reached the hot dog cart and stood on line behind a couple of young boys in baseball uniforms. "Wow," said one of them, "cool dog! Can I pet him?"

I looked at Gordon, who nodded.

"Say hi, Mingus," I said, and the big dog wagged his tail and licked the sticky hand held out to him.

"He's great with kids," Gordon said with paternal pride.

"I can't believe he was a police dog. He seems so gentle."

"A well-trained dog turns it on and off like a switch. Mingus was one of the elite, a SWAT team dog."

"How did he come to be with you?"

"His handler got sick and had to retire. Mingus was six, too old to reassign, and the handler couldn't keep him. So he came back to me." Seeing my puzzlement, he added, "He's one of mine. I bred this fellow out of the best bitch and stud I ever owned."

"I'm not sure I want a dog with a pedigree better than my own."

Gordon laughed. "It's just a loan, till this thing gets sorted out. After that, Mingus comes back home to his well-earned retirement in the country."

Now was the time to tell him that Mingus couldn't stay. But we'd reached the front of the line, and Gordon was ordering: five hot dogs, two with the works, and three bottles of water. The vendor gave us a cardboard tray. We sat on a nearby bench to eat, and Mingus sat beside me, eyes politely averted from the food.

"Shouldn't we feed him?" I asked Gordon.

"You will, but not yet. Alphas eat first."

I ate quickly, not just for Mingus's sake but because I was hungry; and that hot dog with sauerkraut tasted better than the fancy dinner I'd just had with Teddy Pendragon. When I finished, Gordon had me break off a piece of meat and offer it to Mingus. The dog ignored the food and looked intently at Gordon.

"Chow time," he said, and suddenly the meat was gone, swallowed whole. "Chow time's the release phrase. Dog's trained not to eat without it. Protects him from poisoning."

I went on feeding Mingus by hand, piece by piece. I never felt his teeth touch my hand; he used his lips to pluck the pieces from my palm. When the food was gone, he licked my hand clean, then nosed one of the water bottles.

"He's thirsty," I said. "But we don't have a bowl."

"Cup your hands." Gordon poured water into my hands and Mingus lapped it up. We continued until one of the bottles was empty. I wiped my hands on his ruff.

"Nice job," Gordon said, "You're a natural, Jo."

"Funny—that's what I told you, remember?"

"I'm not likely to forget it. You sure you never had a dog, maybe as a kid?"

"I brought a stray home once," I said incautiously.

"What happened?"

What happened was that she'd taken the leash to me, dear old Grandma, buckle end flailing. That was a bad one, and the reason that I can't wear low-backed gowns or bathing suits.

"It didn't work out," I said. "Look, Gordon, as much as I appreciate the offer—"

"We're not done yet. Ready?" Without waiting for an answer, he gathered up the wrappers and bottles and carried them back to the cart. I watched him take a cell phone from his pocket and make a call. Mingus stayed by my side but never took his eyes off his master. When Gordon came back, he took the leash.

We started back the way we'd come. It was dusk now, and a breeze carried the scent of grass and honeysuckle. Gordon said, "Any German shepherd is going to have a deterrent effect, but Mingus is trained to do a lot more than that. Chances are you'll never have to deploy him, but you need to know how."

We'd reached the lake abutting Strawberry Fields. Gordon looked around, and I followed his gaze. There was no one nearby except a bearded man, homeless, I presumed, because he seemed to be wearing everything he owned. He trailed us by twenty yards, moving stiffly, like a zombie in a horror flick. I sensed movement and glanced down. Mingus had stiffened to attention and was staring at the stranger.

Gordon unsnapped the dog's leash and pointed at the bearded man. "Watch!"

Mingus tore through space like a bullet. Inches before colliding with the man, he stopped short and barked fiercely up at his face.

The man froze. Mingus continued to bark, sharp staccato barks that clearly said how much he'd like to take this confrontation to the next level.

"Out!" Gordon yelled. "Mingus, come." Instantly the dog turned and ran back to us. "Well done, dog."

"Are you out of your fucking mind?" I said, my heart racing. "Please tell me that guy's with you."

Gordon just smiled. "Let's keep walking." He ordered Mingus to heel but didn't reattach the leash. After a few steps, I heard a loud cry behind us and spun around. The bearded man was lumbering toward us, waving a stick and shouting incoherently.

"Pack in!" Gordon said, pointing, and Mingus disappeared in a blur of silent motion. When I saw him next he was leaping on the bearded man, clamping his jaws on the arm with the stick. I heard the impact, a solid *whomp*. The man spun around and fell to the ground, Mingus still attached to his arm.

"Out!" Gordon called, trotting toward them. I stayed where I was, watching. Mingus released his grip but stood guard until Gordon reached them. Gordon reached out a hand and hauled the bearded man to his feet. They shook hands, and the victim patted his mauler on the head.

They came back to me, and Gordon introduced his helper, who I then saw was wearing a heavily padded jacket.

"This dog's out of my league," I said.

"He's powerful," Gordon said. "A German shepherd has a bite force of two hundred and forty pounds, more than most sharks. He can immobilize any attacker, armed or not. The dogs are trained to go for the gun arm, and at the speed they move, ninety-nine times out of a hundred the perp never even gets a shot off. But Mingus will never attack on his own, only on command or if you are attacked. Imagine Fred here had been your stalker, coming at you with a weapon."

I imagined it without difficulty. I pictured Mingus flying through the air and nailing Sam Spade to the sidewalk; I pictured him sinking his fangs into the stalker's arm, and I tested for guilt. None came. As Huck Finn said, there's folks you can sivilize, and folks you just can't.

"I'll take him," I said.

Chapter 11

By ten I was in my pajamas, reading in bed with Mingus snoozing on the rug beside me. Hugo had slept naked, and I did as well while we were married. It hadn't come naturally at first, for I'd been raised by a woman who got dressed under her nightgown and taught me to do the same. But I grew to enjoy the caress of fine cotton sheets and the freedom from restraint, which spilled over into our lovemaking. Many mornings I woke to find Hugo propped on an elbow, gazing at me, tracing the line from hip to shoulder first with his fingertips, then with his lips. When he died I bought flannel pajamas, the bulkier the better.

The intercom buzzed. "It's a Detective Cullen," the doorman said.

"Wait ten minutes, then send him up." I threw on jeans and a T-shirt and checked myself in a mirror. Then I did a quick run-through of the living room, gathering up as many photos of Hugo as I could and tossing them into my bedroom. "Daunting," Jean-Paul had called them, but that wasn't the reason. The photos were personal, and with Tommy there needed to be boundaries.

The doorbell rang. I opened the door with Mingus at my side.

Tommy, dressed in a blue suit and holding my laptop, took a quick step back. "You have a dog."

"On loan from a client. Name's Mingus."

They eyed each other; then the man extended a cautious hand, and the dog sniffed it in the same spirit. "Can we talk?" Tommy asked.

"Come on in." I led him into the living room. He stopped in the center and looked around. I saw the room through his eyes: spacious and high-ceilinged, with tall bookshelves full of first editions and treasures from our travels, a massive fireplace, windows overlooking the park, and French doors to the terrace. "Nice digs," he said. "I see you landed on your feet."

"Better than on my ass." It was meant as a joke, but it fell flat. What was he doing here, anyway? Without Max to buffer the encounter, Tommy's presence in my home felt disturbing and incongruous. Mingus's, on the other hand, was comforting. Before he left, Gordon Hayes had insisted that I practice siccing the dog on his assistant. At first I'd resisted. When I finally gave the command, Mingus flew like an arrow and brought the man down. It should have felt bad, loosing a dog on a fellow human being; it should have felt wrong. What I felt instead was pure elation. All that power, all that strength at my command! The feeling was illogical, of course. I couldn't deploy the dog against the sort of invisible online stalker Sam Spade had evolved into. I couldn't even sic him on Teddy Pendragon, much as I'd like to. But at least, with Mingus by my side, no one was going to lay hands on me.

"I brought your laptop," Tommy said, handing it over. "Figured you could use it."

"That was nice of you." I gestured to the couch and took a facing seat. Mingus positioned himself between us, watching Tommy. "What did you find?"

"No spyware. Clean as a whistle."

His knees were jiggling. He's nervous too, I thought, and somehow that made me calmer. "He wouldn't have needed spyware if he grabbed my laptop in Santa Fe. He could have copied the whole hard drive."

"Sam Spade?"

"Who else?"

Tommy shrugged. "Someone who knew about your stalker and saw an opportunity to get away with some shit."

"What a devious mind you have, Detective."

"Tell me something, Jo. What would happen if you quit the agency?"

"That's never going to happen."

"But if you did," he insisted.

"The agency's mine. I could sell it, but it's more likely that I'd come to some arrangement with the agents who work for me."

"That would be Harriet Peagoody?"

"At the moment she's the only other agent. But Harriet would never—"

"Why not? You stole the business out from under her, isn't that how she sees it?"

"Yes, but—"

"Why do you think none of her clients got hit?"

"Because whoever did this was targeting me. Do you have any reason to accuse Harriet?"

"Apart from motive and opportunity?" Tommy asked. I didn't answer. He sighed. "We're looking for Sam Spade. Your secretary gave us a long list of rejected writers, and we're working our way through it. But you have to consider the possibility that whoever sent those e-mails is someone close to you, personally or professionally. Someone with a grudge who lacks the guts to confront you head-on."

Charlie came to mind. After I fired him, he'd launched a campaign of nasty rumors and attacks on industry websites. But there was a big difference between coming after me and striking at my clients, and I still couldn't believe he'd cross that line.

"Maybe Charlie," I said reluctantly, "but I know you already talked to him. He called my office, pissed as hell. Said you guys gave him a hard time."

"Yeah," said Tommy, stone-faced, "we took turns waterboarding him. Who else is mad at you? Who've you hurt?"

"No one."

He raised his eyebrows. "Come on, now, darlin'. We both know that's not true."

Who's talking, I wondered, Detective Cullen or my old friend Tommy? He had a way of sliding from one to the other that kept me a step behind, struggling to adjust. A tactic, I thought, and hardened my heart against him. "Do not call me darling," I said coldly. "And isn't it time you eighty-sixed the drawl? You've lived here as long as I have."

"There's some might say you've overcompensated."

"Tell me something, Tommy. How did it happen that of all the detectives in New York City, you were the one assigned to my case?"

"Just lucky, I guess."

"No, really: isn't it an amazing coincidence?"

"You're suspecting me now? That's good; you're getting the mind-set. It's time to take off the rose-tinted glasses, Jo, and use those gorgeous eyes for something other than flirting."

"*Flirting?*" I said, outraged. "Is that what you think I've been doing?"

"Can't help yourself, can you?" he said. "But don't worry about me. Once bitten, twice shy."

"You look chipper," my secretary said as I entered the office the next morning. Her face fell as the dog followed me in. "Don't tell me you're keeping that thing."

"Just for a while."

Mouth pursed, she busied herself squaring a batch of message slips.

"Do you not like dogs, Lorna?"

"Filthy animals. If it makes you feel safer, fine by me. Just don't expect me to walk it."

"Morning, Jo," Jean-Paul said. "Hey, buddy," he said to Mingus, who nosed him as thoroughly as a cop patting down a suspect.

Chloe emerged from Harriet's office and said, "I see you've been replaced, Jean-Paul." There was an edge to her voice and a look on her face that made me wonder if something had happened between them. But if it had, Jean-Paul seemed clueless.

"Supplemented," he answered cheerily. "Dogs can't go everywhere. I'm still available anytime Jo needs me."

"She's already got an Alsatian; why would she want a lapdog?"

He stared at her, looking more surprised than hurt. Chloe clapped a hand over her mouth and rushed back to her cubicle. The awkward silence that followed was broken by Harriet's arrival. She wore an ivory silk blouse, a smart, high-waisted black skirt, and heels in place of her usual sensible pumps.

"Morning, Harriet," I said. "You look swell."

"Lunch at La Jolie today." There was a little pause where the name of her lunch date should have come, but didn't. Harriet stared at Mingus. "Is that Gordon's dog? Are you keeping it?"

"For a while."

"But bringing it to the office—is that wise, Jo? A big dog like that . . . think of your liability if it hurt someone."

I wished they would quit calling him "it." "He's trained. He'd never attack except on command."

"A trained attack dog? That's like bringing a loaded gun to work!"

"Guns can be turned against you," I quoted Gordon. "Dogs can't."

She raised a plucked eyebrow and said, "It's your neck, my dear. Better introduce us, then."

"Say hi, Mingus."

He got up, wagging his tail, and accepted a proficient scratch behind the ear. Harriet might have been disapproving, but she wasn't intimidated. "Comes from a musical family, does he?"

"Apparently. His brothers are named Satchmo and Miles."

She sketched a smile and walked past us to her office. I watched her go. Tommy's words lingered like poison dripped in my ear. *Stole the agency out from under her . . . motive and opportunity . . . none of her clients hit.*

"Who's she meeting for lunch today?" I asked Lorna, who shrugged. "Where am I lunching?"

"The Union Square Cafe at one with Marisa Deighton," she said promptly.

"Give her a call—see if we can switch it to La Jolie."

Lorna didn't ask why, just turned to her computer. I poured myself a cup of coffee and filled a plastic bowl with water for Mingus. Then I hurried down the hall to my office and, without stopping to think about it, dialed Molly's number.

She answered on the first ring, as if she'd been waiting. "Hey, kiddo."

"Molly, I am so sorry." I didn't know what I was apologizing for, but I felt better for saying it. Nothing was worth being at odds with her.

"Fuggedaboutit. That was me sticking my nose where it doesn't belong. Old habit. Hard to break."

We went on in that vein for a while, each of us taking the blame on herself, but after we hung up I realized that Molly never recanted those nonsensical things she'd said about Hugo. I thought about that for a while. If Teddy Pendragon had already signed with Random, then Molly was right: he would write the biography with my help or without it. If I didn't cooperate, skewed stories like Molly's would be all he'd have to go on.

That couldn't be allowed to happen. I pulled up an e-mail I'd received from Teddy the morning after our dinner. In it he'd asked for a letter addressed "To Whom It May Concern," stating that he was writing a biography of Hugo with my approval and cooperation, and encouraging Hugo's friends to speak with him "so that the resulting book will do justice to its subject in all his splendid complexity."

I'd written back, thanking him for dinner but ignoring his request, which seemed to me presumptuous and even dangerous: endorsements sent to individuals could easily be withdrawn later, if the biographer proved untrustworthy, while this blanket statement could not. But once again the balance of power had shifted. If there were to be sides, I needed him on mine.

I typed up the letter myself. Normally I'd have had Lorna do it, but it wasn't strictly agency business, and given the dog situation, I was wary of provoking her. Prickly as she was, Lorna was valuable to me. I'd given her two raises already, but in the back of my mind I was always braced for an announcement that she'd found a better-paying job and was leaving us. But this was unjust to her, for like the German shepherds in Gordon's book, Lorna was a loyal soul, and she'd attached herself to me. She certainly didn't stay for love of literature. If the girl read at all, I'd never caught her at it. I'd asked her, when she first applied for the job, why she wanted to work in publishing. It was a standard question, and I'd expected the usual English-major twaddle in response, but Lorna's answer had been memorable.

"It's clean work," she'd said. "Books are clean."

I looked at Mingus, lying beneath my desk with his head resting on his front paws. He didn't seem to me the least bit filthy, but I supposed that filth, like beauty, is in the eye of the beholder.

———

New Yorkers, like denizens of all great cities, cope with its unfathomable vastness by carving out small communities. Some are based on location, others on affiliation. Lawyers have their hangouts, stockbrokers have theirs, and we publishing professionals have ours. Some restaurants are perennials: the Union Square Cafe, Michael's, and the Four Seasons. Among the fashionable newcomers were Maison D'être, where Rowena had had her book launch, and the current favorite, La Jolie. The chef was a young Frenchwoman who'd been a sous-chef at Le Cirque. La Jolie was her nickname, a dismissive one in the male-dominated world of haute cuisine, so there was a pleasing sassiness in her adopting the name for her first restaurant.

It was a charming little place on East Fifty-Fifth, not far from Michael's, with a small but comfortable bar and a dozen well-spaced tables in the dining room. The décor was French rustic, as was the menu; only the prices referenced Manhattan. I found Marisa waiting in the bar, radiant with secret knowledge. Either she's pregnant, I thought, or she's got an offer for me, and judging by the wineglass in her hand, she wasn't pregnant.

The maître d' led us into the dining room. The moment we entered, I spotted Harriet at a table in the center of the room. Opposite her sat a man I recognized at once, though his back was to me. They leaned across the table with the quiet intensity of lovers or conspirators.

I let Marisa go ahead and paused beside their table. Harriet glanced up, smile in place, and did a double take. Her companion, seeing her reaction, turned to discover its cause. Charlie Malvino didn't blink an eye. "Hello, Jo," he said, sketching an ironic little bow.

"Charlie," I said coolly, "Harriet. Catching up on old times?"

She stared at me. "What are you doing here?"

"Isn't it obvious?" Charlie said. "She's checking up on the help."

"Enjoy your lunch," I said, and went back to Marisa. I ordered the goat-cheese salad and a glass of Sauvignon Blanc, and she said she'd have the same. Definitely not pregnant, I thought. Then she broke the news.

"Marty read the Keyshawn Grimes and he loved it. We're prepared to make an offer."

"Nice," I said. "What's the offer?"

"Modest."

"How modest?"

"Eight thousand?"

"That's not modest, that's downright chintzy."

I know she would have been given a range, not a figure; the trick was figuring out the upper limit of that range. We haggled amicably over our salads and settled at last on $12,000. Better than eight, but still low enough that unless we got extraordinary early reviews or major award nominations, they'd just shove the book out with no support, which is like dropping a toddler off to play in Times Square. But with no other bidders, I had very little leverage.

Still, it meant that Keyshawn's first novel would be published by a prestigious house. There'd be reviews, maybe some subsidiary rights sales: not a bad debut for a twenty-three-year-old writer. Suddenly I couldn't wait to get back to the office to call him. The sale of a first novel is a moment that lives forever in a writer's mind. It's the start of his career, a before-and-after moment he'll remember for the rest of his life. I would be a part of that memory: a modest sort of immortality, but my own.

Chapter 12

I was on the phone with Keyshawn when Harriet stormed into my office. Waving her to a seat, I continued my conversation.

Keyshawn attempted to take the news coolly but was undermined by the break in his voice. "You're the man, Jo. I can't believe it. I owe you for this."

"I take it you accept the offer?"

Harriet, who'd been scowling at the floor, looked up at this.

"Oh, hell yeah!" Keyshawn said.

I congratulated him again and warned him that contracts would take several weeks. We talked for a few more minutes, then I eased him off the phone.

"Who'd you sell?" Harriet asked.

"Keyshawn Grimes."

"Well done." Her tone was begrudging but sincere. For all the nos we have to give and receive, we agents live for the yeses; and the sale of a first novel is the sweetest deal of all.

Harriet recomposed her face into a scowl. "*Were* you checking up on me?"

"Why would I?"

"You tell me; you're the one who showed up at La Jolie."

"We've crossed paths at lunch before, and you never asked that question. Feeling guilty?"

"Why the bloody hell should I? Charlie may be on your blacklist, but he still has some friends." Her voice had taken on a grating upper-class English edge. Mingus sat up and stared at her. "Lie down, you silly dog!" she snapped, and to my surprise he obeyed.

"Harriet," I said mildly, "it's no business of mine who you lunch with." And yet I couldn't help wondering. Charlie had good commercial sense but no real taste; Harriet was the opposite. They'd never gotten along in the office, and I'd never known them to meet outside it. Why now?

"No, it isn't," she said sourly.

"How is Charlie, anyway? Still fuming?"

"What do you expect? It's not pleasant being grilled by the police."

"Beats being fried," I said. Harriet was not amused, and I remembered that she, too, had been questioned. "I told the police they were wasting their time. No agent would have sent those e-mails."

"Yes, well, apparently you didn't tell them forcefully enough."

"Charlie called me to complain," I said, "but what he really wanted was to find out exactly what the police were investigating. I can't imagine he didn't ask you."

"Of course he asked. I told him nothing."

I thought of their two heads, canted together like lovers'. Charlie hadn't looked disappointed.

The door opened and Lorna walked in, carrying a stack of letters. "I need signatures," she said.

Harriet turned on her with the fury she hadn't dared show me. "Can't you see we're in a meeting, you stupid cow?"

I was on my feet before I knew it, and so was Mingus. "How dare you talk to her like that? Apologize at once!"

"Or what, you'll sic the dog on me?" Harriet took a deep breath and composed herself. "I apologize, Lorna. *You* didn't deserve that."

"No, she didn't," I said, quelling an impulse to slap the older woman silly. Striking out at Lorna like that was like kicking a stray dog, and I wouldn't have it in my office. "Thanks, Lorna, leave them on my desk. Harriet and I have some things to discuss."

"Actually," Harriet said, "we're done. I've had enough interrogation to last me for a while, thank you very much." She got up and marched out of my office with the perfect posture of one whose governess had made her walk with books on her head.

I started to call after her, then stopped myself. If this conversation continued, it would end with Harriet quitting or being fired. Maybe that's where we were headed anyway, but I didn't want it to happen now, in the heat of the moment. I sat back down and rested my head on my hands.

"Nasty old witch," Lorna muttered. I pretended not to hear.

I worked late. The sun had set by the time I left the building, but Manhattan by night is as bright as most cities by day. I'd changed into sneakers and planned to walk home through the park. Mingus needed the exercise, and I needed to clear my head.

The rush-hour crowd had abated, but there were still plenty of people on the streets. I stood for a moment, adjusting to the clatter and clanks, honks and beeps, the incessant polyglot hum of the city. Then I stepped onto the pavement, and the city cradled me in its towering arms, cloaking me in anonymity. Mingus trotted at my heel, ears perked, vigilant. All he needed was an earbud to be the consummate Secret Service agent.

Hugo used to hate me running in the park, or even entering it at night, but that's because he didn't understand my situation.

The city was his birthright, not mine. I had to earn it; and to make a city yours, you must inhabit it. So whenever Hugo fussed, I'd said "Yes, dear" and "No, dear," and then I'd done as I pleased.

I was willing to cede the outer boroughs, but within Manhattan, there was nowhere I would not go. Central Park was relatively safe. The main paths were well lit and well patrolled, and I took sensible precautions: I never walked through late at night, and I avoided secluded places. But at seven thirty on a clear summer evening, with Mingus at my side, I had no fear.

The evening was warm, and a fine mist rose from the lake. We had just passed the tall boulders along the lakefront when Mingus stopped and swung his head around, pointing like a bird dog at a spot amid the rocks. The hair on his ruff rose, and I believe my own hair did as well, for I felt it too: the sense of being watched, followed . . . stalked.

I stared hard at the boulders. At first I saw nothing. Then my eye caught a flicker of movement where none should have been, and gradually I made out a deeper darkness in the shadow of the boulders: a crouching human figure.

There were people around but no one close. I thought of running, but to run was to invite pursuit. I felt for the clasp of Mingus's collar and called out, in a voice much braver than I felt, "Who's there? Show yourself!"

A moment passed. Then the dark shape unfurled, and through the mist I glimpsed a male figure in dark clothes and a hoodie. A moment later it swung around the side of the boulder and was gone. Mingus leapt forward, straining against the leash, and for a moment I was tempted to let him loose. If it was Sam Spade, this was my chance to catch him. But what if it wasn't, and I ended up siccing Mingus on some harmless vagrant who'd been sheltering in the boulders?

"Leave it," I said. "Let's go, Mingus." The dog threw me a reproachful look but followed as I turned toward home.

To call or not to call, that was the question. Whether 'tis nobler in the mind to be taken for a poor frail woman in need of protection, or to swim alone through a sea of troubles? If I called Tommy, would he take it personally? Even the question made me angry. What did I care what he thought?

I took a steak from the freezer and stuck it in the microwave to thaw. Poured myself a glass of wine, which I sipped in the kitchen while the dog lapped water from his bowl. I thought of all the novels I've read in which witnesses withhold information from the police, only to show up dead in the next scene. Tommy's card was in my wallet, cell phone number scrawled on the back. I laid it on the counter and looked at it. When the microwave beeped, I put the steak on to broil and threw together a salad. Mingus stationed himself beside the stove, drooling so much that a little pool of saliva collected on the floor. "Poor guy," I said. "You're not used to city hours, are you? How do you like your steak? Medium-rare work for you?"

It seemed to. His half of the sirloin, mixed with kibble, was gone before I took my second bite.

"No, I don't think you're paranoid," Tommy said when I finally phoned him. "I think you're stupid."

"What?" I sat up straight on the couch.

"Walking alone through the park at night? Jesus wept, woman. Why not pin a target on your back?"

"I wasn't alone. Mingus was with me."

"Can he stop a bullet?"

"Easy there, Detective. No one's been flashing any guns. Sam Spade's the white-collar type."

"His namesake wasn't."

"Oh," I said. "You've read Hammett."

There was a little pause, and I found myself listening for background noises on his end—footsteps, a TV, a woman's voice—but all I heard was his voice in a vacuum. "You gave me *The Maltese Falcon*. Said if I insisted on being a dick, I might as well learn from the best."

I laughed. "I don't remember, but it sounds like me. Fiction trumps reality every time."

"Now there's a surprising flash of insight."

Definitely alone, I thought. He wouldn't use that tone if he weren't. Somehow conversations with Tommy seemed to start out professional and take a sharp turn toward personal. He had an encroaching way about him: that much I did remember.

I told him about Harriet and Charlie. He didn't seem impressed.

"You don't think that's kind of suspicious?" I asked.

"La Jolie, you said?"

"That's right."

"I know it," Tommy said. "Expense-account joint. Publishers' hangout."

"Yeah, so?"

"Silly place to meet if they're conspiring."

I hadn't thought of that, but he was right. La Jolie was more the type of place you take someone you want to impress. "So now you think Harriet's OK?" I asked.

"Didn't say that. She's no fan of yours, that's for sure. My advice would be don't take any poison apples from her. And stay out of the damn park."

"Brilliant, Detective."

"My pleasure, ma'am."

Chapter 13

The next blow fell the following morning. Jean-Paul was with me; we were going over his plan for resubmitting the work of each of our targeted clients. Lorna walked into my office and said, "Amy Patel from *Publishers Weekly* called."

I looked up impatiently, having told her to hold my calls. Amy's call was nothing unusual. I had several friends at PW, and we regularly passed on news of sales and suggestions for features. "So?"

"She asked if it's true you're leaving the agency."

"*What?*"

"She said she heard you're leaving, and Harriet is taking over." The breath caught in my chest. "What did you tell her?"

"I said I didn't know anything about it."

I stared at her.

Lorna, normally phlegmatic, now looked distinctly uncomfortable. "I said she should ask you, only you weren't available at the moment. What was I supposed to say?"

"You should have said no, you twit!" Jean-Paul exploded. "You should have found out where she heard such a ridiculous story."

"No one asked you," Lorna retorted, but her heart wasn't in it.

"Take it easy," I told Jean-Paul. "Don't kill the messenger." Although in truth, I felt like flinging a large book at the messenger.

"What should I do?" Lorna asked me.

"Call her back." But just then the phone rang.

Lorna answered it. "Hamish and Donovan." She listened for a moment. "What press release?"

Jean-Paul groaned.

Lorna scowled and put her finger to her lips. "Could you forward us a copy right away? . . . No, of course it's not true. . . . No, sorry, she's in a meeting. I'll have her call you as soon as she gets back."

She hung up. "Bill Dietrich from the *Times*. They received a press release in your name. He's forwarding it now."

Bill was the *Times*' publishing beat reporter. I logged into my e-mail, and no one spoke a word until it came through. I read it aloud.

> *Dear Publishing Friends and Colleagues:*
>
> *As some of you may know, this agency and some of its clients have recently been the objects of a malicious attack. Twelve of my clients received e-mails, supposedly sent by me, containing book and movie offers for their work. The discovery that these offers were phony caused great distress to them and to me.*
>
> *Our attempts to identify the perpetrator of this cruel hoax have been unsuccessful. The police, too, have failed to find the person responsible. Because all the targeted writers were my own clients, I have concluded that this malicious act was intended to undermine these valued relationships. There is only one way to protect this agency and its clients. As of today, I am*

severing my ties to the Hamish and Donovan Literary
Agency, which will henceforth be directed by my faith-
ful and trusted associate, Harriet Peagoody. I take
comfort in knowing my writers will be in such capable
hands.

It has been a pleasure to know and work with you
all, and I wish you all the best.

Sincerely,
Jo Donovan

When I looked up, Jean-Paul was on his feet, pacing the room
and punching his palm with his fist. Lorna's eyes were glued to
my face. I opened the address list, and even as I ran down the list
of names, I knew, without yet knowing how, that this would
change everything. The list was a Who's Who of the New York
publishing scene. *Publishers Weekly,* the *New York Times, Pub-*
lishers Lunch, Vanity Fair, Mediabistro, and Gawker were on it.
So were all the major publishing websites and agent blogs, along
with the personal e-mail addresses of a dozen top publishers and
editorial directors. If I had compiled it myself, I couldn't have
done a better job.

We would deny it at once, of course, but now there was no
containing the story. Before the day was through it would be the
talk of the industry. I had no idea what to do, where to begin.
Lorna and Jean-Paul were looking at me fearfully. I forced down
the panic that rose inside me. Later, I promised myself. I'll fall
apart later.

"Write a refutation, and explain the backstory," I told Jean-
Paul. "Bring me a draft in twenty minutes." He turned and ran.
I looked at Lorna. "Let all calls go to voice mail till I get this
sorted. Is Harriet in?"

She nodded silently, owl-eyed behind her thick glasses.

"Ask her to step in, would you?"

Harriet swooped in, all elbows and British hauteur, dressed today in lady-of-the-manor tweeds. "What's going on, Jo? Lorna looks like she swallowed a toad."

"Shut the door." I hardly recognized my own voice, which seemed to issue from some cold, dark place deep inside me.

She closed the door and approached my desk but remained standing. I handed her a printout of the press release. "This went out to the entire publishing community this morning."

The blood drained from her face as she read. Even her lips went pale. Halfway through, she sat down heavily.

"Who sent it?" she said when she finished reading.

"You took the question right out of my mouth."

"How can you ask me that?" she cried. "But how could you not? I quite see that. I see how it looks. And after yesterday. But even so, Jo, even so."

She looked genuinely stricken, so ill I edged the wastebasket toward her. "Maybe you told Charlie more than you meant to."

"I didn't! I swear to you I didn't. He did ask, but I hardly said a thing." She stared at the printout, running a hand through her hair until the gray spikes resembled a turbulent seascape. "'My faithful and trusted associate,'" she read aloud. "'Her capable hands.' You see what this is?"

"A vote of confidence?"

"He wants you to suspect me. I'm the scapegoat here. I'm as much a victim as you are."

"Who would do that?"

"Not me. And it couldn't have been Charlie. He didn't know enough."

"Because you 'hardly said a thing.'"

She bit her lips and didn't answer.

"Maybe it was a thing or two too many," I said. "I'm not blaming you. But I have to know."

Patches of color returned to her cheeks. She read the press release again. "Whoever wrote this knew there were twelve phony offers. Charlie didn't know that. Isn't it obvious who it is?"

What was obvious was that she was ratcheting back her claim to have told him nothing. Now it was just the number he didn't know.

"Not to me," I said.

"It's that stalker of yours, that Sam Spade." She said "stalker" as if she were saying "husband" or "lover," as if he were someone I had willfully allowed into our lives. But I observed this without feeling it. I felt nothing at all, except cold.

"It must be," she went on in the face of my silence. "It's his MO: phony e-mails, impersonation. Only now he's trying to destroy us from within, casting suspicion on me. Don't you fall for it, Jo! I told you I'd see you through this, and I meant it. But I have to know you trust me. I can't go on working here if there's any doubt in your mind."

There was plenty of doubt in my mind. Harriet was a skillful saleswoman, but I wasn't buying. Anyone who knew about our cyber-stalker could have written that press release, including Sam Spade himself. But only someone in publishing could have put together that distribution list, and chances were I was looking right at her. Or so I'd thought before she came in. Now I was less certain. Anyone can fake shock, but she'd actually turned white.

I looked away from her, and my eye fell on a photo on the opposite wall. Taken at a mayoral inaugural ball, the photo showed Hugo and Norman Mailer embracing warmly. In fact, Hugo had disliked Mailer, who'd once written an essay about the state of contemporary American fiction without so much as mentioning Hugo's name, and Mailer had loved Hugo about as much as any alpha wolf loves an upstart male challenger; but you'd never know it from the photo. Keep your friends close, Hugo always said, and your enemies closer.

"Of course I believe you," I told her.

The first person I called was Tommy, despite having sworn last night never to call him again. I was in crisis mode, blindered, full-speed ahead. Tommy gave me his e-mail address, asked me to forward the phony press release, and put me on hold. When he came back, his voice was grim. "This isn't good. It's escalating."

"You were right about one thing. Look at the addresses it went out to. Whoever made up the distribution list knows his way around publishing."

He grunted. "Seen Harriet yet?"

"She was shocked, shocked!"

"Again with the Bogie references. A guy could get jealous."

And he accused *me* of flirting. I was in no mood. "The thing is, she really did seem shocked. She turned white. How do you fake that?"

"You'd be surprised what people can fake. How bad is this, Jo?"

"Bad enough. I expect I'll lose some clients." I felt a pang as I said it.

"I thought all publicity's good publicity."

"For writers, maybe. Agents are supposed to be effective and invisible."

"Any chance your media friends will keep quiet?"

"Not a chance in the world. They don't do quiet."

"Then I guess you'll be issuing a denial."

"Working on it as we speak."

"You want to downplay the damage. Refer to the incidents as

'unfunny jokes'; try not to mention the perp at all. Remember he's out there obsessing, feeding on every bit of attention he can squeeze out of you. I've got to go. I'll be over later."

"Are you going to talk to Charlie again?"

"So now you suspect Charlie?"

I looked at the door to my office, gauging the silence behind it. "At this point, I trust the dog."

"Now you're talking sense," Tommy said.

Jean-Paul brought in a draft statement. I edited out the indignation and downplayed the villainy, borrowing Tommy's phrase, "unfunny joke." The result was short on detail but dignified in tone. "Print it on agency stationery," I told him. "I want it faxed to everyone on that distribution list."

"Not e-mailed?"

"Faxed and e-mailed, then followed up with phone calls. And that's just for starters. I'm going to need to reach out to every writer in our stable." Telling the story over and over, listening to the same expressions of shock, issuing the same reassurances—my stomach curdled at the thought.

"What kills me," Jean-Paul said, "is that I actually had my hands on the bastard. I wish I'd broken his fucking neck—sorry, Jo."

"I wish I'd brained him with my umbrella, but wishes ain't horses. Now, go fix that statement. I want everyone in my office in half an hour for a staff meeting."

He left. To save time, I forwarded the phony press release to Molly and Max, then conference-called them. She was home in Westchester; he was on tour in Houston. I filled them in, and they read the statement. Max was the first to speak.

"The hell with the tour. I'm coming to New York."

"Don't you dare," I said. "I need you out there flogging books and charming booksellers. Don't forget, your income is my income."

"This is serious, Jo. It's escalating."

"The cops are taking it seriously. There's nothing you can do that they're not doing."

"How can I help?" Molly asked.

"Just do what you do. Talk to people. Let them know it was a hoax. Tell them the agency's on solid ground and I'm not going anywhere."

"Won't that make them suspect the opposite? It would me."

"Can't be helped," I said. "The false story's out there; we have to deny it."

"I'll get right on it."

"And I'm calling Detective Cullen," Max said.

"Keep your chin up, kiddo," Molly said. "You're not alone."

"You guys," I began, but couldn't go on due to something stuck in my throat.

We sat around the conference table in my office, as we did at our monthly slush-pile treasure hunts, but the atmosphere this time was very different. Chloe, seated opposite Jean-Paul, looked everywhere but at him. Harriet was physically present, but so distracted and silent she hardly seemed there at all. Only Lorna was her usual efficient self, anchoring the foot of the table with notepad and sharpened pencils at the ready. The phone rang constantly, two rings per call before voice mail picked up.

"We've got to start answering that phone soon," I said. "When we do, I want to make sure we're on the same page. Our attitude is that someone played a nasty prank on us. We're annoyed but not worried; and despite the recent unpleasantness, it is business as usual here. I want a batch of submissions out of here by the close of day. Any calls from the media should be directed to me.

Any appointments you have, keep 'em. Lunch dates, whatever. Business as usual."

Harriet shuddered. "As if I could eat. I'm feeling quite ill, actually. I may have to go home."

In the silence that followed, there came a loud snort from the foot of the table. We all looked at Lorna, who rarely spoke in staff meetings. "If anyone should feel sick, it's Jo," she said to Harriet. "*She's* the one getting battered and her name dragged through the mud, and I don't see her running home."

"Nonsense!" I said, bristling. "Do I look battered and muddy?"

"Hell no," Jean-Paul said loyally, and Chloe gave him a sharp look. Lorna seemed taken aback, and I regretted my reaction. In her own awkward way, the girl was just trying to support me, and I'd nearly taken her head off.

"Personally," Chloe said, "I think you're taking this really well, Jo. What this creep did was criminal. My dad says you'll have a humongous civil suit against him, too, if the police ever find out who it is."

I'd met her parents once, shortly after Chloe joined the agency: tall, dark, angular people, high-powered attorneys in a large city firm. Very fine people, touchingly proud of their only child. I'd marveled at the lack of any resemblance between them and their petite, kewpie-doll, blue-eyed daughter until the obvious explanation occurred and was later confirmed by Harriet: Chloe was adopted, a much-loved only child.

I wondered what else her parents had said.

"Wait," Jean-Paul said. "You talked to your father about this?"

Chloe turned on him combatively. "Yeah, so?"

"So Jo specifically asked us not to discuss these incidents with anyone."

"It just so happens that we talked this morning, after the *New York Times* and PW and everyone else already had the story. I thought he might be able to help. You are such a suck-up, Jean-Paul, it's pathetic."

"Just because I'm concerned—"

"Concerned? Try obsessed!"

"Knock it off, both of you," I growled, and they subsided, glaring off into different corners.

Lovers' quarrel, I thought. All I needed.

If that meeting had had a soundtrack, it would have been by Bartók. And yet despite the disharmony, my little crew pulled together over the next week as never before, including Harriet, who did not, after all, go home that afternoon. Later that day, Tommy and another detective came by the office to do a second round of interviews. Harriet emerged from hers with reddened eyes; yet within minutes I heard her on the phone, reassuring someone that I was still at the helm of Hamish and Donovan. The reason I heard it was that she had taken to leaving her office door ajar, in a show of openness.

Though they still weren't speaking, Jean-Paul and Chloe worked like demons, while Lorna guarded my office so zealously that Mingus began to feel redundant. Like so much of her solicitude, it was well-meaning but tone-deaf. Solitude was the last thing I wanted or needed. Like Harriet, I took to leaving my office door open.

My first calls were to the journalists on the distribution list. They were sympathetic but unbending. The story was already out on various blogs and websites; they had no choice but to cover it themselves. I spoke to dozens of book editors and publishers, all full of indignation on my behalf and Harriet's, for she, too, was seen as a victim. During that week, every agent and editor I knew called to commiserate and share their own horror stories about obsessive writers. No one seemed to wonder about the distribution list, which to me had been the most disturbing aspect of the incident. They assumed that the pushy writer who accosted me outside the office was the same person impersonating me on-line. I was glad about that, and kept my darker suspicions to myself.

Everyone worked overtime to keep submissions flowing while we coped with the phone calls. I went to two dinner parties and a book launch; I kept all the lunch dates on my calendar and insisted that Harriet do the same. "Business As Usual" was our mantra.

My greatest fear was that the phony press release would prove a self-fulfilling prophecy, leading to wholesale defections until the agency collapsed around me. But once again I was unjust to my clients. Their support gave me strength I could never have summoned on my own. The first one I called was Rowena Blair. She was the client I could least afford to lose, and the one who could most easily leave, since a writer who churns out a bestseller a year can have any agent she wants.

"I'd kill him," she said after I told her the story. "I'd feed him to the pigs. I'd cut off his balls and serve them on a bed of fucking rice." After that, Rowena called at least once a day. She offered me a private detective, the services of her masseuse, the use of her country house in East Hampton. I was tempted to take her up on the last, just to get away, but I knew that house: secluded in the woods, it had towering glass walls. I'd have felt far more exposed there than in the city.

And it wasn't just Rowena. Gordon Hayes phoned daily. He said he was checking on Mingus, but I knew he was checking on me. Keyshawn Grimes stopped by the office to offer himself and a cadre of friends as bodyguards. I explained about Mingus, but Keyshawn wasn't impressed. "Dogs can't go everywhere," he said, and a strange thought came to me then, like a wisp of a dream that dissipates even as you reach for it: where I grew up, dogs were welcome in places black men were not.

I didn't want a bodyguard or posse, for that would only draw more unwanted attention; but I understood that for my young author, this must seem the perfect opportunity to repay a debt in a currency he actually possessed. I looked at him, and an idea came to me.

"I'm going to a PEN reception next week," I said. "Mingus certainly can't go there. Why don't you come with me? Not as my bodyguard, though. As my guest."

Keyshawn went away happy, and I went back to the phones. Incoming calls were stacked up like planes circling a landing field, so constant that I hardly had a moment to myself. Lorna disapproved, but keeping busy was a good thing. Fearsome beasts lurked in the crevasses between tasks. Denied access by day, they came out at night when I was defenseless. Every evening I'd fall exhausted into bed, and sleep would claim me quickly—only to creep out a few hours later like a faithless lover, leaving me alone with my revolving thoughts. *Who hates me enough to do this? How could a stranger bear so much malice? How could a friend conceal it?*

Chapter 14

I took as much care preparing for the PEN reception as a debutante for her coming-out ball. This would be my first major outing since last week's sabotage, and I needed to project the very opposite of what I felt: an image of serene confidence and invulnerability. Thursday afternoon, one week after the phony press release, I left work early to get my hair and nails done, then went home and riffled through my closet, still full of clothes Hugo bought me. When we first married, my wardrobe had consisted of three pairs of frayed jeans and an assortment of consignment-shop finds. Hugo took me on forays into Bloomingdale's and trendy SoHo boutiques he read about in the *Times'* Style section. Effortlessly attracting the attentions of every saleswoman in the shop, he'd stride through the racks snatching up garments, never glancing at price tags or bothering with sizes; then he'd enthrone himself in an armchair (armchairs tending to materialize as needed in Hugo's vicinity) and watch as I modeled his selections. He'd dressed me the way a child dresses a paper doll, and with as little resistance, for in those days I was a blank slate with no taste of my own but absolute faith in his. Hugo's choices were, I believe, designed to elicit envy in other men; sexy but not slutty, they said "Eat your heart out," not "Come and get it."

I tossed half a dozen dresses onto the bed, considered them for a moment, and narrowed my choices down to two: a Laila Azhar scoop-necked number and a black-and-white Nicole Miller jersey with a wrap front. The Laila Azhar looked casual but elegant; the Nicole Miller was that and sexy, too. Hugo would have chosen the second for me. He had enjoyed the envy of other men because he was devoid of jealousy, too sure of me to worry. I, on the other hand, had suffered agonies of the stuff in the early days of our marriage. Before I met him, Hugo had a long and storied career as a playboy and philanderer, and Molly warned me that he'd never change. For a long time I believed her. Hugo's second wife had been one of the most beautiful women in Hollywood, and he'd cheated on her, so what hope was there for me?

And yet he never did. In the ten years we were married, Hugo never strayed, though plenty of women tried their best. I would love to say that this was because I satisfied him so thoroughly that no other woman could tempt him, but the truth, I believe, is that by the time we met, Hugo was tired of sowing wild oats. He'd sown enough for ten men already; he had nothing left to prove. At that point in his life, fidelity suited him. The energy he saved on women he invested in his work, and the results of that choice were four brilliant novels.

I tried both dresses on and studied my reflection in the bathroom mirror. Mingus declined to weigh in. Finally I chose the wrap-front. "Man's lust is woman's capital," Hugo used to say, and I have never had cause to doubt it.

"Whoa," Keyshawn said, rising from an armchair in the lobby.

"Whoa yourself," I said. He looked very handsome in a one-button charcoal jacket, gray slacks, and a pristine white shirt with the store creases still in it. I should have brought Jean-Paul, too, I thought. Strolling in on the arms of those two hotties, I'd have given Rowena a run for her money. Keyshawn was twenty-three but looked even younger, except for his eyes. He had a writer's eyes, watchful and a bit remote. Had I really needed a bodyguard, I'd never have chosen a writer, because writers are rarely fully present in the moment; there's always a piece of them standing aside, taking notes. Even Hugo; especially Hugo. Sometimes I would say something to him, and he'd look at me in that absent, writerly way; and a year or two later, my words would pop up in his work.

We took a cab to Joe's Pub in the East Village. The PEN symposium was sponsored by the Freedom to Write Program, which defends writers around the world who are threatened or persecuted for their work. It was a cause Hugo and I had supported for years, and I continued to support it after his death, taking on endangered writers as clients and bullying American publishers into giving them a voice. Not that much bullying was required, to be fair, because this particular cause appealed to the best in people who were normally fixated on the bottom line. Tonight's speakers included Salman Rushdie and a Burmese woman who was on everyone's short list for the Nobel.

Joe's was an attractive space, half theater, half pub, with fuchsia banquettes and tables illuminated from within. The usual suspects were there in force. I introduced Keyshawn to several writers and his own publisher, the head of Doubleday, who congratulated him on his book and drew him aside to chat. Rowena was late as usual. I kept a wary eye out for Teddy Pendragon, who was bound to be around somewhere. He wanted Hugo's papers, and I'd had no time to sort through them. The biographer was circling my life the way a vulture circles a battlefield, and I hated it. It had occurred to me that all my troubles began right around the time Teddy started campaigning to write Hugo's bio; but not even I could find a connection there. Teddy might well have resented me while I was holding out on him, but once I gave in, I was his new BFF, at least until the next book came along.

A group of agents had gathered by the bar, and one of them, George Levy, waved me over. George had been the publisher of a Simon & Schuster imprint until he was ousted in a palace coup. Like so many in that position, he'd taken the leap into agenting, bringing on board a number of his bestselling authors. This act of blatant piracy had ruffled feathers in our insular world, but George was a first-class editor and a fierce, savvy advocate for his clients, and I liked him for that.

"You look stunning," he said with a genial leer. "I knew there was a reason I stayed in publishing. Bartender! What'll you have?"

I ordered a scotch, and the other agents closed ranks around me, bathing me in waves of shared indignation and curiosity. I was buoyed by the former but could do little to satisfy the latter. I hadn't heard a word from Tommy Cullen for a week. For all I knew, he'd given up on me and moved on to the next case.

After a few minutes, George murmured that he'd like a private word, and we stepped around to the side of the bar where the waiters pick up their drink orders. I was wary—George was recently divorced and vigorously playing the field—but I misjudged him.

"Sorry to be the bearer of more bad news," he said, "but in your place I'd want to know. One of your clients called me."

I steeled myself. "Which one?"

"Tracy Simons."

I breathed again. Tracy was a legacy from Molly, and the only client on my list I disliked. Her first book, which Molly sold, had been a roman à clef about her affair with a married governor, the exposure of which cost him his job and his marriage. The book had captured the zeitgeist of a popular disgust with politicians and sold well enough to make the bestseller list for about a quarter of a second. Since then she'd written two more novels to dismal reviews and plummeting sales, for which she blamed me. This was particularly galling, as she'd refused every editorial suggestion I gave her, on the grounds that her writers' group thought the book perfect as is. When we spoke last week, she'd oozed sympathy and sworn undying support. She must have gotten busy the moment she hung up the phone.

"Take her if you want her," I told George. "It's fine with me."

"Not interested. Sort of a one-trick pony, isn't she? Besides, if she'd leave you now, she'll leave me, too, eventually. Who needs that?"

Tomorrow, I thought, I'd give Tracy her walking papers. I was too busy with clients who wanted my help to bother with someone who didn't. After that, I suspected she wouldn't easily secure new representation. Publishing is still a small, collegial world, and other agents were likely to feel as George had about the timing of Tracy's move. She had just hurt her career badly, and there was enough meanness in me to be glad of it.

Rowena still had not arrived when our table was ready. Keyshawn rejoined me and we followed the maître d' to a table against the far wall. I squeezed into the banquette seat while Keyshawn folded himself into the chair opposite mine. The table to my right was occupied by an editor from Viking and her husband. We exchanged air kisses, then I looked to my left. Sitting right beside me, staring rigidly ahead of him, was Charlie Malvino.

"I'm starting to think you're stalking me," he muttered out of the side of his mouth.

"That's funny, Charlie."

He glanced at Keyshawn. "I'd heard you've taken to robbing the cradle."

"Excuse me?" Keyshawn said, leaning toward Charlie.

"This is my client, Keyshawn Grimes," I said. "Remember

that name; you'll be hearing a lot of it when his book comes out. Keyshawn, this is Charlie Malvino, whose sorry ass I fired months ago. He still hasn't gotten over it."

"Was it the whiny voice?" Keyshawn asked.

Just then the panelists filed onto the stage. Charlie settled back in his seat, looking like thunder. The moderator was an NPR host whom I knew and liked, but I couldn't focus on his remarks; I was too aware of Charlie glowering beside me. Five minutes into the program, he couldn't contain himself and leaned over and whispered, "Just so you know, I had nothing to do with it."

"I never thought you did."

"Yeah, well, tell that to your pet detective. The bastard's hounding me. I had to hire a fucking lawyer."

Shushing sounds came from all around us. Salman Rushdie, in white pants and a Nehru shirt, was approaching the podium. I'd met him once at a White House dinner, which he attended with his wife at the time, the beautiful Padma Lakshmi. I found him charming, Hugo less so. I'd put that down to the usual writer's jealousy until later that night, in the cab back to our hotel, when Hugo burst out, "How does a guy like him get a woman like that?"

"Why not?" I said. "He's brilliant, she's stunning."

"He's old enough to be her father."

"You're old enough to be mine."

"*Au contraire, chérie,*" Hugo said. "You're older than I am."

"Really? And how do you figure that, Sherlock?"

"Elementary, my dear Jo. You never had a childhood, and I never left mine."

Rushdie was talking about his years in hiding when Charlie let out a sudden gasp and sank down in his seat. I turned to follow his eyes. Tommy Cullen was striding toward us. By the time he reached us, Charlie had his BlackBerry out and was frantically scrolling through numbers. But Tommy barely spared him a glance.

"Jo?" he said, and nodded toward the door.

It must have rained while I was inside. Neon lights reflected off the street, and music seeped upward from an underground club. Tommy led me toward the curb, where a portly, grizzled man in his fifties leaned against a parked Ford.

"Jo Donovan," Tommy said, "Detective Juan Suarez."

The man straightened up and we shook hands. Suarez had walnut-colored skin, empathetic brown eyes, and the sad, jowly face of a basset hound. He said, "I believe you know Rowena Blair?"

I knew at once, just as I had that night in the Parisian hospital, that something terrible was coming. And just as it had that night, a rebel force inside me took to the barricades, determined to stop it.

"Of course," I said. "She's my client and my friend."

"When did you last speak with her?"

"Yesterday after lunch. She called the office."

"What did you talk about?"

"We made plans to meet here tonight, but she's late. Later than usual, I mean. Are you looking for her?"

"No, ma'am," Suarez said, with a finality that breached the barrier. I looked at Tommy, but it was hard to read his expression in the neon-studded darkness. Two boys strolled past, arm in arm, then a woman on Rollerblades. I said nothing.

"Was she expecting anyone?" Suarez asked.

"She didn't say." I couldn't pretend anymore. "Just tell me, please: what's happened?"

"I'm sorry to tell you that Ms. Blair was found this morning, shot dead in her apartment."

The words were clear. I'd been primed for bad news. And yet I couldn't process it.

"Is she all right?" I said.

"No, ma'am," Suarez said patiently. "She's dead."

I closed my eyes and I saw her, draped in a green and gold gown, borne aloft on a litter. That bawd, that vital, earthy spirit, gone? I turned and walked away, with no idea where I was going. Tommy came after me, took my arm, and led me back.

"Shot, you said?" I asked Suarez. He nodded. "Who shot her? How did it happen?"

"Seems like she let someone in, and they shot her."

There was a hole in that story I could drive a truck through. Rowena was always security conscious; she had to be, living as she did in a duplex on the two lower floors of a brownstone. The ground floor was her office and library, which opened out onto a private garden. Upstairs were her living quarters, a spacious two-bedroom flat with exposed brick and a wood-burning fireplace. It was a charming apartment, though not the safest for a woman on her own. But Rowena loved her garden oasis and wouldn't have traded it for twice the space in a high-rise doorman building.

"Impossible," I said firmly, for I felt somehow that if I could refute part of their story, it would prove the whole thing untrue. "Rowena was very cautious. She would never have let a stranger into her home."

"What makes you think it was a stranger?"

"Was she robbed? Was she . . ." I couldn't say it.

"Nothing like that," Tommy said. It was the first time he'd spoken since we came outside. He still held my arm, and that firm grasp felt like the only thing tethering me to earth. I was grateful for his presence, but I didn't understand it. Rowena lived on West Eighty-fifth, close to me. Tommy's precinct was on the East Side.

A horrible thought crept into my mind. "Do you think there's a connection, Tommy? Is that why you're here?"

"We do think that, yes."

"No, how could there be? Why would you say that?"

Tommy deferred to Suarez, who said, "There were words on the wall, written in the victim's blood."

I didn't want to know. Or maybe I already knew.

"What words?" I asked.

"'Can you hear me now?'"

Chapter 15

Keyshawn saw me home, and I called Molly. She came with her bottomless Mary Poppins carpet bag, just as she had when Hugo died and I came back to New York alone. We sat up till dawn, drinking and swapping Rowena stories. Over the course of her career, we had optioned the film rights to nearly all her books, half a dozen of which were actually made. From the start, her film contracts contained one ironclad condition: that she have a cameo role in each film. In this Rowena wasn't emulating Hitchcock, but rather was ensuring her access to the set, where she met all her directors, leading men, and leading ladies. Rowena was a convivial soul and shy of no one, for she was as much a star in her world as they in theirs. There were friendships and affairs, and later the fun of dining out on tales of horse riding with Harrison Ford, sailing with George Clooney, and lunching with Nicole Kidman.

We talked until the sun rose over Central Park. Molly's was the greater grief, for she and Rowena had been friends for twenty years, but the guilt was all mine. "It's the stalker," I said. "The same freak who sent the phony e-mails and press release. He killed her, and then he signed his work."

"You can't know that. And even if it's true, it's not your fault."

"Then why do I feel like it is?"

"It's called survivor's guilt. Anyway, we don't know who did it. My money's on a literary critic."

"Never happen," I said, laughing through my tears. "Throw Rowena in the ring with a critic, you *know* who's coming out alive."

Molly stayed with me for five days. I could not have managed without her help. Beyond grieving for Rowena, we had to act on her behalf. Molly had been Rowena's designated literary executor until her illness forced a change and that responsibility passed to me. Rowena had more than forty publishers around the world, not counting the pirates, and all of them had concerns that needed addressing. On my desk in the office was the first draft of her next novel . . . her last novel. I needed to read that and figure out what to do with it. There were countless calls from journalists with questions, clients and colleagues with consolations. Because the police withheld the detail of the writing on the wall, no one made the connection between my stalker and Rowena's murder; only Molly and Max knew. We also had to run interference between Rowena's family, who wanted to bury her back home in Kansas, and the police, who weren't ready to release her body and wouldn't even give us a date. There was no telling when the funeral would be, but Molly and I, along with Rowena's publisher, began planning a memorial service in New York.

All of this on top of my usual full-time load meant that instead of staying home chugging scotch in my pajamas all day (as I'd no doubt have done if left to my own devices), I was forced by necessity and by Molly to go into the office and work hard every day.

Scattered among these days were interviews with the police—so many that they began to blur into one long repetitive marathon against changing backdrops. The police had determined that

Rowena died sometime between eight and ten Wednesday night, and everyone in the office was asked for alibis. I'd been home reading that evening, alone except for Mingus, who couldn't testify. The doorman could confirm that I'd neither entered nor exited the lobby all night, but that didn't preclude my having snuck out the basement door, to which all the tenants had keys.

After the detectives left, my staff gathered in my office, and we compared notes. Their alibis were as feeble as mine. Harriet, who had gone to the movies, complained bitterly about the detectives' attitude. "Who the bloody hell saves ticket stubs? If I were a copper and someone handed me a stub, I'd arrest him on the spot!" Lorna had been home alone in her little studio in Bensonhurst, with no doorman to back her up. Jean-Paul had gone running in Central Park, also alone, and Chloe had been food shopping.

After a week of constant intrusions, my staff was looking frazzled. What the detectives seemed to want was everything we could tell them about Rowena: her past, her professional life, her finances, and her love life. I didn't know much about her love life. Rowena had enjoyed the company of younger men, but whether she slept with them or just displayed them I had never cared to ask. About her finances I was able to be more helpful, since nearly all her income came though the agency. Advances, royalties, film and TV options and residuals, translation, and all other subsidiary rights were subject to our commission, so our records were detailed and up-to-date. With a new hardcover each year and her backlist constantly in print, Rowena was making north of three million a year, some years considerably north.

"Which means," said the police forensic accountant who was sitting in my office, poring over our books, "that your agency made at least $450,000 a year in commissions."

"Well, yes, less the subagents' share," I said, taken aback; I had not yet begun to think what Rowena's death meant for the agency.

"Who gets her royalties now?"

"I don't know, her family, I suppose. She had a will."

"How will her death affect her earnings?"

"She'll enjoy them a lot less," I snapped.

He sat back, blinking mildly behind his glasses. "I'm sorry, did I—"

"No, *I'm* sorry. It's just . . ." I took a deep breath and started again, trying to match his dispassionate tone. "I expect there'll be an immediate spike in sales because of all the publicity, and because some of her publishers are putting out new editions. Then there's one more book in the pipeline. After that, without new books to bolster the old and Rowena to promote them, her sales will start to decline."

He made a note. "That's very clear; thank you, Ms. Donovan. And how will this affect your agency's earnings?"

"In direct proportion," I said bleakly. It occurred to me that if the killer's motive was to hurt me or destroy my business, he could hardly have taken better aim. There was nothing random about this. No stranger could hate me this much. No stranger could know so much.

I looked past the auditor at the closed door of my office. Just beyond it, my faithful staff manned the phones and sheltered me from everything they could. Outside them was a concentric circle of friends, people like Molly and Max and Gordon, who had involved themselves deeply in my troubles, who talked to and counseled and helped me every day. And beyond them was a wider circle still, dozens of clients and colleagues who did not burden me with daily demands for updates but stayed in touch with e-mails and handwritten notes urging me to bear up, assuring me of their love and support. (And if some of my clients could not resist appending apologetic little requests that I read their latest pages or look at jacket copy or run interference with their publishers, that only warmed my heart the more; for writers can't help being writers.) Without the concern and support of all these people, I would surely have flown apart, for the truth is, I lack a center of gravity. If Hugo was an oak, I was a vine twined around greatness; and this was as true of my working life as it was of my marriage. As an agent, my one talent lies in recognizing talent in others and nurturing it. Whatever I'd given to them was coming back to me tenfold. No one could have been more grateful than I for the friends who had closed ranks around me . . . and yet I couldn't help wondering if Rowena's murderer was sheltering among them.

This constant grain of suspicion was so irritating that it would have been almost a relief to learn that Charlie Malvino was the culprit, which seemed less far-fetched than any other explanation. He was, after all, the only person I knew who hated me, and he had the savvy to carry out well-aimed attacks. Rowena knew him too, and wouldn't have hesitated to open the door to him. But one of the few things I'd been told about the investigation (by Tommy, in confidence) was that Charlie had an alibi for the time of Rowena's murder. "Do you have any suspects?" I'd asked, and gotten no reply, which was typical. With the police, I was discovering, information flowed one way only.

I'd given the homicide detectives everything they asked for. I'd opened my books and files, let them trawl through my computers, given permission for phone taps and e-mail surveillance in case the stalker tried to contact me again. I'd gone further than I should have in surrendering my privacy and that of my clients, but I didn't care; there was nothing I wouldn't do to help catch Rowena's murderer.

By way of return they fed me vague talk of promising leads and a methodical investigation, but never any specifics. Maybe Max could have gotten more out of them, but he, for the happiest of reasons, was unable to come to New York. His baby had been born, two weeks early, and he had flown home to be with Barry when they brought the baby home. It was a little girl whom they were naming Molly, to the tearful delight of my Molly. This event was a great consolation to us both, and we spent a couple of therapeutic evenings shopping for the new arrival. In the midst of death, we are in life. Or in our case, Bloomingdale's.

As day followed day with no arrest, the detectives seemed to focus more intensely on Rowena's ties to the agency and to me. On Monday, the last day of Molly's stay, I was asked to come into police headquarters for another interview. By "asked" I mean that two patrolmen were sent to fetch me from the office. Lorna tried and failed to keep them out. "Am I being arrested?" I asked, only half joking, for the feeling that I was responsible for Rowena's death still lay heavy upon me.

"No, ma'am," the taller patrolman said, while his partner looked around with the sort of frank nosiness only cops and small children display. "We're just here to escort you."

"That's his job," I said, nodding at Mingus, who had positioned himself between me and the cops. "He's my bodyguard."

"I can see he's a good one. But there's no dogs allowed at headquarters, except police and assistance dogs."

"He was a police dog, and he assists me in staying alive."

But in the end I went peaceably, and Mingus stayed behind.

I was shown into a small room with a mirror at one end, a solid oak table, and upholstered chairs. Three people rose as I entered the room: Tommy Cullen, Detective Suarez, and a tall black woman of fifty or so, whom Tommy introduced as Lieutenant Boniface. It could have been a meeting in any large publishing house, except that the detectives were better dressed. There was a faint whiff of acrimony in the air, as if I'd interrupted an argument; but the men greeted me politely, while the lieutenant, who had warm brown eyes and a ready smile, shook my hand enthusiastically. "Thank you so much for coming, Ms. Donovan, and for all your cooperation. You've been a great help." She gestured toward the chair beside hers, which put Tommy on my left and Suarez across the table. I felt surrounded.

Boniface swiveled her chair toward me and leaned forward, as if what she had to say was just between us girls. "We've asked you to come in today because as this case has developed, we've grown concerned for your safety. The writing on the wall of the crime scene keeps bringing us back to you and your mysterious stalker."

There was something in the way she said "mysterious stalker" that made it sound like "imaginary friend." I felt immediately defensive, though I'd no idea why I should, and took refuge in silence.

"One theory of this case is that Rowena's murder was in some way aimed at you. We've already looked very carefully at Rowena's life. Now we need to look closer at yours."

"It's an open book," I said. "Just Google me; you'll get everything you could possibly want to know and more."

"I've done that. You've led quite a life for someone so young. But what I want is the stuff that's not public."

"Like what?"

"Let's start with the message on the wall, the same message you previously received in an e-mail. 'Can you hear me now?' I'm sure you've spent a lot of time thinking about it. Do the words remind you of anything? Have you ever heard them before?"

"Only as a catchphrase from an old Verizon commercial. I've tried to remember, but nothing else comes to me."

"'Can you hear me now?' suggests that at some point you could not or would not hear this person. Did you ever tell someone 'I can't hear you'?"

A vague recollection stirred, nothing I could pin down. "On the phone, maybe. A bad connection?"

"Is there anyone in your life now or in your past who might feel that way about you, that you don't hear them?"

"Harriet often thinks that. She feels that because she's been in the business longer, I should be guided by her. But I promise you that Harriet is quite incapable of shooting anyone, let alone Rowena. It has to be the stalker. People whose work we reject often think that we're deaf to their unique voices. Sam Spade was one of those."

"We're searching for him," she said with a reassuring nod. "We're looking at everyone your agency rejected over the past year. But the person who did this knows a lot about your agency and your industry. And you yourself told Detective Suarez that Rowena wouldn't have opened her door to a stranger. I think we're looking for someone closer to you, someone you know, even tangentially."

"I understand," I said. "But there's no one I know of who bears that kind of grudge, except maybe Charlie Malvino, and you know about him."

"Tell me about your family. Are you close?"

"Don't have any," I said, unsettled by this abrupt change of subject.

"What happened to them?"

"Parents died in an accident when I was an infant. My grandmother raised me. She's dead too."

"Boyfriends? Lovers?"

"No."

"Not just current. I'm talking about prior relationships as well."

I was careful not to look at Tommy. I felt him not looking at me, either. "I was married for ten years," I said. "I've been widowed for three. I've had no other relationships in all that time. Am I going back far enough, or do you want the name of my sixth-grade valentine?"

Boniface raised her eyebrows the way people do when they're thinking something they don't mean to say. Then she said it anyway. "I know that's what you told my detectives, but that was before Rowena died. Now we need you to be frank with us."

"I was frank. Painfully so."

"I just find it hard to believe that an attractive young woman like yourself, free and unencumbered, wouldn't have relationships."

"It's a tough town."

"Not that tough." She looked at me like she knew me. "The thing is, if there was someone and you didn't want to tell us on account of he's married or female or whatever, that would have to change right now. There's no more privacy in a murder investigation than there is a delivery room. We need to know everything. We'll be as discreet as we can be, but we have to know."

"That's the third time you've asked, Lieutenant, and the answer is still the same. Do you have any other questions?"

"I do, actually, and I hope you won't take them personally. In any murder investigation we have to look at who benefits." She waited for an acknowledgment.

"OK," I said, curious to see where this was going.

"Rowena made a lot of money for your agency, didn't she?"

"We like to think of it as the agency making a lot of money for her. But yes, either way you look at it, it was a very successful partnership. She was by far our best earner."

"How will her death affect the agency's income?"

"It will decline as her sales decline."

"So on the face of it, the agency stands to lose by her death."

"On the face of it?" I looked around the room. No one had moved, and Boniface was still smiling pleasantly, but the atmosphere had changed.

"Well," she said, "you personally stand to realize quite a windfall, don't you? Several million, paid out over several years, according to the accounts you so kindly shared with us."

"What are you talking about?"

Boniface looked surprised. "You know the terms of Rowena's will."

"I know that I'm her literary executor."

"And your compensation for that work?"

"The same as it is now: our commission."

"But Rowena was asking you to undertake a lot of work and responsibility on her behalf. Surely you're entitled to be paid for that. Did you discuss a specific amount with her?"

"There was nothing to discuss. It was understood that I would continue to represent her estate as I'd represented her. Our commission was ample payment."

Boniface looked worried on my behalf. "Be careful here, Jo. If you tell us you didn't know, and later it turns out you did, it wouldn't look good for you."

"Didn't know what?" I said impatiently.

"That Rowena left you ten percent of all future earnings."

"We get fifteen percent," I corrected her.

"I'm not talking about the agency commission. I'm talking about the additional ten percent she left you personally."

Blood rushed to my head; amid such a welter of conflicting emotions I could not speak at once. If Rowena had died of natural causes, I'd have been touched and grateful for this bequest; tickled, too, by the form it took. It was a great deal of money, an extremely generous gift, but she had not left it to me outright; I would have to work for it by perpetuating the sale of her books, thus ensuring her legacy. This mixture of slyness and generosity was so utterly Rowena that a part of me couldn't wait to tell Molly.

But Rowena hadn't died of natural causes; and under the circumstances, her bequest only exacerbated my sense of guilt. "I'll give it to charity," I said. "I don't want it."

"Oh, now that's rash," Boniface said. "It's a good deal of money, isn't it, Jo? Ten percent of three or four mil a year? Quite a healthy annuity."

I stared into her kind, placid face and realized I'd been played, lulled into stupidity. They weren't worried about my safety. They saw me as a suspect. All of them? I wondered. I glanced at Tommy, whose face bore all the expression of sheet metal.

One theory of the crime is that it was aimed at you, Boniface had said. *Your mysterious stalker*, she'd said. When I finally understood what the alternate theory was, a calmness came over me. From a cave deep inside myself, I said, "You're suggesting that I murdered my friend for money?"

"My detectives don't believe that. I don't either, now that I've met you. But it's not like we can just ignore inconvenient facts, can we? Because if we do, I'll tell you what's going to happen. Somewhere down the road, some smart-ass defense attorney's going to point a finger at you and say, 'Why is my client being charged? That woman had a million dollars' worth of motive and no alibi for the time of death!'"

"That was careless of me. I must remember the alibi next time."

"Easy, Jo," Tommy murmured.

Ignoring him, I stood and shouldered my bag. "Apart from being insulting, it's a stupid theory. I'd have earned that money ten times over if Rowena were alive to keep writing."

"Sit down, Ms. Donovan," Boniface said. Now the gloves were off. "We're not done yet."

"I'm going back to work. Maybe you people should do the same." I walked out. No one tried to stop me.

I sat up late that night, drinking scotch and trying to watch TV while Mingus snoozed beside me. Molly had gone back to Westchester. For the first time since Rowena's death, I was alone with my thoughts, and they were not good company. When the buzzer rang, Mingus jumped up barking, with no transition at all between unconsciousness and full alert. I answered the intercom.

"Sorry to ring so late, Ms. Donovan. It's Detective Cullen again," the doorman said, disapproval stamped on every syllable.

Of course it was. I'd half expected him. No doubt Boniface had sent him. I could just hear her. *Go see her yourself, Tommy. You've got a relationship. Maybe she'll open up to you.* I'd made up my mind that if he really did have the nerve to show, I'd refuse to see him.

"Send him up," I said.

Tommy wore the same suit he'd worn earlier that day, minus the tie. "Sorry about the time," he said. "Figured you'd be up." As he passed me, I smelled liquor on his breath.

The living-room windows were open, admitting a soft, soothing murmur of traffic and a breeze from the park. Jon Stewart was on, muted. I turned off the TV and picked up my glass, which was half-empty or half-full, depending on how you look at these things. "I'd offer you one," I said, "but I know you can't drink on the job."

"I'm not on the clock. I'll have what you're having, if it doesn't come with little umbrellas."

"Do they teach condescension at the academy, or is it on-the-job training?"

"I'm sorry, did you not use to drink piña coladas?"

No defense was possible. I poured him a scotch and replenished my own while I was at it. Just a splash, though. It wasn't like drinking with someone you trust.

We sat on opposite sides of the coffee table, as if we were playing chess. "If you've come to apologize, go right ahead," I said.

"I don't need to apologize for doing my job."

"Then why are you here?"

"I was worried about you. That was rough, this afternoon."

"It was fascinating. I've never been accused of murdering a friend before."

"She wasn't accusing you. Those questions have to be asked."

"'A million dollars' worth of motive and no alibi'? Sure sounded like an accusation to me. And you just sat there."

He sipped his drink before answering. "I said my piece before you came in."

"Maybe I should hire a lawyer. What do you think, Tommy?"

I was certain he'd say no. Instead he stared into his glass, opened his mouth as if to speak, and shut it without uttering a word.

"What an interesting pause," I said.

"I'm not the right person to ask."

"And yet I feel as if you've answered. But we both know that any lawyer would order me to stop cooperating with the police. Is that going to help find Rowena's murderer?"

"No," he said carefully. "But you have to consider your own position."

"I am considering it. If you people don't catch this bastard, all my clients could be in danger. Besides, the police couldn't really be idiotic enough to seriously suspect me."

Another eloquent silence. Now I was shaken. "Why are you telling me this?"

"Why do you think?"

"Do they know we were . . . do they know about us?"

"Their impression is that we knew each other casually."

"Masterful use of the passive voice," I said.

"If I'd told the truth, I'd have been off the case. And that wouldn't have been good for you."

"You did tell the truth."

He stared at me, and to my annoyance I found I could not quite meet those hooded eyes.

"We were friends," I said. "Today they call it friends with benefits. We had a good time. But it wasn't a long-term kind of thing."

"That's your story, is it?"

"It's not a story, it's the truth."

"Sometimes I wonder what-all you remember."

I bristled. "It just so happens I have an excellent memory."

"For fiction, maybe. Just for the record, and not because it matters anymore, you and I went together for over a year, exclusively as far as I know. Thirteen months, to be precise."

"That can't be right."

"It started the summer before our senior years and ended the day you left me for Donovan. Do the math."

I did the math. Technically he was right, but it didn't jibe at all with my recollection of a fling, an interlude. This dissonance troubled me. It was as if life before Hugo was foreshortened in my mind, like Saul Steinberg's famous map of America. As if my life as Hugo's wife and then his widow had taken up all available memory.

But if I was mistaken about the duration of our affair, I was sure about its nature. "We had fun, but it wasn't serious. We both knew that."

"You knew it. The day you dumped me, I had a diamond ring in my pocket. I'd been carrying it around for a month, waiting for the right moment."

He stated this with no emotion, in a voice I could imagine him using in court. Could it be true? Had he really meant to propose? Suddenly, vividly, I recalled his face when I told him we were through. We'd met in Central Park, the Columbus Circle entrance. It was early August, a hot summer afternoon. I could smell the carriage horses' sweat. Tommy was stunned. I once saw a boy get hit in the back of the head with a baseball bat. Tommy's face wore the same catastrophic look. He never saw it coming, but neither did I. Hugo just happened, like an act of God.

But that was the old Tommy. The one sitting in front of me, if you hit him with a bat, the bat would shatter. This Tommy was a little scary.

"I didn't know that," I said. "I'm sorry. But even without Hugo, it never would have happened. I was looking for something else."

"Found it, too, didn't you? I've read all your interviews. You always tell the same fairy tale about meeting Hugo, falling madly in love, a whirlwind romance in montage that ends in happily ever after."

"It happens to be true."

He held his glass up to the light. "Excellent scotch, Jo. Well distilled, like your version of the truth."

"Clever, Tommy."

"It's not even a good story. Where are the impediments? Where are the jilted lovers? Life's a lot messier and more interesting than your fictional account."

"I believe you're drunk," I said.

"Just a hair, but that's irrelevant. *Irrelevant.* You're missing the point. It's not about us; that's ancient history. It's about you needing to wake up and remember."

"What's that mean?"

"It means Boniface asked you some questions worth pondering. Maybe there was someone in your life, someone you couldn't hear or wouldn't listen to."

"Apart from you, you mean?"

The silence in the room was total; even the distant murmur of traffic seemed to pause.

"That's right," Tommy said without expression. "Apart from me."

Chapter 16

Five weeks after Rowena's murder, on a crisp autumn afternoon, we held her memorial in the concert hall of the New
York Society for Ethical Culture. The society was housed in a
beautiful old limestone building overlooking Central Park, in the
heart of the neighborhood Rowena had loved. Originally Molly
and I had planned to use the social hall, which seated 280, but it
soon became clear that this would not suffice, and we switched
to the 800-seat auditorium. Color-coded tickets had been distributed. Rowena's friends and colleagues were seated in the orches-
tra and mezzanine, among them a sizable Hollywood contingent,
representatives of the various causes and charities that Rowena
had supported, and the Mayor of New York, to whom she had
been a generous donor as well as a friend. Pellucid Press was of
course there in force, from the publisher to the salespeople, all
looking suitably grim. A writer who sells millions of copies a year
supports many people besides herself, but their sorrow was personal as well, for Rowena had known and cultivated just about
everyone in the company. Many writers had attended, friends and
protégées of Rowena's as well as clients of mine and Molly's
who'd turned out in a show of support and solidarity. The bal-
cony was reserved for Rowena's fans, several hundred of the

thousands who'd applied for seats. They'd gathered from all around the country and the world, almost all women, dressed in black for the occasion.

And somewhere, among all these mourners, all these dear friends and colleagues, was Rowena's killer. I felt it, a small seed pearl of malice hidden somewhere in the room.

I wasn't the only one who thought so. There were uniformed police on the door and plainclothes detectives milling about inside, Tommy Cullen among them. We exchanged nods when our eyes met; nothing more. I hadn't seen him since our late-night stroll down memory lane, which turned out to be two separate lanes.

I sat in the front row, between Molly and Rowena's sister, Janet Hubbard. On her other side sat her son, Chris, a newly minted lawyer dressed in a black Brooks Brothers suit. Molly and I had met the whole family when we flew to Kansas for the funeral. We'd stayed at the farmhouse, at Janet's insistence, and were treated like visiting royalty. Janet's black dress was dowdy and frayed at the collar, and her figure had settled into what Mma Precious Ramotswe would have called a traditional build. But her face and smile were so like Rowena's that people coming up to pay their respects froze in momentary shock.

Molly and I had come early to see to the arrangements, although in truth, Lorna, hustling about with a clipboard, had everything well in hand. The auditorium looked beautiful. Huge urns of calla lilies, black-eyed Susans, purple trachelium, and brilliant orange roses anchored the corners of the stage; on the podium was a smaller bouquet of autumn flowers from Molly's garden. I could smell their earthy, pungent scent from where we sat. The musicians and singers sat to one side of the podium while a screen at the back of the stage played a continuing montage of photos from Rowena's life.

All of my staff had worked hard to arrange this memorial,

with help from Pellucid, but no one had done more than Lorna. It was my good fortune that her twenty-fourth birthday had fallen last week, for it gave me an opportunity to thank her. I spent hours choosing her gift, a beautiful shoulder bag to replace the old tote she wore to work every day. At first I looked at Juicy Couture, whose satchels were popular with the twentysome-things; Chloe owned two at least. But they didn't seem right for Lorna, too whimsical and pleased with themselves, and in the end I went with a classic Coach bag in supple black leather. Feeling that we all needed a break, I took everyone to lunch that day at a little Italian place two blocks from the office. The birthday girl was made to sit at the head of the table where she presided, red-faced, lumpish, and more than usually silent. Chloe flirted ex-travagantly with the handsome young waiter, while Jean-Paul affected not to notice. I ordered wine and we drank a toast; then Harriet demanded a speech. "This is the nicest birthday party I ever had," Lorna said, which saddened me because it rang true. Lorna was a lonely soul, a young Eleanor Rigby. She lived alone in a basement studio in Brooklyn and had no family to speak of. Her parents were Irish immigrants who never managed to set down roots in America. When Lorna was eighteen, they'd taken their meager savings and moved back to Ireland, leaving their only daughter behind. When she first told me her story, I'd felt a bond with her, though of course my parents hadn't chosen to leave me, and I wasn't eighteen when they did.

Now Lorna hovered about me, scrutinizing everyone who came near and competing with Jean-Paul for the privilege. She had dressed with more care than usual, in a white rayon blouse and a black skirt (too long) over patterned black tights. The Coach bag would have been perfect with her outfit but was no-where to be seen. Was it petty of me to mind? It was a beautiful bag, but one meant for everyday use, not special occasions; yet Lorna still used her battered old hobo carryall. Most likely, I thought, she'd returned the Coach bag, and how could I blame her? The money would have paid half her monthly rent. I hoped she hadn't, though. Every woman needs a few nice things, as a hedge against despair.

On stage, the cellist and violinist had begun tuning their instruments, while the pianist and singers arranged their song sheets. Rowena had loved Broadway musicals, the hokier the better, and Molly had chosen the songs accordingly. She found the musicians and singers, too, through a friend at Juilliard.

Rowena's murder, and our subsequent trip to Kansas, had taken a visible toll on Molly. She'd lost the hair that had been growing back and was thinner than ever. Friends who came up to greet us tried unsuccessfully to hide their shock. "It'll be my turn next, that's what they're thinking," Molly whispered to me between visitors.

I, too, had seen that thought cross their faces, but it was one thing to think it, quite another to say it out loud. "Shut up, Molly! Sufficient unto the day and all that."

"You're right." She squeezed my arm apologetically, but I wouldn't look at her. Molly fixing to die felt like a betrayal of the worst sort. She knew I couldn't spare her. Who would I turn to for strength and comfort when their very source was gone?

Someone was calling my name, a man's voice, deep and diffident. I looked up through a scrim of unshed tears at Gordon Hayes. I hardly knew him in a suit; he looked like a soldier in civvies. "Didn't mean to intrude," he said. "Just wanted to say I'm sorry for your loss."

I hugged him, thanked him for coming, and congratulated him once again on the sale to Animal Planet. The offer had come in last Tuesday: the one bright moment in a dismal week.

"It's beyond anything I imagined," he said. "I'm so grateful, Jo."

I beckoned my assistant, who was standing a few feet away

with his back to the stage. "Much as I'd love to take the credit, it was all Jean-Paul."

"No, it was Jo's idea," Jean-Paul said. "Turning lemons into lemonade for all the writers who got those fake offers."

"And have you done that?" Gordon asked, shaking his hand. "For me, obviously, but for the others as well?"

"A few. It's still a work in progress."

"Strange that something good could come out of such a malicious act."

Gordon was innocent; he had no idea that we were here today because of my stalker.

"Come over afterward," I said. "I'm having a few friends. There'll be food, and you'll get to see Mingus."

Then Molly let out a whoop. I spun around. A tall man with a shiny bullet head was walking toward us, arms outstretched. I could hardly believe it. I'd talked to him just yesterday and he never said a word. "Max, what are you doing here?"

"I couldn't not come." He reached out with his free arm and pulled Molly and me into a group hug. I introduced him to Janet and Chris Hubbard, and he offered his condolences. Then he and Molly and I sat down together, and Molly thrust out her hand imperiously. "Pictures!"

Baby pictures were produced and exclaimed over, and for once the object of our adoration fully deserved it. Little Molly was a black-haired, apple-cheeked beauty. Max had limited himself to a dozen or so prints out of what were undoubtedly hundreds. There were pictures of Molly lying in her crib, gazing up at a mobile; Molly cradled in Barry's arms, drinking from a bottle; Molly napping on Max's bare chest. "And here she is in one of those gorgeous outfits you two sent."

We weren't three feet away from Rowena's sister. I glanced back to see if she minded, but she, too, was smiling at the baby pictures. "What a beautiful little girl," she said. "Yours, Max?"

Max studied the pictures. "We don't know. I think she's the image of Barry, but he says she has my eyes."

"Definitely your eyes," Molly said. "His mouth, though."

"I don't actually think that's possible."

"Strange things happen in centrifuges."

Max laughed. I'd never seen him so happy, and I wished him and Barry every joy in the world; yet I could not look at those pictures of their baby without thinking of my own, mine and Hugo's. How do you let go of someone who never was? How do you cease mourning her? She would have been nine, if she'd been born. Or he. I never knew.

It does no good to dwell on old sorrows, but my defenses had been battered and breached. Seeking distraction, I turned toward the podium, but the bright stage lights carried me back to another room, a cold room where I lie on a cold hard table, staring upward into the glare. Voices speak over me, some of them to me, but I have lost my French and my English, too. Inside me is an aching emptiness. I am hollowed out, a jack-o'-lantern, no woman at all.

Now I pressed my hands to my temples and squeezed hard. *Wake up and remember,* Tommy had said, but some things don't bear remembering. Suddenly the smell of dying flowers and the press of people all around me were suffocating. I rose from my seat, meaning to seek refuge in the ladies' room, but just then Rowena's publisher approached the podium and asked everyone to take their seats.

The ceremony began with music. The female singer was a pale, slender girl who looked like one deep breath would knock her over, but when she began singing the old *Funny Girl* classic, "Don't Rain on My Parade," the voice that emerged was big and brassy enough to fill the room. Molly and I exchanged smiles. Rowena would have approved.

Next came a series of eulogies and reminiscences: from her

publisher, the mayor, and a young writer whose career she'd mentored. "She changed my life forever," the young woman said, a perfect segue to the next musical number, a duet from *Wicked*. When the singers reached the chorus: "Because I knew you, I have been changed for good," tears welled in my eyes and Molly's, too, but they were different sorts of tears. The secret inside me felt too big to contain; it swelled on the music, morphed into lyrics that played in my head. *Because she knew me, her life has ended.*

When our turn came, Molly spoke for both of us, while I stood beside her like a mute. I have no idea what she said. She must have told Rowena stories, because people laughed. I looked out over a sea of familiar faces. In the second row, protectively arrayed behind my seat, sat the agency staff; even our accountant, Shelly, had come. One chair was empty: Harriet's, I realized, and spotted her a moment later, several rows back, sitting beside Charlie Malvino. That irritating sight woke me from my stupor. They saw me looking. Charlie sketched a bow. Harriet met my gaze defiantly.

It was nothing to me whom she chose to befriend, although what those two could have had in common was beyond me. "The Soufflé," she used to call him; he'd called her "Old Ironsides."

Nearly every seat was occupied, and latecomers lined the back of the auditorium. I was surprised and touched by how many of my clients had come, given that few of them actually knew Rowena. When I first returned to the agency as a partner, I had suggested to Molly that we host an open house, so I could meet our clients and they could get to know one another.

"Like one big happy family?" she'd said with a snort.

"Why not?" I'd asked.

"Because it *is* like a family. We're the parents and they're the children, every one of them seething with sibling rivalry. Trust me, kiddo, you don't want them comparing notes."

She was right, of course; I knew that now. Writers recognize intellectually that their agents have other clients, but most prefer to think of themselves as only children.

Molly finished her speech to a burst of laughter, and we left the stage arm in arm. The next singer was a young man as dark and stocky as the girl singer was pale and waifish. He sang "Ol' Man River." After that, representatives from some of Rowena's charities spoke. She hadn't chosen the fashionable causes, the boards of cultural institutions and conservancies that attracted New York's social elite, but rather had given her time and money to causes close to her heart: campaigns for adult literacy, scholarship programs, women's shelters, grants for writers, and support for rural libraries. Because there were more than a dozen, these speakers came up in a group, and each took a couple of minutes to talk about Rowena's contributions to their causes. The cumulative effect was stunning. The Rowena I knew had worked hard and played hard, but this was a whole new side of her, one she'd kept on the down-low.

After more music it was time for the final eulogy, delivered by Rowena's nephew. Chris Hubbard bounded up to the stage with some folded pages in his hand. He laid them on the podium but never referred to them.

"My aunt," he said, in a clear, strong voice, "was the youngest of four children, born to a hardscrabble existence on a small Kansas farm. The farm produced barely enough to sustain the family and pay the mortgage. Everyone worked, children included. These were honest, hardworking, thrifty people, with a thick streak of stubborn in them. 'Waste Not, Want Not' was the family motto, and it wasn't just words with us. Until she started making her own money writing stories, Rowena never owned a stitch of clothing bought new, nor a book she could call her own. She loved to read, though, and from the time she was big enough to walk the two miles into town by herself, my aunt was the library's best customer.

"Now, you might think, hearing this, that the Rowena you knew came a long way from where she began, and you'd be right. Certainly to us back in Kansas, her life in New York City seemed larger than ours, full of adventure and foreign travel and friendships with brilliant, accomplished people. Yet as I sat here today, listening to all the things she did in her life, I realized something about my glamorous aunt that I'd never quite understood. The woman was the same person as the girl. She lived larger, but her values were the family's values, and they never changed. She still worked hard. Wrote a book a year, come hell or high water, and I don't have to tell anyone here what that took. She was honest with her readers: she did her research and gave them the best she had in her to give, every time. And she was thrifty, because she wasted nothing: not one penny, not one experience, not one minute of her life.

"Now I'll tell you some things you maybe don't know. When my aunt's first novel became a bestseller, she paid off the mortgage on the family farm. Didn't ask anyone, didn't tell anyone, just went to the bank, paid, and brought the papers home to her parents. I don't know if you can understand what that act meant to the family. For her parents it meant security, and the chance for once in their lives to invest the farm's earnings into growth and improvement instead of paying interest. For her siblings, it meant freedom, options they'd never had before. For her nieces and nephews . . ." He stopped, sipped some water from a glass on the podium, then continued steadily.

"Rowena had no children, but she took a parental interest in her nieces and nephews. She wasn't one to shower the people she loved with money. Instead, she encouraged us to set goals, and when we met them, she made sure that lack of money never stood in the way. When my cousin graduated veterinary school, Rowena paid off her loans and enabled her to open a much-needed large-animal practice in our own county. My cousin Ralph opened a pediatric clinic, the only one in a fifty-mile radius of our hometown, where most folks don't have health insurance. Only way he can afford it is he's got no loans to pay back either.

"She didn't pay off my loans. She said lawyers can pay their own debts, and I agree with that. But here's what she did. The day after my graduation, which she flew to Chicago to attend, she took me shopping at Brooks Brothers and Neiman Marcus. She bought me an entire wardrobe, a watch, and a Gucci briefcase. Nothing I could say would stop her, which if you knew my aunt you'll understand. 'If you want to make a million, you gotta look like a million,' she said, which I believe is something Molly taught her. I got my first job wearing one of the suits she bought me. I'm wearing another one now. She said I needed a black suit. I just never expected I'd be wearing it to her funeral."

His voice broke, and he lowered his head. After a minute, during which there was not a sound from the assembly, he straightened and resumed in a steady voice. "It wasn't just family. When the town lost its only fire engine, Rowena donated a new one. There's four kids a year from our town attending college who wouldn't be if it weren't for her. My aunt Rowena lived a full, rich life far from her origins. She blasted her way through many doors; but she never forgot where she came from, and she never closed those doors behind her. May the murderer who took her life roast in everlasting hell; and may our dear Rowena rest in peace."

Chapter 17

W hy does death sharpen the appetite? Do we feel a void and mistake it for hunger? Or is it a way of exalting life over death, like making love after a funeral? Whatever the cause, the effect is predictable and I'd planned for it. There was to be a cold spread in my apartment for a few dozen friends and out-of-town visitors immediately after the memorial, and if I was to arrive before my guests, I had to leave quickly.

And yet for several minutes after Chris Hubbard's eulogy, I sat without moving and heard nothing that was said to me. *The woman was the same person as the girl . . . she lived a full, rich life, but she never forgot where she came from.* High praise, the very definition, it struck me now, of integrity. And yet, although my eloquent young friend could not have known it, those very words were a reproach to me. I, too, have led a full and useful life, far from the place of my origins; but unlike Rowena, I have forgotten where I came from. I, too, have pushed through many doors; but unlike Rowena, I locked them behind me and swallowed the key.

There is no connection between the girl I was and the woman I am, and I'd always believed that a good thing. Hadn't Hugo admired that quality in me? I came with no baggage, which meant plenty to a man with so much of his own. His phoenix, he'd called me, his fabulous creature born from the ashes of her past. I took a less romantic view. For me, amnesia was the better part of valor, or at least the only part I could lay claim to. What can't be fixed had better be forgotten, I'd thought, but Rowena had made different, perhaps more honorable choices. If her life was a tapestry woven through with themes and motifs, mine was a patchwork quilt with missing panels.

Perhaps that's why, when Teddy Pendragon ambushed me in the aisle, I didn't shy away. Lorna stepped forward to intercept him, but I waved her off and offered him my cheek.

Teddy kissed it and took my hand in his. "It was a beautiful tribute."

"She was a beautiful person."

"And the nephew—what a grace note that was! Look, Jo—"

"I know, I know. You've been very patient." Now that I'd paused, people were starting to clump up around us, waiting for a chance to speak to me. "I have to run. Why don't you come back to my place? I'm having a few people over. We can talk." I saw Lorna's face over his shoulder. She looked shocked, and no wonder; I'd been ducking his calls for weeks. Enough ducking, I thought.

"That's very kind," Teddy said. I reclaimed my hand and hurried on. Outside, Lorna hailed a taxi. Just as I started climbing in, I noticed Tommy Cullen standing a few yards away, gazing at me. "Hold the cab," I told Lorna, and crossed the pavement toward him. Last time we'd met we were both a little worse for drink. He was sober now, and somber, but he cobbled up a smile when I reached him.

"Hey, Jo."

"Tommy. Any news?"

He shook his head.

"How is that possible?" I said. "It's been weeks since the

murder, months since the stalking began. How long can this go on?"

"Until we catch him," he said. "Which we will. Hang in there, Jo."

The caterers had set up while I was out, and by the time I walked in with Lorna, the dining room had been laid with a cold buffet, extra chairs and tables scattered around the living room, and my meager bar supplemented with bottles of wine and Champagne. The rich, earthy scent of brewing coffee perfumed the air.

My guests followed close on my heels. Molly came first, with Max and Harriet in tow—Charlie Malvino, I was happy to see, had not tagged along. The Hubbards arrived with Keyshawn Grimes, then Teddy Pendragon with Rowena's publicist and a contingent of Pellucid brass. The rest were a mix of clients, agents, and editors. The mayor stopped by for a plate of lobster salad and mentioned a book he planned to write when his term ended. Gordon Hayes came in with Jean-Paul; they had brought Mingus home from the office, where I'd left him so that the caterers could get into the flat. "He looks great," Gordon told me when I met them at the door. "Maybe put on a pound or two."

"City living," I said. "All those yummy leftovers." Mingus sat beside Gordon, gazing up adoringly. I felt guilty about shutting the dog in my bedroom, but with so many people milling about, it had to be done. I hadn't had such a crowd over in a very long time. Hugo and I used to entertain constantly between books, everything from intimate dinners to large, raucous parties; but when he was writing, he detested intrusions. It was my job to prevent them. Keeping one's friends at bay is a treacherous skill, and it's possible, I sometimes thought, that I had gotten too good at it.

It felt unexpectedly good to see the rooms filled again, buzzing with laughter and conversation. Waiters kept replenishing the buffet, a bartender saw to the drinks, and Lorna had stationed herself at the door to take coats, which she hung on a rack the caterers had supplied. There was little for me to do but drift from one group to another, welcoming, introducing, dipping into conversations, and then moving on. I ate nothing, but drank several glasses of wine.

I looked around for the Hubbards. Chris was engaged in conversation with Rowena's editor, but his mother hovered alone in a corner of the dining room, looking shy and ill at ease. I went and found Teddy, who could talk to anyone, and drew him away from his group. "Let me introduce you to Rowena's sister," I said, slipping my arm in his. "She doesn't know anyone here."

"Gladly," he said. "But you're the one I need to talk to, Jo. I've been filling in as best I could, but the project has reached a point—"

"Come Sunday afternoon," I said. "I'll have his papers ready for you."

Teddy stared at me. He probably thought it was the wine talking, but in fact it was the eulogy. "And we'll talk?" he asked.

"We'll talk." I introduced him to Janet Hubbard. When I left them, he was telling her a story, probably apocryphal, about meeting her sister on a Nile cruise.

Presently the salads, cheese, and sandwiches disappeared from the table, replaced by platters of pastries and fresh fruit. Wine goblets gave way to coffee cups, and a feeling like flat Champagne settled over the company. That's always the way of it: bereavement outlasts its ceremonies.

Janet and Chris Hubbard left for LaGuardia, and the others took that as their cue. By eight thirty, everyone but Molly, Max, Lorna, Jean-Paul, and Chloe had taken their leave, and the caterers had finished clearing up and slipped away. I was anxious to talk to Max and Molly privately, so I shooed Lorna out after pressing money on her for a taxi home; but Jean-Paul seemed reluctant to leave us, and Chloe to leave him.

"Can I walk Mingus for you, Jo?" he asked. Behind him, Chloe scowled.

"Gordon did already," I said. "You kids go on now. I'm sure you have better things to do on a Friday night."

"Not really," he said.

Chloe took his arm and dragged him toward the door. "C'mon, genius. Can't you see the grown-ups want to talk?"

"Call me if you need anything, Jo," Jean-Paul was saying as the door closed behind them.

Max burst out laughing. "What did I tell you? Did I call it?"

"Shut up," I said.

"I'm so good I scare myself. Just don't break the kid's heart."

I wondered how else it could end, if Max was right. I looked at Molly, who shrugged. "What do you expect?" she said. "You're older, powerful, beautiful. Don't look so stricken, kiddo. Everyone gets crushes, and most of us survive them."

I've been sleepwalking, I thought. Tommy Cullen had said so, and it seemed he was right. I wondered what else I'd failed to notice.

The caterers had left a pot of coffee brewing, and Max got up to prepare three cups. Molly kicked off her shoes and stretched out on the sofa. Her bare legs were covered with gooseflesh. I went into my bedroom to fetch an afghan.

She opened her eyes as I tucked the throw around her. "It really did go well, don't you think?" she said.

"I think Rowena would have loved it."

Max handed out the cups. "*I* think she would have expected the Rockettes and the Mormon Tabernacle Choir."

I laughed. "Tough combination. How long are you staying, Max?"

"I'm catching the red-eye home tonight. Any longer away from

home and I'll start lactating. What's going on with the investigation, Jo? Do they have a suspect?"

"Apart from me, you mean?"

"No!"

"Rowena left me a bequest in her will, which naturally means
I murdered her." I spoke lightly. It was old news to me, and despite Tommy's warning, I couldn't believe anyone could take that
theory seriously. But Max slammed his cup down so hard that
coffee sloshed into the saucer.

"Morons!" he cried. "Everything else aside, she was surely
worth more to you alive than dead."

"I pointed that out. I think they've moved on, but I don't really
know. They won't tell me anything."

"Not surprising, if you're on their list of suspects. What about
your boy Tommy; won't he talk? Guy's got a soft spot for you."

"More of a sore spot."

"Well," Molly said reasonably, "you did dump him for Hugo."

Max looked at her, then back at me. He ran his hand along his
bald pate. I wondered if bald men retain a sense of their hair, the
way amputees still feel their phantom limbs. He said, "You told
me it was casual."

"That's how I saw it. I guess he saw it differently."

"So you were lovers. How long?"

"About a year. It ended when I met Hugo." I should tell them,
I thought, about the ring Tommy had carried around in his
pocket. But I knew what Max would do with that information.
His mind was an express train; it skipped the local stops.

"So," he said, "all this time Cullen's been questioning you
about jilted lovers or someone with a grudge, he's been describing
himself."

"Who says he has a grudge? It was ages ago; we were kids.
Everyone's moved on."

"And you know this how?" Molly asked. "Is he married?"

"I don't think so. There's no ring, and he doesn't feel domesticated."

"The point is, he never should have taken the case," Max said. "Why did he, I wonder."

"Duh!" Molly said. "He wanted to see her again."

Max flicked her a smile. "That's certainly one possibility. Of course, if *he* was the stalker, he'd naturally want to control the investigation."

"If he *were* the stalker," I corrected him. "He's not. No motive, for one thing."

"Revenge. You ruined his life, now he's going to ruin yours."

"But I didn't. And even if I had, why come after me now, nearly fourteen years later?"

"Some stressor in his life, maybe."

"Feeble."

"Feeble for fiction, maybe. Real life has lower standards." Max peered at me, as if uncertain whether I understood the difference. "In the real world, people do terrible things for the most trivial reasons. Sometimes they get obsessed; they blame one person for everything that's gone wrong in their lives. Sometimes they do it just because they can, because the opportunity's there and the malice is there, and they think they can get away with it. Cullen has the expertise to hack into your computer without leaving a trace. And he's a cop; Rowena would have opened the door to him."

I forced myself to consider it. I could see Tommy standing on Rowena's doorstep, saying with his best country manners and the Kentucky drawl he turned on and off like a faucet: "We're talking to all Ms. Donovan's clients, ma'am, if you could spare a few minutes." She'd have wanted to help . . . and she'd have liked the look of him, too.

I could see all that. What I could not envision was the sequel: Tommy pulling out a gun and shooting Rowena in cold blood.

"No way," I said. "Impossible. I know this guy."

"Do you?" Max gave me his standard-issue inscrutable FBI look. After a moment, when I failed to implode, he smiled and was himself again. "I don't believe it either. Just playing devil's advocate. Molly probably got it right the first time: he wanted to see you, and be seen."

"Or maybe it was just the luck of the draw," I said. "That's what he said when I asked. Chance, serendipity, they're part of the *real world* too, aren't they?"

"Touched a nerve, did I?"

"Not at all."

"You still like him, is that it?"

"Not at all," I said again, realizing even as I spoke that I was lying. I stowed that useless revelation away for the next millennium, when I might have time to consider it.

"If you say so." Max looked at his watch and stood. "Gotta scoot. Nice 'do, ladies. Jo, do me a favor: stay away from Tommy Cullen."

I walked him to the door. "I thought you were just playing devil's advocate."

"Sometimes," he said, "even the devil gets it right."

Chapter 18

Saturday morning, Mingus and I went for a walk. Tommy had advised me to stay out of Central Park, but that stricture could not possibly have applied to a beautiful autumn day like this one. We strolled down a tree-lined path beneath a thinning canopy of gold and scarlet until we reached the baseball fields, where the change of season was marked by overlapping ice-cream and hot-chestnut vendors. A woman in spandex jogged past us in the opposite direction, a sleek saluki high-stepping it at her side. Mingus turned his head to watch them pass, and I swear he'd have whistled if he could have. He'd been neutered, according to Gordon, but apparently nobody told the dog.

"Knock it off," I said. "You're on duty." He grinned up at me and wagged his tail.

We went home. Mingus settled in the kitchen with his breakfast and a big bowl of water. I took a key from the utility drawer, walked down the hall, and unlocked the door to Hugo's office. Intended as a third bedroom, it had been converted long before my time into a writer's den. The room faced east, and two tall windows overlooked the park. The opposite wall was all custom cabinetry, the others were lined with mahogany bookcases. Atop the cases was a seemingly artless but endlessly fussed-over array of framed photos, prizes, and small treasures. There was a Hopi mortar and pestle, given to Hugo by the composer Isabel Delgado, an inscribed photo of Sonny Rollins, an Oscar wedged between a Pulitzer and a candid shot of Hugo arm-wrestling with Rudy Giuliani (and winning, as he was always quick to point out). The Oscar was for Best Adapted Screenplay, based on his novel *Colossus*. Hugo had bought this apartment with that movie money. He also met his second wife on the set, but there were no pictures of the beautiful Noelle Braeburn, or any of his other former wives.

"Why is that?" I'd asked him once. We were at that stage early in our marriage when we could not be in the same room without touching, and I sat on his lap, my hair damp from the shower. "I hope you don't think I'd be jealous of a few pictures."

"Don't have any," Hugo said, nuzzling my neck.

"Why not?"

"Tossed 'em."

I leaned back to examine his face. "All of them, really? Why?"

"Why, why, why," he said teasingly. "You're like a little kid. When a snake sheds his skin, does he carry the old skin with him?"

"Are you a snake?"

He laughed. "Let's just say I'm a shedder."

"But don't you think about them sometimes?" I asked. "Wonder how they're doing?"

Hugo cupped my face between his hands. "Silly girl," he'd said. "Why would I?"

Now I crossed the room to open the blinds, which I kept shut against the sun. Light flooded the room, which looked much as it had when Hugo was alive. The desk was neater—I'd gathered all the loose papers and stuck them in a storage box, leaving only his computer and the lucky Yankees cap he always wore while writing. His annotated manuscripts, drafts, and galleys had gone to his alma mater, as Hugo had instructed. Otherwise the room was untouched and hideously quiet.

It wasn't a shrine; I hated that word. If anything, it was a testament to my inertia. This space could have served me well these past few years, if I'd cleared away Hugo's stuff. I'd thought about doing it, planned to do it, even blocked out time on my calendar; yet somehow it never got done. Teddy's incursion was an opportunity.

No, not an incursion. I had to break the habit of seeing the biographer as my enemy. Hugo's cupboards were not the only ones that needed airing out.

I took a storage box from the cupboard and assembled it. Then I turned to the filing cabinet, but it was locked. It took half an hour of searching till I found the key in an earthenware bowl on the bookcase, buried in an assortment of old stamps, rubber bands, and paper clips. It was a Hopi bowl, incised with stylized antelopes: another gift from Isabel Delgado, Hugo's partner in the musical adaptation of his first book, *Distant Cries*. We'd spent a week in Santa Fe, staying at the La Fonda while Hugo worked with Isabel on the project. She gave me the bowl on the last day of our stay. It was of museum quality and really deserved a place of honor in the living room, yet somehow I'd never loved it as much as I should have; and eventually it migrated into Hugo's office.

The key fit, and the cabinet drawers slid open. I started with the files on each of the novels, figuring that publishers' correspondence would be safe to share. Hugo's letters to his primary editor, David Axelhorn at Random House, were particularly meaty, ranging in tone from charming to tempestuous. I was mentioned in several, as in "Jo thinks the first scene's a bit hinky; what do you say?" Hugo accepted editorial advice from very few people, but those whom he trusted, he trusted implicitly and credited generously. It was his boasting about my editorial prowess that had other writers—friends and protégés of Hugo's—lining up to have me read for them, too. Pimping out my services, he used to call it, but I built my career on that start. Molly didn't bring me back into the agency purely out of friendship. I had a name and a following, and many of the writers whose work I'd edited became clients when I turned pro.

There were many letters to and from Molly, who'd been his agent throughout his career. As I read through them in order, I noticed a certain stiffness in tone that set in around the time Hugo and I met. Molly's letters were suddenly all business; Hugo's replies were uncommonly terse. Then, several months after our marriage, Hugo had appended a P.S. "Your little chick thrives in my nest, dire predictions notwithstanding, and is far more useful to me than she could have been to you. It's not like you, my dear, to begrudge a man his comforts. The world is full of bright young things. Choose another, and be friends again."

An olive branch, and Hugo the one to extend it! It shed an interesting light on their relationship. I tossed it in the box for Teddy, then pulled it out and read it again. "Useful," he'd called me. "A comfort." Someone who didn't know us could get a skewed notion of our relationship. I replaced the letter in its file.

I worked steadily for several hours and got through dozens of files. The box was filling up nicely. Teddy would be too delighted to inquire closely about what was missing, not that I had to justify myself to him. Most of the withheld letters had unkind comments about writers or other people we knew. A few referred to me in ways that would look different in print from the way they were meant, like this one to his editor: "Jo's a fine, lusty wench. She wears me out, yet I work the better for it. Life right now consists of fucking and writing, with an occasional meal thrown in. At this rate I'll be dead in three years and count it a bargain."

Probably wrote it drunk, the idiot. Now I understood the gleam
in David's eyes every time we met.

I took a break, walked the dog, brought home some Cuban-
Chinese takeout. Mingus and I ate together in the dining room
while I listened to phone messages: a bunch of people thanking
me for Rowena's memorial, and Max, checking in from L.A. to
repeat his warning to stay away from Tommy Cullen. As if I had
any intention of seeking him out! I would avoid Tommy, I decided, not because I suspected him but because I felt uneasy
around him. Ever since our last encounter, vivid but useless memories had been welling up, and with them longings of a sort I
thought I'd put behind me. Tommy hadn't been my first lover, just
my first good lover. Hugo was the second, and he had eclipsed the
first; but Hugo's eclipsing days were over.

Mingus finished his kibble and looked sideways at my plate. I
off-loaded my leftovers into his bowl and cleaned up. Then I went
back to Hugo's office. This time, I opened a window. It hadn't
been touched in a long time, and I had to wrestle the sash up. At
once, cool, fresh air rushed into the overheated room, and the
oppressive silence gave way to the ceaseless murmur of traffic
ebbing and flowing. Hugo's desk stood in the middle of the room,
facing the windows, whose framed views of the park were like
living Monets. *My* desk, I thought. *My* office. Hugo doesn't need
them it anymore.

I hadn't come back in for Teddy's sake. There was more than
enough material in the carton to keep him off my back for weeks.
Rather, I'd returned to reclaim the room for myself by clearing it
out. Hugo may have been a shedder of women, but he was a
world-class hoarder of paper. In files dated by year, he'd saved
ancient taxi receipts, laundry lists, utility bills, canceled checks,
fading bank statements, and stock prospectuses yellowed with
age. Some of this minutiae might conceivably have interested

Teddy Pendragon, but as far as I was concerned, it was all dross. I shook open a plastic garbage bag and set to work, starting with the oldest files. Every piece of paper had to be checked before I discarded it, in case anything important had been misfiled. After a couple of hours, I reached the year of our marriage, 1996. The file contained the usual mishmash of bills and receipts, plus a few odd ones: rent receipts for an apartment on Coney Island Avenue in Brooklyn, dated September through December. I opened the file for 1997 and found three more receipts, through March.

This made no sense. I couldn't imagine why Hugo would have rented an apartment in Brooklyn. I knew what Molly would say, cynic that she was, but this was no love nest. Once he came back to the city, Hugo and I were inseparable. I left my apartment to live with him. At his request, and despite Molly's admonitions, I'd quit my job at the agency to help him with his work. They say that when John Lennon and Yoko first got together, they went everywhere together, even to the bathroom. Hugo and I didn't go quite that far, but we weren't apart long enough for him to eat a sandwich, let alone travel all the way to Brooklyn to bed some woman. There had to be another explanation for the Brooklyn apartment, but even though my mind kept turning in circles like a neurotic dog, I couldn't think what it was.

Putting the rent receipts aside, I turned to the utility bills. Hugo had spent all of that summer we met in a friend's guest-house in Sag Harbor. His city apartment had stood empty, so the bills should have been minimal. And they were, all except the phone bill. In July and August, someone had made hundreds of dollars' worth of long-distance calls to a number I recognized instantly as Hugo's Sag Harbor number.

Teddy Pendragon came on Sunday afternoon, carrying a briefcase and a big bouquet of mums. He was especially resplendent today, in a fawn cashmere jacket, a red bow tie, and a walking stick that was pure affectation. I wore jeans and a Henley shirt, showing no more flesh, though a bit more face, than you'd find in a Saudi souk. Not that Teddy noticed; he was ogling the carton on the coffee table with a look that reminded me of Brer Rabbit eyeing the briar patch. For some reason I never understood, Uncle Remus's *Tales of the South* had been the only book in my grandmother's house, apart from the Bible, so I pretty much knew it by heart before I was seven.

"Is that for me?" he asked.

"Yes. You can keep them; they're photocopies."

"Bless you, Jo."

I managed a smile. I'd been anticipating this visit with the same blend of determination and fear I felt on my annual excursions to the dentist. Rooting through Hugo's papers had stirred up questions and fractured memories. After photocopying the papers, I'd stacked the copies in a cardboard box and carried them out of the office; and as I did, I had a sudden, visceral memory of doing the same thing once before. Hugo had just come back from Sag Harbor, and I was moving in with all my worldly possessions: a small suitcase full of clothes and toiletries and half a dozen boxes of books. As I began to settle in, I found empty drawers waiting for me, but also bits and pieces left behind by other women. I'd tossed them all in a cardboard box, covered the box with a lid, carried it out to the trash chute, and tossed it.

I put the flowers in water and offered Teddy a drink. He said he'd have what I was having, swallowing his disappointment when that turned out to be coffee. We sat in the living room and I asked him how the book was coming along.

"Really well," Teddy said. "Of course, a lot of the research was done in advance for the *Vanity Fair* piece. Now I'm focusing on the books." He was rereading them in chronological order and had to come see them as falling into three periods, as distinct as

Picasso's Blue, Rose, and Cubist periods. The first was Hugo's angry-young-man phase: raw talent fueled by Irish working-class rage. In the second period, he abandoned the conventionally structured plotting of his earlier work to experiment with language and perspective, layering one version of a story over another. And in the third, which Teddy called the culmination, everything came together: the intense narrative drive, the passion, the technical virtuosity, and, for the first time, female characters that equaled the males in complexity and gravitas.

"Those," Teddy said, "were the books he wrote while married to you. I suspect that you were not only his editor but the model for those characters."

"Aha! A theory is born."

"I'm not married to the period idea, but it is a starting point for exploration."

"With three trailheads."

"Nicely put. I may have to steal that."

So he *is* a writer after all, I thought. It reminded me of the time I saw a Chihuahua trying to mount a Lab and realized that they're all just dogs, regardless of breed. I warmed toward him, just a degree or two. Then Teddy took a small recorder out of his briefcase and placed it on the coffee table.

"But I didn't come here to talk about Hugo's work," he said, "so much as his life. Specifically, his marriage. I need to know more about you, Jo."

"You know all that."

"Next to nothing. And no one I've talked to, which by now is lots of people, knows anything about your life before Hugo."

I told him what I'd told the police. "My life's an open book."

"Highly abridged," he said, "and one senses that the story's in the gaps. Tell me about your childhood."

I stared into my mug and within the dark liquid a room took shape, a room with a cast-iron, wood-burning stove, a cottage sink with a drainer beside it, a padlocked refrigerator, a chipped linoleum table, pegs on the wall for a flyswatter and a switch. A mutinous spirit rose up in me. What business is it of his, this pompous little mole? But Chris's eulogy came back to me, and I thought of all the doors I'd shut and locked behind me. I wanted to be one person again, like Rowena was.

I was born in Memphis, I told Teddy. When I was three, my parents died together in a car crash. Their names were Jesse and Rose LeBlanc. I believe my father was Cajun, although I don't know for sure. At the time, he was working as a studio musician, backing up bluegrass and Cajun singers, but when he first met my mother, he was traveling with an itinerant revival meeting. A couple of preachers, father and son, had set up a big tent near the crossroads of three little towns in the hills of southwest Virginia, and all day long for a week, they took it in turns to preach fire and brimstone. It was a good show. There was snake handling and speaking in tongues and much laying-on of hands, not all of it in the tent. At night there was gospel music under the stars.

Jesse LeBlanc was one of the musicians. He preferred the fiddle, but he could play guitar or banjo or just about anything with strings. He was there for the music and the money; the preaching just rolled right off his hide, and that was something he and my mother, whose name was Rose Cunningham, had in common. Rose, who to her mother's despair was not saved and cared more about this world than the next one, attended the revival that first night only because her mother made her.

Bertha Cunningham would have cause to regret her insistence. At the end of the week, Jesse quit the revival, and my mother ran away with him. He was twenty-three, and she was seventeen. They married in Memphis. Rose never went back to Hoyer's Creek, and from the day she left she had no contact with my grandmother. Bertha had no idea she was a grandmother until the day the sheriff came knocking at her door.

My grandmother did her Christian duty; she took me in. But no power in heaven or on earth could force her to love me or regard me as anything other than a burden and a trial. I never had a kind look or word from her, never a word of praise. She told me there was bad blood in me, swamp-nigger blood. She said my mother was a whore.

My grandmother did not hold with sparing the rod. For ordinary infractions she used a paddle, but for special occasions there was that switch kept handy in the kitchen. The worst offenses were sassing her, taking the Lord's name in vain, and telling stories.

"Which is ironic," I said to Teddy, "when you think of who I married."

Teddy straightened the recorder and when it couldn't get any straighter, he picked a tiny bit of lint off his jacket. Finally he said, "I've been to Hoyer's Creek; through it, more accurately. Real Dorothea Lange country. What I can't fathom is how you got from there to here." His wave took in the large, high-ceilinged living room, the park views outside my windows, the city beyond.

"I ran away, like my mother before me."

"But you didn't elope, and you didn't join the army, which is how most folks who want out get out. You went to *Vassar*. How would it even occur to you? It's a whole other world, isn't it?"

"That's what I wanted, another world. I'd been planning my escape since I was twelve years old. I meant to live in New York, and Vassar seemed a good step toward that goal. And the school was very generous."

"Had you been to the city?"

"Never."

"Why New York, then?"

"Because it was the furthest place on earth from where I grew up."

"It is that," Teddy said, and it struck me that he must have had a New York dream of his own.

"It started with books," I said. "Everything I could get my hands on. *Eloise; Breakfast at Tiffany's; The Thin Man; Rosemary's Baby; Marjorie Morningstar; Bright Lights, Big City;* Paul Auster's *New York Trilogy.*"

"Your grandmother didn't object?"

"She didn't know. I used to cover my library books with brown wrapping paper, the same as my schoolbooks. The librarian had been a friend of my mother's, and she was kind to me. She let me watch films on the library's VCR, which is how I discovered Woody Allen's New York."

"Oh, isn't Woody wonderful? I saw him just the other day; had lunch with him and Soon-Yi. Let me guess: your favorite film was *Manhattan.*"

"How did you know?"

He smiled. "A beautiful young woman falls for an older, accomplished man. Clearly a case of life imitating art."

"It's not like I set out to do that," I said stiffly. "Hugo just happened."

"I see. And yet you were such a determined young person, weren't you? Did Hugo know your story?"

"Of course. We had no secrets from each other."

"Did he ever meet your grandmother?"

"No. I never saw her again once I left for Vassar."

He blinked. Teddy was a Southerner, and Southerners are a tribal breed, whippings be damned. "Is she still alive?"

"She died five years ago. We were in Paris."

"So you couldn't go to the funeral."

"I wouldn't have gone anyway." I sipped my coffee, cold now. "We paid for the stone."

"What did it say?"

I gave him an approving nod; it was the pertinent question. "Her name and dates." Nothing more, no "Beloved Mother" or "Adored Grandmother." For country folk it was the closest thing to spitting on the grave.

Teddy was quiet. I looked out the window. Not five yet, and already getting dark. Rain was coming.

Mingus whined. It was his dinnertime. I went into the kitchen and Teddy followed with his recorder. He leaned against the doorpost while I measured out the kibble.

"People say you're tough," he said. "I can see why. You've had a hard life."

"The first part, maybe. But then I married Hugo."

"And now I understand the fairy-tale depiction of that marriage. And yet it couldn't have been easy, being the great man's wife."

"Nothing could have been easier," I said. "I was with Hugo, he was working, and I was helping him. Nothing else mattered."

"He was kind to you?"

"Very kind. And generous. I came into the marriage with nothing but the clothes on my back. He loved buying me things, dressing me up."

"Like a doll," Teddy said, and even though I'd had the same thought myself, I didn't like hearing it from him. "Was he respectful, would you say?"

"Of course. Why would you even ask that?"

"Several people told me about an incident at a party you gave here, a few months after your marriage. Do you remember that incident?"

I opened the refrigerator and bent down to look. There was half a chicken left over. I tore off a piece of breast meat and shredded it into Mingus's bowl. Gordon had said that kibble is all dogs need, but I'd noticed that Mingus preferred human food, daintily picking out the pieces and devouring them first. Dogs aren't big on delayed gratification.

"Chow time," I said, and Mingus fell to.

Teddy, too, had a hungry look about him, but I had nothing for him. "There were so many parties," I said vaguely.

"In this one, Hugo was huddling with some of his writer friends, the old-timers who'd seen him through his first three marriages and divorces. They were ragging on him for doing it again. 'Fuck you,' he told them. 'You don't know her. This girl cooks like Julia Child, fucks like the Happy Hooker, and edits like Maxwell Perkins. I'd be a fuckin' moron not to marry her.'"

Teddy paused. I said nothing. Mingus licked his bowl and looked up hopefully.

"They said you grabbed him by the ear and marched him out to the terrace. You shut the door, and everyone pretended not to watch while you yelled, and Hugo laughed and tried to kiss you."

"That was nothing," I said scornfully. "I told him he was an idiot. He said it was high praise and I should be flattered. But he knew he'd crossed the line, and he never did it again." Until that note to David Axelhorn, I thought, and I walked past Teddy into the living room and poured myself a drink. Then I had to offer him one. We sat down and I said, "You have to understand that Hugo liked to present a certain macho, Hemingway-esque image. He would have hated to seem what he really was."

"Which was?"

"A loving, faithful husband."

Teddy's mouth opened, then closed.

I glared at him. "What?"

He looked down and chose his words as carefully as a man picking his way through a swamp. "When you met Hugo, you must have known his reputation. Was sexual fidelity a big issue for you?"

His delicacy was an affront, in that it suggested delicacy was needed. "Fortunately," I said, "I never had to find out. You talked about the deepening of his work in those last books. Where do you think it came from? Monogamy suited him at that stage of his life. Less energy spent chasing women meant more for his work."

"I see," Teddy said in that superior way, and I wanted to slap him, because every time he said "I see," I heard "Bullshit."

"Spit it out," I said. "It's obvious you think you know something."

"It's not my place to say anything."

"The hell with that, Teddy. This is a two-way street. I've answered your questions. Now you're going to tell me what you've heard."

"Honestly, I don't think that's a good idea. Suppose someone asked me what you and I talked about, you wouldn't want me giving chapter and verse, would you?"

"I'm not *someone*. Apart from being Hugo's widow, I'm his executor." I gave him a moment to think about that. "And let's not pretend there are confidentiality issues. You're putting it all in a book, for Chrissake. Did you really think I'd just wait and buy a copy?"

Teddy looked distressed, but whether this was real or feigned I could not tell. I waited for his answer, which came at last with a little shrug of resignation. "I'm sure he was a loving husband. I heard he wasn't all that faithful."

"Someone told you he had an affair? Did they name the lucky lady?"

"Isabel Delgado and Valerie Lepetit. Sorry, Jo."

I hooted. "And you believed that? Who told you?"

"They did."

I stared, my face stinging as if he'd slapped me.

"In fact," Teddy said, watching me closely, "both of them said they thought you knew."

Someone's lying: if not Teddy, then Isabel and Val. But why would they tell such hurtful lies? That's what I thought in words, but below that, memories were stirring, struggling toward the surface. I caught glimpses—Val on the pavement outside the ER, Isabel and Hugo emerging from her house, laughing, his arm around her shoulders—but I forced those images down. Now was not the time, not with Teddy Pendragon strip-mining my face for every nugget of emotion.

"Bullshit," I said firmly.

"You didn't know?"

"It never happened."

"Have you read Michael Holroyd?" Teddy asked. "Brilliant biographer and essayist. Not as well-read as he deserves to be. He wrote, 'The lies we tell are part of the truth we live.'"

"You think I'm lying to you?"

"Not to me."

"To *myself*? You have some fucking nerve."

"Jo, please. You asked. You insisted—"

I cut him off, my voice shaking with anger. "And just when did these alleged affairs take place?"

He closed his eyes, opened them again. "With Isabel it began before your marriage and continued during their collaboration on the opera."

"Ridiculous. Hugo and I were newlyweds, crazy happy. That makes no sense."

"I see." Teddy got up, brought over the bottle of Johnnie Walker, and replenished both our drinks.

"If you say 'I see' one more time, I swear to God I will brain you with that bottle."

He drained half his glass in one nip. "She said you almost caught them once. You don't remember?"

"No," I said, but I was lying. I hadn't so much forgotten as dismissed the incident. Every day, while Hugo and Isabel worked,

I'd occupied myself exploring Santa Fe. I visited every museum, every gallery on Canyon Road, the shops around the plaza, and the Indian vendors outside the Inn of the Governors. On the last day of our stay, I came back early. Isabel's car was in the drive, but the studio was empty. I sat down in the shady courtyard to wait. Lilacs perfumed the air, and I dozed off to the murmur of the fountain and a chorus of birdcalls. I woke suddenly to familiar laughter and the sound of a door opening. Hugo and Isabel emerged, not from the freestanding studio but from her house. His arm was slung around her shoulder. His shirt was half-unbuttoned. Her hair was loose. The moment they saw me, they stepped apart.

"Isabel has the most exquisite collection of Indian pottery," Hugo said. "You must see it."

They took me inside and showed it to me. When I admired one Hopi bowl in particular, Isabel gave it to me. I didn't want to accept, but she insisted. "A belated wedding gift," she'd said.

I'm not an idiot. I wondered; of course I did. But I couldn't imagine them in bed together. Isabel was old, Hugo's age or even older. Beautiful, but old. And Hugo loved me. I'd chalked up my doubts to insecurity and pushed it out of mind, till now.

"I'm sorry, Jo," Teddy said.

I glared at him. "And Val?"

"Let's give it a rest, shall we? I don't want to upset you any more than I already have."

"Then answer the question."

He finished his drink. "Valerie said the affair began when she painted Hugo's portrait and ended the night he died. He was with her that night. She called the ambulance; she went to the hospital with him. And then she stayed a little too long. She said you saw her leaving."

"I did, but she wasn't . . . she said a neighbor cut herself."

He gazed at me pityingly. Hot blood flooded my face. Of all

Hugo had to answer for, this may have been the worst: that this Nothing Man should pity me.

"She made it up," I said. "She's looking for attention. Great men attract leeches. She wouldn't be the first. How many women claimed they slept with Jack Kennedy?"

"Most of them did."

"I bet you never even bothered to check. You just took it as gospel, whatever lies those women fed you. And you call yourself a biographer!"

"Knock it off, Jo," Teddy growled. Finally I'd hit him where it hurt. "I spent two weeks in Paris. I went to the hospital. I talked to the triage nurse, the doctor who treated Hugo, and the paramedics who picked him up at the Hôtel de Crillon on the Place de la Concorde. He was there with her that night; that much is certainly true. As for the rest of her story . . . she knew a lot."

"What do you mean?"

"Did *you* tell her about your pregnancy?"

I gasped. Mingus came over and studied my face. I buried my face in his ruff. No one knew about my pregnancy, only Hugo and me. I didn't tell Val, and there was only one conceivable way Hugo would have confided that particular item.

Pillow talk.

Chapter 19

I didn't sleep that night. Two scenes played through my mind in an endless loop: Hugo and Isabel emerging from her house, and Val coming out of the hospital. In the darkened bedroom I did what I would not allow myself to do in front of Teddy: I wept with anger and shame. I wished Hugo alive so I could kill him. I devised mad plans to hurt the women who'd injured me. But my greatest contempt I saved for myself. How stupid I'd been, how willfully blind! Right under my nose, both women, and somehow I'd contrived not to see. If I'd read those two scenes in a book, I'd have drawn the obvious conclusions; yet in my own life I saw everything and understood nothing. I was all three monkeys rolled into one, a willful fool.

So much anger, and no outlet. The worst betrayal wasn't even the sex; it was Hugo telling Val about my pregnancy. Did he tell her how it ended, too? Did Teddy know? Every time I thought about that, I had to jump out of bed and stride around the apartment.

Morning came at last. At eight thirty, my eyes burning with tears and fatigue, I called the office. Lorna was there early, as usual. I told her I felt unwell and wouldn't be in.

"It's getting to you," she said, with the grim satisfaction of a

Cassandra. "I knew it would sooner or later. Why not take a few days?"

"I'll be in tomorrow. Just messenger over a manuscript, would you? Send me the one Chloe and Jean-Paul wanted me to read, that texting novel."

After that I fed Mingus and took him out for a walk. It was my favorite time in the city. Gradually my aching head cleared in the clear, crisp air. We walked through the park for a long time, neither of us in any hurry to return to the apartment, and came by a circuitous route to the Central Park Carousel.

It was a beautiful old wooden carousel, with brightly caparisoned chargers rising and falling to the sound of a calliope. It was always the same, the carousel; it had stood there long before I was born and no doubt would remain after I died, the unchanging center of a city that was constantly morphing around it. Mingus stared in amazement, wagging his tail, while giddy children eddied about. The smell of roasted chestnuts reminded me that I hadn't eaten. I bought a bag for me and, for Mingus, a sausage from the next cart over. I sat on a bench to eat and watch the carousel turn.

Mingus had finished his sausage in one gulp and was now eyeing my bag of chestnuts. I took one out. The shell was as smooth as a riverbed stone, but brittle; when I squeezed it, the slit popped open to reveal the crenellated yellow flesh inside. I peeled off the shell and popped the chestnut into my mouth, chewing slowly, savoring the warm, buttery flavor. There is nothing better than roasted chestnuts on a brisk fall day.

As I ate, I felt stronger. The dark cloud had receded, if only for the moment. Raymond Carver was right, I thought. It *is* the small, good things that save us. Not lofty ideals, not hope or faith or religion, but concrete, tangible things: the aroma of fresh-baked bread, the taste of roasted chestnuts, the sound of a calliope. These things undermine our stubborn grief, bind us to life.

I heard a burst of high-pitched scolding, like a very indignant bird, and I turned to look. A little girl was berating two older, towheaded boys, twins by the looks of them, who were playing keep-away with a rag doll. As I watched, one of the boys over-threw his brother. The doll sailed directly toward us; I raised my arm to catch it, but Mingus intercepted with a leap.

"Whoa!" the boys cried in unison, and the girl wailed, "Oh no!"

I held out my hand to Mingus, who relinquished the doll. The moment I felt its weight in my hand and looked down at its face, I knew I'd seen it before. I had, of course, many times; it was a Raggedy Andy doll, brother of the more famous Raggedy Ann. But I had seen it somewhere very particular. I closed my eyes, and this time the memory did not elude me. I saw a cardboard box full of odd bits of clothing. I was tidying up, making room for my things while removing the scattered residue of Hugo's former lady friends. A pair of pantyhose, daubed with nail polish where a run had started; a bright-red lipstick; a brush full of long blond hair. I averted my eyes as I tossed them into the box, just as I would avoid looking at a dead roach as I swept it up. Between the dryer and the wall I found a black satin bra, C-cup, a small Mickey Mouse T-shirt, and a Raggedy Andy doll.

Into the box they went. I shut the lid and carried the box out to the trash chute. It wasn't heavy. I asked no questions.

"Lady! Hey, lady! Can our sister have her doll back?"

The twins were standing in front of me, the little girl just be-hind them.

"Of course," I said, reaching past them to hand it to her.

"That was an awesome catch," a twin said. "Could we pet your dog?"

"Sure. Say hi, Mingus."

All three showered him with pats and praise. Mingus accepted this as his due and unbent enough to relieve one of the boys of some excess facial ice cream. The dog swaggered all the way home. I trudged behind him, lost in thought.

In the lobby, I stopped to talk to the doorman. "Ray, how long have you been here?"

"Be twelve years next month, Mrs. Donovan."

"Have any of the other doormen been here longer?"

He thought for a moment. "Only Morris, the weekend guy. He's been here since before the Flood. Can I help you with something?"

"I'm expecting a package from work. Bring it up when it gets here, would you?"

"Sure thing, ma'am."

Upstairs, I did what I always do when I'm upset; I called Molly.

"You're home?" she said. Molly never bothered with hello.

"I needed a break."

"What's the matter? You sound terrible."

"Teddy Pendragon was here yesterday."

"And?"

"I hate him."

"What did he do now?"

"Nothing, if you leave out the bamboo shoots and water torture. I don't want to talk about him. Molly, tell me again about that mystery mistress of Hugo's."

"Why?" she said.

"Because my life is full of holes, and I need to fill some in."

In the silence I heard a car passing and pictured Molly on her porch, the afghan wrapped around her, watching the world go by, or what passed for the world in Westchester.

"I never met her," she said. "No one did. He kept her very quiet."

"Who was she?"

"No idea."

"So what makes you think there was a mistress, much less a kid?"

"Hugo complained that he couldn't work with the child underfoot. That's why he went out to Sag Harbor to finish the book."

"But when we came back from there, we came together, and no one was living in the apartment."

I could almost hear her shrug. "Well, that's Hugo, isn't it? Out with the old, in with the new. What's it matter, anyhow? She was before your time."

"*She* was," I said, then stopped myself. Molly had enough trouble of her own; she didn't need mine.

"Jo, are you going to tell me, or do I have to schlep all the way into the city?"

She would, too. I knew that voice.

"Teddy claims Hugo had affairs while we were married."

A moment passed. "So what if he did?"

"You're saying it's true?"

"If he was fucking around, I'm the last person he'd have told," Molly said, which was no answer at all. "What's it matter now? Hugo was Hugo. You know he adored you."

"I feel like a goddamn self-deluded fool."

"Listen to me, kiddo. Wherever Hugo stuck his dick, you're the one he loved and needed. He worshipped the ground you walk on."

"Only because he walked on it, too."

She cackled. "I have an idea that'll cheer you up."

"Does it involve a killing spree?"

"More like a drive upstate. It's that time of year. I'd like to see the leaves changing—" She stopped abruptly.

One last time? Had we come to that? I couldn't think about it. We made plans for the upcoming Sunday to drive up the

Taconic to Old Chatham and have lunch with Molly's friend Leigh Pfeffer. "It's Macoun season," Molly said, and my spirits inched upward. Another small good thing: Macoun apples.

After we hung up, I gathered up all the photos of Hugo from the living room except the wedding photo with Molly on the steps of City Hall. I put them in a carton and stashed the carton in a closet in the study. Then I removed Val's portrait of Hugo from the study wall and tossed that into the box too, along with the Hopi bowl and the mortar and pestle Isabel had given him, a gift whose significance struck me only now.

Just as I finished, the doorbell rang. I opened, expecting Ray with my manuscript, but it was Jean-Paul. His face was glowing, as if he'd run up the stairs, and his curly black hair was tousled.

"What are you doing here?" I asked ungraciously. "I told Lorna to messenger the manuscript."

"I thought I'd bring it myself."

I couldn't help remembering Molly's version of the way I met Hugo, and the coincidence made me uneasy. I pointed to the foyer table, and Jean-Paul set down two packages. Then he shut the door, which I'd left open. "The other one's from the doorman; someone left it for you. Lorna said you're not feeling well. You do look flushed." He pressed the palm of his hand to my forehead, a surprising, sweet gesture. I imagined his mother doing the same to him as a child.

"I'm OK."

"What do you need? I could walk Mingus for you." He bent to pet the dog with a fluid grace as poignant as youth.

"We already took a nice long walk in the park."

Jean-Paul straightened, frowning. "Central Park? By yourself?"

"With Mingus, my SWAT-team protection dog. Don't you start, too."

"Everyone's worried about you, Jo. *I'm* worried about you."

He was too close. I took a step back, which he interpreted as permission to enter. As he walked past me into the living room, I caught a scent of Ivory soap and musk. I sat in a corner of the couch and curled my legs beneath me. Jean-Paul sat beside me. We talked about the office and the morning's calls, which included a nibble from one of the small regional presses currently considering Edwina Lavelle's first novel. We rarely submit to those houses, because the advances they pay are minuscule, and there's never any money for co-op advertising or promotion. But Edwina was one of the writers who'd been victimized by Sam Spade's hoax, so money wasn't the object. Jean-Paul had found several small publishers with lines in Caribbean or immigrant literature, and it was one of those who'd called this morning.

This was very good news, because no one ever called to say no. "No" comes in an e-mail or a note; "yes" comes by phone. "They'll plead poverty, of course," I said.

"Don't you think they'll offer more because you're her agent? They wouldn't want to look minor-league in front of you."

"Oh, much more," I said, laughing. "What's three times nothing?"

He looked shocked. "Really?"

"They're used to dealing directly with authors, and most writers are so eager to get published, they'll work for paper clips. But we'll do better than paper clips for Edwina."

"So we hold out for stick-its and staples?"

"Maybe even a stapler." We smiled at each other. There was a silence that went on a beat too long. "Well," I said, standing, "you'd better get back. One of us has to work today." He rose too, but instead of moving toward the door, he came and put his arms around me.

The hug was comforting at first, then discomfiting. His arms were strong. It had been a long time since any man held me, apart from Max, who didn't count in that way.

Then I felt his lips on my neck, and I pulled back. But Jean-Paul held on, standing so close I could feel the heat of his body. "Jo, there's something I need to tell you."

"No, you don't." I pushed him away.

"I do, though. Chloe says I'm nuts, but she doesn't feel what I feel."

"I think maybe she does. You should pay more attention."

He shrugged that off so dismissively that I felt a pang of vicarious heartbreak for Chloe. I was glad she hadn't seen it; but she'd probably seen and heard worse. "I'm crazy about you, Jo. I'm totally in love with you. I want to—"

"Stop!"

"Don't fire me," he said quickly.

"I'm not going to fire you, you idiot. Look, Jean-Paul, it's been a tough time for all of us, and emotions naturally run high. I know you care about me. So does everyone in the office. You guys are like my family."

I'd thrown him a lifesaver, but he swam the other way. "That's not what I meant. There's nothing brotherly about the way I feel. I can't believe I'm saying this. What kind of moron hits on his boss? But I can't help it."

"You'll have to. We can't have that sort of relationship. For one thing, you're my employee."

"If that's all you've got, I'll quit. Don't you like me a little, Jo?"

"I like you a lot. You're a great guy. But I'm not in the market, and even if I were, you're too young for me."

"Hugo Donovan was twice your age."

"That's different."

"No, it's not. You know age doesn't matter." His dark eyes bored into mine. I felt the heat coming off his body and felt the urge to run my fingers through those beautiful black curls, knowing full well where that would lead. I imagined Jean-Paul in my bed, the bed I'd shared with Hugo. It seemed a very pleasurable means of getting my own back.

Something must have shown. Jean-Paul, sensing weakness, reached out and pulled me to him. The strength of his embrace unleashed a terrible hunger inside me. Three years of abstinence, three years of dammed-up yearning, three years of not being touched . . . three years of starvation, and suddenly a feast lay before me. It would be so easy. All I had to do was acquiesce, and he would do the rest. *Go for it, girl,* I heard Rowena whisper. *If it's a mistake, it's a divine mistake.*

Jean-Paul bent his head toward mine. My eyes were closed, but I felt his breath on my face.

Mingus growled.

Chapter 20

I sat in Hugo's office, which I was determined to colonize, and tried to read the texting novel. Jumping into someone else's story is usually a surefire way to escape my own, but not today. When I realized I had read the same page three times, I put the manuscript away. I kept thinking about Jean-Paul, the way his body felt against mine, and my own internal meltdown. Over the years since Hugo died, quite a few men had tried their luck. Some were attractive, yet I never felt even a twinge of answering desire. I'd thought that part of my life was buried with Hugo. Jean-Paul's move took me by surprise but shouldn't have. Max had warned me, and Molly, too, yet I blundered on, blinders firmly attached. If I'd seen this thing coming, I could have averted it. But I only see what I want to see.

Even when I tore my thoughts away from Jean-Paul, they found no safe landing place. The home strip, strafed by Teddy's revelations, had been torn to pieces. Though I sat in a comfortable cage in a fortress high above the city, I felt assailed on all sides.

Searching for a distraction, I turned to the package the doorman had sent up. It was wrapped in brown paper, addressed in block letters to "Jo Donovan"; no address, no stamp, and no return address. I tore off the paper and found a standard-size manuscript box with an envelope taped to the lid, addressed to me. I opened it up and read:

My dear Jo,

The recent death of Ms. Rowena Blair was tragic on many levels. While not a great writer, I'm sure she was a fine person and a lucrative client. I'm very sorry for your loss.

The good news is, I'm here to make it up to you.

You need a major writer to take the place of Ms. Rowena Blair. I need a top agent to represent my work—and not just any top agent, as you'll understand once you read the enclosed. We each have what the other needs.

I've taken the liberty of delivering my manuscript to your home, because when I followed the conventional submission routine, my work was summarily and, I'm sorry to say, rudely rejected by someone on your staff. You never had the chance to read the novel that you yourself inspired. I know you'll love it, Jo. I just wish I could watch your face as you read it, but that will come in time. For now I must content myself with imagining it. I told you the first time we met: just as you were Hugo's muse, so shall you be mine.

Take your time; read carefully. I will call you in a few days, and we'll make plans to meet. I look forward to a long, cozy chat. Until then, my dear Jo, happy reading.

Your devoted,
Sam Spade

———

"What did you touch?" Tommy Cullen asked.

I felt a Pavlovian twinge of dread, for when I was a child, those words often preceded a beating. "Nothing," I said, though the evidence was right between us on the desk. "Just the wrapping paper when I tore it, and the letter."

"Was the envelope sealed?"

"No, the flap was tucked under."

"Did you open the manuscript?"

"I wanted to, but I didn't."

"You *wanted* to? After reading that?" He jerked his head toward the letter, now encased in a plastic bag as if it were a body part.

"I have to read it," I said. "You need to get the manuscript back to me as soon as you're done with it."

"You really want to let this guy into your head?"

"I want to get into his. People reveal themselves in their writing. I'm a good reader."

"Reveal themselves how? I thought he writes fiction."

Teddy Pendragon's quote came back to me then, and it seemed apt, though I hadn't much liked it at the time. "'The lies we tell are part of the truth we live.'"

Tommy didn't answer at once, but studied my face. I'd called him the moment I'd finished reading the letter, and fifteen minutes later he'd been at my door, dressed not in a suit this time, but jeans and a forest-green sweater, the color of his eyes. Maybe he was off duty; I'd called his cell. Max would disapprove. But how could I get through this without trusting the people I felt I could trust?

"Look, Jo," Tommy said, "if we don't catch this guy before he contacts you, I'm going to need you to talk to him, set up an appointment. You think you could do that?"

"I've got to read the manuscript first. I'll need to say something about it."

"Wouldn't 'I love it' suffice?"

I smiled. "It never does. They always need to know why."

"Fine; I'll see you get a copy, if not the original. Now, tell me again how the manuscript reached you."

"Jean-Paul got it from the doorman. I don't know who Ray got it from. You should ask him."

"I talked to him before I came up. He said a teenage Latino kid dropped it off. Not a regular courier; no paperwork. We're looking, but it's probably just some random kid paid to deliver it. Why was Jean-Paul here?"

"I was working at home today. He brought me a manuscript from the office."

"Did you ask him to do that?"

"I told Lorna to send it. Jean-Paul volunteered. What's your point? Sam Spade has crawled out of the woodwork again, still obsessed. He practically admits killing Rowena; at least, he gives us his motive on a platter."

He cocked an eyebrow. "Clearing the decks? Making room for the next big thing?"

"Exactly. It's him; it was always him." The corollary was that it wasn't anyone else, which was very good news indeed and a great weight off my heart. Yet my detective friend seemed curiously unconvinced.

"Maybe. Until we know for sure, I'm interested in everyone who's interested in you, including Pretty Boy."

"Pretty Boy," I scoffed. "You've been watching too many old gangster movies."

"Is it mutual, the attraction? Is Jean-Paul your lover?"

I stared at him but couldn't penetrate the surface. Whatever became of the old exuberant Tommy, who wore his heart on his face?

"No," I said coolly. "Is this still business, Tommy?"

His voice was colder yet. "What else would it be? Jean-Paul's obviously smitten. If there's a relationship, we need to know."

"We have a relationship. It's called boss-employee." I glanced at Mingus as I said this. *Thank God dogs can't talk.* I owed this one a big debt. That growl had worked as well as a bucket of cold water, on me at least. We'd jumped apart like guilty teenagers. "Put him away," Jean-Paul had pleaded, but by then my fit of madness had passed. I gave the kid a lecture on appropriate behavior and sent him away, praying he didn't know how close he'd come—how close *I'd* come to doing something cruel and stupid. I owed Gordon Hayes more than he'd ever know. He said the dog could save me; I'd just never imagined how.

"No one would blame you," Tommy said. "He's a good-looking kid."

"'*Kid*' being the operative word. If I wanted someone, it wouldn't be a boy." I held his eyes as I said this. Tommy started to answer and thought better of it. What am I doing? I wondered in the sudden quiet. Flirting while Rome burns? Jean-Paul had loosed something in me, which maybe wasn't such a bad thing in itself, but Tommy was a hopeless case. *Once bitten, twice shy,* he'd said. *Ancient history.* Those bridges were burnt.

"An unrequited lover, then," he said. "Our favorite kind."

"Where are you getting this? Surely not Jean-Paul."

Tommy snorted. "According to him, he sees you purely as a mentor, which I guess is why he can't take his eyes off you. When I asked you to imagine a motive for everyone in your office, remember what you came up with for Jean-Paul?"

"That was before Rowena died. I wouldn't have played your stupid game after."

"You said he was secretly in love with you and wanted to play the rescuer."

"I also said Lorna was an anarchist out to kill all bosses. Did you believe that, too?"

He smacked his forehead. "You are such a fucking Pollyanna!"

"*You're* such a cynic. You've changed, you know. You used to see the best in people. Now you see their worst potential."

"Comes with the territory. You've changed too."

"How?" I asked.

"Stronger," he said, studying me with that sleepy-eyed, hooded look that could fool you into thinking he wasn't paying attention. "Sadder."

Even though the police hadn't yet captured or even identified Sam Spade, his reappearance buoyed the spirits of everyone in the office. There were still unanswered questions, as Max was at pains to point out. We had no idea how the stalker had accessed my clients' submissions histories in the first cyber-attack, or how he'd put together the distribution list for the second, or how he'd persuaded Rowena to open her door. Nevertheless, my staff took his return the same way I did: as a sign that we could stop looking askance at one another and focus our anger on the outsider.

Fate, or the goodwill of my publishing colleagues, seemed determined to support us with daily infusions of good news. Max's novel clung tenaciously to the bestseller list, while Rowena's last novel reoccupied the top spot. The brilliant Sikha Mehruta, whom I'd met in Santa Fe, called to ask if I would take her on, as her current agent was retiring. I said I'd be proud to represent her, but felt obliged to ask if she'd heard about the agency's troubles; Sikha said she had and it didn't matter.

We sold British rights to dear old Alice Duckworth's novel on the same day our film subagent optioned rights to a small but prestigious studio. Keyshawn Grimes's first novel was tapped by one of the major bookstore chains for its "New Voices" program, which meant a larger print run and guaranteed front-of-the-store placement. And the best news of all: an offer for Edwina Lavelle's

Haitian-American first novel. A small but respectable Chicago publisher offered an advance of $3,000, which Edwina would have accepted in a heartbeat if I'd told her about it; I managed to get it up to $5,000 before the publisher dug in his heels. Fifteen percent of $5,000 was petty cash, but it wasn't about the money. For Edwina, the offer would be a life-changing validation.

I summoned Jean-Paul into my office before calling Edwina on speakerphone. She had to hear the news from me, or she might have suspected another hoax, but I wanted my assistant, who'd done all the work, to share in the joy of telling her. Her reaction was everything I could have hoped for. Jean-Paul was beaming by the time I hung up.

"I feel like I should be handing out cigars," he said, and I laughed. There'd been no repetition of Jean-Paul's declaration in my apartment. If anything, he seemed anxious to reestablish our old footing—afraid, perhaps, that I'd fire him after all. It suited me, too, to pretend the incident never happened; but I did not allow myself to forget it. I was done playing ostrich.

Harriet reacted to the news about Sam Spade by abandoning the unnatural deference she'd assumed ever since the phony press release came out. I took it as a sign of progress when she started disagreeing with me again. At our monthly submissions meeting, I announced that, after reading the Vigne manuscript, *I Luv U Baby, but WTF?*, I agreed with Chloe and Jean-Paul. The novel was clever, well-written, and potentially salable. It needed work, but if the author was amenable to that, I was willing to take it on. Chloe beamed, and Jean-Paul reached across the table to high-five her, but Harriet scowled. "At least make her change that repulsive title," she grumbled.

Our assistants rolled their eyes at this but refrained from answering. The two of them seemed to have settled their differences; at least they'd quit sniping at each other, and Chloe was her perky self again. Only Lorna, of all my staff, seemed untouched by the general zeitgeist. She remained on high alert, bristling each time the door buzzer sounded, fussing needlessly over me. This wasn't surprising. Lorna, though bright enough, was a stolid, deliberate soul, as slow to change course as an ocean liner. But it was worrisome, because she answered the phones. When Sam Spade called, it would be Lorna's job to keep him on the line as long as possible before passing him on to me. The longer we kept him, Tommy had stressed, the better their chances of tracing the call. Lorna would have to be friendly and encouraging, apologetic for the delay but insistent that he hold on because I really, really wanted to talk to him. Was she up to it? She insisted she was, but I had my doubts. With Lorna, what you see is what you get, and charm was not among her many estimable qualities. Lying was, though; she did it every day on my behalf. All I could do was wait and hope for the best.

Personally, I was as prepared as I could be for that call. True to his word, Tommy had sent over a copy of Sam Spade's manuscript, entitled *The Hand-Me-Down Muse*. It was the same story he'd pitched in Santa Fe. A poor but brilliant painter soars to greatness when the widow of a famous painter becomes his muse and lover. It was the worst sort of wish-fulfillment crap, but as awful as the story was, the style was even worse, full of info dumps, head-hopping, and cringe-making sex scenes. Manuscripts like these are the reason agents need assistants and the reason assistants burn out so quickly: for just as great writing elevates the soul, so does bad writing depress it.

I'd forced myself to finish, skimming the last few chapters, looking for something to praise if I actually had to talk to this sicko. There was nothing. I would have to fall back on empty adjectives like "heartfelt," always useful because it was usually true; writers can pour as much of themselves into bad books as good ones.

Tommy called a few days after sending the manuscript. "What

can you tell me about this mope?" he asked, assuming correctly that I'd read the novel.

"The main character's what we call a Mary Sue: an idealized projection of the author, perfect in every way. He's a brilliant artist and an incredible stud. Even his poverty is presented as confirmation of his artistic purity. I would expect the author to be the opposite of his character. He's not an artist. He has a boring, routine sort of job, which is OK with him because he knows his true vocation is writing, and pretty soon the world will discover him and he'll be able to quit the grind. He's probably college educated, not stupid but not half as smart as he thinks he is. He has zero writing talent: no ear, no taste. Also, my guess is he's impotent, or at least unsuccessful with women."

I heard the scratching of a pen. Then Tommy said, "You got all that just from reading his novel?"

"Sure."

He lowered his voice. "I'll tell you something. We brought in a behaviorist. Real smart guy; I've worked with him before. We gave him the manuscript and a lot else besides. He came up with virtually the same profile. You're good, Jo."

"*He's* good," I said.

We were ready for the call. Lorna was prepped; the tracers were good to go. But a week went by and nothing at all happened. Like a groundhog, Sam Spade had stuck out his nose and pulled it right back in again.

Chapter 21

W e left early so that the ride home would be by daylight. The night chill was still in the air when I reached West-chester, and a thin white rime covered the suburban lawns. Molly must have been waiting by the window, because as I pulled into her driveway she came out lugging a purse, two travel mugs, a walking stick, and a cloth Trader Joe's bag so heavy she listed to one side. I hurried out and relieved her of the stick and bag, which was full of books—for Leigh, no doubt. Lately Molly had been giving away her possessions. I stowed them in the backseat, next to Mingus.

"He's safe with books?" Molly asked.

"Unless they have cats in them."

She settled herself in the front passenger seat and we set off. I drove north on the Taconic. It was a narrow highway hemmed in by towering cliffs. Now and then the cliffs receded and we had open views of rolling hills, crimson, orange, and gold. Our plan was to take the scenic highway all the way north to Old Chatham, where we would lunch with Molly's old friend Leigh; then home through the Catskills. I had suggested taking an extra day and extending our trip to Saratoga Springs, which was a charming old town, and not far from Gordon Hayes's kennels. We could have taken Mingus home for a visit. But Molly had been reluctant; these days, she said, she sleeps better in her own bed.

Molly gazed out the window, exclaiming now and then at the colors of the foliage. We'd hit it exactly right this year. Her jeans were a size too big for her, tightly belted. She wore a purple sweater and a denim jacket and an orange kerchief, tied at the nape of her neck, to cover her head.

For the first hour we hardly spoke at all. It was an easy silence, Molly drinking in the colors and me trying to decompress; for today I meant to leave all my troubles behind me and enjoy our time together. As we crossed into Dutchess County, forests gave way to orchards and rolling farmland. Eventually, Mingus grew restless, and we stopped at Lake Taghkanic State Park. We followed a trail into the woods, Molly holding her stick in one hand and my arm in the other. There was no one around, so I let Mingus off the leash. He gave a little shiver of excitement, then bounded ahead. The ground felt strangely soft and giving under my feet, which had grown used to pavements. Except for these annual jaunts with Molly, it had been years since I'd spent any time in the countryside. During our marriage, Hugo and I had divided our time between New York and Paris, and when we traveled, it was to other cities. Friends urged us to get a place in the Hamptons, but Hugo, a city boy through and through, preferred fresh air in moderation and nature contained within the bounds of city parks. That suited me fine; growing up, I'd had enough of both to last me a lifetime. We were urban creatures, Hugo and I; we did not amble, we strode. Thinking this, I unconsciously lengthened my stride, until Molly protested. "What's your hurry? We're not catching a bus."

"Sorry," I said, slowing to her pace. Mingus forged ahead, nose to the path.

"I heard Vonnegut speak once. A commencement address, only without all the usual gobbledygook about following your dreams and staying true to yourself while making pots of money. He talked about taking time to enjoy the good moments in life instead of rushing by them. When you see something beautiful, he said, stop and look, and ask yourself, 'If this isn't great, what is?' It sounds simplistic, but it stuck with me, and lately I find myself thinking of those words more and more."

"They're good words," I said, and as I looked around me, the world suddenly came into focus. Dappled sunlight filtered through a canopy of gold and red boughs, and the air was rich with that fecund, foresty blend of growth and decomposition. I squeezed the arm linked in mine. "If this isn't great, what is?"

Leigh Pfeffer lived just outside the village of Old Chatham, on a hilltop surrounded by acres of meadowland. As we drove up the gravel track to her house, an enormous, shaggy gray beast rose from the porch and ambled down the steps toward the car.

"Good God," I said. "Is that a dog or a pony?"

"That's Sasha. He's a Russian aristocrat, I'll have you know, so treat him with respect."

As if I'd treat him any other way. Molly opened her door and got out, and the dog rushed over to her, nosing her hands and pockets, then raising its long, narrow head to lick her face. It looked like the Knopf colophon: some kind of wolfhound, I guessed, though I'd never seen any dog as big as this one. On its hind legs, it would have towered over Molly, and it certainly outweighed me.

Mingus was staring out the windshield, front paws on the console, hackles raised. "Behave yourself," I said. "That dog could kick your butt." I got out of the car, meaning to close him inside, but he jumped into the front seat and was out before I could shut the door. The two dogs eyed each other warily. Then

Sasha advanced slowly, ducking his head and wagging his tail, and they introduced themselves in the usual way.

A screen door slammed, and Leigh Pfeffer came running down the porch steps with her arms outstretched. She was a tall woman, almost Molly's height, but rounded where Molly was gaunt. She had long black hair, which she wore gathered in two braids, and large, competent hands with traces of paint around the nails. Except by Manhattan standards, where anything over size 6 is obese, Leigh wasn't fat but solidly female, with the abundant breasts and thighs of ancient fertility sculptures. We'd met before, at Molly's and once at an exhibit of Leigh's paintings. She'd seemed awkward and shy to me on those occasions, out of her element. On her own turf, she had the presence of an Amazon.

She embraced Molly ferociously, then pushed her back to arm's length. "You look like you've gone a few rounds."

"You oughtta see the other guy," Molly said.

Then I got a hug too, but a gentle one, as if I were a porcelain doll. "Jo, beautiful as ever and *très, très chic*. I'm so glad you came. And who's this?" she asked, turning to Mingus.

"That's Mingus, her bodyguard," Molly said. "We brought him in case the deer attack."

"I wouldn't put it past them," Leigh said. "Come on in."

We had tea in the kitchen, an enormous, old-fashioned room with a stone-clad hearth and a massive, butcher-block island. Clay pots of ivy lined the windowsills, and cast-iron pots and pans hung from a rack above the island. The house felt deeply lived in, as if Leigh had occupied it all her life, although she'd moved in only a year earlier.

Leigh had prepared a picnic lunch, which she proposed eating at a spot beside Kinderhook Creek. "Unless," she added, with a forthright look at Molly, "it's too chilly for you, in which case we can picnic right here."

Outdoors, we all agreed, and the dogs could come too. "But

first I want to see what you've been working on," Molly said, and Leigh was quick to comply. She took us out to her studio, a converted barn behind the house. I'd seen her work before, and admired its technical virtuosity without being in any way moved by it. The new paintings were very different. Since her move upstate, Leigh had switched from oil to watercolor and from portraits to landscapes; and somehow the landscapes seemed more animated and sentient than the portraits ever had. Infused with light, they were beautiful to look at but difficult to assimilate in a single viewing. The tall trees leaned toward one another, boughs intertwined, and seemed to have relationships unknowable to the viewer; and along with the intense luminosity came equally intense shadows. These paintings I felt in my gut; they were exhilarating, unexpected, and a little scary. I walked all through the studio, looking and looking, and then I turned to Leigh. "Who *are* you?"

"Seriously," Molly said. "I've got goose bumps."

"Goose bumps are good," Leigh said.

One particular painting kept calling me back. In the center of the frame, bisecting it from top to bottom, a wild, foaming stream rushed through a glade and, it seemed, through time itself. In the background, the bordering trees were black and wintry-looking, the light a sullen gray. In the foreground, rays of golden sunlight haloed trees in full bloom. The picture seemed to tilt outward, as if the stream were about to overflow its frame and sweep the viewer along. I turned to find Leigh watching me. "Does it have a title?"

"I thought of *The Same River Twice,* but I'm not sure about it. What would you call it?"

"*Swim at Your Own Risk?*"

Leigh laughed. "That's where we're having our picnic, by the way. You'll be able to judge if I did it justice."

———

In fact she'd done it an injustice. No actual landscape could compare to the magical scene in her painting. Real nature is mute; it is what it is and nothing more, whereas Leigh's rendition was infused with purpose and meaning. That an imitation should outshine reality could not surprise me, who saw it all the time in fiction. I subscribe to the view of British novelist Ivy Compton-Burnett, who, when asked if she based her characters on real people, replied, "People in life hardly seem definite enough to appear in print. They are not good or bad enough, or clever or stupid enough, or comic or pitiful enough." I have known only one man as vivid and outsized as a proper fictional protagonist, and reader, I married him.

If this spot was not as mystical as it appeared in Leigh's painting, it was nonetheless a charming place for a picnic. The noontime sun was warm enough for us to shed our coats. The stream was wider and less precipitous than its portrayal, the boulders smaller, the trees less majestic; only their color, brilliant autumn hues of orange, gold, and scarlet, surpassed their depiction.

Leigh had prepared everything with an eye to Molly's comfort. We lolled on cushions atop a large, flat rock, overlooking the stream. While the dogs cavorted below, daring each other into the water, Leigh decanted a feast from her wicker picnic basket onto a checkered cloth. There were four different types of sandwiches, potato salad and cole slaw, Macoun apples and ripe pears from a local orchard, homemade oatmeal cookies, and two bottles of chilled Riesling.

While we ate, we talked about Leigh's painting. "What caused such a radical departure?" Molly asked her.

"I needed a change. You can't just go on doing the same thing over and over."

"But how did it happen?"

Leigh stretched out her long legs and raised her face to the sun. "It happened when I moved out here. I'd been in the city for ages, and I loved it. I thrived on the faces, the whole wonderful mish-mash and all that jangling energy. I thought I'd stay forever. Then one hot summer day, I had a meeting in Midtown. I took the uptown local, and it was hideously crowded, steamy, and stinky despite the MTA's feeble stab at air-conditioning. I got off in Times Square and climbed up to the street, which was even more mobbed than the subway, full of tourists who don't know how to walk. Suddenly I felt suffocated, totally claustrophobic. I had to get out of the city. The Hamptons were out of the question; too expensive, and I don't like the art scene out there. A friend of mine had a place in Old Chatham, so I knew the area. I called an agent, and one week later, I had a summer rental, a sweet little cottage in Ghent with two acres and a separate studio.

"I started doing landscapes just to clear my palate—pun intended, thank you very much!—and because there wasn't anything else up here to paint. Pretty soon I found myself fascinated by formations and shapes around me, and above all by the light. After all the portraits I'd done indoors, in artificial light, I'm embarrassed to say that I had to rediscover sunlight, which is as different from the fake stuff as Häagen-Dazs is to fat-free yogurt. To try to capture that light, I switched to watercolor, which I hadn't used since I was in art school. This time, I discovered a whole new vocabulary.

"It was a paradigm shift, a different way of seeing the world and working with it. When the summer ended, I realized that I didn't want to leave. I was into this new series, and I wanted to see where it would take me. So I sold the loft, bought the farm-house, and here I am."

"You found your place," I said, feeling that I understood her completely. Hadn't I found mine in Hugo? "Like Rousseau found Tahiti, like Van Gogh found Arles."

"Oh, really!" Leigh said, blushing. "Why stop there? Like Michelangelo in Rome, like Mark Twain on the Mississippi."

"Like God in his heaven," Molly added, and we laughed so hard that the dogs came over to investigate and stayed to eat.

Back at Leigh's, I asked to see the paintings again. Molly stayed behind to rest while Leigh walked me over to the studio. "How is she really?" she asked as we crossed the yard.

"Not great. The chemo wasn't working, so they stopped it. But at least she doesn't have to deal with the side effects anymore."

Leigh said nothing; what was there to say? They'd been friends since grade school, though you'd never know it to look at them now.

I was drawn again to the same landscape, which on second viewing pleased me even more than at first. I thought of all the blank walls in my apartment, where photos of Hugo used to hang, and I asked if the painting was for sale.

Leigh tried to give it to me. I refused. An odd negotiation ensued, in which the buyer bid the price up and the seller pushed it down, until at last we arrived at a figure both of us could live with. I wrote a check. Leigh wrapped the painting in cardboard and brown paper, and we laid it carefully in the trunk of my car.

Molly, who had taken some pain pills, struggled against dozing on the way home. "Who knows if I'll ever see this again?" she asked, sending a shard of glass through my heart. "Talk to me, kiddo. Keep me awake."

"I bought a painting from Leigh. It's in the trunk."

"The one of our picnic spot? That's great, Jo. She's brilliant, isn't she?"

"She's amazing, as a painter and a person. I came up here thinking of her as your friend; now I feel she's mine as well."

Molly beamed, and it occurred to me that she'd taken to bequeathing people as well as possessions. Suddenly a deer bounded out from the woods into the road in front of me. I slammed on the brakes, thrusting an arm out to restrain Molly. Mingus thudded hard into the back of my seat, but I held the wheel steady. The car juddered to a halt while the deer, unscathed, disappeared into the woods.

"Jesus," Molly said, her hand at her throat.

I looked back to check on Mingus. He was clambering back onto the rear seat, looking indignant but unharmed. My heart was pounding. "Leigh said they might attack. I thought she was kidding."

I drove on, more slowly than before. Just outside the town of Hudson, we stopped at a farm stand and bought a bushel of Macoun apples, more than we needed, but I wanted plenty for the office. We drove through Hudson and onto the Rip Van Winkle Bridge. From the top of the bridge, the land on either side looked like brilliantly hued Persian carpets.

For once I felt sorry to be returning to the city. Rowena's killer was still at large, and so was Teddy Pendragon. Just thinking about the biographer curdled my mood. He knew too much, but how much? I couldn't think of any way to find out without revealing the very thing I wanted to conceal. Was there any way to control what he wrote, any leverage I could apply?

Lost in these thoughts, I forgot to notice the foliage, forgot even about Molly until her voice brought me back.

"What's eating you, kiddo?" She was studying my face with those wise brown eyes. "I know there's something. You're barely here."

"It's that bastard Teddy Pendragon. He found something out, and I'm afraid he's going to publish it."

"What, those so-called affairs of Hugo's? Even if it's true, they meant nothing. Hugo was Hugo. I told you before you married him: you don't take a wolf into your home and expect it to act like a poodle."

"It's not that." I hesitated, torn. I never wanted her to know but now, if I didn't tell her, chances were Teddy would.

"What then?" she said.

"If I tell you, will you promise not to repeat the story ever?"

"Trust me, kiddo, I'll take it to the grave."

"Very funny. Three years after Hugo and I married, while we were living in Paris, I got pregnant."

She swiveled her whole body toward me. "You never told me that!"

"It wasn't planned. I knew Hugo would be upset, but he was more than upset; he was furious. As soon as I told him, he demanded that I get an abortion. I said I was damned if I would. We had a huge fight; it went on for weeks. Hugo played good cop/bad cop all by himself. One day he'd be cold and aloof; he'd accuse me of trying to trap him, scheming to undermine his career. The next day he'd be kind and forgiving; he'd pet me, comfort me, talk about all the great things we were going to do together. About one thing, though, he never wavered. He said that if I insisted on having the baby, he'd leave me."

"That lousy bastard! Even for Hugo, that's abysmal."

"Yes. But he was straight with me from the start. Before we married he told me he didn't want children, and I agreed. I *agreed*, Molly. The way he saw it, I'd reneged on our deal."

"So what? There's a hell of a difference between not wanting kids and forcing your wife to have an abortion."

I kept my eyes on the road. "He didn't force me. It was my choice."

"Your choice my ass. You were obsessed with the man, and he knew it."

"I was in love with him," I said, with what I hoped was quiet dignity.

Molly shrugged impatiently. "Same difference. And he knew just how to play you. I'd like to dig him up just to slap him silly."

"Jesus, Molly, you're talking about my husband."

"I know who we're talking about! I loved Hugo with all my heart, but you got to admit, the man was a swine."

"He was a genius. You know how far an artist will go to protect his gift."

She blew a raspberry. "He'd have been the same selfish bastard if he'd been a butcher or a pipe fitter. I can't believe you're defending him."

I couldn't believe it either. But Molly was always too hard on Hugo, and too easy on me. The pressure he put on me, the threats and accusations—I remember them vividly. The pain was like nothing else I've ever known; certainly no whipping ever came close. Not even Hugo's death hurt as much as those weeks of fighting and the choice I had to make. But it was my choice, no matter what Molly said. I loved Hugo, and I loved my life as his wife, and in the end that is what I chose. He didn't force me. I know what he did was wrong. But I also know you can't judge a man like Hugo the way you'd judge an ordinary man. Why couldn't Molly see that?

I drove on. The closer we got to the city, the more Sunday-night traffic we encountered. Molly rested her head on the door and closed her eyes, but I knew she wasn't asleep; I could hear her thinking. We didn't speak again until we reached her house. By then it was fully dark. The house next to Molly's was tricked out for Halloween with jack-o'-lanterns and a dancing skeleton on the lawn. The street was deserted save for a man walking a dachshund. Molly's face, lit by a streetlight, was hollow with exhaustion.

"Come in for coffee?" she asked.

I hesitated. A cup would have fortified me for the drive home, but Molly looked like she needed to dive into bed. "I'd better push on."

She gathered her possessions: walking stick, empty mugs, and the Trader Joe's bag, now full of Macouns, but she didn't get out.

"Finally I get it," she said. "I understand now why you fought this bio tooth and nail. You were afraid all along this story would come out, and you couldn't allow anything to tarnish Hugo's precious memory. How could you, when you believe your entire life rests on your perfect marriage? 'The foundation,' you called it; oh yes, I remember."

"First of all," I said, "I wasn't afraid the story would come out, because as far as I knew, Hugo and I were the only ones who knew. And second, my whole life *is* built on my marriage. Where would I be if Hugo hadn't married me?"

"Exactly where you are today, you ninny! Running the best damn agency in town."

"That's very kind, but both of us know that when you brought me back as a partner, it wasn't for anything I'd done; it was for who I was."

"Exactly: who *you* were, not whose widow you were. I saw what you did for Hugo. He was a brilliant writer when he met you, but you made him even better. That's your gift, and I'm proud to say I recognized it from the first. How do you think you got that internship with me?

"Because I begged?"

"You didn't beg," she said, laughing. "You were eager, but they were all eager. No, it was the test. Remember the test?"

I'd never forget it. Eight openings to eight novels, and on the basis of just a few pages, I had to say which ones I'd read and which I'd reject. It made me so nervous I nearly walked out.

"Of course," I said.

"The good ones were obscure books by great writers. The others were from the slush pile, not the dogs, but the close-but-no-cigar category. You aced it, kiddo. I'd been giving that test for years and never saw an applicant come close. You not only made the right choice every time, you knew why it was right. You heard those writers' voices, and you went for quality every time. Hiring you was the smartest move I ever made."

I felt too much to speak. I squeezed her hand. But Molly wasn't finished.

"Remember what Leigh said about a paradigm shift in her way of seeing the world? That's what you need, kiddo. You're not who you are because Hugo married you. He married you because of who you are." And before I could think of an answer, she kissed my cheek and was gone.

Chapter 22

I fell asleep with Molly's parting words still playing through my head, burrowing inward like benevolent tapeworms, and woke to full daylight and the sight of Leigh's painting propped up on my dresser. There was frost on the windows, but I was as warm in bed as a coddled egg. Nothing had changed, but something inside felt different. It was like going to bed with a cold and waking up without one. I could breathe again. The ceaseless clamoring inside my head was gone at last.

I got up and made coffee, fed the dog, and ate a couple of Macoun apples for breakfast. They were as sweet as I remembered. Before leaving for the office, I called Molly. She didn't answer; sleeping in for once, I supposed.

Lorna was at her desk when I got in. She ignored Mingus, who ignored her back. "You're early," she said.

"You're earlier."

"I always am. Gives me a chance to get organized. Coffee?"

"Thanks." I put a bagful of apples on her desk. "For everyone. Macouns, fresh off the tree."

She brought the coffee to my office and watched as I drank it.

She wore a tweed skirt, plaid shirt, clunky shoes. Maybe Chloe could take her in hand, I thought. She knew how to dress. Granted, Lorna didn't have Chloe's figure, but she could certainly do better than what looked like Salvation Army castoffs.

"Did you and Molly go upstate?" Lorna asked.

"We did. Hit it just right, too. It was beautiful."

"You look better."

"It's amazing what a little country air will do."

"*You're* amazing," she blurted. "All the stuff that's been happening, just one thing after another. If it was me, I'd be curled up in a little ball by now. You're something special."

I stared. Who was this woman, and what had she done with my secretary? That Lorna so rarely showed her feelings made this outburst all the more touching. I thanked her. She shrugged and hurried out.

The others arrived and poked their heads in to say hello. I was on the phone when Harriet looked in. *"Talk later?"* she mouthed, and I nodded.

I dialed Molly's number again. Still no answer. Thinking I might have missed her, I tried her cell and left a message. For the rest of the morning, I had back-to-back meetings, followed by lunch with an editor from Simon & Schuster. Lorna handed me half a dozen message slips when I got back to the office, but Molly's name wasn't on any of them.

Worried, I tried both her home and cell, without success. She could be sick, I thought. She could have had an accident. But why wasn't her aide, Maria, answering?

I found Maria's cell phone number and called it. When she picked up, I heard music and children's voices in the background.

"No, ma'am," she said, "I am not working today. Ms. Hamish gave me the day off for my daughter's birthday."

I had another emergency number, Molly's across-the-street neighbor. No answer there, either. This is stupid, I thought. She's gone out somewhere and left her cell phone home. Or she's home, but the phone's out of order. I called the operator. There was nothing wrong with the line.

I put Mingus on his leash and went out to Lorna's desk. "Call the garage and have them get my car out, please."

Jean-Paul looked up from his desk across the room. "Where are you going?"

"Molly's. She's not answering her phone."

He jumped to his feet. "I'll go with you."

"You've got a meeting at four with that Twitter girl," Lorna said.

"Apologize for me, tell her I had an emergency, and let Chloe take the meeting," I said, and closed the door on their protests.

From the outside everything looked normal. I left Mingus in the car and prepared my excuses for barging in. Before climbing the porch steps, I detoured to peek in the window of Molly's garage. Her old Volvo was in its usual spot. Wherever she'd been, she was back.

I climbed the wooden steps to the porch, rang the doorbell, and waited. There was no sound, no movement inside when I peered through the side light window. The door was locked. I took Molly's spare key from my bag, opened the door, and poked my head in.

"Molly?"

It was quiet in there, empty-house quiet. I went in, and a faint but sickening odor hit me. It reminded me of Chinatown on a hot summer day, and it was all wrong in this context. I left the front door open behind me and forced myself down the hall toward the kitchen. The smell grew stronger. I stopped just outside the door.

I've already admitted that I'm a coward, maybe not in my day-to-day conduct, but in all the ways that matter. I'd tried to filibuster the news of Hugo's death; I'd averted my eyes from his affairs; I'd cleared away the detritus of former lovers without ever asking a question. My instinct now was to run. Whatever was in Molly's kitchen, whatever the source of that smell, I wanted desperately not to see it. Only the thought that Molly could be hurt kept me from bolting.

I opened the door. The kitchen was a mess. A stool lay on its side. The Trader Joe's bag was overturned, and apples were scattered across the floor. There were dark splatters on the counters, cabinets, and walls; what looked like caked blood on the butcher-block island.

The island blocked my view. I inched forward and saw two feet sticking out. They were wearing Molly's sneakers. There was a terrible stillness to those feet, which seemed to lack even the potential for movement. There was too much blood.

I stepped around the island. Molly lay on her stomach in the center of a black stain shaped like the wings of a snow angel. Her head, with its patchy growth of silver hair, was uncovered. The orange scarf, now a deeper shade of red, lay on the floor beside her face. Her eyes were open but sightless. Her lips were drawn back, her chin bloody. I glimpsed letters written on the side of the island but made no sense of them.

I heard a scream, and time seemed to stutter. I don't remember leaving the house. When I came back to myself, I was in my car. The windows were shut, the doors locked; Mingus was in the front seat and my arms were wrapped around him.

I couldn't comprehend what I'd seen, and I couldn't stop seeing it: Molly sprawled on the floor, the smell of blood and apples. That blood would never come out. The floor was ruined. Molly would be so upset, I thought. She loved that old plank floor.

But no. Molly was dead. What should I do? Not a soul in sight in this suburban desert. Call for help, I thought, although I knew she was beyond it. I let go of the dog. My hands were shaking so badly, I couldn't get the phone out of its compartment in my bag. I closed my eyes and saw again the blood, Molly's empty eyes. My stomach heaved. I threw open the car door, bent over, and vomited into the street.

Now my teeth were chattering. I shut and locked the door, upended my bag, and shook the contents onto the seat beside Mingus. My wallet tumbled out, sunglasses, keys, checkbook, loose change, ATM receipts, and, finally, my phone. I flipped it open but drew a blank. Couldn't think of whom to call. Couldn't think at all. I scrolled through the address book. Tommy Cullen's name came up, and I hit DIAL.

He answered on the second ring. "Jo? What's up?"

"Molly's on the floor," I said. "She's dead. There's blood all over. Apples, too. Macouns," I added helpfully.

"Jo," he said, his voice very calm, "where are you?"

Like a child, I recited Molly's address.

"Are you in the house?"

"Outside, in my car."

"Stay there. I'm on my way. Have you called 911?"

"I called you."

"I'm going to hang up, and you're going to dial 911 immediately, OK? And then you sit tight. I'm coming, Jo. Call 911 now."

He hung up. I did what he said. I was OK as long as I didn't have to think. I called them, and told them about the blood and the apples and Molly, and I gave her address, and I waited.

They gathered like carrion crows, first two police cars, then dozens of patrol cars, unmarked cars, and ambulances, too, with sirens wailing, though surely it was too late for that. They boxed me in. Someone tapped on my window, but Mingus barked and lunged and sent him reeling backward. Two policemen ran yellow tape around the entire front yard, trampling Molly's beautiful garden. People in white booties walked in and out of her house as if they owned it. One man carried a camcorder. I wished I'd put her scarf back on her head. Molly would hate to be photographed without it. Even at the worst times, sick from chemo or burnt by radiation, she'd never gone out without her war paint on. She'd joked about it, a stupid Tom Swift pun. *"'Vanity's the last thing to go,' she said baldly."* I should have covered her head.

A man in a suit approached the car. Mingus barked again, but this man wasn't deterred. He beckoned me out of the car. I held on to Mingus and looked away. I didn't know him. He could be anyone. A reporter. Sam Spade.

He took out a detective shield and held it up. "Open the window," he said. I pushed the window button, but nothing happened. My keys were on the floor of the car. It took three attempts to insert the key in the lock, but I finally succeeded.

I rolled the window down three inches. Mingus snarled.

"Ma'am, can you control that dog?"

That, at least, I could do. I ordered Mingus into the backseat and told him to stay. He was more obedient than my own body. The detective asked me to unlock the door and step out of the car. The unlocking part went OK. But when I tried to step out, my knees buckled and I would have fallen if he hadn't leapt forward to catch me. "Oh no," I said, for he'd stepped in the puddle of vomit. He lowered me into the driver's seat and hunkered down outside the car. I felt humiliated.

The detective was a man of about Molly's age, with sleek silver hair and a gray mustache. He asked my name. I said it. My voice sounded strange, as if I had water in my ears.

"Was it you who found her?"

"Yes."

"Do you live here?"

"I live in the city. Molly lives alone."

"How did you come to find her?"

"I kept calling. She didn't answer. I was worried, but not worried enough. I should have come hours ago. She shouldn't have had to wait so long, lying on the hard floor. And the apples are ruined. Even if you washed the blood off, who would eat them now?" I could tell by his face that I sounded like a lunatic. But I had no more control over my mouth than my body.

"Was the door open when you got here?" he asked.

"Locked."

"How did you get in?"

"I have her keys, she has mine."

"What's your relationship to Molly?"

Molly indeed, I thought. Never met her in his life and he's first-naming her. The dead get no respect. It was starting to sink in: Molly was gone, irretrievably gone. I was alone again.

"We used to be business partners. She's my best friend." *Was* my best friend, I thought. Something was wrong with my breathing. The air wasn't reaching my lungs.

"Are you OK?" the detective asked, reaching toward my shoulder.

I shrank away. "Fine."

"You're doing great, ma'am. Just a few more questions and we'll get the medics over here. When did you last see Molly?"

"Last night. We drove upstate for the foliage and then I dropped her off. I should have gone in. She asked me to. But she looked so tired."

"What time was that?"

I tried to focus, but it was like wading through cotton. "It was dark. Nine, nine thirty. I watched her go in and then I drove away."

"Did you see anyone hanging around?"

I would have laughed if I could have. "In this neighborhood?"

"Any unfamiliar cars? People walking by?"

"No," I said, then remembered. "A man with a dog."

"Detective!" The call came from somewhere behind him. I looked past the silver-haired man and saw Tommy Cullen approaching, holding out an NYPD gold shield.

I caught a flash of anger as the detective stood and turned to face Tommy. They walked away together, Tommy talking fast and gesticulating. He didn't look at me. He only looked at the detective.

I shut the car door and rolled the windows up. I felt safer that way. I watched Tommy and the other detective. Gradually the other man's posture relaxed. They talked for a while more, then entered Molly's house without knocking. Time passed. Tommy came out alone and walked straight over to my car.

He tapped on the passenger-side door. I let him in. Mingus jumped up, but Tommy spoke to him and he sat back down.

"I'm so sorry," Tommy said.

"Did you see her?"

"I did."

"What happened to her?" It was the first time I'd thought to ask. The fog was getting patchy.

"We'll talk about that later," he said softly, in a rush. "I only have a moment, and you need to listen carefully. You need a criminal lawyer before you say another word to these detectives. Do you hear me, Jo?"

I heard him fine. I just didn't understand him. "Why would I need a lawyer?"

"Because Molly was murdered. She was shot, just like Rowena. Didn't you see the writing on the side of the island?"

"I saw something. There was so much blood, and all those apples, and Molly's face. Her scarf fell off. I wish I'd fixed it."

He gripped me by both arms, then quickly let me go. "You're not tracking. Listen to me. You're tied to two murders. Molly was shot sometime last night. You may have been the last person to see her alive. For all I know, as close as you two were, you could be her heir." I started to speak, but he raised a finger. "I'm not asking. That detective will be back in a moment with more questions. You tell him you can't talk; you're sick and in shock and you need to go home now. Tell him you'll see him tomorrow. But don't talk to him again until you've got a lawyer." He peered into my face. "Are you following, Jo?"

I was, but three or four steps behind. "What did it say?"

"What?"

"The writing."

Tommy grimaced. On Molly's porch, a man with an old-fashioned doctor's bag was pulling on booties. I watched him enter the house.

"Same as the last time," Tommy said. "'Can you hear me now?'"

Chapter 23

The EMTs, having come too late for Molly, wanted to take me in instead. I said I wanted to go home, and the silver-haired detective didn't argue but asked permission to search my car and swab my hands. I had no objection except the cold, which seemed to have crept into my bones. Tommy put me and Mingus into his car and turned the heat on full-blast before returning to Silver Hair's side. Two men in jumpsuits came out of Molly's house carrying a stretcher. I covered my eyes.

After that Tommy drove us home in my car. At the end of Molly's block, the police had set up barricades, and beyond the barriers there were media vans, photographers, and reporters. As Tommy ran the gauntlet, they trotted beside the car, peering in, but the windows were tinted and I knew they couldn't see me.

"They already know?" I asked.

"They're like flies. Takes them no time at all to sniff out a crime scene. And Molly was somebody."

I rested my head against the door and closed my eyes, just as Molly had done last night. We didn't speak again until Tommy pulled up in front of my building. Without asking, he came upstairs with me and walked briskly through the apartment, looking in every room, as if I, like Molly, had surrendered ownership. I went into the kitchen to feed Mingus.

"All clear," Tommy said, appearing in the doorway.

"Why wouldn't it be?"

He watched me mix a raw egg in with the kibble. "You're doing that now?"

"He's hungry now." I put the bowl down. The dog waited, eyes on my face. "Chow time," I said, and he fell to as if he hadn't eaten in a month.

"You remember what I told you, Jo?"

"Get a lawyer."

"A criminal lawyer. Do you know any?"

"Sean Mallory. He's a client."

"I know Mallory. He'll do." Tommy handed me his cell phone. I looked at him. "All yours are tapped." He left the kitchen.

I looked up Sean's number on my cell phone and dialed it on Tommy's. Sean answered and listened to my rambling explanation for no more than a minute before cutting me off. "I'm coming over," he said.

I found Tommy in the living room, pouring a scotch. He handed the glass to me, and took back his phone. "Did you get him?"

I took a long pull of the drink. Feeling and sense were returning, and I needed a buffer in place before they arrived. "He's coming," I said. "But he's just going to give me advice I won't take."

"You'll take it if you're smart."

"Strange advice from a cop."

"Strange like Benedict Arnold was strange. You'd be doing me a favor if you forgot we had this conversation."

"What conversation?"

"There you go," Tommy said with a flash of the old smile.

"Max was wrong about you."

"What did Max say?"

"That you weren't to be trusted. That you hadn't forgiven and forgotten."

"He got it part right, anyway. You're not so easy to forget."

I sat down on the couch, Mingus beside me. Tommy's cell phone beeped. He read the message and said, "I have to go back. Is there anyone I can call for you?"

"Molly," I said automatically, and didn't realize my error till I saw Tommy's face. I knew she was dead, but the knowledge wasn't continuous; it was more like a series of speed bumps.

"No one," I said.

"Out of the question," Sean Mallory said, with all the authority inherent in his bulk. He'd been a boxer in his youth, and with his broken nose, massive chest, and long arms, he looked the part still, though he didn't dress it. I'd changed into jeans and an old sweatshirt, comfort clothes, while Sean, despite the hour, had appeared at my door in a fine blue suit and pristine white shirt. It gave him an extra edge in what already felt like a contest.

"Not till I say so," he went on, "and only in my presence. Also, we will have to rethink the phone taps. Really, Jo, you should have called me sooner."

"I didn't want a lawyer," I said, "because I knew what a lawyer's knee-jerk reaction would be, and I wanted to help the police. Now more than ever. Catching this monster is the number-one priority."

"Yours, maybe. Theirs is closing the case. Mine is keeping you safe. You're the real target here. You're as much the victim of these crimes as Molly or Rowena, yet right now those detectives could be building a case against you. You're the last person known to have seen Molly; you found the body; and you stand to inherit the bulk of her estate. They're gonna think they hit the trifecta."

"They can't be that stupid. There's no motive. I love Molly, and everyone knows it. Hugo left me very comfortable, and I make a good living. Her money means nothing to me. As for her house . . ." I shuddered. "After tonight, I'd burn it down before I'd set foot in it again. If the police have questions for me, I want to answer them. And you can forget about taking those taps off my phones."

"Preferences duly noted," Sean said smoothly, "and just as soon as I am satisfied that you are not a target of their investigation, I will make you available for questioning."

I could not gain any traction with him. This was a whole different man from the one who'd sat in my office, hat in hand, hoping I'd sell his book. Then I was the expert, he the supplicating client. Now our roles were reversed, and I was finding it a lot harder to accept guidance than to give it. But my objections bounced off Sean like pebbles off a steel fortress. I could see I had only two choices with him: I could take his advice or I could fire him. And I wasn't at all sure he'd agree to the second.

Sean's thoughts must have run along the same lines, for he said, "You're in my ball park now, Jo, and you've got to let me call the shots. Think about your own business. Without you standing between your writers and their publishers, how screwed would the writers be?"

"Totally."

"I rest my case."

I didn't rest mine, though, but went on arguing until finally we reached a compromise. The phone taps stayed, but I would allow Sean to run interference with the police. Soon after that, heavy with weariness and sorrow, I walked the lawyer to the door and submitted to a bear hug I hardly felt. "Leave the investigation to the police, and the police to me," Sean said. "You have your own work to do."

I stared at him. Could he really believe I was going back to the office as if nothing had happened?

He squeezed my shoulder. "You need to mourn your friend and tend to your own wounds."

We buried Molly on Thursday, one day after the police released her body. By then the story had gone national. I tended to forget it, because we were so close, but Molly was indeed, as Tommy had said, "somebody": lifelong agent to Hugo Donovan, mother hen to generations of great writers, "the Max Perkins of agents" the *New York Times* called her in their obituary. Although the police withheld the one definitive piece of evidence that linked Molly's murder to Rowena's, reporters on the twenty-four-hour-a-day one-upmanship treadmill made their own connections; they also dug up the earlier items about the agency's "prankster." Any way you connected the dots, the agency was right in the middle. Reporters gave the case a name: the Publishing Murders. There was such a media frenzy that it took a hundred police officers to secure the funeral route and the Westchester cemetery where Molly would be laid to rest beside her husband. My apartment building had been staked out by reporters, one of whom tried to sneak in disguised as a masseuse and was summarily ejected, folding table and all. Just outside the funeral home, a Fox News van collided with a CNN van as both maneuvered for a vantage point. No one was hurt in the collision, but two reporters and a cameraman were injured in the scuffle that followed.

But all that happened on the periphery, while I sheltered in the eye of the hurricane, surrounded by protective bodies. Since Tuesday morning my apartment had turned into Grand Central Station. Friends, colleagues, and clients formed a procession that never ebbed, most of them bearing platters from Fairway or

Zabar's. The kitchen was always full of women doing something to food: preparing it, serving it, putting it away. The office was closed for the week, but instead of taking the time off, the staff gathered every day in my apartment. Max flew in with Barry and the baby, and together with Max's mother, Estelle, they spent most of every day at my place. Max's mother made chicken soup from scratch and stood over me until I finished a bowl, clucking over how much weight I'd lost. There were people in my house when I went to bed at night and when I woke in the morning. The whole thing stank of coordination. I suspected Lorna, who could have organized leaves in a hurricane, but I didn't object. Unlike Garbo, I didn't want to be alone.

And I never was, except in bed. Then images of the scene replayed over and over in my mind. Eventually, I knew, those flashbacks would stop. What I dreaded was the emptiness that would follow, when nothing stood between me and the dreariness of loss, which is like a wound that will not heal.

A small fleet of limos had been ordered for ten a.m. to take us to the funeral home. The younger agency staff would go in one limo, along with our accountant, Shelly Rubens. Max, Barry, Harriet, and I would occupy another. There were three more for old friends of Molly's who'd gathered for the funeral. Max's mother had volunteered to stay behind with baby Molly to prepare for the gathering afterward; for it had been decided, with my passive acquiescence, that we would sit shiva for Molly in my apartment.

By seven of that morning, I was showered and dressed and had embarked on an attempt to restore a semblance of life to my face. Sitting at my vanity table, I coated my swollen eyelids with taupe powder and applied mascara—waterproof, just in case, though I had no intention of needing it. Molly's dignity had been assaulted by cancer's depredations, by her murderer, and by the police, who had left her lying in her blood while they took pictures and talked over her. I was determined that her funeral would restore what it could of that stolen dignity. She deserved a stately departure, and by God she would have it. There would be no scenes of extravagant emotion, no weeping and wailing, no hugging of coffins. I would drown in my tears before I would shed them in public.

Dabs of concealer covered the dark circles under my eyes. I put on a lipstick that Molly had bought me the last time we went shopping, and studied the results critically. What I really wanted was a veil to hide behind, but that would have looked melodramatic. Makeup would have to be my mask.

I left my bedroom, trailed by Mingus. Keyed up by all the tumult, the dog stuck to my heel like a shadow. When I went to bed last night, Jean-Paul had been dozing on the living-room sofa. Now Keyshawn Grimes lay there, sound asleep under an afghan. My self-appointed bodyguards, the boys were switching off, so that one of them was always within earshot.

In the kitchen I made a pot of strong coffee and drank two cups in quick succession. Jean-Paul and Chloe came in together and left again at once to take Mingus for a walk. I hadn't been outside since Tommy Cullen drove me home from Molly's house.

Soon the others began to gather. Harriet arrived alone and uncharacteristically enveloped me in a hug. "I just want you to know," she said gruffly, "I'm here for you. You're not to worry about the agency. I've got your back."

Then my back had better watch out, I thought, and was instantly remorseful. Molly had been Harriet's mentor as well as mine; they'd been colleagues and friends for many years. The hard feelings that arose when Molly installed me as a partner must have made this loss all the more painful. And Harriet had been wonderful these past few days, undertaking tasks that should have been mine, if I'd been functional. She notified clients, handled the press, and set in motion the process for Molly's pre-planned funeral. She worked from my apartment, hardly leaving except to go home at night and once when the police summoned her to an interview. She'd come back from that interview hours later, paler than ever, with a pinched mouth and nothing at all to say.

More people came. Leigh Pfeffer, queenly in purple, cried when she hugged me and again when she saw her painting above my mantel, a bittersweet reminder of our last day together. Molly used to joke that in this city you can't tell a funeral from a wedding, because New Yorkers wear black to everything. Today, though, there would have been no mistaking the occasion. I'd never seen a sadder room.

The doorman called up to say the limos had arrived. The mourners made their way out to the hall and into the elevator, which had to make several trips. The last to leave were Barry, Max, Harriet, and me. While the men waited in the hall, Harriet approached me with a glass of water. She took my hand and pressed a small white pill in my palm. "Take it."

I looked at her.

"It's just a Valium, to take the edge off." When I hesitated, she laughed awkwardly. "Don't you trust me?"

Molly trusted you, and look where she is now. A vile thought, totally unwarranted. I was ashamed of myself. Molly and Rowena were murdered by a stranger, a twisted wannabe writer who styled himself Sam Spade. I knew that.

But I didn't take the pill. I slipped it in my pocket.

"I don't want the edge off," I said.

Jean-Paul and Keyshawn were waiting in the lobby when we descended. Together with Max and Barry, they formed a wedge that funneled me and Harriet from the building into the waiting limo. Lights flashed. I heard people shouting my name and caught a glimpse of overcast sky before I was bundled inside. Barry and Max followed, and Max slammed the door shut. The limo slipped into the stream of traffic and bore us away.

———

Harriet and I sat in the front row of the chapel, for Molly had no living relatives. The service was short, and much of it was in Hebrew. I stood when told to stand, sat when told to sit.

Harriet spoke. It should have been me, but I couldn't. There were, by arrangement, no other eulogies; those would come in the memorial service, whenever I had the heart to arrange one. Behind me I heard weeping and snuffling, but I kept my eyes on the coffin, which lay atop a bier in the front of the chapel. It looked too short for Molly, and I conceived the notion that the undertakers had folded her into it, knowing the casket would be closed. I worried, too, that she wouldn't have enough air. Though I realized these concerns were stupid and absurd, they ran though my head in an endless loop.

There was a rabbi and a cantor. The casket was bare of flowers. There was no incense, no organ, no music except the cantor's deep, mournful chanting. Unlike most funerals I'd been to, not a word was spoken about joyous reunions in the afterlife. "Jews don't sugarcoat death," Molly once told me, "and they sure as hell don't celebrate it. They just look it in the face." Not my forte, looking things in the face. It would have been nice to imagine Molly meeting up with Hugo and Rowena in some book-lined version of paradise, but I didn't believe in that any more than they had.

Molly was gone. I would never see her again. I would never hear her voice again.

After the service, Harriet and I stood in the front of the room greeting people as they filed out to the parking lot. Many were crying. I clung to my threadbare composure and did my best for Molly's sake. I thanked the mourners for coming, comforted the weepers, and assured everyone who asked that I was fine. I endured their inadequate praise of Molly and hackneyed phrases of consolation, willing myself to see past the banalities to the sorrow underneath.

The line inched forward. Suddenly Charlie Malvino stood before me in a somber black suit and tie. "I hope you don't mind my coming," he said. "I was very fond of the old girl."

"She was fond of you, too," I said, which was true. Charlie had come to her straight out of college; she'd made him an agent. We shook hands. Less restrained with Harriet, he gave her a hug and whispered something in her ear. Harriet shook her head reprovingly and turned to the next person on line.

Molly was buried beside her husband, whose headstone, commissioned from an artist, was engraved with wildflowers that encircled the inscription. We huddled together beneath a gray sky before the open grave. Harriet stood beside me, her arm linked in mine, tears and mascara streaming down her face, stiff upper lip quivering. I could feel her body shaking, but my own felt as heavy and immobile as the stones around us. Max was on my other side, his arm around my shoulders. Someone had handed out leaflets with the Hebrew prayers transliterated. When the rabbi led the Kaddish, I read the words aloud. *"Yis'gadal v'yis'kadash, shmei rabba."* I didn't know what they meant, but for once it didn't matter. They were the right words, the necessary words.

Then something happened that I should have foreseen but hadn't. The rabbi pulled a shovel from a pile of dirt beside the grave and handed it to me.

Harriet released my arm. Max stepped back. Unmoving, I stared at the rabbi.

"It's the last service we perform for our loved ones," he said gently.

It seemed a poor return for the woman who had given me my

life, my mother in all but birth. But it was the way of her people, and I had to honor that.

I forced myself forward, scooped dirt from the pile, and pivoted toward the grave. As I looked down at the coffin, it hit me full on that my Molly was in there. For a moment my knees buckled; but I recovered, stood up straight, and turned the shovel over. Gravel and dirt rained down, striking the coffin with a sound like hail.

Chapter 24

Shiva, Max had explained, was the Jewish equivalent of the wake, except that it came after instead of before the funeral. We sat shiva for Molly from Thursday through Sunday. During this period, the television was unplugged, and copies of the *New York Times* in their blue cellophane wrappers piled up on a side table, untouched. It didn't bother me to be cut off. It actually felt soothing, as if I'd entered a sort of temporal cocoon. I knew I'd be told if the police made an arrest. Short of that, there was no news I cared to hear.

Once again my home was full of people, food, and drink. Max and Barry came every day with baby Molly. The jealousy I'd suffered when Max first told me they were expecting had long since dissipated, and so I took my greatest comfort in holding the baby and looking into those wise, dark eyes, which reminded me of her namesake's. Lorna, Chloe, and Jean-Paul took it in turns to man the lobby, screening out reporters but letting all other visitors up; and there were so many that gradually these gatherings took on the aspect of an endless publishing salon with me as hostess, Nora Charles sans her Nick. I felt Hugo's absence these days as acutely as I did Molly's, as if the new loss had exacerbated the older.

Most of the shiva calls were kindly meant and gratefully received. Many came from clients, Molly's and my own. On Friday, Gordon Hayes drove down from Saratoga Springs, and the reunion between him and Mingus had me smiling for the first time in days. Our colleagues, too, came in droves, agents and editors, movie agents and producers, publishers and reviewers. With me they shared stories about Molly, reminisced about her toughness in defense of her clients and all the matches she had made, and not only between writers and publishers: Molly had been a natural matchmaker, with half a dozen marriages to her credit, not counting mine and Hugo's, which she'd opposed right down to the wire. My gaze drifted toward the framed wedding portrait on the table beside the couch. Even as she was buying my wedding dress, Molly had inveighed against the marriage, a contradiction so perfectly *her* that the memory of it made me smile.

Other callers were less welcome. Teddy Pendragon stopped by, but I'd anticipated this and left orders. Jean-Paul intercepted him in the lobby and told him I was not receiving visitors, even as a group of editors emerged from the elevator. There were others whose expressions of sympathy could not disguise their avid curiosity. Though they dared not question me, they didn't hesitate to buttonhole members of my staff. I caught wisps of conversation. "Did Jo really find the body? How is she holding up? What do the police say?" I could excuse it, barely, in the writers. Waving a half-told story under their noses was like teasing a chained dog with a marrow bone. But I found it harder to forgive in the publishing colleagues who gathered every afternoon and evening in my living room. The constant flow of liquor didn't help, loosening lips that ought better have stayed tight.

The fate of the agency was another hot topic. There were rumors that I would not return. I was silent on the subject, for I'd not yet decided what to do. Even though Molly had been retired for two years, she'd remained my closest ally and adviser. It was hard to imagine diving back in the water when I felt there was no ground beneath my feet. And it wasn't just about me. As long as Molly and Rowena's killer was on the loose, the safety of others was at stake. Chloe's parents, I knew, were frantic. They'd called me on Friday morning and begged me to fire their daughter, because Chloe had refused their entreaties to quit. "We're so sorry for your trouble," her mother said, wringing her hands, "but she's our only child, and we are frightened for her." I promised to talk to her. That afternoon I took Chloe into Hugo's study—mine now—and offered her an indefinite leave of absence, with a guaranteed job when she was ready to return, assuming there was an agency to return to.

Chloe's eyes filled with tears, and she looked at me the way I used to look at Molly. "I'm not going anywhere, Jo. If you want me out you'll have to fire me, and if you fire me, I'll, I'll . . . sue you for wrongful termination!"

I spoke to each of the others separately, made the same offer, and received the same reply. A person would have to be made of harder stuff than I was not to be moved by such loyalty. Yet it didn't solve my problem. The killer was still out there; and instead of summoning up the balls to come at me directly, he seemed intent on killing the people close to me. I was a danger, not only to my staff but to my clients as well. The only way I could think of to protect them was to close down the agency, or sell it to Harriet . . . just as that phony press release had claimed.

But how could I quit the agency? The very thought was treacherous, for it meant the killer would have succeeded not only in destroying Molly but also her life's work, and my own. And what would I do with myself, if I couldn't do what I do best?

Because I could not address the rumors, Harriet once again stepped in to fill the breach. "Of course we'll soldier on," she said stoutly, every time the subject arose. "Molly would have it no other way."

It was the right thing to say. Sorrow having rendered me neither blind nor deaf, I'd noticed other agents cozying up to my writers. None would be so crass as to openly solicit a client of mine, but that didn't stop them from maneuvering to reap the spoils if I should drop out. Our clients needed to know we're still there for them, and the industry needed reminding that we're still a force to be reckoned with, so Harriet did well to take the line she did. But I couldn't help wondering what she really thought. Did she see herself as my heir presumptive? I certainly didn't see her that way. Harriet was an excellent agent for certain writers, but she was too conservative, too wedded to the traditions of our industry: a dangerous trait when those norms were in flux. If she took over, the agency would gradually dwindle into the ranks of all the hundreds of midlist players with no particular clout. The thought of it curdled my heart, what was left of it. But Harriet had to be hoping, and perhaps she had some moral right to her expectations. Once I heard her talking to Martha Gale from Random House. They were in the kitchen, washing and drying wineglasses, and didn't notice me entering with a tray. "The agency will absolutely go on," Harriet was saying, with more than her usual emphasis, "whatever she personally decides to do."

I delayed my decision, hoping the police would finally do their job and catch the killer. But no arrest came; and according to my lawyer, the police were wasting precious time investigating me instead of searching for Sam Spade. I don't know where Sean got his information, but he clearly had sources inside the investigation. Forensic tests had borne out the tie between the two murders, the same gun having been used in both. Despite the different jurisdictions, the two investigations had merged into one. The police were pursuing two different theories of the crimes; the fact that they were contradictory showed, I supposed, a certain greatness of mind in the constabulary—that or total idiocy. The first theory was that I had killed both my friends, alone or with a confederate. The second was that I was the indirect target of both murders.

Even without Sean's information, I would have known which way the wind was blowing. My building's doormen were questioned, along with every member of the agency, past and present. Even Max was interviewed, his alibis checked. The police examined surveillance cameras in the building and my garage, E-ZPass records, and my phone records. All of this, along with the negative results of the gunshot residue test, must have confirmed my innocence; and yet it took three precious days for the police to reach that conclusion, and another to convince Sean that they'd reached it.

He still wasn't taking any chances. "We've worked out parameters for this interview," he said, as we sat in the back of his chauffeured Lincoln. It was three o'clock Saturday afternoon; shiva was suspended until sunset, the end of the Jewish Sabbath. "But they may test the boundaries. If I tell you not to answer a question, you don't answer; *capisce*?"

"Got it," I said. We were driving north on the West Side Highway. Rain sluiced across the windshield, and the wipers flashed hypnotically. I stretched out my legs. For the first time in days, I'd given some thought to my attire. What does the well-dressed murder suspect wear to an interview with the police? I remembered Sharon Stone's ploy, but I was in no mood to flash my legs or anything else at these idiots. Instead I went the other way, covering up from head to toe in a black cashmere sweater over jeans, with the same black raincoat I'd worn to the funeral.

The silver-haired detective from the murder scene was waiting when we reached the station. He led us into a small interview room with a mirror on one wall. The only furniture was a table with three chairs, two on the side facing the mirror and the other on the opposite side. It looked a lot like the interview rooms in the city precinct houses: familiar territory these days.

The detective shook our hands and handed me a card with his name on it: Lt. Steven Rosenbaum. "You look better," he said.

"I'm fine." I'd said those words so often they'd worn a groove down my tongue.

"I appreciate you coming in."

"We have agreed," Sean said, in a for-the-record sort of voice, "that this conversation will not be recorded. I will decide what questions my client will or will not answer. Are these conditions accepted?"

"Of course," Rosenbaum said genially, as if they were of little account. He took a pen and notebook from his jacket pocket. "Sit down, won't you? Coffee? No? Then let's begin. I'd like to start with the day Molly died. You and she spent the day together?"

I described our day: the drive upstate, the picnic with Leigh, and the return home.

"Did anything happen out of the usual?"

"We almost hit a deer. But that's not so unusual up there."

"Did you notice any cars following you?"

"No."

"What time did you get to Molly's house?"

"Around nine, maybe a bit after."

"What did you see as you approached her house?"

"Nothing much. A man walking a dog; Halloween decorations on the lawn next door."

"Any other pedestrians?"

"No."

"Any cars parked or standing on the street?"

"If there'd been a car right in front of Molly's house, I'd have noticed. Other than that, I wasn't looking."

"Did you go in with her?"

"No. I wish . . ." I bit off the words, because they were empty now. If I'd gone in, if I'd stayed the night, it might never have happened. But what's the use of wishing? You either do something or you don't. I hadn't.

"Was she expecting anyone?"

"No, I'm sure she wasn't."

"Did you see her enter the house?"

"I waited till the door closed behind her, then I left."

"We found the guy with the dog," the lieutenant said. "He remembers seeing Molly get out of your car. He said she was carrying something."

"Her cane, her purse, and a bag of apples," I said, and I saw it again: Molly on the floor, bloody apples strewn around her. *Don't take any poison apples*, someone had said, but I couldn't remember who. "Did he see me leave?"

"Yes, he did."

I glared at him. "So your theory, which you spent the better part of a week pursuing, was that I dropped Molly off, drove away, remembered that I'd meant to kill her, and came back?"

Rosenbaum appeared unscathed. "It's nothing personal. In a murder investigation, everyone's a suspect till proven innocent."

"I don't care about the insult. It's the wasted time that kills me." I could hardly believe the words gushing from my mouth, the propulsive anger behind them. Sean put his hand on my shoulder, but I shook it off. This was the Peter Principle in action, I thought, people rising to their level of incompetence. Molly deserved better than a bunch of Keystone Kops.

"The next morning," the lieutenant continued, as if I hadn't spoken a word, "you called her number half a dozen times. Why is that?"

"At first just to make sure she was OK. Then I got worried because I couldn't reach her."

"But why did you feel the need to check on her?"

I stared at him. "She was sick. I thought you did an autopsy. Molly had stage-four cancer."

"So you left work and drove up here to check on her. Tell me what you did when you got here."

"I looked in the garage to see if her car was there. Then I rang her bell. No one answered, so I let myself in."

"Before you got to the kitchen, did you see anything out of order in the house, anything that alarmed you or seemed out of place?"

"The smell," I said reproachfully, though that, surely, was no fault of his. I was blaming the messenger again. I'd hated Molly's oncologist, too, for no fault of her own.

"After you found her, what did you do?"

"I called the police."

"You called Detective Cullen first, before you called 911. Why was that?"

I glanced at Sean, hoping he'd object, but he too seemed to be waiting with interest for my reply. "I don't know why," I said. "I was panicked. His number was in my phone. I just did. He told me to hang up and call 911."

"Perfectly understandable," the lieutenant said, "considering that you two are old friends."

Something in the encouraging way he said this made me wary. Sean cut in. "Hang on, Lieutenant. What's that got to do with the price of eggs?"

Rosenbaum looked at him. "If your client is the indirect target of these crimes, as you've argued and we now believe, we're interested in everything about her, including past and present relationships."

"If you mean Detective Cullen," I said, "there is no relationship. He's just someone I used to know a long time ago."

"By 'know' you mean . . . ?"

"We hung out with the same crowd."

Rosenbaum let it go and changed the subject. If he'd been a

boxer, he'd have been light on his feet. The next series of questions were identical to those asked first by Tommy Cullen, then
by the detectives on Rowena's murder. Did I know what the
words on the wall meant? Did I have any enemies? Any spurned
lovers, disaffected clients, murderous rivals? No, I said, no and
no and no, until finally something snapped. "I've been through
this a thousand times. Don't you people talk to each other?"

"It's important to go back at things," Rosenbaum said mildly.
"Sometimes people know things without knowing them."

Thank you, Dr. Freud. "Where's Sam Spade? Why haven't you
caught him yet? What kind of investigation are you running,
Lieutenant?"

Rosenbaum stared at me for a long moment.

"I knew Molly," he said at last.

"You did?"

"We belonged to the same temple. I knew her and I liked her
enormously. You couldn't help it, the kind of person she was. For
her to die like that was an atrocity, and it happened on my watch.
We'll get her killer, Ms. Donovan. It might not play out like it
does in the novels you sell, but it will happen; and I don't need
attitude from you to motivate me."

I muttered an apology.

"Nah," he said, "I get it. It's horrible to have a friend murdered that way. And to find her, as you did . . . Of course you're
angry. But you and me are on the same side here: Molly's side."

He had a sympathetic face. Lots of people would have trusted
that face. I wasn't one of them. "Then why are you wasting time
on the people who loved Molly? You've got to find this Sam Spade
monster before he goes after someone else!"

"We'll get your stalker, but we're not limiting our investigation
to him." He glanced at Sean, then back at me. "There are some
indications that Molly knew her killer."

"What indications?"

"No sign of forced entry or a struggle. Molly opened the door and let the killer in. Seems like someone she trusted."

I imagined her in her house, tired after our long day. It's dark outside, and the street is deserted. The doorbell rings. She peeks through the window and sees a strange man. Does she open the door? Hell no, she doesn't! Molly wasn't the nervous type, but after what happened to Rowena, there's no way she opens that door.

I realized I was shaking my head and stopped. "He must have tricked her somehow. Or maybe he was already inside, waiting. And how can you say there was no sign of a struggle? I saw that kitchen."

"Molly was standing in front of the counter when she was shot. She slumped forward onto the counter and knocked over her purse and the bag of apples before falling to the floor. There was no fight, no struggle. Apart from the gunshot wound and some surgery scars, there wasn't a mark on her body. If it's any comfort, she probably never knew what hit her."

It wasn't.

Rosenbaum turned to a new page in his notebook. "Are you aware of a bequest Molly made—"

"Don't answer that," Sean interrupted. "Lieutenant—"

Rosenbaum raised his hand. "Sorry, Counselor, let me re-phrase. Molly left a bequest of eighty thousand dollars to Harriet Peagoody. Was Ms. Peagoody, to the best of your knowledge, aware of this bequest?"

"I have no idea," I said.

"Why do you think Molly left her so much money?"

"It's not so much, considering that Harriet worked for her for ten years and stayed on even after Molly left. She deserves it."

"What's your relationship with Harriet like?"

I felt the blood rising to my face. If I'd had any confidence in the police, it would have been easier to answer that question truthfully. As it was, I feared they'd make too much of anything I said and set off on the wrong path again.

"She's a loyal and productive employee," I said stiffly.

"That bad, huh?" Rosenbaum said. "You kept us waiting long enough, Ms. Donovan. Least you can do now is be frank. Molly made you partner over Harriet's head, even though Harriet had ten years' seniority. Unless the woman's a saint, and I've never met one of those, she had to resent that."

I shrugged. "Maybe she did, but she stuck with us all the same. I don't judge people by how they feel, Lieutenant; I judge them by what they do. Harriet's been stalwart and kind. I couldn't have gotten through the last week without her. She was with me constantly, looking after me. On the day of the funeral—" I stopped abruptly, aware I was blathering on. Both men were looking at me strangely.

"On the day of the funeral . . . ?" Rosenbaum prompted.

"She gave me a Valium."

He looked astonished. "You took a pill from her?"

"I didn't, as it happens. The point is, she was trying to help."

"What'd you do with it?"

"I don't know, shoved it in my pocket, most likely." I remembered that I was wearing the same raincoat now as then, and felt in the pockets. The pill was still there, soggy but intact. The lieutenant took it from me and dropped it into a clear plastic bag.

I felt my temper rising again. "If you focus on Harriet, you'll just be wasting more damn time. Harriet loved Molly as much as I did. There's no way in hell she could walk up to Molly and shoot her."

Rosenbaum leaned back in his seat and regarded me for a long moment before answering. "Molly was killed by the same person who murdered Rowena Blair, but there's one significant difference. Rowena was facing the perp when she was shot. Molly took a bullet to the back of her head."

"What does that signify?"

"It suggests," he said, "that whoever did this couldn't just—what were your words?—walk up to Molly and shoot her."

Chapter 25

The doorman must have been watching. As soon as Sean's Lincoln glided into the no-standing zone in front of my building, Morris ran out holding a big black umbrella. I kissed Sean's cheek and stepped into a cold, driving rain. The weather had done what nothing else could have: cleared away the reporters and gawkers. "Some night," the doorman said as we hurried into the lobby. He summoned the elevator and lingered by my side. "Just wanted to say, ma'am, I'm sorry for your loss. Mrs. Hamish was a real nice lady."

"Thanks, Morris." I smiled up at his grizzled, bulldog face. Morris was the oldest of our doormen, semiretired, working just a few weekend shifts.

"You expecting more visitors tonight?"

"Maybe, though in this weather . . . Morris, you've been here a long time, haven't you?"

"Sure have. Thirty-five years in this building, longer than I been married. When I die, they gonna bury me in the lobby."

"Do you happen to remember who was living in Mr. Donovan's apartment before we married?"

"Ma'am?" he said, stalling. I could see the wariness in his eyes. Doormen have their codes of conduct, as all professions do, and discretion had to be a large part of theirs. No one likes a gossipy doorman; they see too much.

"Was there a woman living there? With a child, maybe?"

"Oh, jeez," he said. "That was a long time ago." I waited. "I think maybe he had a housekeeper for a while. And the housekeeper had a little one."

Of course, I thought. A maid, not a lover. Suddenly it all made sense. "What was her name?"

"Oh, you got me there, Mrs. Donovan."

"And the child? Was it a boy or a girl?"

He squinted into middle distance. "A little boy, I think. No, a girl, definitely a girl. Or was it a boy?" The elevator arrived while he was still debating with himself, and I rode up alone. It was satisfying to have one small puzzle resolved, but less than it should have been without Molly to enlighten. For me that was the hardest part of her death to absorb, even more than its brutality: the suddenness, which left me choking on all the things I should have said.

I'd thought we had time.

Though shiva had resumed at sunset, the weather had kept everyone away except Max, who'd brought the baby, and my faithful staff. I found it hard to look at Harriet after hearing Rosenbaum's insinuations. I knew they were false; I knew the police had tried to pin the murders on me, too. And yet they'd sullied her in my mind, and left me feeling angry without knowing why.

Maybe that's why I reacted the way I did to her remark. She wasn't the first. Others had voiced similar idiocies in my hearing and I'd merely tightened my lips and turned away. But Harriet should have known better.

Someone had lit a fire in the living room, and we gathered

around it, drinking mulled whiskey that Chloe, who'd spent a gap year tending bar in Dublin, had prepared for everyone. The absence of outsiders was a relief. I slipped off my boots and curled up on one of the sofas, while Mingus stretched out on the floor beside me. Jean-Paul asked what the police said, and everyone turned to me.

"They're clueless," I said. "They're chasing their tails."

"You don't know that," Max said. He was feeding the baby, who kept falling asleep on the bottle and then jerking awake to suck vigorously for a moment or two before dozing off again. "They're not going to tell you what they know."

"They asked all the wrong questions."

"The lead guy, Rosenbaum, is no slouch. I asked around. He was an NYPD homicide detective before he moved to Westchester."

Lorna said, "I heard once on TV that if the cops don't solve a murder within forty-eight hours, chances are they never will."

My heart sank, for she'd touched on my greatest fear. As long as the killer was free, I was in limbo.

"Thanks, Lorna," Jean-Paul said. "That's real helpful."

She lowered her eyes. "Sorry."

"Of course they'll catch him," Harriet said in her brisk, English nanny tone. "Molly and Rowena were not some inner-city riffraff killed in a drive-by. They mattered."

In the silence that followed this remark, Chloe and Jean-Paul exchanged glances, and Max raised an eyebrow. I knew then that if I quit the agency, Max would, too. Without me, and without the income generated by Max's and Rowena's books, the spoils would be meager indeed. Harriet could lose other clients, too. Some writers would be too afraid of losing representation to jump ship, but the most successful ones knew they had choices. An agency is a nebulous thing, constructed of relationships. Harriet might inherit the kingdom only to find it a ghost town.

"The important thing," she continued, "is to keep a positive outlook and take comfort where we can."

"What comfort is that?" I asked.

It was a rhetorical question, but she answered it. "Well, I for one find some in knowing that even though the end was sudden, it was relatively painless, and Molly was spared the suffering we all knew was coming."

Her words shot through me like a bolt. I sat up, glaring. "How can you say that? Are you really that stupid?"

Instead of getting angry, she shrank back in her chair. "Jo, please! All I meant is that I've seen people die of cancer, and it's a terrible way to go."

"So it was a mercy killing. Maybe we should find this monster and thank him, what do you think?"

A chorus of protests broke out. "Easy, Jo . . . Harriet didn't mean . . . no one's suggesting . . ." Only Lorna was silent, looking wide-eyed from Harriet to me like a child watching her parents quarrel.

I had the feeling, so familiar of late, of a breached levee within me. Words gushed out of my mouth, as unstoppable as the stream in Leigh's painting. "Molly could have ended it herself if she'd chosen to. She had the knowledge and the means. That's *not* what she wanted. She told me she meant to squeeze every last drop of juice out of her life. She wanted to revisit places she'd loved. She wanted to see her garden bloom and her writers prosper. She wanted one more Shakespeare in the Park. She wanted to see this little baby walk, and maybe she could have. She wanted to spend time with the people she loved. And it was *her* time to spend. Every day was precious, more precious than a hundred of ours, because she had so few left. That's what this murdering bastard stole from her. And for this you are thankful!"

Harriet was hunched over in her chair. One hand covered her

eyes, and her spiky gray head bobbed with muted sobs. I came back to myself feeling as if I'd stabbed her with a knife.

"I'm sorry, Harriet, I'm so sorry!" I rushed over and tried to embrace her, but she pulled away. Then I fled, like the coward I was, down the hall to my bedroom with the dog at my heels. I slammed the door and threw myself onto the bed. Mingus nudged me with his muzzle, his brow contracted in a very human expression of worry. "I'm fine," I said automatically, then groaned with despair: now I was lying even to the dog.

A knock came at the door. I ignored it. The door opened, and Max walked in with Molly on his shoulder. He sat beside me on the edge of the bed and shifted her to his lap. When Mingus came over to investigate, the baby gazed back at him with huge eyes and a wide-open mouth. I stroked her fine black hair, soft as dandelion wisps, and felt the steady pulse beneath the fontanel.

"How are you?" Max said. "And if you say 'fine' again, I'm going to smack you."

"Is Harriet all right?"

"Who cares?"

"I was awful to her."

"Yes. It was quite a relief."

I sat up. "My losing it is a relief?"

"You acting human is. I was starting to wonder."

"But Harriet of all people. She's been solid, Max."

"It was a moronic thing to say. One of a series from her."

"That's not the point."

"No," he said, "it's not. The point is, you're a Spartan. I know exactly what Molly meant to you, yet all week long I've watched you stonewall your grief. It's admirable as hell; you broke my fucking heart at the funeral. But my God, woman, don't you know you're allowed to cry? It's the one privilege your sex is allowed; you ought to take it."

"I can't," I said. "I'm afraid to. Once I started, how would I stop?"

"It sort of stops by itself. And you can. In fact," he said, handing me the diaper from his shoulder, "you're crying now."

He held me tight as the last levee collapsed, and murmured in my ear. "It's OK, let it come. When it's over, you'll still be here."

"And Molly still won't," I gasped.

"And Molly still won't."

What happens, I discovered, is that you run out of tears. Afterward, my nose was stuffed, but my spirit felt less congested. The body, it seemed, had its own mourning to do.

Max let go and studied my face. "Better?"

"If you think one good cry will wash away all my sorrows, you've been drinking the water at Disney, my friend."

"Now, that's the Jo we all know and fear! And a good thing, too, because you look like hell. Who'd have guessed you were the type to get all bloodshot and blotchy when you cry?"

"Everyone does," I said, wiping my face with the diaper.

"Nonsense. Your average romantic heroine turns dewy and ethereal when she weeps. I learned this from Rowena."

I laughed—couldn't help it. "What am I going to do, Max?"

"What everyone does when they've lost someone. Go on with your life and fake it till the feeling comes back."

The baby had fallen asleep with her fist in her mouth. Max laid her down between us. She had tiny, perfect hands, translucent fingernails the size of diamond chips. I stroked the palm of one hand, and it closed around my finger. I felt a tug inside me.

"So that's it?" I asked. "Molly is dead; long live Molly?"

"What else is there?" Max said.

On Monday I went back to work. Max flew home with Barry and the baby, but only after coming into the office to meet with building security. We were once again on full alert. Visitors would be screened twice, downstairs by security and upstairs by Lorna. Our doors were to be kept locked, our phones were tapped, and the police were on speed-dial. Mingus would accompany me to and from work, and Jean-Paul would escort me anywhere the dog couldn't. All these precautions created a siege-like atmosphere in the office. But even within the gates, all was not well. Harriet greeted my arrival with a cool stare. "You're back, then," she said.

Clearly I was not forgiven.

"Of course," I said, as if I hadn't spent most of the night wavering back and forth. By forging on, I was endangering the people I cared for. But the best way of protecting us all was to catch Sam Spade, and the best way to do that was to put myself out there as bait. I had to go back.

But no sooner did I make that decision than I began to second-guess it. What if he didn't come for me? What if, instead, I got a call one day informing me that Jean-Paul or Chloe or another of my writers had been murdered? How would I live with that?

I didn't know what was best, and with Molly gone, there was no one to ask. In the end, my choice was a selfish one. I would go on because I wanted to go on. Molly's last words were etched in my heart. *You're not who you are because Hugo married you. He married you because of who you are.* For the first time in my life, faced with the loss of the agency, I acknowledged the truth in that. Hugo was a genius and I am far from that, but I had been as good for him as he had been for me. When I read his drafts, I saw not only what the story was, but also what it wanted to become. The first time we met, Hugo and I didn't bond over sex and a shared predilection for May-December romance, as everyone assumed. Our first night together was spent chastely talking about his work. I'd read all of his published books, most of them more than once, and I'd read the new manuscript on the train from New York. Of all living writers, Hugo was the one I admired most. Did I, as Molly claimed, purposely misunderstand her instructions in order to engineer a meeting? If I did, I have no memory of it; but I wouldn't put it past the starstruck little bookworm I was back then. I'd loved Hugo's stories before I loved him, and he'd loved my understanding of them before he ever thought of loving me. Perhaps it was always what he loved best.

I marched past Harriet to my office and sat at the desk I'd inherited from Molly; and from somewhere deep inside my head, I heard the echo of her voice. *Once more unto the breach, kiddo.*

There was a ton of work to catch up on, starting with several hundred e-mails. I worked my way steadily through them, deleting the ones from reporters, delegating others to Jean-Paul and Lorna. Two hours later, I was down to a few dozen that needed a personal response when Harriet walked into my office without knocking. "We need to talk."

Never a harbinger of good news, that phrase. I waved her to a chair and waited with what I would call a sense of impending disaster, if that were not now my normal state. Harriet lowered herself stiffly into the chair. She did not look good. Her face was pale, with red splotches on her cheeks, and her gray hair was in a state of anarchy. She looked like I felt, which was where we differed.

"I need to know where I stand," she blurted.

"Where you've always stood," I said. "Nothing's changed."

"That's not good enough. I've been with this agency for longer than you have. It's time I became a partner."

It was out now, the five-hundred-pound gorilla crouching between us, and I hadn't so much as a banana to feed it.

"Harriet," I said, "I'm incredibly grateful for everything you've done, not only this past week, but in all the time you've been here. I understand your feelings, and I'm willing to discuss your future here, but frankly, your timing amazes me. You must understand that I'm in no shape to make major decisions right now."

"No—*you* must understand that I can't go on waiting and hoping for you to do the right thing. I know this is a bad time; it's a bad time for me, too, in case you haven't noticed. But this should be a no-brainer. I've earned this. I deserve it."

She had a point. She'd paid her dues and then some. But a partnership is a bond almost as profound as marriage, and as I looked at Harriet's haughty, pinched mouth and censorious eyes, I felt the dawning of something like dread. It was one thing to work with her, but the agency would be different with Harriet as a partner, and not, I feared, in a good way.

And yet I didn't want her to leave, either. Prickly though she was, I respected both her taste and her toughness. Her clients were a reliable bunch who brought in a steady stream of revenue and added heft to the agency. If she left, she would take them with her; I could not and would not do to her what I'd done to Charlie. If it was simply a matter of money, if she wanted a larger share of the pie, I could accommodate her. But how could I submit to a shotgun wedding?

I told her I needed time to think. Harriet didn't soften at all, which, under different circumstances, was one of the things I liked about her.

"Think fast, then, because I do have other options. I love this agency and it would break my heart to leave it. But I won't go on as before."

I wondered then if she knew about Molly's bequest. "If you're thinking of going solo, that's your right, of course. But I'm sure we can come up with a less risky solution."

"That is *not* my only option," she said testily.

Mingus didn't like her tone. He sat up and gave her a hard stare, which she ignored. I nudged him with my foot and motioned him down. The trouble with a German shepherd for an ally is that you can't actually deploy him. What was Harriet talking about? Where would she go if she left me? She wouldn't leave just to go work for another agent; someone must have offered her a partnership, but who? No sooner did I ask the question than the answer came to me. I gasped. "Not Charlie Malvino!"

"Never you mind," Harriet said, but a blush broke through her pale skin and I knew I was right.

"No, really, Harriet? How could—I mean, the two of you are so different."

"You and I are different; that never stopped us working together."

"Yes, but you and Charlie are at opposite ends of the spectrum."

"Which some people might say makes us perfect for each other."

"Some people meaning Charlie?" It explained so much: their lunch, her indignation on his behalf, even the whispering at Molly's funeral. And yet I could hardly wrap my mind around it. When they were both on the agency staff, they used to squabble incessantly in staff meetings. Harriet was nearly twenty years older and far more experienced, but Charlie, always a cheeky devil, had no respect. He used to imitate her accent and manner right to her face. "Queen Harriet," he'd called her, and "Your Ladyship." If Charlie was courting her now, it could only be to hurt me.

I looked closely at Harriet, who now wore a smug, secretive little smile, and a dark thought struck me. Could Charlie have gone so far in his malice as to actually seduce her? I tried to banish that thought to the pit from which it had escaped, but it left its traces, which mingled with those left by Lieutenant Rosenbaum into a noxious brew.

"Class and crass, he calls it," Harriet said, dropping all pretense now. "I'm the class, he's the crass. We balance each other out."

"Or cancel each other out. Harriet, be careful."

"*You* be careful." It sounded like a threat. We stared at each other. The room was so quiet I could hear Mingus breathing.

Harriet composed her features. "I meant you should consider the matter carefully. I belong here. We both do. But things have to change."

I thought about that, disliking both my options. Losing Harriet now would leave a big hole in the agency. I'd never replaced Charlie; so I'd have to find another agent or two. Jean-Paul was too green for promotion, and Lorna wasn't agent material. Chloe was, but she was Harriet's assistant and would probably go with her. I'd lose all those clients, too.

Maybe I could I live with Harriet as a partner, I thought. Would it really be so different from the way things were presently? Maybe if she got what she'd wanted for so long, she'd be less abrasive. Still, something in me recoiled from the thought of giving in to her. Why now of all times? Was Charlie pressuring her, or had Harriet herself decided to strike when I was most vulnerable? I wished I could talk it over with Molly.

"I'll think about it," I said.

The door had barely closed behind her when Lorna staggered in under the weight of an enormous vase of lilies. She set it down on my desk.

"What's this?" I said.

"No idea. There's a card."

I opened the card.

> *Dear Jo,*
> *My deepest sympathies for your loss.*
>
> *Your devoted, Sam Spade*

Chapter 26

For the next two days I subsisted on black coffee and aspirin, sleeping in fits. When I wasn't obsessing over Sam Spade, I was dithering over Harriet's ultimatum. On the second night I dreamed that Molly called me from Frankfurt. There was static on the line, other conversations bleeding through, but I knew it was her. "Molly?" I called, pressing my ear to the receiver. "Molly, I can't hear you." Men were shouting in the background, and a woman cried out in pain or fear. There came another burst of static, then, in a sudden patch of clarity, Molly said, "Can you hear me now?"

After that I quit my bed and trudged into the kitchen. By the time the coffee had brewed, the sun was rising over Central Park; beyond it, the spectral city glowed. I carried my cup onto the terrace. A film crew was setting up across the street for an early-morning shoot. The morning air was chilly, but I was warm, wrapped in Hugo's cashmere robe. I breathed the textured city air and let the bitter brew revive me.

Later Wednesday morning I was sitting in my office reviewing contracts when the door burst open and Lorna hurtled in, holding a phone to her ear in one hand and gesturing wildly with the other. "Can you hold on a moment, Mr. Spade? She's on the other line, but I know she wants to talk to you."

My whole body jerked. Coffee sloshed onto the contract I'd been reading, but I didn't stop to wipe it up. I speed-dialed Tommy on my cell. He answered immediately.

"It's him, Sam Spade," I whispered. "He's on the office line now."

"You know what to do," Tommy said, as calmly as if discussing the weather. "Keep him on as long as you can. Make an appointment to meet, preferably in your office."

I hung up and nodded at Lorna. "Mr. Spade?" she said. "I slipped her a note. She said don't hang up, she'll get off as soon as she can. She's very anxious to talk to you. Was it you who sent those beautiful flowers?"

She was supposed to stall him at least three minutes before I picked up, then I would stall some more. If all went optimally, we'd hear him arrested. Lorna's words were right, but the music was all wrong. She sounded like a bad actress reciting lines. If this guy was half as antsy as he ought to be, she'd scare him off for sure.

I made an executive decision and picked up the phone. "Is this really the elusive Mr. Spade?" The words came out in a flirtatious Southern drawl. I don't know why. Maybe it was easier to play a part with a voice other than my own.

"Jo, is that you?" His voice was deep and raspy, as if he, too, were playing a part.

"It's me. Thanks, Lorna, I've got it now."

Lorna hung up but didn't leave the room. Harriet, Jean-Paul, and Chloe hurried in, drawn no doubt by Lorna's unprecedented scramble. I signaled for silence and put the call on speakerphone.

"Sam," I said, "I have to tell you, I loved the novel."

There was a pause so long I feared I'd lost him. Then he said, in a voice crackling with emotion, "You don't know how long I've waited to hear you say those words."

"Well, you've kept me waiting too. Quite a tease, sending a manuscript like that with no contact information. I started reading the day you delivered it and couldn't stop till I'd finished. I've been hoping you'd call ever since."

Was I laying it on too thick? But there is no "too thick" for writers. They're all gluttons for praise.

"I knew you'd feel that way," Sam Spade said, proving the point, "if I could only get your attention."

"You've got it now."

"I'd have called sooner if it weren't for recent tragic events."

I squeezed the phone so hard my knuckles turned white. I wanted to reach down the line and shove it down his throat. Instead I picked up my letter-opener, a short dagger with a mother-of-pearl hasp that Hugo bought me in Marrakesh, and started jabbing my mouse pad.

"Thank you for the lilies," I said.

"You're welcome. Sorry to cut this short, Jo, but I can't talk now. We should meet."

I glanced at my watch. What felt like the longest conversation of my life had lasted less than a minute. "Absolutely, as soon as possible. Just a few questions first, while I have you on the line. Do any other agents have the manuscript?"

He sounded hurt. "Of course not. You're the only agent I ever considered."

Lucky me. "Have any publishers seen it?"

"No, that's your job."

"I know half a dozen who'll be interested. We may even get an auction going, though I'm not one to count my chickens before they're hatched. Is this really your first novel?"

"The first of many, now that we're together."

"I find that amazing, considering the level of maturity and sophistication in the writing. How long did you work on it?"

"Twelve weeks," he said proudly. "I was on fire. It felt like the story was being dictated, if you know what I mean."

"I do," I said, avoiding the eyes of my staffers. "Many great writers have described that feeling. What's your real name, by the way? I can't keep calling you Sam Spade."

"Why not? You christened me; I've adopted the name."

"You can publish under any pen name you like, but as your representative, I need to know who you really are."

"When we meet, I promise you'll find out all you need to know about me."

"Then let's meet soon. When can you come in?"

"To your office? No, I think not. Sam Spade, like many writers, is an intensely private person, as tongue-tied in person as he is eloquent on paper."

Pompous asshole, talking about himself in the third person, reciting from some imagined biography. I looked at my watch. Only two minutes had passed.

"Lunch, then," I said, "or a drink. I know some quiet places where we can talk. Before we get together, though, I'd like to do a little preliminary planning, maybe put out a feeler or two. Have you given any thought to who you'd like to publish you?"

"We can talk about it when we meet."

"Of course. Can I take you to lunch? Michael's, maybe, or the Four Seasons? Or would you rather meet for a drink?"

"Columbus Circle," he said, "in the entrance to the park. We'll take a carriage ride."

Jean-Paul was shaking his head violently.

"Not a fan of carriage rides," I said. "Unlike you, I'm an intensely public person."

Chloe had to clap a hand over her mouth to mute a nervous

titter, but from Sam Spade I got only a reproachful pause. "Indulge me, if you will," he said. "I've been planning this for a long time. Six o'clock this evening, Columbus Circle. Till then, my dear Jo." At once, as if to stave off a refusal, he hung up.

"Wait," I said uselessly, then dropped the phone into its cradle and scrubbed my hand on my skirt.

The others stared at me. "Well, hello there, Scarlett O'Hara," Harriet said, mimicking my drawl. "If you're not just full of surprises."

I ran past them to the bathroom, slammed the door, and spewed black coffee into the sink.

"You don't have to do this." Tommy Cullen turned away as the female tech positioned a tiny transmitter inside my bra. "We have an officer on standby, your height, your shape. Slap on a wig and a pair of dark glasses and your own mother would mistake her for you."

"She might," I said, "but this guy knows what I look like." The three of us were alone. I'd sent the others home for the day. Jean-Paul left last, under protest, to take Mingus back to my apartment. Neither he nor the dog could come with me tonight, lest they spook our quarry.

"You'll be fine," the tech said, snipping a piece of tape. "There'll be more cops than pigeons in the park. Just try not to sweat."

"How?" I asked, sweating already. Sam Spade wouldn't show, I told myself. He'd been smart enough to call from a prepaid cell phone and keep the conversation short enough to evade capture, so why would he walk into an obvious trap? This was just another torment, another game for him. No doubt he'd be watching from a distance, laughing.

But in my gut I didn't believe it. I know writers' fantasies, and during our brief conversation, I'd played into every one of Spade's. I'd hooked him good, with the help of his monstrous ego, which told him he was a genius who deserved every word I said. There was another reason why I knew he'd come too, one closer to the heart of his obsession. Every story needs an ending. Everything Sam Spade did, he did to get at me. He'd invented a fantasy; then he sabotaged my business, tormented my clients, and finally murdered my friends just to bring it about. If he wasn't building toward a personal encounter, none of it made sense.

The tech finished and left, shutting my office door behind her. Tommy and I were alone. I tapped the transmitter. "Is this thing on?"

"Not yet," he said.

"That Westchester detective asked me about you."

"Figured he would," he said dismissively.

"About our history. I said we were casual acquaintances."

"Figured that, too, since I'm still on the case. Look, Jo, are you sure you're up—"

"Positive."

"OK. There'll be plainclothes police all around you. Don't look for them. Chances are this skell won't show, but if he does, try to engage him in conversation. Don't interrogate him, but if he's inclined to boast, encourage it. Whatever happens, you do not get into a carriage or any other vehicle with him. If he tries to force you, if he shows a weapon, we will take him down. If he walks away from you, we will take him down. Do you understand?"

I nodded, not trusting my voice.

"You have to act normal. Let's see a smile."

I flashed one. A corner of his mouth twitched in response. "Atta girl. I heard tape of the phone call. You'll do fine."

"I'm sweating like a pig."

He came toward me, took a handkerchief from his jacket

pocket, and dabbed my brow. When he finished, he didn't step away. My back was to the desk. I couldn't have backed up if I'd wanted to, but I didn't want to. I held his eyes and raised my face.

He kissed me.

He was a great kisser, always was. How could I have forgotten? All his nature was in his kiss, the sweet and the hard of it. What started as a question ended as a statement. My body recognized the smell and feel of his body pressed against mine, and I responded. For a moment all the fear and sorrow were gone, and I thought, If this isn't great, what is?

It was Tommy who pulled away. We stared at each other, both of us breathing hard.

"I'm sorry," he said. "That was totally inappropriate."

"But nice."

"*Nice?*" he said, pretending outrage—or was he pretending?

"Timing's a bit iffy," I said.

"There's always something. Are you ready?"

"Give me a moment, will you?"

After he left, I took the Moroccan dagger from my desk and slipped it into my jacket pocket.

I was the tethered goat in *Jurassic Park*. For months I'd been living in purdah, unapproachable. Now, sitting alone on a bench just inside Central Park, I felt as exposed as if I were naked. I knew there were police around but couldn't identify them. That canoodling couple on the bench across from me? His hand kneaded her thigh; would cops do that? Those tourists studying a city map? The chestnut seller? The maintenance man? The girl in horn-rimmed glasses reading a book and munching an apple?

I'd arrived alone by taxi, fifteen minutes early, and taken possession of an empty bench just inside the park entrance, beside the horse carriages. The air smelled of horse sweat and roasted chestnuts. I spread out my bag and book carrier beside me to discourage casual loiterers and waited. Normally I'd have brought a book or manuscript to pass the time, but to an egomaniac like Sam Spade, that would be like arriving for a date with another man in tow. Just as I was the only agent for him, so must he be the only writer in my life. I'd been tempted, though, to bring along the book I was currently rereading: *The Wolves Among Us,* by a client of mine, Dr. Avery Broome. Sam Spade, I'd concluded, fit squarely into Avery's definition of a psychopath. He was utterly self-centered, shallow, and manipulative; lacked empathy and shame; and was willing to mow down anyone who stood between him and his goal. For Spade, I was an object to be cajoled, terrorized, and coerced into playing the role he'd determined for me.

There was logic in this concept of my tormenter, but no possible satisfaction. According to Avery, psychopaths are human in appearance and intelligence only. Their physiological responses are different from those of normal people, and their social orientation is that of a solitary predator, a lone wolf or grizzly bear; so labeling Spade a psychopath took human causality out of the picture and rendered my most pressing question—Why?—as irrelevant as if my friends had died in a tsunami.

Six o'clock came and went. The streetlights came on. A brisk breeze cycloned leaves through the park; the carriage horses tossed their plumed heads and clanked their bits. I shivered. A young man in a trench coat strode in under the park arches and looked around him, smiling with anticipation. I froze, but his eyes slid past me and fastened on the girl in the horn-rimmed glasses. She snapped her book shut and flew into his arms. *Young love,* I thought, and it was only then I remembered that I, too, had once waited there for a man. In my case, though, it hadn't been to run to him, but to break up with him.

The rising wind seemed to penetrate my pores and swirl

around inside me. *Another coincidence?* I heard Max ask. But what else could it be? Sam Spade was real, corporeal. I'd whacked him with an umbrella, I'd spoken to him on the phone, and any moment now he was going to appear. This had nothing to do with me and Tommy.

I wished Mingus were with me.

Hand in hand, the young couple strode off into the park. I turned to watch them go. When I turned back, a man was standing in front of me. He smiled hopefully, but I knew at a glance that this was just some random doofus trying his luck. He was too old, too ordinary—a nebbish, Molly would have called him. His thin hair was the color of dirty dishwater, and his features were so indeterminate, so inconsequential, that I forgot his face even as I looked at it, which I did for just a moment before turning away.

"Hello, Jo," he said.

"*You?*" Outraged, I whipped my head around. "You're Sam Spade?"

"In the flesh. May I?"

I cleared a space for him to my left, keeping my bags between us. Could this really be the man who had ripped my life apart, this little sad sack of a man? He wore what he no doubt imagined was a writer's uniform: a tweed jacket with patches on the elbows and corduroy slacks that swished when he moved.

"You're a hard woman to reach, Jo," he said.

"So I'm told. Didn't stop you, though, did it?"

"I can be very persistent. Good thing for both of us."

"Not so good for my friends."

His colorless eyes blinked at the unscripted line. "What's that?"

Slow down, I told myself. Draw him out; make him confess. "You attended that writers' conference in Santa Fe, didn't you?"

He beamed. "You remember."

"I remember you gave me a plot summary, but you never showed up to discuss it."

"Wasn't the right time. All those wannabes. You wouldn't have seen me in the right light."

"It would have saved a lot of trouble if you'd spoken to me then."

"It would have saved even more," he said, with a touch of asperity, "if you hadn't rejected me in the first place. Not that I blame you, Jo. I blame the people around you who kept us apart." He leaned toward me, and I thought he was going to touch me. *Go ahead,* I thought at him. My right hand was in my jacket pocket. *Give me an excuse.*

He kept his hands on his thighs. "All I wanted was for you to read my book."

"You don't feel you went too far?"

"No, why would I? Artists are meant to push the boundaries. We're outliers; the usual rules don't apply. You know that, surely. You couldn't have been married to Hugo Donovan without knowing it."

It didn't escape me that this was the very argument I'd made on Hugo's behalf. It sounded specious, coming from him. It sounded foul.

"Writing's a job like any other," I said. "It doesn't convey absolution."

"It did for him," he said serenely. "It will for me."

"Seriously, man, you dare compare yourself to Hugo?"

"I know he was a better writer. But he's gone, and I'm just coming into my powers. There's greatness in me, Jo, I've always known that. All I needed was the right muse to bring it out, and now I've found her."

He smiled. His breath stank of tuna fish and mints. It made me sick. Beyond loathing, though, I felt a jarring dissonance, like the feeling you get when a novel you're enjoying suddenly lurches off track. How could it be, how was it possible that this puffed-up nothing, this waste of skin, could bring down two great women who towered head and shoulders above him?

"You promised," I said, "that when we met you'd answer my questions."

He lowered his watery eyes and whispered, "Stanley."

"What?"

"Stanley Drucklehoff. You can see why I'd need a nom de plume."

"I don't give a fuck what your name is. I want to know why you did it."

"Did what?" he said.

I have read Hannah Arendt; I know all about the banality of evil. But "banal" was too banal a word. This was murderous vapidity, lethal stupidity. The question came to me again, more insistently this time. How could this nebbish have tricked two of the world's smartest women into letting him in?

A cold draft ruffled the hair on the back of my neck, and suddenly I felt the presence of Rowena and Molly hovering behind me. Back in Hoyer's Creek, people used to say that a murder victim never rested until the blood of his killer was sprinkled on his grave. I'd rejected that superstition along with all the rest, but it came back to me now with the force of conviction. Something was owed these ghosts, and it had fallen to me. I closed my hand on the dagger's hasp. Its blade was sharp enough to slice envelopes, but too dull and short to kill. It would do damage, though, and damage needed to be done.

"Why Molly?" I said. "Why Rowena?"

"Why ask me? I'm not God, though I may write like him." He tittered. His laugh, surprisingly high-pitched, sounded like a neighing horse.

"You promised me answers."

"I thought you meant my real name, not the meaning of life.

But since you ask, sure, I'll take a shot. Why do bad things happen to good people? I believe there's always a reason. Maybe old relationships have to die to make room for new ones. Death is nature's way of opening our eyes to what else is out there."

"Which makes you what, a force of nature?"

"Me? I'm just a writer."

"No, you're not."

He blinked, puzzled but still smiling, like a man waiting for the punch line to a joke. "What do you mean?"

"I mean you have zero talent. You can't write. Not even a vanity publisher would touch that so-called novel of yours. It was the worst drivel I've ever read."

He looked like Dracula in the moment the stake enters his heart. "No, that's . . . What do you mean? How can you look me in the face and say that? You love my work. You said so yourself."

"I lied."

"You're lying now."

I leaned in close. "All the talent in the world wouldn't justify what you've done, but you have none. No talent, no taste, and nothing to say. You did it all for nothing."

I might as well have used the dagger. He was bleeding out in front of me. Never in my life had I spoken such words to a writer; wouldn't have thought myself capable of it. I've always respected the effort, if not the result, for a writer can pour as much of his heart's blood into a bad novel as a good one. Now I felt like one of those perverts who gets off on crushing small animals underfoot. But he murdered Rowena, I told myself. He murdered Molly.

Sam Spade stumbled to his feet. He reeled away from me, and without thinking I flew after him. Suddenly the entire park seemed to explode into motion. Two men appeared out of nowhere to grab Spade and hurl him to the ground. A pair of arms caught me around the waist and swung me away. "Put it away, you idiot," a voice said, close to my ear. Tommy Cullen's voice. I had no idea what he meant until I glanced down and noticed the dagger in my hand. I shoved it into my pocket, and Tommy let go.

Sam Spade writhed on the ground, hands cuffed behind him, surrounded by a knot of men. After a moment, one of them separated himself from the group and trotted over. I recognized Suarez, who'd led the investigation into Rowena's murder.

"You did good, Mrs. Donovan," he said. "You're a gutsy lady."

"He didn't confess."

"This ain't *Columbo*. You did good." Suarez hesitated. He looked like he had something more to say and it was giving him agita. "One of my guys saw a knife."

"No, he didn't," Tommy said before I could answer.

"He's pretty sure."

"He's mistaken."

They stared at each other. Behind them I saw Sam Spade being hoisted to his feet. Dead leaves and bits of gravel clung to his face. The murderer lunged at me, but his captors held him back. "You bitch, you fucking bitch! You'll pay for this!"

Suarez looked at Spade, then back at Tommy, and finally at me.

"Tricky thing, lamplight," he said.

Chapter 27

"Ladies, gentlemen, and writers," I began, to the accompaniment of much laughter and the clinking of forks against glass. Being for the most part unseated, my guests could not rise; but they quieted and turned toward me. Standing on a platform at the end of the room, I continued. "As you know, the police have arrested the man we believe responsible for the murders of Rowena Blair and Molly Hamish. Although this man has not yet been charged with the murders, he is being held on related charges, and I fully expect that once the police finish their investigation, he will be held to account for all his crimes."

A burst of applause greeted this announcement. I beamed at the crowd, which consisted of the people who'd sustained me over the past months: the editors who'd made a point of signing my books, the clients who'd stood by me despite their own victimization, friends, fellow agents, and, above all, my faithful staff. At the margins of the room, the sleek, black-clad waiters held their trays and waited for me to finish.

"No arrest or conviction can restore what was taken from us. But I have learned—you have shown me—how much remains. Without the love and support of the people in this room, plus a few who couldn't be here tonight, I never would have made it through. To you, my friends." I raised my glass.

Another round of applause, then the waiters plunged back into the fray, holding high their trays. Renting Maison D'être for the evening, even a Monday evening, had been a great extravagance, but my gratitude demanded expression, and there could not have been a more fitting venue than the restaurant where Molly, Rowena, and I had last been together, the night Rowena made her entrance on a litter carried by four half-naked men.

I stepped off the platform and made my way around the room, greeting my guests. Keyshawn Grimes, looking every inch the up-and-coming writer in a suit jacket and jeans, broke off a conversation with his editor to kiss me on both cheeks. We exchanged a few words and I moved on through the crowded room. Most of the writers victimized by Sam Spade had come, along with other clients who'd gone out of their way to express their concern and support during the whole ordeal. Jean-Paul and Lorna were tasked with making sure none were left standing alone, a duty Jean-Paul performed with his usual social fluency and Lorna with a grim doggedness that normally would have annoyed the hell out of me but today seemed a welcome sign of normality. Their ministrations left Chloe free to make the rounds of editors, and I could tell by the swath of smiles and handshakes that she was introducing herself as Hamish and Donovan's newest full-fledged agent. I looked about for Harriet but couldn't spot her in the mass of people, nearly all taller than me.

Near the bar, my client and lawyer, Sean Mallory, was chatting with Leigh Pfeffer, whose painting he'd seen at my place and admired. Beside him, Teddy Pendragon held forth to a group of people including Larry Sharpe, publisher of Pellucid, and a couple of agents. Teddy was the only person in the room I was not happy to see, but I had no one but myself to blame for his presence.

The arrest of Sam Spade (as I continued to think of him,

though his real name was in fact Stanley Drucklehoff) had affected me in strange ways. Terror, it seemed, had iced over a number of other emotions that came welling to the surface once the threat was removed. I still missed Molly every day, but my mourning was punctuated by odd eruptions, like patches of melting ice on a frozen pond: euphoria at having my life back, gratitude for those who'd helped, inchoate longings for something more . . . even a sense that more was possible. It was during one of those soft spots that I'd picked up my home phone without checking caller ID and found myself talking to Teddy Pendragon. Ever since I'd refused his shiva call, Teddy had besieged me with flowers and notes apologizing for whatever he'd done to offend me. Now he begged my forgiveness again; and this time, feeling churlish for having turned him away, I granted it freely and threw in for good measure an invitation to tonight's soiree. Regretted it at once, of course, but the invitation could not be rescinded, and so there he was, working the room as only Teddy could.

As I approached the bar I heard him saying, ". . . the same sort of obsession. Mark David Chapman thought he was Holden Caulfield. This guy thinks he's the second coming of Hugo—" He broke off when he noticed me and assumed a bedside sort of voice. "Dear Jo, what a time you've had."

"Got it all figured out, have we, Teddy? Neat and tidy and wrapped in a bow?"

"It's human nature to try, don't you think? Although in this case, the mind boggles."

"Not yours, surely."

He laughed. "Now there's the old Jo. Warm and fuzzy doesn't last long with you, does it?" Then, in an aside to the others, "I'm afraid our hostess subscribes to the novelist's view of literary biography; that is, she hates it."

"I don't hate it," I said. "My husband used to say that biography's goal was to cut great men down to their biographer's size . . . but Hugo could be harsh. It's true that biography satisfies a certain voyeuristic curiosity we all share, but the important thing about an artist is surely his work, not his life."

"Ah," said Teddy, raising a pudgy finger, "but where does that work come from?"

"Does it matter?"

"Of course it does. For as long as art has existed, people have wondered about its source: hence the ancients' invention of muses. If you rule out supernatural inspiration, which we tend to do these days, what's left but the artist's life and times?"

I patted his arm and addressed the spectators. "If you gave Teddy a horse, he'd not only look it in the mouth, he'd give it a colonoscopy."

"Charming image." Teddy was still smiling, but there was a lot going on behind those pale blue eyes. "I could put out a shingle: 'Proctologist to the stars.'"

Even as we traded barbs, I found myself scanning the crowd for a gleaming bare head, though I knew perfectly well I wouldn't find it. Max had declined my invitation, and not only because he was in L.A. "It's too soon," he'd said last weekend when we talked on Skype.

"It's been two weeks since the arrest," I said. "How is that too soon?"

"They haven't charged him with the murders yet. Last time I spoke to Cullen, all they had on him was stalking."

"You talked to Tommy?"

Max leaned back and crossed his arms over his chest, so he looked more than ever like Mr. Clean. "That's what interests you, that I talked to *Tommy*? What are we, back in high school?"

"No," I said, hoping the webcam wasn't good enough to register slight changes in color. "It's just that I haven't heard from him lately."

"And that matters because . . . ?"

"It doesn't. Why should it? He's got his perp, case closed and on to the next. I get that." So what if it left me with one more hole in my Swiss cheese of a life? I suppose all crime victims feel this odd sense of loss when their case is resolved and the investigators move on. Or maybe it was the kiss, which I couldn't quite get out of my mind. At the time I'd thought it meant something; but sometimes, I guess, a kiss is just a kiss.

"The point is," Max said, "there are still a lot of unanswered questions. How did this Drucklehoff get to Molly and Rowena? How could he have written those spot-on e-mails and put together the distribution list?"

"He is a printer, you know."

"He's a clerk in a retail print shop: hardly a publishing maven!"

"He could have stolen my laptop in Santa Fe, downloaded a bunch of stuff, and put it to use."

"Maybe. The point is, we don't know and he's not talking."

"He might never talk," I said. "We may never know." Though Max's frustration with this answer was evident, I had made my peace with uncertainty. There is no understanding the mind of a psychopath. Just the other day I'd read a story in the *Times* about a man charged with murdering a woman simply in the hope that her brother would come out of hiding to attend the funeral. There are people among us, people who look and, for the most part, act like the rest of us, for whom a human life has as much value and weight as a pawn in a game of chess. Cross the path of such a person and your life may be lost or upended for reasons so petty that they defy detection by the normal mind.

I could live with not understanding why. Unlike fiction, real life is full of plots that never get resolved. What bothered me was the how of it. How did Stanley Drucklehoff do all the things he did? How did he get to Molly and Rowena? Unless he confessed, we'd never know.

Eventually, I was certain, the police would assemble their case, and Drucklehoff would be charged with both murders. But I was in no mood to wait for the law to wend its stately way. After several weeks of blissful routine, I'd begun to breathe normally again. Somehow I needed to draw a line between the past hellish months and the future; and the dinner at Maison D'être, I'd decided, would be that line.

The maître d' announced that the buffet was open. At once the margins of the room thinned out as my guests gathered around the serving table. On the sparse outskirts I noticed Gordon Hayes, standing like a sentinel with Mingus at his side.

I flagged down a passing waiter. "Bring me a sirloin steak, would you, please?"

"Yes, ma'am. How would you like that? Rare, medium—"

"Raw, cut into chunks, and packed in a doggy bag. It's for my bodyguard there."

The waiter followed my eyes, nodded, and hurried off to the kitchen.

I joined Gordon, gave him a hug. Then I hunkered down next to Mingus and hugged him, too. He licked my cheek once with his warm tongue, then squirmed until I let him go.

Gordon reached down and hauled me to my feet. "Are you sure about this?"

I ran my hand through the dog's thick black ruff. Giving him back was harder than I'd ever imagined it would be, but seeing the way he'd greeted and now cleaved to Gordon made it easier. "Got to cut the umbilical cord sometime. He deserves his country retirement."

"If you ever need him again—"

"I won't hesitate. Thanks, Gordon."

His narrow eyes crinkled. "Just looking after my interests."

Well-trained as Mingus was, there was no point in torturing him at the buffet table, so I went and filled a plate for Gordon. The menu was eclectic but hearty: there were crab cakes and

Black Mission fig salad, wild mushroom risotto, chicken pot-au-feu, and tender short ribs. I'd eaten nothing all day, and the smells rising from the buffet reminded me how hungry I was. I gave Gordon his plate—Mingus's dinner, I noticed, had already been delivered—and went back to get one of my own.

By then everyone was seated at the tables, eating. The noise had died down to a muted thrum of conversation amid the tinkling of cutlery and glass. Silvery light reflected off the tin ceilings. Finding myself alone for a moment, I looked around the glittering room at my guests, New York's finest publishers, editors, agents, critics, and writers. These are my friends and colleagues, I thought. This is my life. I started as a scrawny, unloved orphan, and look where I am now. And then, with a bow to Molly: *If this isn't great, what is?*

Holding my plate, I looked for a congenial table and noticed two people alone at a table for six: Harriet, with Charlie Malvino by her side. I hurried over, unhappy to see them alone. If anyone suspected our parting was less than amicable, my sitting with them should refute it.

"Nice speech," Charlie said as I joined them. He wore tight jeans and a graphic tee under a blazer. Harriet wore a black wool dress with crisp white cuffs and looked like his maiden aunt.

"Is it official?" I asked. "I didn't know if I should say anything or not."

"Signed the papers this morning," he gloated while Harriet, picking at a crab cake, eked out a sour smile.

"So what is it? The Malvino-Peagoody Literary Agency?"

"Peagoody Malvino Literary Management, actually," Harriet said stiffly. She'd done something to her hair, tamed it into a kind of pixie cut that perched uneasily atop her long, angular face.

"Sounds fine. I wish you both every success."

Charlie thanked me, but Harriet pursed her lips and would not meet my eyes. She hadn't believed I would call her bluff, and in fact I nearly hadn't. Harriet was an accomplished agent with a serious client list. It should have been, as she'd said, a no-brainer. And yet Molly had never offered Harriet a partnership; she chose me instead. I thought about that, and about Harriet's habit of lecturing me in staff meetings, and the timing of her ultimatum. I churned it over in my mind until gradually my thoughts clarified into a decision to let her go. Like Tolkien's Galadriel, I would diminish and yet remain myself.

She was shocked when I told her, disbelieving at first, then furious. A generous settlement had, I hoped, taken the edge off that fury. I'd allowed her to take her clients' backlist with her, although contractually those books belonged to the agency, not her. This gave her fledgling company a small but vital float and accounted, I presumed, for Charlie's smugness. In return, though, I'd kept Chloe. Given a choice between accompanying Harriet as her assistant and staying with me as an agent, she hadn't hesitated.

Now Charlie wore the sly, sated look of a fox who's raided the chicken coop, while Harriet looked like one of the chickens. "Be careful what you wish for," Molly always said.

Chapter 28

I slept in the morning after the party, and when I woke, I was
alone. It felt strange and rather sad not having Mingus underfoot, not fixing his breakfast while my coffee brewed. It was nine
thirty; I had just stepped out of the shower when the phone rang.

"You're there," Lorna said.

"So it seems. I did say I'd be late."

"I know. Only there's a problem." My secretary lowered her
voice. "Harriet's here. She said she just wanted to pick up some
personal items, but she's been in there for like an hour."

"Doing what?"

"Nothing. Just sitting at her desk; Chloe's desk, I mean."

Damn. "I'd better come in."

"No, wait. There's something else . . . I didn't think much of
it when it happened, but now I think you need to know."

I sat down on the edge of my bed, towel wrapped around me.
Lorna wasn't the brightest girl in the world, but she was never
fanciful. If she thought something was wrong, it probably was.
"What is it?"

Silence for a moment, then she whispered, "I can't talk about
it here."

"Come over here, then."

"OK, but it would be better coming from you, not me. Could you call Jean-Paul, tell him to send me over with a manuscript or something?"

This seemed unnecessarily circuitous, but I did as she asked, refusing Jean-Paul's offer to come himself. Once I'd dressed, there was nothing to do but wait. I carried the manuscript I was reading into the living room, which was full of flowers from last night's party: spray chrysanthemums, roses, and Asiatic lilies in shades of red, yellow, and orange. Curling up by the unlit fireplace, I tried to read.

She arrived without any announcement, and I made a note to talk to the doormen. Of course they knew my staff well—Lorna and Jean-Paul in particular were always coming and going—but there was no excuse for laxness. Lorna stood awkwardly on the threshold, dressed in stretch pants, a plaid blouse, and a bulky brown cardigan that put an extra twenty pounds on her extra twenty pounds. She carried a thick manuscript under one arm, her oversized bag on the other. "Come in," I said, relieving her of the manuscript and jacket.

She glanced around as she followed me into the living room. "You finally got rid of that beast?"

"Never did warm to him, did you? He's back in retirement." We sat on facing sofas. Lorna clutched her bag on her knees as if she expected a purse-snatcher to dash by. I offered her some coffee.

She shook her head. "I can't stay long." And yet she seemed in no hurry, gazing around at the flowers, studying Leigh's painting over the mantel, even fingering the wedding photo of Hugo, Molly, and me on the steps of City Hall.

"So what's up?" I asked, and finally she looked at me, an odd expression in her small brown eyes.

"You are," she said. "You're something else."

"What are you talking about?"

"Nothing gets to you, does it? The agency's torn apart, your top client and your best friend murdered, and what do you do? You read manuscripts and throw parties."

If this was a compliment, it was an idiotic one. Though she always meant well, Lorna often annoyed me, and this time she'd surpassed herself. But I bit back my first intemperate response, reminding myself that I wasn't the only one who'd suffered these past few months. Everyone had been afflicted; and no one had been more loyal than Lorna.

"What choice do I have?" I said. "It's ridiculous to say nothing gets to me. I got hit so hard I feel like I went ten rounds with Muhammad Ali. I'm just trying to pick myself up off the mat."

"And doing a fine job of it. Everyone admires you. 'Jo's so brave; Jo's so gutsy; you must be so proud to work for Jo, however menial your position.'"

However menial her position? Was this her clumsy way of asking for a promotion? A reaction to Chloe's elevation, maybe . . . but that made no sense. Lorna, whose lack of ambition was the very reason I hired her, had never aspired to be anything more than the perfect secretary.

"Lorna," I said, as patiently as I could, "what was it you had to tell me?"

"More show than tell," she said, smiling as if there were a joke in there somewhere.

"Are you OK? You don't sound like yourself."

"What self is that? Fat, dull Lorna? Unambitious, work-for-peanuts Lorna?"

I stared at her, and she held my gaze with that incongruous little smile. Her usual slump was gone; she sat erect and still, eyes sparkling with restrained exuberance. I looked around for Mingus, wondering what he'd make of this transformation, but of course he wasn't there. Uneasy, I stood.

"Where the hell are you going?" Lorna said, in a decidedly unsecretarial tone.

"Making coffee." I tried to sound normal; I thought I succeeded.

She followed me into the kitchen, still clutching her bag, and perched at the counter. I measured out the coffee grounds, carried the carafe to the sink, and filled it. I could feel her eyes on the back of my neck. Was Lorna having some sort of belated breakdown, now that it was all over? My BlackBerry was charging on the counter beside the coffee machine. With one hand I poured water from the carafe into the machine. With the other, I eased the phone from its cradle and dropped it into the front pocket of my jeans, taking care, though without thinking about why, to shield this movement from Lorna.

"You put in a dishwasher," she said.

"What?" I turned to look at her.

"And you moved the refrigerator. It used to be over there." She pointed to the corner where the old fridge had indeed stood, before Hugo and I updated the kitchen.

Goose bumps prickled my arms. "How do you know?"

"I used to live here."

"What, in another life?"

"My room was the second bedroom down the hall. Your guest room now."

"That's impossible, Lorna. Hugo bought this apartment ages ago, before you were born."

"We lived here together."

"*We* being . . . ?"

"Mama, Hugo, and me."

"Really," I said, crossing my arms. "And this was when?"

"Right up until you got your claws in him."

I didn't speak. The silence between us was so dense, it had its own gravitational field, sucking in sound from outside. I heard a

doorman whistle for a cab, heard the rise and fall of a siren passing by far below.

"Tell me you don't believe me," Lorna said.

An image rose before my eyes: a Raggedy Andy doll, crammed
into a box full of women's clothing and shoved down the chute.
But that memory had nothing to do with Lorna; whatever it
meant, it was none of her business.

"Of course I don't believe you."

"I knew you wouldn't. You're the Queen of Denial." She
reached into her bag, and I flinched.

Until that moment I hadn't admitted that I was afraid. I'd told
myself it was pity I felt, pity and concern. Lorna's sudden movement shattered that illusion. She noticed my reaction and seemed
to feed on it, keeping her hand hidden, prolonging the moment.
Then she drew it out slowly, and I saw that she held a snapshot,
lovingly preserved in a clear plastic case. She looked at it rever-
ently, then handed it to me.

Despite the protective casing, the color photo was faded and
creased through much handling. The setting was unmistakably
the Central Park Carousel. A plump little girl of five or six sat
beaming with pleasure atop a gray charger. Behind her, his hand
on her shoulder, stood Hugo. I studied the child and recognized
those small brown eyes, that pugnacious chin.

The picture blurred before my eyes. Lorna snatched it away,
wiped it on her sweater, and stuck it back in her bag.

I couldn't look at her. "He wasn't your father. Hugo had no
children."

"He had me. I called him Papa."

The coffee maker beeped. I took two clean mugs from the
dishwasher.

"Not for me." She glanced at her watch, as if she had some-
place to be and I was keeping her. "Put that fucking cup away."

Once, walking through the woods behind my grandmother's

house, I stumbled on a black bear nursing a cub. The mother bear jumped up and roared, flashing her long white teeth. I froze, inside and out. The bear didn't move, and for that one endless moment full of latent possibilities, it seemed as if there was no one in the world but me and her. Looking at Lorna now with the same funnel vision, I was met with the same predatory stare; and at last I understood that she was not the prissy-mouthed, dull little girl I thought I knew. This was a whole other person.

I put the second mug away and filled mine with steaming brew. My back was to the corner; I felt trapped. I didn't drink my coffee. There was more comfort in holding it.

"Why are you here?" I asked.

Her eyes widened in a look of dopey innocence. "Because you needed me to bring you a manuscript. Isn't that what you told Jean-Paul?"

I could throw the scalding coffee in her face and grab her bag. My fist tightened on the mug's handle . . . but I hesitated. I was scared, but I wasn't sure. Sam Spade was in jail. So far this was all just crazy talk. Unlike the bear, Lorna hadn't shown a weapon.

I asked her again: "Why have you come?"

"To tell you a story," she said. "I know you like fairy tales. I read the ones you told Teddy Pendragon in that magazine article. So sweet they made me puke."

"And this from someone who takes four sugars in her coffee."

"You think this is funny?"

"No," I said carefully. "I don't understand it, but I don't think it's funny. Let's go back to the living room."

She made no move to stop me, but stayed between me and the front door. We resumed our former places in the living room, in front of the fireplace, with the coffee table between us. Lorna clutched the bag on her knees like a tourist riding the subway.

"Once upon a time," she said, in a singsongy voice, "there was a little princess who lived in a castle with her mother and father, the king and queen. The king and queen doted on the little princess and were kind to her, showering her with gifts and treats. One day, when the king was abroad, an evil enchantress cast a spell on him that turned his heart to stone. At her command, he banished the queen and the princess from the castle to make way for the witch."

"No," I said, holding out a hand. "Wait."

She raised her voice. "When the queen fell ill with grief, the little princess sent many messages to the king. But the king never got those messages, because the evil witch intercepted them all. Fearing that in time the king would return to himself and remember his beloved queen and princess, the witch sent minions who captured the queen and threw her in a dungeon. They kept her in darkness; they tormented her until at last she took the only escape open to her: she hanged herself."

Mad, I told myself. Totally delusional. But there was an ache in the pit of my stomach, the kind you get when chickens come home to roost.

"And the princess?" I asked.

"Exiled to the wilderness, where she was raised by wolves."

"Not a very happy ending."

Lorna glowed from within, looking, strangely enough, like the woman I always thought she could be. "It hasn't ended yet," she said.

"So you're that girl. You were raised by wolves."

"Duh!"

"And I'm the witch who destroyed your life?"

"Finally!" She raised her arms in benediction. "It's unbelievable how stupid smart people can be."

Indeed. Eighteen months working side by side and I never had a clue, although surely there were clues to be had. I thought about the gifts I'd given her: the clothes she never wore, the Coach bag she never used. Now it made perfect sense; who accepts gifts from someone they hate? I thought about her indifference to books, combined with her determination to work in publishing. Why had I never realized what a strange combination that was? All that behavior I'd attributed to protectiveness—the drinks she put in my hand, her vigilance in guarding my door and my phone, the many times she urged me to stay home or go away—I saw now as attempts to isolate and weaken me. Oh yes, there had been signs; but in my egotism, in my certainty that everyone loved me, I had misread them all. I'd seen everything and understood nothing.

Even now I struggled. "You said your parents went back to Ireland."

"Leaving me all alone, boo-hoo." She smirked. "You liked that one, didn't you?"

"Then who were they? And don't tell me Hugo was your father. I know that's not true."

"My mother's name was Irina Kassofsky. She was a Russian immigrant, very beautiful, much more beautiful than you. We lived here together, the three of us. On Sundays we went to the park. Hugo loved us. He was my father, the only father I ever had." She sounded rehearsed, like a child reciting her catechism.

I wanted to deny it. Molly had said there was a live-in lover, but I never believed that. There *was* a housekeeper, though, and the doorman had said she had a child. *A boy, I'm sure of it . . . or was it a girl?* And suddenly it was clear.

"Your mother was the maid!"

Her brown eyes blazed. "How dare you call her that! She made his bed, yes, but she slept in it too. You destroyed our lives. You killed my mother. Everything I had, you stole from me. You're a thief and a murderer."

"Lorna, I swear I never even knew you existed."

"I knew you'd say that. You can't see me. You can't hear me. You never could." Once again she reached into her bag. This time I didn't hesitate. I threw my coffee at her, mug and all. Lorna ducked and raised her arm, and the cup deflected off it and fell harmlessly to the floor.

For a moment both of us remained as we were, frozen. Running wasn't an option. Even if I made it out the door, she'd catch me in the hall or the stairwell. To have any chance at all, I had to get that bag away from her. I grabbed a crystal vase from the coffee table, but before I could throw it, the gun appeared.

"Put it down," Lorna said. "Gently."

I set the vase down within easy reach and sank back onto the couch, trying not to cringe. It was a smallish gun, with a long, tubular attachment on the barrel, and it was aimed at my heart. Beside me was a large throw pillow. I clutched it to me.

She sniggered. "Yeah, that'll help."

Coffee was seeping into the ivory silk rug that Hugo and I bought on our trip to China. It is a testament to my grandmother's hands-on training that, despite the situation, I had an overwhelming urge, as reflexive as a sneeze, to fetch a bottle of club soda and some rags. Maybe Lorna had the same sort of upbringing, for she, too, glanced at the spreading stain with distress.

"Look what you did," she said reproachfully.

I thought of Mingus then with a regret and longing so intense that I almost expected him to materialize on the spot. He didn't. But it occurred to me that I wasn't entirely weaponless. There was an ice pick in the bar and a poker beside the fireplace.

Lorna seemed to read my mind. "Move one inch and you're dead."

I wondered why she hadn't pulled the trigger already. What did she want from me? Using the pillow as a cover, I slipped my hand into my pants' pocket, found the BlackBerry, and started easing it out.

"I understand your anger toward me," I said. "But why take it out on my clients? Why kill Rowena and poor Molly? What the fuck did they ever do to you?"

"You destroyed my life. I wasn't going to put you down till I'd destroyed yours."

"You organized Rowena's memorial service." Each new realization was hitting me as a distinct shock; I couldn't get ahead of it. "You sat in that room and listened to the life she led, the kind of person she was. How could you, knowing what you'd done?"

"It was tough," Lorna said. "Tough to keep from laughing. Rowena was nothing like all that pious bullshit. She was a snotty bitch, so full of herself she never even bothered to learn my name."

"And for that she deserved to die?" The phone was out of my pocket. I ran my fingers over the keys, trying to visualize the keyboard. Tommy Cullen was number five on my speed dial. I pressed what I prayed was the right number.

"If she hadn't deserved it, she wouldn't have made it so easy." Lorna smiled in what looked like fond remembrance. "It was so perfect. She opened the door and said, 'Laura, dear, what are you doing here?' 'Jo sent me,' I said, and of course those were the magic words. She invited me in, and I didn't waste any time. But here's the kicker. After I shot her, she didn't die right away. I leaned over her, so my face would be the last thing she saw, and I said, 'Actually, *dear,* it's Lorna.'" Lorna had been sniggering throughout this recital. Now she laughed so hard that she didn't hear what I heard: a muffled voice between my stomach and the pillow saying, "Jo?"

She wiped her eyes with the heel of her free hand. "You have no idea how badly I've wanted to tell that story. And you're such a good listener now."

Was it Tommy? I couldn't tell. It was someone, anyway. If this ended badly, someone would know.

"And Molly?" I said loudly. "What did Molly ever do to you, Lorna?"

"Nothing," she said, turning truculent. "Molly was OK,

except for thinking the sun shone out of your asshole. But she was your crutch. If you'd given up after Rowena, if you'd stayed down like a normal human being, there would have been no need for Molly to die. But no, you had to be better than anyone else, tougher than anyone else, the invincible Jo Donovan. Molly's your fault. They both are."

Fear acted like Novocain on my emotions, but I felt the impact of those words. They would hurt later, if there was a later. "Lorna, I didn't know about you and your mother. Maybe I should have, but I didn't. You were treated unfairly; you have a legitimate claim. We can resolve this to your advantage. Look at this apartment. You loved it as a child. It could be yours again. Killing me gains you nothing."

"Nothing but satisfaction," she scoffed. "Nothing but achieving my life's goal."

"People who've been damaged are entitled to compensation. Why don't we settle this the American way?"

She waved the gun. "This *is* the American way."

"I meant money."

"And I suppose Molly and Rowena will be our little secret? Damn, woman, you still think I'm stupid. Must be a hard habit to break."

"Of course I don't think you're stupid, how could I? You fooled everyone. No one looked twice at you."

"You never even looked once," she said, with a lifetime's worth of contempt. "Fooling you was easy. I knew you'd never suspect me. 'Poor dumb Lorna, such a good little filer. Just don't ask her to walk and chew gum at the same time.'"

"I never said anything like that!"

"Thought it, though, didn't you?"

Odd, I thought, that the truest lines in this conversation were coming from the crazed murderer. "I think we've established that I had no idea who I was dealing with. The point is, you'd never get away with this one. The doorman saw you; Jean-Paul knows you came to my apartment. If you shoot me, you'll be caught in two seconds and rot in prison for the rest of your life. Where's the justice in that?"

I was afraid, mentioning the apartment for the second time, that Lorna would catch on. But she was too busy gloating, proud of herself and eager to show off her cleverness. "No one saw me. I came in the basement door and I'll leave the same way. Thanks for the keys, by the way; good of you to trust me with them. After I finish with you, I'll go around front and deliver that manuscript to the doorman, just like your little boyfriend told me to. With you gone, the agency will fold; and I'll drift away, the way little people like me do."

"They'll find you, Lorna." I hoped Tommy had gotten the message by now, because if I said her name once more, I thought she'd shoot me on general principle.

She shrugged. "It'd be worth it if they did, but they won't. It's a big country, and I've got the perfect invisibility cloak: a few extra pounds and some dowdy clothes. Worked with you, didn't it?"

"I hope you don't expect a reference."

"Good one, Jo. Too bad it's just you and me here."

"Seriously, think it over. Everything else aside, it's a hell of a time to be out of a job."

She flushed. "Everything's a fucking joke to you, isn't it? You should be on your knees, begging for your life."

"Like that's gonna help."

"You never know. I might take pity, if you beg hard enough."

Finally I understood what she was waiting for. Humiliation, the final station of the cross. She must have pictured it for years, fantasized about it. The Lorna I'd thought I knew was rigid in her routines and expectations. I had a feeling this Lorna wasn't so different.

I didn't budge. She raised the gun and took aim, left hand supporting her right. "Kneel before me, you evil witch!"

Even though she held the gun and all the power, her voice was shrill, shaking like a child's. And suddenly I knew that voice. I'd heard it before. The memory rushed over me.

"Put him on, witch. Put Hugo on." A young voice, high-pitched and agitated.

I move the phone away from my ear. "Stop calling. Leave us alone."

"I need to talk to him right now!"

Noises in the background: men shouting, a woman screaming. Some vile prank, I think.

"I can't hear you," I say, and hang up the phone.

Now I looked at Lorna, and I could see the young girl from the photo in her face. "You called the apartment."

"Oh, so now you remember. I called many times. I called the day they took my mother away. You hung up on me."

"I thought you were one of his girlfriends."

"No, you didn't," she said flatly. "On your knees!"

I heard the elevator stop on my floor.

If Lorna had any sense, I'd be dead already. But she must have envisioned this moment a thousand times, me on my knees, begging for mercy, and she didn't want to settle for less. She'd heard the elevator, though, and it spooked her. As she threw a quick glance over her shoulder, I jumped up, raised the crystal vase above my head, and hurled it at her.

I missed. The vase flew past her head, hit the wall, and shattered in a shower of glass shards, mums, and roses. Both of us were on our feet. There were footsteps in the hall. Someone banged on the door. "Help!" I screamed.

Lorna raised her arm and sighted down the barrel. I grabbed the closest thing at hand, my wedding photo, and aimed for her chest. She ducked, but the heavy metal frame clipped her shoulder. As she staggered backward, the gun roared.

I felt a searing pain on the side of my head and fell back onto the couch. Blood dripped past my eyes like a red bead curtain. Through it I saw uniformed policemen rush in, shouting, guns in hand. "Drop it. Drop the gun!"

I heard a thump; then Lorna spoke with astonishing composure. "Don't shoot. It's not what it looks like. She attacked me."

I wanted to deny it, but my head was on fire. A large body knelt beside me. A man's voice said, "She's shot. Call a bus."

I closed my eyes and waited to die.

Chapter 29

After the sentencing, Max and I left the courthouse together. The Criminal Court building was an imposing white edifice on Centre Street, whose carved portico and columns made the perfect backdrop for the attorneys who were already outside talking to the press. We skirted the knot of reporters, our faces averted, and crossed the street to the little park on Foley Square, where we sat on a bench facing the courthouse. A year had passed since Lorna's arrest; winter had come again, but the weather this week had been unseasonably warm, almost sultry.

"Well," Max said, wiping his brow and the dome of his head with a red handkerchief, "that's that."

"Thanks for coming, Max."

"No thanks necessary. It was worth it just to hear the words 'consecutive sentences.' She'll never get out. That's something to celebrate."

"Yes," I said, but I didn't feel like celebrating, and I didn't believe he did, either. Lorna hadn't testified during the trial, but a great deal about her early life had come out in the sentencing phase. She was not, as she had claimed, Hugo's daughter. Lorna was four years old when her mother, a Russian immigrant named

Irina Kassofsky, quit her job with Jolly Maids and moved into
Hugo's apartment; she was seven when they left it.

Nor had Hugo thrown them out on the street. He'd rented
them an apartment in Brooklyn, paid the rent for six months—
those receipts I'd found in his study—and turned over to Irina a
bank account with $20,000 in it. It was a perfunctory, business-
like dismissal, particularly cruel to the child, though I doubt
Hugo ever considered that. Nevertheless, it was a loss Lorna
could have overcome if her mother had moved on with her life.
Irina did not. Her ascent had been too steep and her descent too
precipitous. She obsessed endlessly over Hugo and especially over
me, and she made her daughter into her confidante. Growing
depressed, she began to use and eventually sell drugs. Child services got involved. For the next five years, until she hanged herself
at Rikers, Irina shuttled in and out of prisons and hospitals. Each
time she got out, she regained custody of her daughter; and the
cycle began again. For Lorna, the intervals with her mother were
devoted to retelling the story of their betrayal and plotting elabo-
rate schemes of revenge, while the stints in foster care were spent
waiting and planning.

Which, I supposed, was how she got so good at it. It took
Lorna years to carry out her revenge: to acquire skills that would
be useful to me, to insinuate herself into the agency, and to learn
what she needed to know to strip me of my life before taking it.

The judge wasn't impressed by Lorna's miserable childhood;
perhaps he was inured to hard-luck stories. In his sentencing
statement, he spoke about the astonishing degree of premedita-
tion that went into her crimes, as well as their cold-blooded cru-
elty. My feelings were more conflicted. The jury had found her
guilty on all counts, as did I. Rowena and Molly could finally rest
easy; their murderer would never again walk free. And yet I remembered, as the court could not, desperate phone calls from a

voice I chose to hear as a woman's; and I knew there was guilt enough to go around.

"The worst part," I said to Max, "is that none of it had to happen. If I'd known back then, if I'd allowed myself to know—"

"Hugo knew," Max said firmly. "They weren't your responsibility. Nor his either, really. You ask me, he treated that woman more than decently. She got three good years and a windfall in the end. There was no need to make a soap opera out of it, much less drag the kid into it."

"Haven't you noticed? Everyone's life is a soap opera."

"Nuh-uh. Mine's a Broadway musical."

I laughed, thinking of his books. "But a dark one, like *Sweeney Todd*."

"Not at all. Something frothy, with Julie Andrews in it."

"*Somebody's* happy."

"It's called marital bliss. Highly recommended, Madame Workhorse."

"Been there, done that."

"Done what?" said another voice.

We turned. Tommy Cullen was approaching, looking cool and businesslike in a charcoal suit. I should have been prepared; I'd glimpsed him in the courtroom and lost track of the proceedings for five full minutes. But I was unexpectedly struck dumb, and Max, for the second time, stepped into the breach.

"Detective Cullen, our savior!" He stood and shook Tommy's hand warmly. "Which, you should know, is not something a Jew says lightly."

"I'll pass, if you don't mind," Tommy said with his old, easy smile. "You folks are tough on saviors. Saw you in the courtroom. Guess I'll be reading all about the case in your next book."

"I don't think so," Max said. "Fiction's easier on the heart."

"Too bad. I already had the movie cast."

"Yeah? Who plays you?"

"That would be Matt Damon."

They laughed, but I thought Matt Damon wasn't a bad choice. Same all-American type, though Tommy was even better-looking. He turned to me, and a scrim of wariness fell over his face. "How are you?"

"OK," I said. "Better than the last time we met." In the ambulance, that had been. The sound of his voice calling my name had roused me; I'd opened my eyes to an ashen version of his face, bending over mine. That stricken look had given me hope; I didn't see how it could come from an indifferent heart. But he hadn't come to the hospital, where other detectives took my statement. I thought he would call after I got out, but months stretched into a year and Tommy never sought me out.

Not that I sat home waiting. In my free time I tended the garden of hardy friendships that had sprung from the soil of my devastation. Though Rowena and Molly were irreplaceable, friendship itself turned out to be fungible. In my free time I saw Gordon, Keyshawn, and my legacy friend, Leigh Pfeffer. Max and Barry were family; I was with them in L.A. when baby Molly took her first steps.

There wasn't much free time, though, because despite three new hires to supplement Jean-Paul and Chloe, I was busier than ever. Sikha Mehruta had delivered an exquisite novel, as good as her first two but more accessible. I thought it could be her breakthrough book. Her publisher agreed, and with just a little prodding doubled her advance and offered a three-book contract. Chloe sold Katie Vigne's book, *I Luv U Baby, but WTF?*, to a new imprint at Penguin. Keyshawn's novel had come out to respectful reviews and sufficient sales to pave the way for a second book, which he was busy writing. Despite Harriet's decampment, the agency was thriving.

Other things had changed in my life. I'd given Rowena's

bequest to her charities and ended up on the board of one of them, a fund that supports rural libraries. Most of Molly's money went to endow a college scholarship fund for students from Hoyer's Creek. I acted anonymously, for I had a horror of ever going back there; but like Rowena, I had opened a door for others.

And yet I yearned for more. The fierce hunger for life that had gripped me in the face of death didn't dissipate once the threat was removed but grew stronger as the shock wore off. Appetites had wakened that were not easily satisfied. I thought a lot about Tommy Cullen. Fantasized about him. Thought of calling him, but resisted every time. If he'd wanted to see me, there was nothing to stop him. I figured he had his reasons. He didn't owe me a second chance; and anyway, what were the odds that a straight, good-looking man like Tommy would be unattached in a city full of hungry women?

"How's the head?" he asked now, sitting beside me on the bench.

I pushed back my hair to show him the scar on my left temple. The bullet, skimming past, had torn off a swath of flesh and bruised the bone, but left the skull intact. One inch to my right, the doctors said, and the story would have had a different ending. As it was, I got away with a concussion and a scar. A plastic surgeon could have fixed the scar, but that didn't feel right. I hadn't emerged unscathed, and shouldn't look as if I had.

"Max is right," I said. "You sent in the cavalry and saved my life; then you rode off into the sunset, before I even had a chance to thank you."

"Like the Lone Ranger," Max said.

"Like Shane," I said. The first movie that ever made me cry. *Come back, Shane! Shane, come back!* He hadn't, though.

"You've got nothing to thank me for," Tommy said. "You were smart and gutsy enough to make that phone call right under her nose." He nodded toward the courthouse. "Were you satisfied with the outcome?"

"It doesn't bring Molly and Rowena back," I said. "But the sentence was just. She deserves it."

"She deserves worse," Max said darkly, "but New York doesn't have the death penalty. What bothers me is not knowing the whole story. I'd have liked to know how Drucklehoff fit into the scheme. Was he part of it? Did Lorna deploy him, or just take advantage of his appearance?"

"We wondered that, too," Tommy said. "We kept searching for a connection, but we never found any. I think she was biding her time, collecting intelligence and making plans. When that nutcase came along, she seized the opportunity to use him for cover."

"Lucky break for her," Max said.

"Yeah, she got a lot of mileage out of him."

"So you never suspected her?"

"We suspected everyone," Tommy said reprovingly. "But she wasn't a focus of the investigation till we caught Drucklehoff. Then we started wondering why he hadn't been on our radar before. I went back and checked the printout of submissions that Lorna had given us. Drucklehoff wasn't on it, and neither was his novel. She kept those records; so either she just happened to miss that particular one, or she'd purged it from the list to impede our investigation. We already knew from background checks that she'd changed her surname, but we didn't know why. We were about to bring her in when she made her move on you."

Poor Sam Spade, I thought. They'd dropped all charges against him after Lorna's arrest, and let him go with a warning to stay away from me. All he ever did was write a really bad book and try to get me to read it. And I said such vicious things to him.

"I keep thinking I should write him a note," I said.

"Hell, no!" both men replied as one. They looked at each other, and Max gave a go-ahead wave.

"Don't even think about it," Tommy said earnestly. "This is still a guy with a major obsession, and you don't want to feed it."

No, I did not. As it was, I kept looking over my shoulder. The ordeal I'd been through had left scars less visible than the one on my temple. I'd become hypervigilant about my surroundings and the people near me, looking outward with the same critical eye I'd honed on the interior world of fiction. This change was, perhaps, not so surprising, but others were unexpected, like the feeling that cataracts had been removed, not just from my eyes, but from all my senses. Color flooded the world; details emerged. My appetite returned, and I'd put back all the weight I'd lost. Even my sense of smell seemed more acute, and strangely infused with emotion. Tommy's odor, for example, a blend of Ivory soap, pine-scented aftershave, and sweat, brought back a time when I'd known it well.

An ambulance shouldered its way through rush-hour traffic, siren blaring. Tommy glanced at his watch. This is it, I thought. In a minute he's going to say good-bye and walk away, and we could share this city for the rest of our lives and never meet again. I didn't have to ask myself how I felt about that.

"I don't know about you guys," I said, before he could speak, "but I could use a drink."

"Sounds about right," Tommy said at once.

Max grimaced. "Wish I could, but I'm afraid I have a plane to catch. In fact"—he glanced at his watch and stood—"I've got to run."

I stared at him. His flight wasn't until late that night, and we'd planned to have dinner together.

The men shook hands; Max kissed my cheek. "See ya, Jo. Remember what I said." As he stepped toward the street, raising his arm, an empty taxi glided to the curb. He climbed in and waved good-bye.

"Impressive," Tommy said.

"He leads a charmed life." I felt embarrassed being alone with him, like a schoolgirl on a blind date, which was ridiculous. "Where should we go? I don't know the neighborhood."

"I do. There's a place just across the square." He hesitated. "Kind of a cop hangout, though. You'd probably want something nicer."

"They got scotch?"

"Yes, ma'am."

"Let's go," I said, and we fell into step as if we'd been doing it every day for a lifetime. It was four thirty, and lawyers in dark suits streamed from the courthouse like ants from a colony. When Tommy's arm brushed mine, I felt a heat that spread inward. On West Broadway we passed a bookstore with a full window display of Teddy Pendragon's *An Audacious Life*. Eighteen months from contract to publication: Teddy and Random House had pulled out all the stops to capitalize on the publicity surrounding Lorna's trial. It would have been impossible if Teddy hadn't done so much of the work in advance for *Vanity Fair*; even so, I feared the haste had taken a toll on the work. On the front cover was a photo of Hugo in his midforties, with a wild shock of prematurely gray hair and a penetrating stare. I kept walking and would have averted my eyes if I weren't trying to quit that habit.

"Did you read it?" Tommy asked.

"Not yet." My copy, fulsomely signed by the author, lay untouched on a shelf in my study. It was strange to remember how obsessively I'd worried about this book, dreading the exposure of secrets I never even acknowledged to myself. Someday I'd read it and finish the job of sorting the marriage I'd thought I had from the marriage I actually had. For now, I was focused on the present, not the past.

"I did," he said.

I looked at him. "Really?"

"I do read, you know. And the subject interested me."

"What'd you think?"

He didn't answer for half a block, long enough for me to regret a question that left me wide open. Finally, with an air of restraint, he said, "I think your husband was a better writer than he was a man. Here we are." He opened the door of a little bar and grill I would never have noticed on my own. New York was like that, not one city but a series of concentric cities that rarely overlap. Inside it was dark and cool and noisy. There was sawdust on the floor, and the Knicks were playing on a flatscreen TV mounted above the bar. Tommy took my elbow and led me toward a booth in the back, nodding at the bartender as we passed. We sat facing each other across a pitted wooden table, and right away a waitress came over. She had spiky platinum hair and a skirt short enough to display the butterfly tat on her thigh. "Hey, Tommy," she said, laying a red-tipped hand on his arm. "Haven't seen you in a while."

"Hey, Crystal, how's it going?"

"Getting fat on takeout. The stove's busted at my place, and my cheapskate landlord won't do nothing about it. Maybe you could come around and talk to him, Tommy?"

"Sure thing. How about I shoot him for you?"

She tee-heed and punched his shoulder lightly. "What'll it be, big guy? The usual?"

"That'll work. Jo?"

"Let me guess," the waitress said, sizing me up. "Strawberry daiquiri."

I gave her a gunslinger's slit-eyed smile. "Johnnie Walker Black, straight up."

She switched away, and we watched her go.

"Sweet kid," Tommy said.

"I could tell."

He smiled down at the table.

"Matt Damon, huh?" I said.

He laughed. "So much for dreams of glory."

"You never know. Max says he won't write this story, but that's what writers do. It'll pop out one way or another."

"He's a good guy, your Max."

"He likes you, too, now."

Tommy raised his eyebrows. "Now?"

"You were high on his list of suspects for a while."

"Not yours, though?"

"I always trusted you," I said, and it was almost true. The waitress shimmied back with our drinks and Tommy paid, ignoring my protests. She served his draft with a smile, my scotch with a frosty glare. Jealous, I thought, which oddly enough evoked the same emotion in me.

I'd thought that if I could just meet him once and thank him properly, his hold on me would be broken. I hadn't figured on how good it would feel to walk down the street with him, or to look into his face, which was everything a man's face should be, or to be looked at and really seen by him. Maybe it was because he came from the same world I did, but I felt he knew me from the inside out.

The exorcism hadn't worked. I had feelings for Tommy Cullen, useless as they were, sad as they made me. I knew where he stood, kiss notwithstanding. Rejection leaves scars. *Once bitten, twice shy.*

We drank in silence for a while. There was a pool table in the small back room behind us, and a couple of guys were playing while others kibitzed. Between each click of cue against ball, a chorus of profane commentary arose, rich in the ethnic slurs that are New York's vernacular. I felt a surge of affection for my adopted city.

"What brought you down here today?" I asked. "Did you come for the sentencing?"

"Sort of," Tommy said. "I figured you'd be there. Wanted to see how you're doing."

"I'm fine," I said. He ignored that automatic response and waited. "The trial was tough. Living through it again stirred up a lot of emotions. But basically I'm doing OK. Life is good, despite everything."

He nodded. "Lorna should have picked her fights better. You're a hard woman to knock down."

"One of my worse traits, according to her." I held my glass in both hands and stared into the amber liquid. "She said she wouldn't have killed Molly if I'd quit the agency after Rowena died."

"She would say that. Fits her MO perfectly."

"You don't believe it?"

"You do?" Tommy sounded incredulous.

I looked up at him and shrugged. Until that moment, I'd never doubted it.

"She was just twisting the knife, Jo. Molly was always on the agenda, the final blow before she finished you off."

"Did she tell you that?"

"She never talked to us; she lawyered up in the squad car."

"Then how do you know?"

"It just fits. The whole thing was carefully, obsessively planned as an escalating series of blows. First the e-mail to your clients, then that targeted press release, which made it all public, and then the two murders. She meant to cut the legs out from under you, bring you to your knees."

I wanted to believe him. The thought that I could have saved Molly's life by quitting the agency was one agony time had not allayed. "Are you sure, Tommy?"

"I'm sure about that," he said firmly. "What I wonder about is the message she left at the crime scenes, 'Can you hear me now?' Did she ever tell you what that meant?"

Heat flooded my face. Of all the questions he could have asked, this was the most painful; but he deserved the truth. "Back when I first moved in with Hugo, Lorna called the apartment. There were plenty of women in his life who weren't shy about calling. My orders were to keep them off his back. I told myself she was one of them, a woman with a girlish voice. She asked to talk to Hugo. I never let her. I told her to stop calling. I pretended I couldn't hear her. Finally I changed our number."

Then I had to stop talking and turn away. Another residual effect of the ordeal: inappropriate fits of weeping.

"Hey," Tommy said. "Hey, now."

"I'm sorry," I said, blotting my eyes with a paper napkin. "You asked me so many times. You told me to wake up and remember, but I didn't, not until the very end. I had the key all along. And look what it cost."

"Jo, look at me." His green eyes drew me in until I felt like I was swimming underwater. "None of this is your fault. Those calls meant nothing to you. Why would you remember?"

"Oh, but I didn't want to remember, any more than I wanted to know in the first place. I had my perfect marriage to protect. Never mind that Hugo was living with someone when we met; never mind that I was with you. I made up a fairy tale, just like Lorna did."

"Everyone does that. People have to, to make sense of their lives. You see it all the time on the job. Every confession comes wrapped in a story."

"But stories have consequences. Wouldn't you think I of all people would know that? For good or for bad, stories have con-sequences."

He leaned back and studied me critically. "You know what your problem is?"

Survivor's guilt, I thought he'd say: everyone's diagnosis du jour, which is why I'd pretty much given up talking about it.

People don't understand that just as paranoids can have real enemies, so can survivors have cause for guilt. I'd turned a deaf ear
to the child and a blind eye to the woman. There were signs, but
I misread them all. The Queen of Denial, Lorna had called me,
and she nailed it. I was an expert at other people's stories, but
when it came to my own, I'd heard only what I wanted to hear,
seen only what I expected to see.

"Your problem," Tommy said, "is you've been snake-bit. I recognize the signs. Still got the venom in you."

"You're not going to cut me and suck it out, are you?"

He laughed the way he used to when there were no barriers
between us. Emboldened, I asked, "What's your story, then, since
you say everyone has one?"

The laughter went away. Tommy studied me for a long time.
Finally he said, "You know my story. Oldest one there is. Boy
meets girl, boy loses girl."

"That's it? No third act?"

"Not really."

"Are you married?"

A pause, then: "No."

"Girlfriend?"

"Why ask now, Jo? You never did before."

"Just trying out life with my eyes open for a change."

His mouth twitched. "How's that working for you?"

"Bit disconcerting, but I'm getting the hang of it. Right now,
for example, I see you avoiding the question."

"I'm single now. I was married once, for a little while. Eight
months."

"Eight *months*?"

"We got married because she was pregnant. After she miscar-
ried, there wasn't much point for either of us."

"I'm sorry," I said.

"I was real sorry about the baby. Always wanted kids; still do.

But the divorce, that part was OK. She's a nice girl, but it wasn't fair on either of us. She wasn't what I wanted."

Shouts rose from the back room, followed by a crash and a sharp crack like a cue stick breaking. I didn't look away, and neither did Tommy.

"What do you want?" I asked.

"I think you know."

Billiard balls came flying out of the back room, and the bartender ran past us, flourishing a baseball bat. Hope flowered inside me; I felt it unfolding, petal by petal.

"Why didn't you call?" I asked.

"Couldn't. Any personal contact between the victim and the investigators could have jeopardized the prosecution." This came out in one breath, with a fluency that sounded rehearsed. It was my turn to wait in silence. Even in the dimly lit booth, I could see the color rising in Tommy's face. He took a long pull on his beer.

"That," he said, "and the other thing. How I felt about you. That hasn't changed. So I stayed away."

"Bit of a non sequitur, that last bit."

"It's not like before, when we were kids together in the big city. I'm not blind. I see the life you've made for yourself, the world you live in."

"Maybe my world could use expanding," I said.

Tommy caught his breath and stared. I'd have stared too. Brazen wasn't my usual style, but there's nothing like having nothing to lose.

"Are you flirting with me, Jo?"

"I think it's way past flirting."

The back-room fight spilled into the aisle beside us. One man punched another, and that one lost his balance and would have fallen on me if Tommy hadn't jumped up and straight-armed him away. Instead of sitting back down, Tommy came around to my side of the booth and held out his hand.

Outside, a blast of exhaust enveloped us. Taxis blared their horns and jostled for position on the street while pedestrians played the same game on the sidewalk. Tommy led me toward the brick façade of the bar, out of the stream. He took me in his arms and we kissed for a long time. It felt as if someone had poured gasoline on me and lit it on fire, except that it didn't hurt. His body felt strange against mine, yet deeply and dearly familiar. All the world flowed by us, yet we were alone together; for there is no place more private than the center of a crowd.

Or almost no place. "Come home with me," I said.

But Tommy didn't move. "I feel compelled to ask your intentions."

"My intentions?" I said. "Kind of old-school, isn't it?"

"I'm an old-school kind of guy."

"At the moment I'd say my intentions are highly dishonorable. Is that normally a sticking point?" I pressed against him, and he held me close, strong hands splayed against the small of my back. Unless that was a gun in his pocket, I was fairly sure he wasn't going anywhere; yet I sensed hesitation.

"Not normally, no," he said. "Just tell me this isn't some incredibly generous sort of thank-you."

"They have cards for that. This is about you and me and nothing else."

"You say that now, but what happens when the next Nobel Prize–winning bastard comes along?"

"Depends," I said, straight-faced. "Is he hot?"

Tommy laughed. "You are a wicked woman, Jo."

"No, I'm not. I know you have no reason to trust me. But Tommy, do I look like I'm playing?"

I held his eyes, and after a moment he smiled that slow, country-boy smile of his. "My place is closer," he said.

"Closer's good." We looked toward the street. West Broadway was teeming with rush-hour traffic. What were the odds of

cab at this hour? I wondered. Maybe Tommy could
trol car. It felt like an emergency. We tacked across the
nt. Just as we reached the curb, a taxi pulled over and
rged two women. Tommy grabbed the door and held it for
t's a sign, I thought, climbing in. Not that I believed in signs
portents. I was trying, these days, to keep a solid yellow line
tween fiction and reality, fairy tales and life. Fictional romance
may end in "happily ever after," but "till death do us part" is the
best mortal lovers can hope for.

On the upside, real people have bodies. We *are* bodies. Tommy's, warm and solid, slid in beside mine. "Where to?" the cabby asked, looking in his mirror.

"Home," Tommy said.